BANEBLADE

Two of Cortein's screens went dead. The battle cannon fired again. The damaged plates in the heavy walker's chest crumpled in. It swayed on its feet, gatling cannon firing wild. Rockets burned off a rack set upon the right shoulder, trailing bright fire. They impacted in a wide burst pattern about the Baneblade, one slamming home on the front of the tank, wreathing Cortein's visual displays in flame.

'Radden…' said Cortein. 'Put that walker down now!'

'I hit it! I hit it!' protested the gunner.

Two more impacts shuddered into the walker's armour, buckling plates, one each from Artamen Ultrus's demolisher and battle cannon. Still it came on.

The walker stopped. A huge cannon on its shoulder above the ruined left arm began to track down.

'Too late!' said Cortein. 'Brace! Brace! Brace!'

By the same author

SKARSNIK
A Warhammer Heroes novel
(June 2013)

STRIKE AND FADE
A Horus Heresy audio drama
Exclusively available from blacklibrary.com

STORMLORD
An Imperial Guard short story
Exclusively available from blacklibrary.com

Short fiction by Guy Haley appears in

MARK OF CALTH
A Horus Heresy anthology
Edited by Laurie Goulding

THE BEST OF HAMMER AND BOLTER, VOLUME 2
Edited by Christian Dunn

More Imperial Guard from Black Library

YARRICK: CHAINS OF GOLGOTHA
David Annandale
*Exclusively available from Games Workshop Hobby Centres,
games-workshop.com and blacklibrary.com*

FIRE CASTE
Peter Fehervari

• THE MACHARIAN CRUSADE •
William King

Book 1: ANGEL OF FIRE
Book 2: FIST OF DEMETRIUS (May 2013)
Book 3: FALL OF MACHARIUS (2014)

A WARHAMMER 40,000 NOVEL

BANEBLADE

GUY HALEY

BLACK LIBRARY

To the many authors of Warhammer and Warhammer 40,000.
Thanks for a lifetime of gaming pleasure.

A Black Library Publication

First published in Great Britain in 2013 by
Black Library,
Games Workshop Ltd.,
Willow Road,
Nottingham, NG7 2WS, UK.

10 9 8 7 6 5 4 3 2 1

Cover illustration by Adam Tooby.

A CIP record for this book is available from the British Library.

UK ISBN13: 978 1 84970 076 4
US ISBN13: 978 1 84970 315 4

See the Black Library on the internet at

www.blacklibrary.com

Find out more about Games Workshop
and the world of Warhammer 40,000 at

www.games-workshop.com

Printed and bound by CPI Group (UK) Ltd, Croydon, CR0 4YY

It is the 41st millennium. For more than a hundred centuries
the Emperor has sat immobile on the Golden Throne of Earth.
He is the Master of Mankind by the will of the gods, and master
of a million worlds by the might of his inexhaustible armies. He
is a rotting carcass writhing invisibly with power from the Dark
Age of Technology. He is the Carrion Lord of the Imperium for
whom a thousand souls are sacrificed every day, so that he may
never truly die.

Yet even in his deathless state, the Emperor continues his
eternal vigilance. Mighty battlefleets cross the daemon-infested
miasma of the warp, the only route between distant stars, their
way lit by the Astronomican, the psychic manifestation of the
Emperor's will. Vast armies give battle in His name on uncounted
worlds. Greatest amongst his soldiers are the Adeptus Astartes,
the Space Marines, bio-engineered super-warriors. Their comrades
in arms are legion: the Imperial Guard and countless Planetary
Defence Forces, the ever-vigilant Inquisition and the tech-priests of
the Adeptus Mechanicus to name only a few. But for all their
multitudes, they are barely enough to hold off the ever-present
threat from aliens, heretics, mutants - and worse.

To be a man in such times is to be one amongst untold
billions. It is to live in the cruellest and most bloody
regime imaginable. These are the tales of those times.
Forget the power of technology and science, for so much has
been forgotten, never to be re-learned. Forget the promise of
progress and understanding, for in the grim dark future
there is only war. There is no peace amongst the stars,
only an eternity of carnage and slaughter, and the
laughter of thirsting gods.

PROLOGUE

BANEBLADE MANUFACTORUM CCIV,
UTOPIA PLANITIA, HOLY MARS
0033639.M39

A thousand thousand triphammers rang out the birth of war's child, the bringer of ruin, the mightiest battle tank in the galaxy: Baneblade, fifteen metres long, as tall as three men, a moving fortress, hammer of the God-Emperor, bearer of firepower to equal a squadron of lesser tanks.

But not yet, not yet. This one was a shell, bereft of tooth and claw, gaping ports where guns should be, tracks limp. No energy flowed through its conduits, no fuel through its pipes. Not for long, for now began the ceremony of activation.

The steady drone of five-score throats singing in chorus built to a crescendo. Mighty chains rattled as scores of men dragged hard, stripped to the waist in the heat, furnace-light glinting from their shaven skulls, shadowing the numerals branded into their foreheads. The work gangs pulled the machine through the final stages of the production line upon a mighty sled, towards the culmination of a year-long process in a forge that covered half a continent. Ruddy, incandescent light caught planes of armour as machines older than memory hammered in searing rivets. The grinding and roaring and hissing of automated systems competed with the chants of the tech-priests and the shouts of labouring tech-adepts. Libations sizzled on cooling plasteel, parchment prayers curled and blackened as they were affixed to the hull, wax ran on hot steel.

A man, or what had once been a man, stood atop a baroque motor-carriage to the fore of the chorus and led the chant, lesser tech-adepts behind him, all robed in cloth the colour of old blood, mirroring his words in the twittering binary language of machines, its meanings the deepest of arcane secrets. Words dragged from aged throats and teased from vox boxes grafted to withered flesh rumbled a glorious litany to the cog and the gear.

'The cowls of victory,' shouted the magos, breaking into the tongue of High Gothic. 'The housings of the weapons of righteousness! Blessed be, blessed be the children of the machine!' The others echoed him, red hoods covering altered faces. Behind them, a choir of servitors droned praise. All were dwarfed by the machine.

A vat-grown homunculus scattered sacred oils upon the hull and the dozens of cyborgs, workers and tech-adepts labouring upon it. Twisted cherubs swung censers, sacred smoke mixing with the stink of hot metal as machine-spirits guided giant arms to attach armoured cupolas to either side of the great tank. Servitors with bolt-drivers in place of limbs moved forwards. Bolts whirred home, the arms and the machine men retreated. Spider-like welders darted in from above, swinging with precision on long, cabled brachia suspended from the roof high above. They spat and shifted, closing gaps with terse arclight. Tech-priests and servitors connected cables amidst darting assembly drones, running auspex and chanting blessings as the Baneblade received the housings for its deadly instruments.

The tank ground forwards upon its plasteel sled, runners squealing on the tracks of the line, work gangs chanting as they pulled it to the next stage of creation; one step closer to birth.

'The teeth of victory!' shouted the magos, his inhuman visage glinting deep within the shadowed folds of his robes. 'The hammers of the Emperor's foes! Heavy boltgun, pattern VI Lucian manufacture,' intoned the magos. His implanted logic engines emanated fat datastreams bearing detailed specifications of all parts as he spoke, subsidiary augmitters studding the length of his mechadendrites chittered the same through the air in hasty binaric, those of his inferiors responded.

'Blessed be he who uncovers the truth!' groaned the cyborg choir. Screeching roars of aurally broadcast datastreams accompanied them.

'Lascannon, timeless, born of dark times, master of the lights of death, Mars created, Primus Standard Template Construct pattern,' continued the magos in High Gothic. 'Bolter, heavy, LXV Lucius type. Swift winged oblivion shalt thou spit, tungsten-capped, solid-fuelled…' He slipped deep into an ecstatic trance as he called the names of the guns intended for the tank before him, blueprints flickering out through his augmitters to enlighten those around him.

As their names were invoked, each of the lesser weapons was brought forth upon an ornate carriage attended by more droning tech-magi, veiled in sacred oilcloth inscribed with holy mysteries too terrible to contemplate, and arrayed about the vehicle. At various points in the last year, each weapon had been singly fitted, tested, retested, and removed. Today, the day of activation, all would be mounted together for the first and last time. For six weeks the tech-priests had been working in shifts, anointing catch and gimbal, praying as they smoothed away burrs of metal, raising praise to the Machine-God as each screw was driven home. Now, the flesh-bound servants of the Omnissiah worked quickly, fitting the fangs and claws of this most terrible of beasts, crooning sweet benedictions to the machine's quiescent spirit, lest it awaken early and incomplete, and consume them all in a fury.

The machine's auxiliary weapons systems in place, many of the tech-adepts retreated, their cyborg slaves clanking dutifully after them, unaltered workers scurrying in their wake.

'Battle cannon, Vulcan-named, death to the unclean!' So spoke the magos. Down came a claw, its grasp seeming mighty enough to clasp a world in unyielding ceramite and shake it all to pieces. In a cradle of plasteel talons rested the main armament of the tank; following behind in the tender embrace of a second claw came the tank's secondary weapon. 'Battle cannon. Demolisher Cannon.' The magos named them both and incanted their specifications. The barrel of the first was ten metres long, capable of hurling rocket-propelled shells over kilometres. The second was shorter, sturdier, wider-mouthed. Its munitions could shatter ferrocrete; the shockwaves alone would turn a man to paste.

Carefully, the claws of the cathedral-factory lowered their deadly cargo. Gently, the tech-priests guided the weapons, directing teams of slack-mouthed servitors and branded workers to tug at chain and tackle, aligning the weapons carefully with their housings. When the work gangs were positioned, the magos nodded. Adepts at the heads of each crew dropped crimson flags. As one, the servitors heaved. The barrels slid into place, the slam of plasteel and clack of bolts engaging announcing their successful situation.

Within the Baneblade others worked, welding, riveting, anointing and praying. Electronic conduits were coupled and opened, the flow of electricity praised and coaxed, resistances tested, switches primed. Energy poured into still machinery, bringing it to life, found it worthy and was shut off, the adepts satisfied.

Two days passed. Around the tank, activity built to a frenzy as the time of activation came near. Hundreds of sweating men pulled hard on hawser and chain, dragging pallets of components, armour plates and external systems towards the unfinished Baneblade. Graspers and claws wired to disembodied human brains attached cupola and hatch, periscope glass and handle. Tech-priests watched carefully through servo-skulls swarming like flies about the whole, checking and documenting the entirety of the process in case the unthinkable happen and the machine did not activate as it should, to lie there stillborn and cold, an affront to the Omnissiah. Reckoning must be made in such a circumstance.

'Pattern, code and number!' bellowed the magos. Soft squeals of ones and zeros announced the same. All eight of his additional articulated limbs rose heavenwards to wave in a serpentine dance as he slammed the base of his ceremonial cog-toothed axe rhythmically upon the floor, setting up a clanging in time with his words. The tech-priests and servitors took up the refrain with their tools and implants until the air vibrated with metallic thunder.

From somewhere high up, far, far from the most holy factory floor, a bell began to sound, counting time to the roar and squeak of audible data-shouts. Fashioned from the melted armour of four thousand holy war machines, fallen in service to the Emperor, it tolled loud enough to alert the Lord of Terra himself, telling him that a new champion was born to him.

Baneblade.

'The first is Mars! Let that be thy pattern, as it is your home. The second is forty-seven-dash-nine three seven two. Let that be thy number! The third is 033639, millennium 39, Terran checksum 0. Let that be thy inception code!'

Slowly, slowly, the tank moved forwards. Work gangs had come and gone, cycling through shifts, the men kept fresh so the machine would keep its speed precise through the last metres of the line. The final machines approached and caressed the tank, the final work teams took up their tasks.

Then, it was done. The Baneblade, completed, passed under a festoon of oilcloths and parchments, of flimsies and blueprints, the blessings of the ages of ancient, holy knowledge, preserved by the Omnissiah for the Adeptus Mechanicus alone.

'Let there be spoken the rites of activation! Shout forth the hymns of awakening! Supplicate the Machine-God!' bellowed the magos, his voice, data-shouts, and augmits growing through cunning means to swallow the din around it. 'I call the Magos Activator!'

'Call the Magos Activator!' echoed the choir, and ceased. The tolling of the making-bell and the clatter and bang of more distant manufactory processes took its place.

The tank ticked as it cooled.

The eyeless face of an autoscribe – part machine, part cadaver – looked on, metal fingers scratching pen on spooling parchments, recording every detail of the ceremony.

A delegation of high-ranking tech-priests walked forwards, a wizened torso upon a spider-legged carriage at their head, the Magos Activator and his followers. Ten deeply cowled acolytes, hands and manipulators hidden in their sleeves, were borne to the side on a palanquin of carved zinc carried on heavy treads. With the faintest impact, the platform came to a rest against the top of the war machine's track guards. One by one the adepts crossed the hull, ascended the turret, and went within, there to take the stations that would one day be filled by the warriors of the Imperial Guard, the ten men who would crew it to war.

Clearly, the Magos Activator spoke the rites of activation,

while runes and mysteries were painted upon the Baneblade's motive parts in oils of utmost sanctity, and the ten within tested the machine's controls, while four diagnosticians pored over a bank of ornate green screens outside, a bundle of cables snaking up and into the tank through its forward hull hatch. For an hour the prayers went on, the murmuring of the activation team growing into song, until gradually the servitors picked up the chant again. Tension built.

Eventually, the Magos Activator and his coterie stepped back. He nodded once to the High Magos. It was done.

'Awaken!' called the High Magos. 'Machine Spirit I call upon thee! To life, to life! Awaken!' he bellowed. 'Prime the pumps! Engage the generators! Start the engine!'

Within, the adepts worked at the tank's stations: First, Second and Third Gunner; First, Second and Third Loader; Driver, Tech-Adept Aspirant, Commander, Commsman, pressed buttons and pulled levers, sibilant prayers on their lips.

The power plant of the Baneblade clicked as it turned over. Then it roared, higher and higher and higher as the diagnosticians outside tested its torque and fuel-to-energy conversion ratios. Armament whined as it rotated. The turret turned, battle cannon and coaxial autocannon rising to full elevation and back again. Its hull-mounted demolisher cannon swivelled this way and that, the twin-linked heavy bolter in the small turret to its right following its movements. The remote weapons banks in the cupolas on the tank's sides whirred with activity; these sponsons were positioned midway down the vehicle on the outer track guards, twin-linked heavy bolters in each, single lascannons contained within miniature turrets atop both.

Inside, mechanisms and screens sprang into life, bathing the interior of the tank in holy machine light. Tactical displays, targeting banks, comms equipment – all glowed and chattered, reeling off information. Wizened fingers caressed screens and buttons, purpose-built manipulators keyed into ports. One by one, the ten men within sang off the holy words of functionality, naming the machines and their intent.

'Activated,' each called, at the end of his litany, and so the next would begin his chant, and conclude 'Activated,' until all were done, and the High Magos Activator informed.

'All systems engaged. Blessed be the Omnissiah,' he intoned.

Outside the tank, the Prelate Master of Diagnostics, a bloated mass of flesh married to a mess of cables, rose up from his bank of logic engines arrayed about him in stepped ranks like the boards of an organ. 'All systems operate within normal parameters, oh high one. Engine function optimal. Systems nominal and ready for command. Weapons primed.'

A leathery tongue licked thin lips. 'Does it live?' asked the High Magos.

'It lives,' replied the prelate, and bowed his head in affirmation.

'Holy life! Cog and Gear!' sang the High Magos. 'Blessed be the Omnissiah!'

'Blessed be the Omnissiah!' echoed the servitors.

'Your Pattern, Code and Number shall be entered into the Liber Armorum Magnus,' chanted the High Magos, now directly addressing the new-born engine of war. 'As shall your name!' He paused. He bent low to a scroll borne by a blue-skinned vat child, a roll a metre thick, bearing the names of tens of thousands of Baneblades, born from this forge down innumerable centuries. 'I name thee Mars Victorius, *Mars Triumphant*!'

The choir reached a crescendo. The bell tolled. The autoscribe scratched the name into its annals beside the names of its forebears.

And so *Mars Triumphant* was born. Its engine roared approval of its name. Its turrets tracked across the room, as if its augur-eyes were already keen to seek the enemies of mankind. The children of the Machine-God gave thanks to their all-knowing master in thunderous reply.

Inside the belly of the beast, a low-ranking tech-adept, young and yet to receive his datacore, carefully placed a brass plaque against a decorated panel the size of a tombstone, and with slow, reverent twists of his screwdriver, attached it to the wall.

The plaque would remain blank until *Mars Triumphant*'s field trials were completed and it was deployed to one of the Imperium's battlefronts. It awaited the name of *Mars Triumphant*'s first commander, the being of flesh who would guide this being of plasteel to protect the worlds of humanity. Metal and flesh, tank and crew, Machine-God and Emperor; together in the greater service of mankind, as was right.

Thus had it always been in the Imperium of Man.

The final work gang led the tank away, chains slack, tracks turning under their own power. The magos turned his palanquin upon its mechanical legs and, acolytes and work gangs trudging behind, headed back to the beginning of the activation run, where another unfinished machine awaited completion. Behind it, another, and behind that, another still, and then another and another, stretching back further than the eye could see on a factory floor that followed the curve of the planet. Truly, the holy work of the Omnissiah was never done, and the High Magos's mechanical heart sang with the joy of that.

INTERSTITIAL

+++ADEPTUS TERRA SYSTEM CLASSIFICATION+++
Kalidar System
Segmentum Tempestus
Chiros Sector
Kalidar Subsector, e 3.000.2.003
STELLAR BODY: 'Kalidar'. Single Type A main sequence
blue-white star. Anomalous elemental composition
sequencing and stellar instability suggests manipulation
in the distant past equating to grade F [X-T Scale].
ORBITING BODIES: Kalidar I, II, III – Planetary husks.
Equidistant placing at orbital distance 3 AU, non-natural
orbital pattern [ref. SUPPRESSED BY INQUISITORIAL
ORDER CLASS EPSILON///ADEPTUS MECHANICUS
DATA ORDINATOR 4///SEQUESTRATION ENTIRE].
Kalidar IV [ref. Kalidar IV]
Kalidar V; Orbital Distance: 5.33 AU. Ringed Gas Giant;
328 Terramass. Moons: None.
Kalidar VI; Orbital Distance: 7.25 AU. Gas Giant; 426
Terramass. Moons: 12. Population 12,137. Orbital
mining platform/ lunar mining personnel. [ref. Lax, grade
XIV habitable moon. Agriworld.]
Kalidar VII; Orbital Distance 12.9 AU.
Asteroid belt 'The Girdle'; Orbital Distance 9 AU.
Population 928,331.
Asteroid belt 'Kalidar's Noose'; Orbital Distance 8.7 AU,
angle 76 degrees from plane of the ecliptic. Possible
stellar collision remnant. Population 2,000,023.

Req. world: Kalidar IV
Orbital Distance 4.78 AU – 8.6 AU
Temp. –37 to 87 degrees C
0.7 G
0.8 Terramass
[Further details ref: Kalidar IV Physical properties
1227/33oIV]
Planetary Grade: Industrial world
DESIGNATED SYSTEM CAPITAL
DESIGNATED SUBSECTOR CAPITAL
Aestimare: Exactus secundus (nominal),
optimare tertio prime
Geography: Grade CLXXVI desert world [subclasses:
minor hive, quinternary echelon death world
(class IV)]
Imperial Planetary Commander:
Lozallio Cann [deceased]
Status: War

Thought for the day: The Emperor protects only the faithful.

CHAPTER 1

Mars Triumphant sat upon a darkened plain, engines quiet, drawn up in readiness for the coming battle. For nearly two years it had lain in its cradle within the depths of a transport barge; tomorrow it would assail the orks of Kalidar.

The tank rocked in time with the barrage; shells flung by artillery batteries ten kilometres behind the tank's position, falling onto the ork army still kilometres ahead. Honoured Lieutenant Cortein felt rather than heard the distant thunder through the Baneblade's armour as a steady metronome of destruction. Fine veils of Kalidar's ever-present dust sifted down from the tank's ceiling with every explosion.

Three days on Kalidar, and already *Mars Triumphant* was being asked to fight.

Cortein was unconcerned by the speed of their deployment, he understood this as his duty. If the tank had been asked, and could have replied, Cortein was sure it would hold similar sentiments. But the new regiments, raised on Cortein's home-world of Paragon, trained as they made their slow, dangerous way through the warp to Kalidar… He was not so sure he could say the same of them. Instinct told him that they needed more time, that this rush to smash the ork force besieging the mine complex of Urta was unwise.

There was little he could do about that. Tomorrow, the 7th Paragonian Super-heavy Tank Company would form the lynchpin of one of two large arrow-headed tank formations, the remainder of them made up of Leman Russ squadrons and mechanised infantry, the two formations part of a large action involving men from three worlds. A hundred tanks, four regiments of infantry, a surprise for the orks besieging Urta at the heart of the lorelei-rich Kostoval Flats.

That was the idea. Cortein was suspicious of ideas like this. Perhaps the thick armour of *Mars Triumphant* had made him cautious, inclined to sit things out, he thought, behind the fortress-like walls of the Baneblade. Maybe, but as they said at home, one does not weather a storm by casting oneself into the sea.

Cortein stood before *Mars Triumphant*'s dimly lit wall of honour, near the reactor, the plant at the heart of the baneblade. Names on brass plaques filled the wall almost entirely, a proud list ending with his own. The green and red glows emitted by *Mars Triumphant*'s dim lights struck strange reflections from the metal, alternately revealing and obscuring the heroisms of the tank's long past.

The first plaque was worn smooth by time to leave but traces of archaic battle honours and the curve of what might have been an S or a G. Perhaps, thought Cortein, other commanders of *Mars Triumphant* had stood here like he did before every engagement, their fingers tracing out the names of those who had come before them. How many times had he stood there? He did not know, the battles and campaigns of thirty years blurring into one endless war, a lifetime of conflict. Such was the sacrifice the Emperor had demanded of him. It was a sacrifice Cortein bore gladly. He'd give his life over again, and again a score of times, having seen what he had seen. Humanity was besieged as surely as the orks out there in the desert besieged the lorelei mine complex. If it were not for the sacrifice of men like him...

But there were men like him, many men, the passing of some remembered on this wall, and so the Imperium would stand. He had faith in the Emperor and in his servants.

Still he felt fear at his own end, its edge dull and worn by experience and hard-won courage; present nevertheless.

He heard a faint scuff behind him and glanced back. Crimson robes moved in the shadows, deeper shadows within the hood.

'Enginseer Adept Brasslock,' Cortein said. He returned his attention to the wall.

'Honoured Lieutenant Cortein,' said the other. He whispered as a priest does in a cathedral, his low voice hard to make out over the hiss of artificial lungs.

'I saw your bodyguard outside and assumed you were within. But I did not hear you approach. In this machine you are as quiet as a monk in a cloister.'

The enginseer gave forth the mechanical cough that passed for his laugh. 'And that I am, in here, within *Mars Triumphant*. Any of the adepts of Mars are but supplicants before such a machine. You hold your vigil?'

Cortein nodded distractedly. 'As always. It calms me.'

'After all these years, you need calming?' Brasslock's voice held the smile his face could no longer show. 'You and I are old men, Cortein. Surely the battle fear has left you now?'

'Never,' said Cortein. 'If it ever does, then I shall be dead. No man can ever conquer the fear of battle, and it is not wise to try. Standing here helps hold it at bay, turn it outwards, use it.'

'To know the Machine-God and the Emperor watch over you,

that is what calms you, and it should,' said the other, certain in his pronouncement. 'Many of your predecessors, the ones that I have known, have felt the same.'

'No, it is not that.' Cortein shook his head, checked himself, not wishing this one night to offend the seer, whose faith was somewhat stronger and deeper than his own. 'Not entirely.' He turned to the enginseer.

Brasslock stood easily within the narrow confines of the main gangway leading from the gunnery deck. Cortein had no idea how old he was. Despite his stealth he suspected Brasslock was ancient, as the followers of the Omnissiah often were. His flesh hand, the left, was wizened as centuried leather, blotched with spots and scars. It was impossible to tell what colour the man's skin had originally been. Brasslock rested this hand on the open bulkhead door, idly stroking plasteel as a mother might soothe her child. Metal glinted in the hood where his mouth should be. A thin, articulated tendril snuck out from under his robes from time to time, tasted the air and wicked back within. His right arm ended in a heavy metal stump, a broad socket ready to accept tools, for the moment empty. To a normal man's eyes he was a grotesque, but Cortein had long ceased to find Enginseer Brasslock disturbing.

'What then do you find here in the heart of *Mars Triumphant*?' said the enginseer.

'Watching the march of the names through time makes me… confident. Near a thousand years of battle, and this machine still fights. So many battles, tomorrow is merely one more. That is why it calms me.'

'The spirit of *Mars Triumphant* is strong,' agreed the enginseer. They both fell silent, the close silence of the tank disturbed by the distant bombardment and the hiss-whirr of Brasslock's mechanical lungs, the two sounding in time, a pair of impacts for every breath.

'I wonder,' said Cortein eventually. 'I wonder who he was.' He nodded at the first plaque, the brass shiny where it had been rubbed away, the edges deepened to a lustre richer than gold. Verdigris scaled the base of the rivets. 'Who was this first man to stand here? Did he come to look at his own name affixed to this wall as I do now and wonder at those who would follow?'

'I do not know,' said Brasslock. 'Men have forgotten as this metal has forgotten.' He pointed with a skeletal finger. 'But the Machine-God does not forget. The flesh is weak, the Omnissiah is not. He knows all.'

Cortein smiled tiredly. 'Perhaps you can ask him for me some time, I would like to know.'

Brasslock took Cortein's blasphemy with good grace. 'Alas it is not my place to do so, Honoured Lieutenant Cortein, but the data is kept by crystal, pen and chisel in *Mars*'s archives. You can be assured that the Omnissiah remembers all the men who serve Him, as He will remember you.'

'That is not as comforting as you might think it sounds.'

'I did not mean it for comfort, honoured lieutenant.'

From deep within *Mars Triumphant* some subsystem or other grumbled, a pulsing thrum of interrupted energy flow, three beats in contretemps to the barrage outside.

'Ah, see? She agrees.'

'*Mars Triumphant* is inactive.'

'They dream when they sleep, honoured lieutenant, as men do. Listen!'

The artificial thunder had ceased. The ground shuddered hard, once, as if in pain. The charms Brasslock and generations of enginseers before him had affixed to the Wall of Honour jangled in reply, a final shower of dust pattered onto the pitted floor of the tank, then the world became still.

'The barrage, it is done.' The enginseer's shadowy face looked up within his hood, rheumy eyes glinting. 'I must rouse the spirit of *Mars Triumphant*; the other machines of the company must also be propitiated,' said the enginseer. 'I have much work to do to ensure optimum functionality of all systems for the morrow.'

'Of course.'

The enginseer inclined his head in a bow and departed, vanishing into the gloom to the aft of the tank.

Cortein reached out to the plaques on the wall and reverently touched the oldest as was his habit, wearing it away atoms at a time, an erosion born of respect. He put on his cap, lifted the mask of his rebreather from the case hanging on his front, a necessary evil. He didn't want to end his career coughing up his own lungs thanks to the dust. He buckled the foul thing about his face and went up onto the command deck, up again into the turret, and then out into the freezing desert dawn.

CHAPTER 2

KALIDAR IV, KOSTOVAL FLATS
3267397.M41

Morning. Battle had begun. The Imperial advance, entirely mechanised, swept across the plains towards the ork siege lines. Around the Leman Russ and the Chimeras, the Baneblades and the Salamanders and the other armoured vehicles of the assault, a storm of shocking ferocity raged, masking their approach, but playing havoc with communications.

'Sta... ation. Comm... s ... itical. Storm is worsenin...' Lieutenant Colaron Artem Lo Bannick's ears rang with Kalidar's electrostatic roar, the directions keeping the 3rd Company of the 42nd Paragon Tank Regiment's echelon true garbled beyond comprehension. In conditions like this, even with the Leman Russ battle tanks so close to one another, short-range voxcasters barely worked, while the comm suite's logic engine had become a lump of inert brass and plastics that did nothing but take up space. Kalidar appreciated no other voice than her own. 'Sig... a... 317... Keep... ormation. Katail, you... squadron... andering to the left.' The vox crackled, a stream of gibberish that might once have been an order rushing out.

'Say again, command, say again!' Bannick's finger clicked off the speaking horn. Nothing but screeching came in reply. 'Damn storm's getting worse.' Bannick hunched over the command suite of his Leman Russ *Indomitable Fury* and checked his squadron's positioning against the overall plan. All bar the simplest instruments showed some kind of effect from the planet's chaotic magnetosphere, but as far as he could tell they were still in formation. The glass bulbs positioned round the circumference of the Leman Russ's vision block were sand-blasted opaque by the planet's accursed dust, revealing only an undifferentiated yellowish blur that could have been sky or ground. The tank's augurs were not much better, screens rippling with actinic ghosts. Thankfully the periscope had been fitted with a cover, or they'd stay blind. He dared not open that yet; he'd learned from veterans of the campaign that supplies could be months in coming. To lose the periscope would be a disaster.

Indomitable Fury bucked and gyred underneath him. Gunner Patinallo glanced up at Bannick from the seat below and to the right of his own, the massive breech block of the battle cannon like a threat between them.

'Squadron Three! Keep your tanks in line!' Bannick shouted into the speaking horn in an effort make himself heard over the roar of the engine. 'I don't want my name read out over the vox like that idiot Katail! Keep us in formation!' Small augur screens showed him his crew: five men. His driver Kurlick, grim-faced and squinting as he wrestled the tank over the soft sand of Kalidar, as blind to what lay ahead as Bannick; Patinallo and the loader Brevant, viewed from an augur-eye at the front of the tank; Arlesen and Tovan, his sponson gunners, one so stoic as to appear petrified, the other mumbling prayers and repeatedly wiping sweat from his hands.

He'd been angered when his squadron had not been given

the duty of going in first at the head of their echelon; that honour had gone to Verlannick. His Leman Russ, *Wilful Destruction*, had been fitted with three heavy bolters in its sponsons and hull mount. These would be firing until they glowed red as the tank hit the enemy, the rest of his squadron on his flanks, covering his charge with their battle cannons. All the glory a man could wish for. He envied Verlannick that, even though the survival of the tank and crew was rated at less than fifteen per cent. It should have been him. The short odds of the point position were no less than he deserved.

He shook himself. Envy was not a virtue worthy of the Paragonian clan nobility.

Bannick blew out his cheeks, sweat trickling into his flesh eye, stinging it. His face itched with grime and salt. He wiped his face. The external screens cleared a little. The pictures remained grainy and jagged with interference patterns, but at least he could see.

'A lull in the storm, Emperor be praised.' Unconsciously he reached up his hand and pressed at the twin medallions under his shirt, the aquila and the cog, side by side, as worn by all the manufacturing aristocracy of Paragon.

The left screen showed a vast expanse of desert, billows of dust from the tanks in front whirling across it. The view to the front and the right was less clear, plumes of the stuff kicked high by the preceding Leman Russ's treads, one of the two in his squadron besides his own *Indomitable Fury*. The third was practically invisible, further out still, its shape lost in the storm. The whole company laboured on a dune as high as a mountain, all ten battle tanks struggling for purchase as they fishtailed their way up to the summit.

The tanks were in a formation designated as Solon's Axe, a *Tactica Imperium*-standard attack mode with trailing edges and a broad, flat front. The 3rd Company of the 42nd Paragonian

Armoured Regiment's job was to cover the left. Out on their right, hundreds of metres away, ran the 2nd Company, tasked with the protection of that flank. The fire arcs were seriously restricted by the formation but that was not important, they were forming a moving wall, a mobile fortress, protecting and supporting the machines in the middle of the two companies.

In between the Leman Russ lumbered the 7th Paragonian Super-heavy Tank Company, four mechanical monsters of prodigious size and power. Their names leapt into Bannick's mind: the Baneblade *Artemen Ultrus*, the Hellhammer *Ostrakan's Rebirth*, the Shadowsword *Lux Imperator*, and the Baneblade *Mars Triumphant*. These were true fists of the Emperor.

Somewhere behind the tank axe rode thirty squads of the 63rd Paragonian Mechanised and 14th Savlar Light Infantry, crammed into Chimera armoured carriers, waiting to leap out and exploit the gap the tanks were to create. They completed the Beta group.

Formation Alpha was of similar composition and rode a few kilometres away, both formations converging on the weakest spot on the ork siege line. The orks had dug themselves in, fighting running battles under and over the ground for more than two months with the lorelei miners and the troops detailed to support them. This attack was intended to break that siege.

The Leman Russ echelons at the sides of the axes would hit first, the super-heavy tanks – slower and more ponderous than the smaller battle tanks – would then advance and destroy the orks and their fortifications in between the Leman Russ echelons across a front perhaps a kilometre wide. Once the orks' lines of trenches had been penetrated by the tank formations, other elements of the Imperial Guard were to move up and exploit the hole, while heavy bombardment pinned down the flanks of the greenskin horde, preventing reinforcements.

Caught between the tanks and mechanised infantry in the rear, the miners and the troops stationed in the mine to their front and a rain of high-explosive fire to either side, the orks would be annihilated.

Bannick desired to serve the Emperor in battle; if he were to die, so be it. But there were a thousand pointless ways to end one's days here on Kalidar before you came within sight of the foe – swiftdust, radiation, temperature fluctuations and the ever-present danger of dustlung from the razor-sharp sand of the place. Right now the biggest threat was swiftdust – if a tank went into a patch of that it wasn't going to come out again. This sector of the front had been declared free of swiftdust by Munitorum Ordinators but that meant nothing; Kalidar was treacherous, the dust moved quickly.

'The Emperor protects the bold,' he muttered. 'Just don't let me die in some damned sinkhole. That's all I ask. If I am to die, let my death count.'

He was jounced out of his thoughts as the engine pitch shifted and the tank heeled to the right and leaned back. His back pressed uncomfortably into the equipment round his chair as *Indomitable Fury* hung at a sixty-degree angle for an impossibly long second and he was forced to grasp at his station to steady himself. Through the scoured glass, the colour of the world outside became lighter as the tank reared up into the sky.

'We're going over!' shouted Kurlick. 'We're going over!'

'Third squadron, stay in line!' Bannick shouted into the horn.

The tank toppled forwards and hit the down slope. Bannick gripped his seat rails as his helmet rang off the vision-port casing before him. The tank's engine howled as it picked up speed, hammering down the dune, slewing from side to side like a snake on the sand.

'Stay together!' Company Captain Malliant's voice, fighting over the roar of static and engines. 'Enemy in …ight. Time to impact is ….' His voice died away, Kalidar's angry scream overwhelming him. '…wait for my…'

This was it. Contact, his – their – first engagement. Two years in the warp, three days in the desert, right off the drop-ship. Finally, a chance to prove himself. 'Squadron, prepare to slow to combat speed,' ordered Bannick. His blood thundered loud enough to compete with the tank's engine. 'Patinallo.'

'Yes, sir.'

'Prepare to open fire with main armament,' Bannick said, then added, 'that's if you can see anything in this mess.' He debated with himself. 'I'm opening the hatch. Masks on!' He fastened his stinking rebreather over his mouth, a heavy, rubbery respiration mask wretched with the reek of his own breath and sweat. Hoses snaking behind the command chair in the turret attached it to the filter system, a bulky machine taking up more than its fair share of the tank's already cramped interior. Bannick had the others sign off to make sure they had attached their masks before he grasped the lever above his head, twisted, and flung the hatch backwards.

Outside was a maelstrom. Kalidar's wind, never quiescent, keened ferociously through the fittings of *Indomitable Fury*. Dust stung his face round his breather and goggles. Although *Indomitable Fury* was practically new, built when the regiment was raised, already the sand had begun to strip the tank's paint. He'd heard of more than one man stepping out to be blinded before putting his goggles on. Such men were shot. The commissars could not rule out the possibility that they had allowed themselves to be rendered unfit for duty.

As Kurlick struggled to keep *Indomitable Fury* on an even course Bannick steadied himself on the tank's turret rail. Out to his right he could make out the shape of Company Captain

Malliant's Vanquisher, protected on the inside of the echelon. Some distance to his left a thicker cloud of dust told him the position of the 4th and 5th Companies' axe formation, more super-heavies at its heart – the Atraxian 18th – moving in parallel to them. He could see nothing of the tanks themselves, as massive as they were. He could barely make out the other two tanks in his own squadron, their blocky forms obscured by plumes of sand churned up by ten sets of tracks. His ears throbbed, the vox noise scrabbled at his concentration, the wind competing with that and the thundering engines of half a tank regiment.

There was something else there too, a noise not of Kalidar. He sought after it, lost it, grew frustrated, and tore his headphones off. Sand instantly infiltrated his ears, but without the static-filled comms chatter, he could hear the noise more clearly, a rising-falling, as of surf beating the shore, though the last ocean of Kalidar had dried millennia ago.

He squinted through the veils of sand whipping towards him. The chant grew louder. A dune obscured the view half a kilometre ahead. The formation was quickly up and over, Bannick bracing himself against the turret edge as Kurlick took the ridge at speed. More than one tank commander had been killed by internal injuries sustained while in transit over Kalidar's unforgiving terrain.

The wind shrieked, the chant was momentarily drowned, and then it was back on, low and guttural.

Skirls of sand whispered up and over *Fury*'s bulk, veils of dust swept in and over him, and suddenly the visibility cleared enough for Bannick to see the blurry outline of Kalidar's fierce blue sun. The shapes around him resolved themselves into tanks. He peered forwards. About three kilometres out over the saltpan of a long-dead sea was a dark wall, a jagged line hard against the desert: thousands upon thousands of orks, all chanting in one savage voice.

'Throne!' said Bannick. 'They know we're coming. They've come out from their trenches.'

The shapes of crude war machines punctuated the orkish ranks, studding the horde with jagged islands of metal. There was little standardisation to them, each different in some way to its fellows. As the taskforce drew nearer to the orks the lurid colours of their armour, equipment and clothing grew brighter and brighter.

They were loosely organised into great mobs of towering warriors, each clutching at unwieldy alien weapons. There seemed to be little hierarchy to them; heavy weapons were scattered amid their ranks, clanking walkers waving pincers and saws stomping backwards and forwards.

A howl went up from the greenskins as they caught sight of the tanks. Instantly the maws of their war machines flashed fire, the pop and crackle of cannon reports sounding moments later.

'Incoming!' shouted Bannick, hoping that the vox pick-up in his mask had not malfunctioned again. Deafening whistles and screaming thrums filled the air, followed by explosions as shells impacted the dessicated seabed and heaved up columns of earth high in Kalidar's low gravity. One landed in the centre of the formation, completely hiding Malliant's command tank behind a fountain of dirt. A Leman Russ further ahead caught a glancing hit from a second shell. A track whipped free, the tank pivoting around its uninjured side and coming to a stop, flank to the enemy. Within moments the turret had rotated to face the orks and returned fire. The following vehicles snaked round it and carried on. Bannick recognised the Leman Russ as Kennerston's, Senior Sergeant in the first squadron. Already he'd landed two shots in the orks' ranks. Smoothly done, thought Bannick.

Bannick ducked inside, slammed the hatch and replaced his

headphones. Dust poured in after him. The tank's off-white interior, near pristine days ago, was already chipped and filthy.

'Sir, are you not to direct my fire?' asked Patinallo, his voice barely audible in Bannick's headphones.

Bannick clawed his mask off, gasped as he took in the clearer air of the tank.

'Too much incoming fire! Storm's abated, so I'll risk the periscope,' he said into the horn. 'Though there is not a chance you will miss.'

'Enemy line impact in six minutes.' Malliant's voice, strong for a moment in the lull in the storm. 'Your coming actions honour the dead. Prepare to scour this world free of the Emperor's foe.'

Patinallo looked to Bannick, his eyes expectant over the rim of his rebreather mask. The face of Brevant bobbed about below him. Bannick nodded at them. What he'd seen had barely shaken his battle-lust. This was what he had come for, this was what he had spent two years on a barge travelling over a segmentum to do, a chance at redemption. Excitement coursed through his veins, and *Indomitable Fury* surged beneath him. A sixty-tonne monster capable of spitting death over a kilometre, and two more like it, were his to command. He felt invincible, as safe behind the tank's armour as if he were enfolded in the wings of the Emperor.

He threw a lever, pulling back the metal eyelid covering the tank's periscope. He put his face to the rubber seal over the eyepiece. The ork horde swam into view, magnified by the scope, a wall of savage green monsters with teeth like bayonets. They were working themselves into a frenzy, discharging their weapons into the air. Suddenly, a large part of the line bellied back and then forwards, a gathering of strength and hate. Ork leaders, taller by a head than their comrades and sporting trophy poles on their backs, ran among them, shouting and striking at the smaller greenskins. But they could not restrain them, the line broke. The orks were as indisciplined as he'd heard.

Captain Malliant spoke. 'The Empe... ...ows the way. Readjust course, aim for the weakening of the line. Enemy in range. Open fire! Fire! Fire! Fire!'

Muffled reports came through the hull of *Indomitable Fury*, the other Russ's commanders jockeying to see who would be first to kill. Not Bannick. He would select his target with care. His first kill would be a big one, he wanted to make certain of it. He scanned the ork line.

'Gunner Patinallo,' he shouted. 'Load armour-piercing high-density shell.'

'Sir! Armour-piercing high-density shell,' said Patinallo. The Leman Russ was noisy, engine, storm and battle noise conspiring to drown out a commander's orders. All conversation was conducted at a shout over the tank intercom. Repetition was essential. Brevant hauled out a green-tipped shell from the rack and slammed it home.

'Track turret. Thirty-two degrees left.'

'Turret thirty-two degrees left,' repeated the gunner. Beyond him the loader had already produced a second shell, preparing to ram it into the breech as soon as the first had been fired. Servos whined as the turret turned.

'Elevate five degrees.' Bannick had his eye on a hulking wagon crammed with orks. Several of these had rumbled forwards in the wake of the infantry hammering across the sands towards the tanks, and were beginning to outpace them. The body of the gun within the tank's turret shifted, halting with a clank.

Patinallo consulted his ranging scope. 'That big ork tank, lieutenant?'

'The very one. Fire.'

Patinallo sat back and his loader rotated aside as he depressed the firing lever. The tank shuddered as *Indomitable Fury* replied to the orkish guns. The noise inside was deafening. The barrel recoiled backwards a third of a metre, fiercely enough to kill anyone stood behind it. The breech door flicked open, ejecting the shell casing halfway and filling the compartment with acrid smoke. Brevant reached his thick gloves between the gunner's and commander's seats to haul the empty casing loose, hurling it back to the tank floor.

Bannick remained glued to his periscope. Bright fire erupted along the length of the ork tank as the shell hit home, pride burning in his heart with it. Armour plates lifted as if punched from within by a giant. Ork body parts pinwheeled away. Black debris pattered down on the sand. When the last had rained down, the tank sat billowing a streamer of greasy black smoke into the wind.

'Hit confirmed. Well done, Gunner Patinallo, our first kill of the day.' Their first kill ever. He curbed an urge to shout like the savage xenos outside. 'Armour-piercing round,' he ordered.

Patinallo echoed him. Brevant brought up the second shell, slid it in to the barrel and shut the breech while Patinallo and Bannick drew a bead on the selected target. *Indomitable Fury* once more gave its deadly shout. A clanking ork walker shattered into fragments, cutting down the infantry about it with red-hot shrapnel. Then the vox blared with static, and the scene was washed away once again by a renewed blizzard of sand. The ork line had vanished, those reckless few who had broken forwards mere shadows in the storm.

'Damn!' swore Bannick. 'Hi-ex! We'll fire blind into the main body! Thin their numbers!' shouted Bannick. His crew dutifully echoed him.

'Prepa... for ...ct.' Malliant's voice began to break up. The end of his statement was lost to the bark of *Fury*'s main gun firing for a third time. When Bannick's ears stopped ringing, there was nothing but interference on the external vox.

'We've lost contact with the captain again! The storm's picking up! Visibility's back down to thirty metres,' said Bannick. 'Sponson gunners keep your eyes peeled for anti-tank. We'll get no infantry support until the grunts debark. Stay on guard.'

'Enemy line two hundred metres and closing!' called out Kurlick.

The four Leman Russ echelons of the twin Imperial spearheads smashed into the charging vanguard of the ork line within seconds of each other. The xenos ran screaming at the tanks, trying to grab on. Many were pulled over, sent head over heels into the dust, more falling under churning tracks. 'Sponson gunners open fire!' bellowed Bannick. Adrenaline coursed through him as the rapid crackle of multiple bolt ignitions joined the racket in the tank. The other vehicles in the formation followed suit, heavy bolters raking the desert. Orks exploded in fountains of gore. Still they came on.

Kurlick shouted, 'Wait, look! Out there, to the left! Contact! Enemy inbound!'

Bannick swung the periscope round, twisting handles to transform a blur of motion into a picture he could understand; out to their flank a score of orks were emerging from the sandstorm, followed by more, and then more. They flung back trap doors and blankets, pulling themselves out of the desert. Many of them clutched crude rockets on poles and limpet mines the size of turret hatches.

'By the Throne! Ambush! Anti-tank, anti-tank! Left sponson concentrate on the missile launchers. Now, do it now!' shouted Bannick.

Rockets corkscrewed through the air on black smoke trails. There was a ringing bang on the hull. Bannick winced, but there was no explosion. Others were not so lucky. Three found their mark on *Ozorian Endures Fatefully*, Bannick's number two, directly in front of *Indomitable Fury*. It lifted off the sand as its magazine detonated, turning over and over in the air with unlikely grace. Bannick stared numbly as it began its downward trajectory, sure it would hit them, then *Indomitable Fury* spun to the side in a grind of protesting gears. The wrecked tank slammed into the ground metres from them. Bannick was thrown out of his seat, and thanked the Emperor for Kurlick's skill as they skidded round the twisted wreck.

Bannick regained his scope to see orks pouring towards them, more and more appearing out of the sandstorm and weaving their way into the formation. 'Sergeant Gallient, concentrate fire to the left, protect the flank, don't let them through!'

'Mai... n form... main...' Malliant said over the vox. Screams competed with frantic orders and roaring static as crews were cooked alive inside their armour.

'They're breaking the formation!' shouted Bannick. This was not how orks were supposed to behave; they were supposed to be indisciplined, chaotic. This was a coordinated attack. What he'd taken for impatience was anything but. As circumscribed as his view of the field was, it was obvious to Bannick that this was not indiscipline.

It was an ambush.

Sponson guns tracked uselessly over the orks' heads as they came in close and low. Rockets rained down from the sides of the formation. As they drew near the tanks the green xenos flung their limpet mines. They stuck with loud clangs to two more tanks ahead of *Indomitable Fury*. The bombs exploded; one tank came through a wreath of fire, guns blazing, the other did not; another Leman Russ gone.

'There's one on the hull! There's one on the hull' yelled Kurlick.

The clank of heavy boots ran up the front of *Indomitable Fury*. Bannick reacted fast, threw open the hatch, hand pulling his rebreather over his mouth.

He rose into the teeth of fury itself. His nose clogged and sand rasped in his throat and lungs before the mask snapped into place. An ork, taller than the tallest man Bannick had ever seen and as heavily muscled as Paragonian swamp cattle, towered above him. Its raised hands held high a metal pole so heavy that Bannick could never have lifted it. Atop the pole a fat, chequered rocket had been wired in place like a hammerhead.

Bannick grabbed for the storm bolter atop the pintle mount. His hands found the cold metal grips, gritty with sand, and he swung it round. The world contracted to a point immediately in front of him – ork and gun, life and death. The storm and the battle were wiped from his perception, his sense of time slowed to a crawl. He pulled the trigger of the storm bolter, watching detachedly as the bolts came out of the weapon's twin barrels, tiny jets igniting at the tail of each as they exited, to accelerate them away. One, two, three… all missed. The ork's rocket came down, inevitable.

The fourth bolt caught the ork in the leg. Mass-activated sensors detonated the miniature missile's charge at a predetermined depth within its warty flesh, blowing the limb free in a spray of blood and meat. The ork went down face first, its rocket clattering harmlessly away. The creature bellowed as it tumbled off *Fury*'s hull, its shout cut short as it went under the treads.

Bannick tracked his bolter round, shooting down orks wherever he could.

'Don't let the greenskins through into the formation centre!' he ordered.

'Sir, something on the scope.' Patinallo's panicked voice was loud in his headphones. 'By the Emperor, sir! Sir, you better come and see this. Sir!'

Through veils of sand like grasping fingers Bannick saw them, ork super-heavy walkers fourteen metres tall, bristling with weapons, crushing orks too slow to move out of the way.

Like all the orks' machines, they were crude and ugly, fashioned as caricatures of fat ork warriors, bulging bellies made of jagged metal plates hammered together with little care and painted in colour schemes of glaring red and yellow, or in garish camo patterns. Crude, but deadly, and seven of them were coming straight at the left echelon. The formation headed blindly towards them.

'Formation! Form... alt!' came Malliant's crackling voice. 'Formation...'

The captain's voice cut out as the ork walkers opened up, heavy ordnance toted on stumpy arms sending shells slamming into the centre of the taskforce.

'Malliant? Captain Malliant... Come in!' shouted Bannick. Useless. 'Lieutenant Verlannick?' He called out to the second-in-command. No reply there either. That left him in command of the depleted company.

The echelon began to break up as the tank squadrons spun tracks, frantically trying to avoid the walkers. Battle cannons barked flame and smoke as turrets rotated, tracking the threat. Shells shattered with fiery bangs against the thick ork armour, but the walkers did not slow.

'All squadrons! Lieutenant Bannick! I am in command! Full reverse! Full reverse!' shouted Bannick. 'Form up on me! Single line! Bring fire to bear...' he consulted his tac display, picking out the walker with what seemed the heaviest guns. 'Point niner-five-zero!'

Hearing his voice, the company began to exhibit some degree of order, forming a wall. They were down to six tanks. Bannick narrowed his eyes. The second company appeared to be doing the same, tanks inching backwards, loosing shots as they went.

He shouted into the horn, internal vox. 'Pantinallo, aim for the...'

He never finished his order. A three-barrelled cannon on a bright yellow walker flashed fire. A second later Bannick's universe became featureless white, shuddering with noise.

He felt himself fall, then felt nothing.

INTERSTITIAL

'Orks are orks are orks, and we're the best in the galaxy! But us, we're the best yet, better than the best of the best. We're Blood Axes, Gorkier than Gork, and Morkier than everyone. We are strong, and we are smart! We're going to tear you all apart, snick snick! Better than a Goff, and sneakier than a Deathskull. We're strong and deadly, but we are cunning too...'

Translated message from Arch-Skarlord 'General' Gratzdakka Wur Mekdakka, prior to the Kalidar invasion.

CHAPTER 3

WARPSPACE
9189267.M41 [NOMINAL]

The feeling in the ship was electric, full of foreboding. Their two-year voyage to Kalidar was nearly done, and the dreams were getting worse – Bannick had not slept properly for days. Lieutenant Kalligen's hand descending on his shoulder was an unwelcome shock.

'I thought I'd find you in here,' said Kalligen, peering into the gloom of Chapel 42, the largest Ecclesiarchical chamber on the transport barge. A statue of the Emperor in armour, three times the height of a man, stared down upon the ranks of pews, flanked by smaller sculptures of saints of the Guard and the Navy. The chapel was getting fuller by the day the nearer the translation came, and now choirs of priests sang constantly, imploring the Emperor for safe passage through the warp.

'Keep your voice down!' muttered Bannick. The transport barge's canon walked by the end of the row of seats, gaze almost as stern as that of the Emperor's statue standing at the head of the chapel. 'Can't a man pray in peace?'

'You do altogether too much praying.' Kalligen sat down on the pew by which Bannick knelt. He at least had the decency to drop his voice and mark the sign of the aquila, Paragonian style, across his forehead. 'I remember a time when you didn't used to pray at all.'

'Times change. Men change.'

'Maybe.' Kalligen nodded. Then: 'Come on, I've got something to show you.'

'Leave me be.'

'You'll like it, I promise.'

'I'm not done.'

Kalligen's face lost its perpetual grin for a moment. 'Yes you are – praying won't change anything, Colaron.'

'I don't see it that way.'

Kalligen scratched his head. 'What's done is done. "Heroes of the Imperium! The time for words is done! Time to live by your actions!"' Kalligen mimicked the thick accent of their commanding officer, Colonel Sholana, a non-Paragonian, like most of the higher-ups in the new regiment.

'You don't know anything about it,' said Bannick.

'I know that you were an idiot to sign up. You could have stayed at home and got rich and fat, not scurrying around in the depths of this tomb with Emperor knows what scrabbling around outside to get in at us.' Kalligen shuddered. 'Gives me the fear. Now, as far as I know you're free right now.' Kalligen stood and bowed to the Master of Mankind. 'I have some orders to deliver to the vehicle deck. And you will want to see what's waiting where I'm going, trust me, but it's a bit of a walk.'

'Time to commencement of realspace translation ritual, six thousand cycles,' intoned a voice, booming across the transport barge in mechanical High Gothic, the syntax mangled in the Navy way, unfamiliar words peppered throughout. 'All personnel prepare for translation. Naval personnel note, Captain Almazan commands free time reduction from thirty to ten minutes daily. Rapid translation preparation protocols alpha ten are now in place. Only the fool shirks his duty, for the Emperor knows all.' A metallic hiss ended the announcement.

'What is that, five days?' muttered Kalligen, his face made choleric by the red lighting of the corridor.

'You're hopeless! Two days, four and a half hours, give or take a few minutes.'

'Come on! Play fair Col, I've never heard the thousand-cycle system used outside the basdack bureaucracy. That and Zero Night, and we... Oh.' He winced when he realised he might have put his foot in it. But Bannick did not react.

'My clan, your adopted family, for the love of the saints, use it in our manufactoria,' Bannick said, 'it keeps the "basdack bureaucracy" happy. If you'd have spent more time learning the ways of your own family and less time drinking and chasing skirt you mightn't find it so confusing.'

Kalligen reached a bulkhead door, grasped the wheel in the centre and turned to his friend. 'Why bother? I was always going into the army, me.' He spun the doorlock with one hand. 'I had a nice, cushy little job in the planetary militia lined up. No war on Paragon for a thousand years, should have been a breeze, just my blasted luck they called a regimental draft two weeks after I signed up. After you, "sir".' Kalligen executed a mock bow.

'Stop it, Lazlo, we'll be up on charges if we get seen. You're a lieutenant too.'

'Yep, well, you have the greater air of authority. All I do is mope about all the parties I'm missing, hardly the stuff of command, am I?' He held up the flimsy clutched in his hand.

'Now where by the High Lords of Terra's collective backsides is berth 29/omicron/iii94a? They could have given me an auspex map. I can barely see this thing it's so dark down here. None of the lights are working. Typical.'

'They could have given you a pass for the tubeway too, but they didn't. Why I agreed to come with you? I could have got some sleep.'

'We both know why you didn't do *that*,' muttered Kalligen, scanning the map hopelessly. 'The nightmares. It's because we're nearly out, it's the worst time.'

Bannick snatched at the map. 'Give it here. Look, the vehicle decks are this way.' He traced his finger round a tangle of corridors. 'But we'll have to avoid this next section.' He pointed down the corridor to the next bulkhead. 'It's not in use.'

Kalligen rolled his eyes. 'You mean go back? I swear this ship has more holes in it than the Emperor himself.'

Bannick gave his friend a level stare. 'They're going to shoot you one day, you know that?'

The route to 29/omicron/iii94a proved long and convoluted. Several times they had to turn around, their way blocked by bulkhead doors welded shut, more sections of the millennia-old craft unused and uninhabitable. They walked kilometres of corridor in the skin of the hull, passing rarely into the vast open spaces at the heart of the barge. Once they walked a catwalk one hundred metres above the training field, a thousand metres square of bare metal deck where they'd spent much of the last two years training on mock battlefields. More corridors, on and on past dim rooms where bunks stretched off into the gloom. The thrum of the engines grew louder until conversation grew impossible between them, then receded. They passed through a gallery where hundreds of Naval personnel toiled at an incomprehensible machine of obscure purpose and immense size, its throaty roar accompanied by the crack of whips and the dirge of a warp-shanty.

After three hours they found themselves walking through colonnaded cloisters running the length of the barge's vehicle decks. Hundreds of Leman Russ, Chimera armoured personnel carriers, Salamander scout vehicles, self-propelled artillery, support vehicles and other, more unusual types rested in their transport cradles, stacked like models in a god's toyshop, the racks disappearing into the gloom. Aside from a few servitors patrolling the place, they were alone. Munitorum and Adeptus Mechanicus personnel would have locked down the place as soon as the twelve-cycle translation warning had come. Having seen to their charges, they'd be preparing themselves now.

A weird howling filled the air and the hairs on Bannick's neck stood on end. The entire craft shuddered.

'What the...?'

Kalligen put his hand on Bannick's shoulder. 'Don't worry. It's always this way when they're getting ready to translate,' said Kalligen, low and conspiratorial. 'That's when it happens; coming in or going out of the immaterium, that's when the Geller fields are most stressed.' He laughed at his friends' dismay. 'Don't worry. It doesn't happen often. The stress sets up all kinds of weird harmonics in the hull, especially in an old tub like this.'

'How do you know that?' Bannick swallowed nervously. A quartet of servitors clanked towards them. They had to move aside or be crushed. Once they had passed, the two lieutenants continued onwards.

'I did pay some attention to my own clan's business. My cousins told me.'

'Just how many cousins do you have?' Kalligen's cousins were an endless source of information.

'A couple of dozen. If there weren't so many I'd never

have been sent to live with you, would I? Four of them are merchantmen, you know that. Typical, I'm the one that really didn't want to go into space, and yet here I am.'

'Stop complaining, it's not worthy of our kind. We're here and... Are those the...?' Bannick stopped, awestruck.

'Well, would you look at that,' said Kalligen with mock surprise. 'See, I told you I had something worth showing you, eh?'

In the racks before them squatted the titanic vehicles of the 7th Paragonian Super-heavy Tank Company. There were four of them, only four vehicles to make up an entire company! Bannick could not imagine what an entire regiment of them would be like, not that such things existed. Aside from the taskforce command Leviathan, the super-heavies were the only tanks of that size and power on the entire transport barge – they were rare.

Bannick looked at the tanks with awe and respect, two versatile Baneblades, a short-range engagement Hellhammer, and a Shadowsword armed with an anti-Titan volcano cannon.

'Are you glad you came now?' said Kalligen. 'Keeping me company for a while a fair trade?'

'Imagine serving on them, Lazlo, imagine commanding one!'

Kalligen shook his head. 'Me, I'd rather serve on that.' he pointed down the ranks of tank cradles. The lower half of one side of the Leviathan could just be made out in the distance, heavy with decoration, three great turrets atop bastions along its flank, a cathedral on tracks.

'On the Leviathan? No Lazlo, they never see much action, too important. These, these super-heavy tanks, that's what does all the fighting.'

'My point exactly,' said Kalligen. 'Stop that will you? Two more minutes and you'll be dribbling. I...'

Kalligen was interrupted. A servitor with a socket in place of a left arm came to life in the shadows, causing them both to start, and marched stiffly across the deck. A faded penal tattoo adorned its bald head. Whoever had provided its organic component had been a giant in life. A harsh machine voice barked out of a speaker in its neck, the lips remaining immobile; half its face was given over to an implanted targeting array, its remaining human eye blank and fixed on the air above their heads. 'State your business. This is a restricted area. No admission to the vehicle decks during transit period for non-authorised personnel.'

'I… we have authorisation. I am delivering this datacapsule on behalf of General Ban Lo Verkerigen,' said Kalligen.

A spread of green light emanated from the cyborg's facial implants, sweeping back and forth over the capsule in Kalligen's hand.

'Authorisation code accepted.' It turned abruptly. 'Follow me.'

'You stay here. I have to go in there,' said Kalligen, pointing at a door in the stanchions of the racks. 'Deliver this to some enginseer or other. Are you listening to me?'

'What? Yes, yes, sorry.'

Kalligen followed Bannick's eyeline to the massive hull of a Baneblade. 'Oh you are smitten aren't you? Makes you proud to serve the Emperor, eh?'

Kalligen huffed when Bannick paid no attention to his sarcasm, and followed the servitor through a door, leaving Bannick alone. A clatter from one of the barge's workshops sounded far in the distance, otherwise the vehicle deck was empty of noise beyond the omnipresent hum of the ship's engines. Bannick had become so accustomed to their constant vibration over the long voyage that it had come to feel a part of him.

He walked over to the Baneblade. His regiment had performed battle drills in their Leman Russ, preparing for the day when they might have to support such an engine in combat, but the super-heavies themselves were far too valuable to risk in training exercises. He couldn't imagine what could possibly harm it; it was even more impressive than he had imagined.

Clamps held the massive machine in place, tracks raised a few centimetres off the floor, hundreds of tonnes of plasteel floating in the air, enwrapped in thick cables. Parchments scrips were affixed to the hull in clusters by seals of deep-red wax, bearing prayers of safe transit in High Gothic and binaric, evidence of the creed of the tech-adepts who shepherded such beasts to war.

He ducked down and leaned his head in close, looking down the line of the tank under the sponsons to the rear. It was bigger than most family habitation units. He reached out a hand. The hull was tacky, the jagged stripes of red and grey-blue camouflage that would hide it in the storms of Kalidar recently applied. Its name, *Mars Triumphant*, was engraved on a plasteel scroll at the fore of the vehicle's track guards.

He breathed out steadily. Here was a machine of heroes! He could only dream of commanding such a tank. Such an honour was reserved for those tank commanders who had proven themselves in battle time and again. A few alone were offered the opportunity to become honoured lieutenants, in command of a super-heavy. To captain a Baneblade, one of the Emperor's hammers, nine men looking to him to lead them... He shook his head. He was not worthy, he never would be. He'd seen to that himself.

Perhaps it was his imagination, but the tank seemed to rumble slightly, as if it growled in its sleep. He took his hand away.

'Hey!'

Bannick jumped to his feet.

'What are you doing skulking about down there? Worshipping it now are you, like one of those tech-adepts? I'd have

thought even you would have had enough of prayers today!'
Kalligen came over and cuffed his shoulder. 'Let's get out of
here. You've had your treat. Whatever was in those orders can't
have been good. That enginseer did not look happy. I don't
want to hang around in case he decides to respond in kind.
Last thing I want to do is rush about this hulk all day. Come
on. I need a drink... No, I need to get drunk, and it's a long
walk back.'

INTERSTITIAL

'Kalidar is not a pleasant place to be. It's a desert, not enough moisture to make a cup of caffeine in 400 cubic kilometres of atmosphere. The star's a nightmare, pumps out solar flares of such magnitude the planet's magnetosphere is constantly in turmoil. Vox communication's nigh on impossible because of that. Commsats get fried in orbit, anything other than a shout won't get through, short-range vox is unreliable, long-range unlikely, and heavy data transmission impossible without direct line of sight. The radiation from the sun would kill you all, in fact, if it weren't for the dust in the air, and that brings me on to the next set of happy facts, gentlemen; the weather. The temperature can swing from iron-cracking cold to eighty degrees plus within a couple of hours. The wind's constant and high, and wind shear is so dangerous you can forget air support.

'Oh wait, wait my brave boys! It gets worse – that dust might keep the sun from filling your bones with cancer, but it gets everywhere, and is sharp as ground glass. Go out without your goggles and go blind. Go out without your rebreather and you can kiss goodbye to the galaxy, because you'll be choking on pieces of your own lungs before the week's out. They got a name for it, dustlung, and unless you fancy getting on personal terms with it, you'll check and recheck your rebreathing unit every fourth hour, every Emperor-blessed day until you're sick of the sight of it. This is your main piece of equipment, not your lasgun, not your helmet, this! Look after it, or die. Simple as that.'

Training-Senior Sergeant Vasco Vanhool,
492nd Cadian Shock Troops, attached to the
63rd Paragonian Mechanised Infantry.

CHAPTER 4

KALIDAR IV, KOSTOVAL FLATS
3267397.M41

'Lock that fire down!' shouted Cortein. He wiped sweat from his face, his eyes stinging with the smoke wafting up from below. 'And shut those damn alarms off! Status report, Epperaliant!'

Second Lieutenant Commsman Epperaliant ran his eyes over the tech feed on his desk, Tech-Adept Vorkosigen being below tackling the damage. 'We're still functional. Engine online and all weapons operational. Damage is minor.'

'Good,' said Cortein and switched frequency, directing his voice through the company's closed datanet. 'Honoured Lieutenant Marteken, concentrate all fire on that lead walker.'

'Affirmative.' It was Colken, the commsman on *Artamen Ultrus* speaking, voice stuttering and cracked by the vox problems. 'We'll follow your lead.'

'Damn right,' muttered Cortein to himself. 'I've been doing this a lot longer than Marteken.' Then, louder into the external vox. 'Piping targeting data over.'

Mars Triumphant's main armament hurled a rocket-propelled

shell at a super-heavy ork walker. The munition exploded in a ball of red-hot metal and billows of fire, shaking the war machine as it scythed an enormous chain weapon towards a pair of Leman Russ. A second shell impacted, fired by *Artamen Ultrus*, *Mars Triumphant's* sister Baneblade in the company. The grind of shearing metal was audible even through the Baneblade's hull as the walker's arm fell off the machine.

An explosion battered against *Mars Triumphant's* armour. Alarms wailed louder, more smoke filtered up into the command deck from the gangway below. 'I said get that alarm shut off and put that damn fire out! Marsello, Meggen, help him!'

Third Loader Marsello, the youngest crew member, nodded and got up from his station, making for the narrow stairs heading below, First Loader Meggen hurrying from his station by the top of the shell lift in the turret.

Cortein coughed and wiped at his streaming eyes. His men were taking too long, the fire had been burning for well over a minute. The Baneblade rocked as another huge impact slammed into its heavily armoured hull. Loaders Marsello and Meggen were now at the side of Tech-Adept Aspirant Vorkosigen, wrestling with extinguishers, directing noisy jets of fire-suppressant gases at the flames. Cortein urged them to greater effort. With two of the loaders on fire control, half the tank's tertiary weapons were inactive, Third Gunner Vand struggling at the station behind Cortein to work both sponson banks and the forward bolter turret without the help of his loader Marsello.

'What's the damage?' asked Cortein.

'It's the rear left side augurs sir, feedback. They've shorted out.' Commsman Epperaliant replied. He punched a button and the alarm klaxon died.

'Again? What's the situation outside?'

'The echelons on formation Alpha have driven deep into the

orks, the Atraxian 18th are following them in, they're crushing everything in their path,' said Epperaliant, hunched over
his the comms suite, face lit a sickly yellow by the glow of its
screens. 'But Beta is stalling. The greenskins must have known
when and where we were coming – their whole strength is
concentrated here.' He flashed up a tac map onto Cortein's
chart desk. Blinking lights pinpointed the main ork force.
'Five hundred metres or so out from their trench line, ork anti-
tank dug in in the desert. We drove right over them. The 3rd
Company has taking a pounding. Half of it's gone, as far as I
can see. The 2nd isn't faring much better. I count over a half-
dozen super-heavy walkers out there, and they're chewing the
Leman Russ to pieces. The 4th and 5th Companies and the
18th Atraxian Super-heavies are faring better, but only because
all the walkers are down our end of the line. Alpha's infantry
support is holding its own, advancing as per the plan, but if we
don't put a lid on the situation here, the greenskins will roll up
our entire front.'

'Our infantry?'

'Half of it's been cooked in the can. General order is out for
main elements of the 63rd Paragonian Mechanised and 13th
Light Savlar to fall back. Artillery bombardment is under way
as planned, but my guess is they're shelling empty sand. All the
orks are here.' He tapped at a screen, his fingernail clicking on
it in a way that cut through the noise inside the tank. Epperaliant shot his commanding officer a worried look. 'Seven heavy
walkers. Where by the Golden Throne did they come from?'

'They've been holding them back, that's obvious,' said
Cortein. 'Those thrice damned kreebirds up at HQ don't know
the ork. This whole affair has stunk of a trap since the outset.'
Cortein jammed his finger onto a vox button, connecting him
to Outlanner, the driver to the fore of the deck below, Ganlick at the demolisher cannon, the second gunner's station,

Radden the first gunner in the turret; all compartments. He spoke rapidly, surely. 'Keep us moving forwards, Ganlick, lay down a sigma pattern, suppressive fire, keep those green scum away from my tank.' He beckoned to the commsman. 'Epperaliant, help Vand, do what you can with the heavy bolters while the loaders are busy.' Cortein scanned over his command suite. 'Orders from Hannick – the company's to cover the retreat of the infantry units. Let's show these ork monstrosities what a full company of the Emperor's finest can do.'

'Sir.' Epperaliant rerouted the main vox from his headphones over the command deck. A barrage of vox chatter swamped the cramped room, screams, weapons fire, voices hoarse with shouted orders, all battling with Kalidar's ever-present roar. He slid his chair along its rails so he could get out, stumbling as the tank took a hit, then joined Vand at the tertiary weapons system fire-control, remotely controlling the bolters and lascannon of the left sponson bank, targets displayed on the screens at the station, relayed by the augur-eyes of the weapons. The muffled report of the hull demolisher cannon joined the faint chatter of the bolters as Ganlick, Epperaliant and Third Gunner Vand set to work, clearing the field in front of the super-heavy tank.

Now for the battle cannon. Radden was doing his best, but he'd do better if Cortein directed him. 'Radden, follow my mark.' Cortein's fingers moved surely over the screens of his command suite, bringing up a weak point on the one-armed walker, a pot-bellied mechanical parody of an ork painted in a camouflage of bright blues. Even bereft of its melee arm, it still bristled with ranged weapons as long as a Leman Russ. The target's information was conveyed by Martian means to the suite in front of Radden's chair up above and out to the company's other Baneblade.

'Hearing you loud and clear, sir!' said Radden over the

internal vox. Tracer fire from the battle cannon's coaxially mounted autocannon tracked across the chest of the ork war machine, ranging the shot. 'Give me a moment and...' *Mars Triumphant*'s main gun spoke and Radden whooped like a simian. The tank shuddered. Cortein's screens whited out as *Lux Imperator*, the company Shadowsword operating to their right, fired its volcano cannon into the heavy walker squadron. Cortein expected the orks to be one walker down after that. Two Baneblades could take down a super-heavy walker in fairly short order if well coordinated; a Shadowsword's anti-Titan main armament needed no help. It was a damned shame its capacitors were so slow to recharge after firing.

'Was it a hit? Confirm Radden, confirm!' Cortein cursed Tech-Adept Vorkosigen under his breath; he'd said he'd applied the necessary libations to ensure the smooth working of the anti-glare cut outs when what he needed, Cortein suspected, was to try a little harder with his tools. 'Obviously didn't pray hard enough,' he growled.

Rattles and banging came from below, Second Loader Ralt working hard alone, shuttling shells from the magazine to replenish the racks by the forward demolisher cannon.

'I'm not getting anything sir, wait... wait... A hit, yes... Hang on... Basdack! Negative, negative. No kill.'

The grainy images of the world outside returned to the tank's screens. The heavy walker hit by *Lux Imperator* was a blazing hulk, molten steel dripping from a large round hole in its hull, but the engine *Mars Triumphant* had targeted was still standing, wobbling slowly round, fire gouting from a hole in its breast, its head grinding to face them. A shell from *Artamen Ultrus* blasted into it, bringing away a section of gantry.

'It's still coming,' said Cortein. 'Keep at it. We've got its attention. Finish it off! Quickly! Before it returns fire.'

'Sir!'

The gatling cannon on the giant metal ork's left arm began to rotate, picking up speed until it was a blur of motion. A hail of shell fire pattered off the hull of the Baneblade, damaging subsystems, augur-eyes among them. Two of Cortein's screens went dead. The battle cannon fired again. The damaged plates in the heavy walker's chest crumpled in. It swayed on its feet, gatling cannon firing wild. Rockets burned off a rack set upon the right shoulder, trailing bright fire. They impacted in a wide burst pattern about the Baneblade, one slamming home on the front of the tank, wreathing Cortein's visual displays in flame.

'Radden,' said Cortein. 'Put that walker down now!'

'I hit it! I hit it!' protested the gunner.

Two more impacts shuddered into the walker's armour, buckling plates, one each from *Artamen Ultrus*'s demolisher and battle cannon. Still it came on.

The walker stopped. A huge cannon on its shoulder above the ruined left arm began to track down.

'Too late!' said Cortein. 'Brace! Brace! Brace!'

A flash of light showed up the ragged joins in the walker's armour. Slowly, the walker leaned drunkenly over to one side, staggering on its massive armoured feet, and toppled to the desert floor. Secondary explosions ripped through its structure, breaking its back, and the walker's hull sank into itself. Cortein breathed a sigh of relief and a ragged cheer went up from the other nine men on the tank.

'Woo! That was my shot! That was my kill! Cut the fuse a little long on that one. Ha ha!' laughed Radden. 'Right in the guts! How do you like that you fat basdack?!'

'Fire's out, sir!' called Meggen.

'Back to your stations!' ordered Cortein. 'Sponson and secondary weapons intensify forward fire.' Cortein quickly appraised the situation. The remaining four walkers were off to the right. Let the Shadowsword deal with them. Infantry was their problem right now. 'Radden, permission to engage targets of opportunity, keep the field round *Lux Imperator* clear. Let it work unmolested.'

'You're a gentleman, sir,' crackled the vox.

Cortein scanned the bank of brass-bound monitors before him, his view of the battle a fragmented 360-degree panorama. Tac screens fed in data from the other three vehicles in the company. The technology in the Baneblade was first rate, Martian secrets far superior to the systems of the Leman Russ on the field about them. But even delivered via the 7th's networked logic engines, the data was scrambled by Kalidar, full of junk, and juddered across screens alive with electric snow.

A wide chart desk projecting a three-dimensional representation of the conflict occupied the centre of his station. There, the Alpha formation showed as red Imperial signifiers buried deep in dots of swirling green. The right side of the battlefield was not so healthy; Beta formation's attack had been blunted by the ork ambush and the walkers. Red chevrons, the armoured fist units of the infantry, were falling back in orderly fashion, regrouping behind the super-heavy tank company to shelter from the walkers' fire.

With the tac screens and the periscope feeds ranged about his command deck, Cortein's view of the battle was broad, the height of the Baneblade allowing him to look down on the fighting orks and men as if they were brawling men and children. Others might find it a godlike position, but not Cortein. Hubris was a fatal trait in an honoured lieutenant. To command a super-heavy tank was to command a target, the storm of incoming fire rattling off the hull of *Mars Triumphant* proving the point.

According to the tac screens, the super-heavy tanks were making their mark. The walker unit had lost three of its number to the volcano cannon of *Lux Imperator* and the combined fire of the two company Baneblades, company commander Hannick's Hellhammer *Ostrakan's Rebirth* taking a heavy toll of the greenskin infantry and their smaller machines. Although the Beta assault had been stymied, now it was the turn of the orks to fall back. The heavy walkers were waddling backwards from the 7th, giving the remaining Leman Russ squadrons in the 2nd and 3rd Companies some respite – these had formed into a wall and begun to reverse, but now they halted to better direct their fire.

Out to the left, the ork line had bowed considerably under pressure from the super-heavies of Atraxia. There, lines of Paragonian infantry marched in gaps between the advancing Imperial tanks, supported by armoured troop carriers moving up behind them, as per the plan. Bright trails of vaporised sand twisted into the wind of the storm as multilaser beams stabbed out, the barrels of the guns running hot. Thin lines of lighter-armed Savlar toxic environment specialists ranged to the flanks, hunting stragglers. Many ork vehicles had been destroyed, undone by superior Imperial firepower. The ork mobs came running in again and again, but were cut down before they were able to close for melee, where they would undoubtedly have triumphed over the weaker humans. Still, Cortein did not think the battle won.

His eyes were caught by the forward left augur screen. A huge shape appeared then vanished in the swirling sand, lost behind the storm-shrouded silhouettes of the remaining four walkers. 'Epperaliant! Sector five. What by the holy Throne is that!?'

'I'm not getting anything... Wait! New hostile approaching, designation unknown... Threat indicators are going wild, honoured lieutenant.'

A hulking shape pushed its way through the ork heavy

walkers, clanging into them as it barged them out of the way. It emerged from the dust storm, gut thrust forwards. Like the heavy walkers it was round-bellied, supported on enormous feet, its stumpy arms a mess of enormous, ramshackle weapons, and thick plates of armour decorated with daubed ideograms protecting its clunking inner workings. The similarities ended there. It was far larger, Titan class at least, an ork Gargant, size matched only by the sense of malevolence preceding it. Two globes on ridged conducting rods projected high over its back, and weird energies played about the thing's grotesque faceplate, darting lightning up to the globes above its horned head, and arcing down in a broad umbrella all about it. Its eyes glowed bright. Cortein felt an uncomfortable sensation at the back of his skull, his teeth itched, and the air took on the taste of aluminium.

'Emperor's Throne,' he breathed. He knew the feeling, not felt for a long time, the sensation that came from the presence of a powerful witch. The ork titan was carrying a psyker.

Honoured Captain Hannick, commanding officer of the 7th Paragonian Super-heavy Tank Company and formation CIC, shouted out over the vox, his powerful override shutting out all other communications and momentarily subduing the planet's incessant roar of electrostatic.

'All tanks, target heavy engine sector five.' The Gargant's outline flashed up in white on Cortein's crackling screens. Tactical info scrolled urgently over it. 'Destroy it!'

The thing's mouth slowly opened, a barbed cannon extruding from its distended jaws. Cannon and lasfire went flying in at the Gargant from all directions, the remaining Leman Russ and the Super-heavy Company all targeting together.

Little got through to the ork Titan's bulging hull. Explosions erupted all around the Gargant as shells detonated, lascannon blasts and plasma shots smeared themselves to nothing well away from its armour, dissipated by its shield of green lightning. The screens on *Mars Triumphant* whited out again as *Lux Imperator*'s volcano cannon discharged once more, terawatts of energy unleashed in one blast. *Mars Triumphant*'s screens cleared for Cortein to see *Lux Imperator*'s beam stopped and spread like molten glass across the energy fields protecting the Titan. Cortein felt blood trickle from his nose. The Gargant's tongue punched forwards, vomiting a braided spout of green lightning. The stream of energy ran across the floor of the dead sea, tearing it up, a spume of earth following in its wake, cutting through Leman Russ and Chimeras as if they weren't there, scattering men in pieces to Kalidar's endless winds. Sensors aboard the Baneblade spiked. Alarms wailed as the wave ran to their left, cleaving the ground perilously close to them.

An explosion buffeted the Baneblade and the lights went out. Cortein reeled. Epperaliant was thrown from his chair. The tank's ancient systems screeched and the hull groaned with stress. Lockers popped open and supplies tumbled to the floor, a lasgun power pack catching the commsman on the head.

Cortein pulled himself up. Half the augur screens were dead. The fire klaxon sounded once more. Emergency lighting flickered on.

'Witch engine! It's a damned witch engine,' shouted Cortein. In thirty years he'd only seen a machine of this type once before, an unholy mixture of technology and the arcane, wielding the unholy powers of the immaterium to deadly effect.

The Titan waddled forwards, trampling all before it, the more mundane cannons, rockets and energy weapons covering its arms and shoulders wreaking terrible destruction on the forces arrayed before it. Tanks exploded, men were rendered into scraps of flesh.

'What?' shouted Marsello, his face white with terror. He was barely a boy, a replacement for an old comrade lost to the eldar back in the Indranis Campaign.

'There's a psyker on board that thing. Some kind of machine to intensify its warp energies,' explained Epperaliant. 'Sir, we don't have anything to go against that. We've no Scholastica Psykana support here.'

Hannick's voice came over the vox. 'Tanks two and three to redirect fire against the heavy walkers. Protect *Lux Imperator* during recharge.'

'Yes, sir,' said Cortein. 'Marteken! Hear that? We won't get through that energy shield. Take out the Titan's support. Concentrate on the leftmost heavy walker!'

'The red one?' came back Colken.

'Aye!' shouted Cortein. 'Outlanner, get us in closer, I want Ganlick in range – let's make this quick.'

Four heavy cannons, two apiece on the Baneblades, spoke in rapid succession and lines of lascannon fire seared the air. The heavy walker disappeared behind a wall of flame. When it reappeared, it came on only slowly, small fires burning all over it, right arm hanging uselessly by its side.

'Finish it!' yelled Cortein.

Artamen Ultrus and *Mars Triumphant* obliged. Shells hammered into it. Internal explosions went off in a long string, fire spurting between joins in its armour. The super-heavy walker stopped dead, smoking.

'*Lux Imperator* – main cannon charged!' came the voice of the tank's honoured lieutenant. Again the volcano cannon spat fire. Again it was stymied by the shields of psychic energy surrounding the enemy engine.

The Gargant replied. Cortein's teeth itched as another wave of energy ripped across the desert, furrowing the sand and scorching it to glass. There came the noise of a massive explosion, and shrapnel dinging off *Mars Triumphant's* armour.

Epperaliant bent over the comms suite. '*Lux Imperator*! *Lux Imperator* is hit!' he said, blood running down his face from the cut in his scalp. On the screens of the command and comms suite, the great shell of the Shadowsword burned.

'Basdack! No!' shouted Radden.

'Emperor's mercy, we'll never beat that,' muttered Cortein, low so his men would not fear. 'Get Honoured Captain Hannick on the vox, now!' shouted Cortein.

'Sir!' Epperaliant wiped blood from his eyes, trying to staunch the flow with his cap while he swept materiel off his comms desk.

'Hannick,' came the CO's voice.

'Sir!' shouted Cortein. His voice was becoming hoarse from making himself heard over the noise of the tank, the tumult of battle and Kalidar's roar. 'That's a damned witch engine the orks have there. We have no Scholastica Psykana support, and there's no way the fleet can lend a hand through this storm. If we do not withdraw it'll be a massacre. The Illudion campaign all over again. We have no way of bringing down a witch engine, not with *Lux Imperator* gone.'

Hannick's voice crackled, fading in and out with washes of static. 'Once more you presume to tell me my job, Cortein, but I am inclined to agree with you. Taskforce Beta to fall back by section. Paragonian 7th Super-heavy Company to cover retreat. Taskforce Alpha, I advise you do the same. Once this witch engine is done with us, it'll be gunning for you. Thank the Emperor for this storm. If it hid the orks, then by the Throne it can hide us. Retreat. Retreat. Order Epsilon 42. Fall back to rendezvous point five. And Cortein?'

'Sir!'

'Nothing foolish. We cannot risk our main assets. Hannick out.'

Cortein reached for the talk button on his headset, to argue that he should stay and cover the guard as they fell back, then thought better of it. Hannick would not change his mind, the machines under his command were always his prime concern, not the men, who were far more numerous. 'How many of our men are detailed to cover the retreat?' asked Cortein.

'Four platoons of the 13th Savlar, five of the 63rd Paragonian have been ordered forwards. They're taking heavy casualties sir. Most of the 42nd Armoured Regiment's gone, only seventeen tanks operational across the whole front. The Atraxians are doing okay, but Grand Captain Olgau has confirmed that he has sounded a retreat in his quadrant also,' said Epperaliant.

Cortein clenched his jaw and worked his teeth together. He removed his vox headset and turned round to face his men.

'We're to fall back, but keep our face to the enemy. Head out reactor-first, I won't have my tank showing its rear to the enemy when it can retreat with honour, spitting fire all the way! Where possible, I want supporting fire for the infantry covering our retreat.'

Epperaliant looked to his commander. 'But our orders sir…' he said levelly.

'Our orders are to not risk ourselves. Our armour is thicker to the front, is it not? And our guns face forwards, if I recall correctly.'

'Aye, sir!'

'Outlanner! Reverse speed, all full,' Cortein moved the heading and speed wheels at his station in time to his orders. A loud bell rang out to inform the driver, in case he did not catch the Honoured Lieutenant's words. 'Gunners, fire at will, let's try and buy those poor basdacks out there some time.'

INTERSTITIAL

'In times of war it is better to consider this: which is of more worth? A man who will serve the Emperor through his death, or a man who lives yet whose life may not serve at all? We face an eternity of war. Those who will not lay down their lives willingly are traitors to all mankind.'

Sayings of Warmaster Ketherion.

CHAPTER 5

KALIDAR IV, KOSTOVAL FLATS
3267397.M41

Bannick should have been dead. The turret of *Indomitable Fury* lay canted on its back, Bannick underneath it. The pintle storm bolter on the turret was jammed against the packed ground of the dry sea floor, preventing the lot from crushing him. It was the second time the weapon had saved him in an hour. He winced as he moved. He hurt all over, his chest bruised. He was sure he'd cracked a rib.

Carefully, he pulled himself out from underneath and stood, body shaking. There'd been a hit on the tank. The turret must have been blown off. It was possible his men still lived. He staggered around in a half-circle, searching for it.

Wind-driven streamers of smoke and of dust shrouded the battlefield, then suddenly he saw it. *Indomitable Fury*'s hull burned furnace-hot, fanned by the wind. Fuel billowed in orange clouds of flame to mingle with the storm. Thick smoke poured out of the aperture where the turret had sat, the crackle of bolter shells cooking off joining with the noise of the larger battle. Bannick stared at the wreck of his first command numbly. No one could have survived that. His men were dead.

He waited for the world to return to normal, for his ears to stop ringing and for his mind to come back into focus. He was not sure what to do. He turned. Behind him was a litter of dead orks, blackened hulks of Leman Russ and Chimeras guttering fire, the sands about them stained with oil. Far to the rear, he could make out the dim shape of Kennerston's tank, gun at maximum elevation, still hurling hi-ex into the orks.

Beta formation had been broken, shattered by ambush and the arrival of the super-heavy walkers. It looked like they'd forced a few hundred metres ahead of Bannick, but the formation remnants were drawing closer to him once again. Men and machines streamed towards and past him. Dimly, through the dust storm, he could make out a crescent line of a vanguard, tanks and infantry, holding the line while the Imperial Guard retreated.

Four Leman Russ stood in line, all exhibiting some damage, starting backwards with each report of their battle cannon. Arrayed next to them was a line of six Chimera armoured personnel carriers, their turrets tracking back and forth, multilasers blazing. In front of the vehicles, a triple line of mixed infantry, uniforms so thick with sand they were indistinguishable, firing by rank into the orkish horde ebbing and flowing towards them, each wave drawing a little nearer to the line. Off to the left he could see the looming shapes of the walkers, weapons fire lighting up the storm as they waddled away after something. He was relieved to see a couple of burning walker hulks nearby.

Bannick groggily made his way forwards, only to realise that he was still tethered to the turret of *Indomitable Fury* by the pipes of his rebreather unit. The unit was fragged, and he realised that he'd been breathing the unfiltered storm-air for the Emperor knew how long. He held his breath as he went back to the tank's severed head, dug into the sand a little so he could open the storage bins at the aft of the turret and, grimacing with pain, dragged out a portable rebreather and a laspistol. He tugged his mask off, and replaced it.

Men ran past him as he walked forwards, many dragging wounded comrades, officers shouting vox-amplified orders, trying to keep the withdrawal from degenerating into a rout.

A panicked face loomed out of the storm, burned hands grasping at his uniform. 'You're going the wrong way! You're going the wrong way! It's coming!' the soldier yelled, then was gone.

Armoured vehicles roared past. Turrets facing backwards, they spat fire behind them to cover their departure. The ground began to shake, the whistle of incoming shells and roar of Manticore rockets audible above the battle and the storm. An artillery bombardment had been called down.

By the time he reached the line of men and vehicles, the ork attack had paused, and the greenskins had disappeared into the shrouds of storm-blown dust, their giant walkers with them. The guardsmen stood nervously scanning the desert. Visibility was down to a score of metres at most. Bannick leaned into the wind as he walked the line, grasping dust-crusted shoulders and turning swaddled heads towards him, looking for signs of rank. Eventually, he found a man bearing the stripes of a Paragonian sergeant on his arm, a statue of sand with eyes of glass.

'Where's your commanding officer?' he shouted. The vox on his respirator was clogged with sand, the wind loud. He could barely hear his own voice; it was worse than it had been inside *Indomitable Fury*.

The sergeant nodded to a mash of body parts crusted with dust.

'All our senior officers are dead,' said the sergeant. 'I guess you're it now, lieutenant.'

'What's the situation?' shouted Bannick.

'The bombardment's keeping the greenies back.' The sergeant pointed out past the line of intermingled ork and human dead, rapidly being covered by sand. 'Our guns won't fire well. Damned dust refracts the beams before they get far. We're down to an effective range of fifty metres or less, but I think they've lost the guts for a scrap. If that green-eyed basdack comes back we're well and truly dead, though.'

'You refer to the walkers?'

'No.' The sergeant shook his head. 'They were just a screen. The orks had a damned Titan in there. We didn't stand a chance.'

'What are your orders?'

'Cover the retreat, fall back when orders come through, sir.' His eyes were resigned behind the yellow plex of his goggles. The man did not expect to live the day out.

'You getting any vox coverage?'

The sergeant shook his head.

'How long since the last men came through?' asked Bannick.

The sergeant shrugged like he'd already given up. 'Five minutes.'

Bannick looked about. A pair of Leman Russ, one in bad shape, sponson missing and left side buckled, ground out of the sandstorm and passed by, its unharmed companion hurling shells blindly behind it. He waited. Nothing else came, neither friend nor foe.

He grabbed the sergeant and shook him to gain his attention again. 'Sergeant! I'll tell you what we are going to do. You and your men mount up, as many as possible aboard these transports.' He indicated the Chimeras behind the ranks of men, all the same camouflage, but emblazoned with a mix of Paragonian, Savlar and Atraxian regimental markings. 'These tanks will cover your retreat. You are leaving in ten minutes, all of you. That's an order, got that?'

The sergeant nodded, hope in his eyes. Bannick went over to the first of the four tanks behind the infantry line. They were from a mix of squadrons, all 2nd Company. The tanks themselves were all just about combat-worthy, but the only lieutenant among them was dead, along with five other crew.

Bannick ran up the side of the lead tank. Grim-faced men looked up to him. The dead lieutenant still sat in his chair, a crater in his chest and a look of surprise on his face. Bannick pointed to his insignia and took command without discussion. He heaved the dead 2nd Company officer's body out of his chair, pulling his tank rebreather and vox set off and replacing his own rebreather with them. He sat down, and tried to ignore the feel of the blood seeping into his trousers. Wind whistled in through a hole in the turret, signs of the shellburst that had killed the lieutenant and turned the command suite into a shattered mess. The turret hatch was jammed open. Sand poured endlessly down into the interior. He stood and signalled the infantry sergeant, and the men quickly boarded their transports, those for whom room was lacking clambering on top. The Chimeras' engines coughed into life. One by one, they spun round and vanished to the rear, swallowed by the storm.

'Designate tank squadron 111, tanks Alpha through Delta,' Bannick said, using the standard regimental term for a battlefield blending of units. 'Aye, sir,' replied the tank crews one after another. 'Half-speed reverse. Gamma and Delta to cover left and right respectively. Load all weapons, hi-ex. Wait for my order to fire,' said Bannick.

The tanks began to reverse at half-speed, keeping their thicker armour towards the orks. Nothing came from the sand. Bannick had his jaw clenched so tight it ached.

Green sheet lightning flashed in the desert.

'Sir! Sir! To the left and rear!' said his tank's gunner. The sandstorm was thicker than fog, and Bannick struggled to see. A further flash followed, then another.

Shapes loomed in the dense caramel air, two massive orkoid silhouettes, one much larger than the other and spurting green fire and lightning. This must be the Titan the sergeant had referred to. By the Emperor it was Gargantuan! The heavy walker looked like a child at the skirts of its mother beside it.

Bannick felt a tickling sensation behind his nose and tasted metal as the Titan cast green energy at the ground. His skin crawled. An umbrella of flickering power shielded the Titan, stopping the shots of the desperate Guardsmen dead. His training had mentioned no energy field like that; all of them, from power fields to void shields, would eventually collapse under weight of fire, but this seemed stronger with every impact.

Conflict resolved itself from a jag of shadows, walker and Titan raining fire down on a knot of retreating tanks and infantry. Explosions, muffled by the storm, sounded unreal and distant, but the damage was real enough. Bannick looked on as a Chimera exploded. Three ragged platoons of men fought desperately against scores of orks, firing, retreating, firing again, trying to stop the massive greenskins from getting to within melee range. The fight was coming towards Bannick's ad hoc squadron, cutting an oblique line across the sand to the rear of the Leman Russ, the heavy walker and Titan reversing as they sought to keep their guns on the humans.

Then a third shape emerged from the storm. Despite the peril of their situation, Bannick's breath caught. A Baneblade, one of the Paragonians, moving slowly backwards. Bright flashes came as demolisher cannon and battle cannon spoke as one, bringing a rain of iron plates down from the smaller ork walker. The Titan replied, crackling energies vomited forth from a spiked tongue to rip the right-hand sponson from the super-heavy, atomising a score of men to the tank's side. Undaunted, the Baneblade fought on.

The whole of the Baneblade shook with the impact of the psychic beam-weapon. Consoles sparked and fizzed. Cortein held hard to his command station as the vehicle bucked under him. He heard Meggen up above swear loudly as the shells in the turret loading-rack clanked to the floor. The smell of ozone, smoke and halon fire- suppressant filled the tank before being sucked out of the air by the tank's atmosphere scrubbers.

'We lost the left sponson bank!' shouted Epperaliant. 'We've damage to main fire control.'

'Fire?'

'Negative. We got a breakout in the forward compartment. Fire suppression is functioning correctly this time.'

'All crew, don rebreathers,' ordered Cortein. The fire-suppression system could suffocate a tank crew as easily as douse flame. They were supposed to be wearing their masks; if the tank's hull was breached they'd all be breathing the planet's deadly dust, but Cortein had allowed his men to wear them as they saw fit – they were cumbersome, and stank.

'Keep up our fire rates!'

'Sir!' replied Ganlick and Radden.

'Vand? Vand!' said Cortein. He half turned to where the third gunner's station was situated on the command deck, to the left behind the commander's station. Vand lay slumped over his twitch sticks, face studded with glass. The whole station had blown, screens gone. Marsello sat there, mouth gaping like a fish.

'He's, he's dead sir…' managed the boy.

'Marsello!' snapped Cortein.

The boy had frozen.

'Marsello! Pull yourself together. Reroute all tertiary weapons systems to your station. You are our anti-infantry defence now. Do you understand? Marsello!'

The boy nodded numbly, fumbling movements becoming surer as he applied himself to his task.

Cortein fixed his eyes on the ork Titan displayed on his chart desk, the lesser walker, the ork infantry pounding wave after wave on the line of Imperial troops falling back by section, tanks at half-reverse covering them. At least the retreat was orderly, but he feared that would not remain the case for long.

'They'll not take another hit like that,' said Bannick. 'We've got to do something.'

The tank's gunner spoke. 'Sir, we have to retreat. There's no way we can take that. No way – it's only a matter of time before it kills the Baneblade. Best we get these tanks back and add our strength to a counter-attack.'

'Gunner, that Baneblade is worth ten Leman Russ. We stay and fight. Squadron, halt!' he called into the vox. 'Follow my mark, we have to be quick.'

Three Leman Russ stood shoulder to shoulder with the Baneblade, heavy bolters carving a gory swathe through the orks. Battle cannon shots from all four tanks slammed into the lesser walker, part of its hull collapsing and falling to the ground. Bannick's pulse quickened.

'Sir!' said the gunner. 'I must protest. No shot can get through that energy field, you haven't seen it, it–'

'Listen!' shouted Bannick. 'Look at the second walker, see how close it stands to the ork Titan.' Bannick pointed, but the gunner was already putting his eye to his ranging glass.

'Yes, sir.'

'See how it is unaffected by its energy umbrella? It's moving right through it without a problem, but it's not covered by it. We fire at the smaller engine. If we target the smaller one's head, there's a good chance it'll collapse into the Titan. That should buy the others time to get away.'

'Yes, sir,' said the gunner, reluctantly.

'All tanks, halt! Drivers, man hull lascannon. I want everything we have thrown at that smaller walker on my mark, do you understand?'

A chorus of crackling 'yes, sirs' came to him. Turrets turned, the tanks manoeuvred into position, then stopped one by one. Their hull-mounted lascannons came to life, tracking the head of the heavy walker, the battle cannons' turrets doing the same, moving with tiny jerks. Bannick watched the giant engines do their ponderous dance; gradually they turned, entirely obscuring the Imperial forces to the front.

'We have only one chance,' he said. 'Do not fire until I give the order. Keep targets locked. He held up his hand. 'Wait for it, wait for it…' he watched intently, watching for the right moment before giving his command. The heavy walker had to be close enough to the Titan to collapse onto it, in the right position and yet not so close that it could benefit from the energy field crackling all around the larger war machine. Further, it had to be in a position where it would cause some hindrance to the larger construct. Bannick prayed to the Emperor that the engine would not have time to recharge its eldritch cannon before they fired. The heavy walker edged closer in towards Greeneye, perhaps trying to gain some protection from the energy shield, perhaps seeking a new target, bringing it closer to the Titan's enormous metal foot…

'Fire!' yelled Bannick.

The Leman Russ unloaded everything into the heavy walker. Two shells went wide of the head, one missing, one impacting into a shoulder. The others struck home, lines of lascannon fire seeming to guide them in. The heavy walker's head exploded with great violence. With the screech of metal upon metal, it fell onto the larger machine, sagging against it, falling onto the Titan's foot and dragging its armoured skirt into the sand. Engines roared as Greeneye tried to move, the whole thing shuddering with mechanical effort, but to no avail. Greeneye was pinned fast.

Bannick permitted himself a deep breath of relief. 'Well done men, now, let's get out of here. All ahead full! Fall back! Fall back!'

Tank engines roaring, the Leman Russ tracked round and made their getaway. Stood in the turret, Bannick watched Greeneye recede, the lesser ork engine leaning against it like a drunk back home in Aronis city. Pinned in place, the Titan spat green fire at the withdrawing Imperials. He couldn't tell how many of the force gathered round the Baneblade had made it away, but surely some of them had.

The energies spurting from the Titan ceased. Its horned head turned to the screech of unoiled bearings, round eyes blazing with the unclean light of witchcraft. They fixed themselves on Bannick and stared unblinking, locking with his own, boring deep into his very soul. The machines became an outline, then a shadow, still the green eyes glared after him, then they too were gone into the anger of Kalidar's storm.

Bannick slumped down into the tank's turret chair. He was filthy and tired, and his head rang. Adrenaline receded, leaving him nauseous and weak. The loss of his men, held at bay by the thrill of battle, hit him like a shell – Arlesen, Kurlick, Brevant, Tovan, Patinallo – men he'd trained with for two years. He was thankful he'd not known any before the raising; that would have made it worse. Dead so far from home, most likely their families would never know what had happened to their sons. He added their deaths to his burden of guilt.

He'd been responsible for their safety, and he had failed, more blood on his hands.

He'd survived. There was that, and he'd done his duty. Perhaps he had redeemed himself.

He wasn't sure if he cared. He was too tired.

He coughed and felt wetness under his mask. He reached up under it, holding his breath as he lifted the mask in a manner that had become instinctive. He pushed his fingers under the stinking rubber, wiping them at his mouth, scratching his skin with the dust layered upon it.

He pulled his hand out. Blood, blood on his fingers.

Pity flicked across the small portion of the gunner's features visible between rebreather and cap. They both knew what that meant.

Dustlung.

INTERSTITIAL

'Only blind fate saved me.'
'Fate is far from blind, my son.'

Astropath Valle speaking with unnamed trooper after the
Kostoval Rout, M41

CHAPTER 6

HELWAT CITY LANDING FIELDS,
THE SIXTH MOON OF PARAGON VI
2259395.M41

Bannick walked down the long carpet to the drop-ship, shoulder to shoulder with the other officers of his newly raised tank regiment, the Paragonian 42nd. He tried to keep his eyes forwards as instructed, but he couldn't keep them from sliding to the side, scanning the crowd of faces in his clan's viewing stand, looking for the old man's face.

Of course his father wasn't there.

Bannick had wrecked the old man's carefully constructed plans to tie Clans Bannick and Turannigen together. He'd cost the clan a 0.3% reduction in gross material costs in interclan trade, and his father a great deal of face. He would not come. Because, according to his father, the Chief Auditor of Clan Bannick, Colaron Artem Lo Bannick wasn't supposed to be there either. He was supposed to be playing politics by his father's side, but he wasn't. After what had happened with Tuparillio, his father had had no choice but to agree to Bannick's request to sign up. His uncle had arranged the rest. But that was that between them. He might have allowed his eldest son to go to war, but he did not have to like it, and the old man had publicly disowned him.

He'd expected it, knew it, but Bannick had hoped that he'd come, prayed for it.

Even now, he was still hoping to lock eyes with the stern gaze of his father, some measure of reconciliation before he left. The clan stands, cantilevered out from the embarkation terminal, flowered high above the heads of the lesser classes of Paragon, gathered in their thousands to see their sons and daughters off to war.

The crowd was immense, a sea of faces round the gothic cliffs of the embarkation building. Forty drop-ships in neat ranks filled this part of the landing apron, sequestered from the endless plain of rockcrete that was Paragon's main spaceport, needfully huge to accommodate the ships that came and went from the planet daily, bringing in raw materials from the rest of the system, carrying away the world's manufactured goods to the stars. All non-essential traffic was suspended for the week of the departure. This raising was costing Paragon dearly.

Bannick marched along a rich carpet laid over the rockcrete especially for the officer cadets of the regiment. His new uniform was uncomfortable in its unfamiliarity, tight and stiff where his old clothes were loose and soft, and his head felt cold where it had been shaved down to blue stubble. The haircut of the penitent, he thought. He and the other officer cadets of the regiment walked together, nearly a hundred would-be lieutenants and others, from where they'd heard the service from the chapel inside the embarkation building and enjoyed drinks at the expense of the Unified Clan Council and Planetary Commander Gondanick Lo Materiak. Theirs was a comfortable send-off, not like the enlisted men, who'd already begun basic training in the swamp outside the spaceport.

He felt lightheaded from both drink and apprehension. This was only his second time in a spacecraft, and this time he would not be coming back. He looked from the corner of his eyes for reassurance from Kalligen, but his friend wore an uncharacteristically serious expression, face set resolutely forwards.

He thought his father might have come because of that, that they'd not meet again. Most men who joined the Guard never came home, falling on some foreign field light years away, or, if surviving, granted land on untamed worlds where they could fight some more. Those that did contrive to return could find themselves arriving centuries later, travel across the galaxy being slow, the strange energies within the immaterium warping time. That Bannick's uncle had come home, along with the three veteran regiments accompanying the two fresh raisings to Kalidar was a near miracle, simply because their homeworld lay en route from one warzone to the other, and they needed reinforcing. Good also for morale, his uncle had confided in him. The Imperial Governor had somehow arranged it, to take people's attention away from the scandals rocking court, or so the rumours went.

If he did come back, it would no longer be home. The veterans who marched alongside the enlisted men up from the swamps had been recruited at three different points over the last century. None of them had ever been back home before, none of them had ever expected to come home, and now, after only three weeks on their birthworld, they were leaving again and they would never be back again. Their faces were grimmer than when they'd disembarked, the world and people they'd known lost to warp-born time distortion.

He'd realised that, at least intellectually, from the moment he had put his mark on the recruitment paper, but now the thought of never seeing his father or mother or the rest of his family again filled him with panic. For the briefest moment he wanted to dash off, to say he had changed his mind, to go back to his father and beg forgiveness, but it was far too late for that. Perhaps that's why the carpet was lined with Navy ratings – they were large men, heavily muscled under their uniforms. The charged belaying pins they carried would put second thoughts out of anyone's mind, and not merely figuratively.

He tensed as the knot of cadets passed by the stand reserved for Clan Bannick. The faces above were proud but free of emotion, as befitted members of the ruling class. There was a large gap in the stands. It looked like the entire fiscal stem of Clan Bannick had been ordered to keep away. He tried to feel angry at his father for that, one last bout of fury at the old man. Although he'd managed it so many times before, often with little encouragement, today it came harder than usual.

He felt ashamed of his doubts. This was not the Bannick way; he might have ruined his life here, but he would not spoil this new one. He tried to hold his head higher.

Still he wished his father had come.

The carpet went in a sweep around the elephantine landing legs of the drop-ship, bringing the officer cadets into line with the column of enlisted men. Ahead of him lay his future, the ship's great square ramp lowered like the jaw of some predator, waiting to swallow him whole and spit him out as living ammunition in one of the Emperor's wars. Even if they made the perilous warp journey intact, he'd probably not survive long, something his uncle had repeated time and time again to him, but Bannick would not be swayed, and his uncle had relented and pulled the requisite strings to free him from the clan exemption. If he died, so be it, it was no less than he deserved. No doubt Tuparillio would agree.

He walked towards the yawning black door to the future, each step taking him one further pace away from a planet he'd never tread again. Paragon. He looked up. The gas giant they called the Mater Maxima crowded the lower half of the sky. The long eclipse was over, the Long Winter it brought done with, warmth returned to Paragon. The first Growth season of the Glory was in full blush. Another thing he'd never see again, among all the people he'd never talk to and things he'd never do. Skating on the canals in the Long Winter, holidays on the plains during Little Summer, drinking nights away with his friends in the city... The list went on as Bannick bade farewell to his privileged childhood.

So be it. He had only himself to blame. Through war he would find atonement.

Cheers went up from the crowd as huge tractors came crawling across the rockcrete apron towards the drop-ships, each pulling a long, treaded trailer crowded with newly minted fighting vehicles made in Paragon's industrial zone, equipment for the new regiments. Everything was festooned in purple-and-white bunting, the colours of Paragon. The celebration would surely become wild and raucous once the brave children of the world had departed. A double raising was rare here, and to see men return home almost unheard of. The crowd was suffused with pride; Paragon was surely amongst the most loyal of the Emperor's worlds, and for that they were blessed. Transporting the twenty thousand men to the transport barges in orbit would take the rest of the week. The celebrations would last all that time.

The lines of soldiers marched up the ramp into the dropship, soft carpet giving way to the ring of plasteel. The ramp was enormous, and led into the hold of the ship, a massive space with room enough for a company to deploy into the heart of battle.

'Company, halt!' bellowed a senior sergeant, resplendent in the vermillion of Paragonian dress uniform, a uniform the recruits would not be able to wear until they had finished training and been formally inducted into the Guard. 'About turn!' The sergeant was one of the few veteran officers that Bannick had met who was actually from Paragon. The rest of the staff were drawn from other units from the same warzone the Paragonians had shipped from, members of depleted regiments merged with the Paragonians, fit to provide a seasoned command structure for the raw recruits.

Bannick and the others turned and looked upon their home for the last time. The crowd shouted, the large band playing to their cheers. The ramp began to rise. It closed slowly, huge cogs in the gloom high above cranking round and round to bring the ramp home centimetre by tortuous centimetre.

Little by little, Bannick's world was shut from view. The landing apron went, then the crowds, then the stands of the clan leaders, where Bannick's father would have stood had circumstances been different.

All went, swallowed by the black of the door. The embarkation building's towers disappeared, as did the smokestacks of the industrial zone about the spaceport.

The last thing Bannick saw of his home were the mountains far to the south of Helwat City Landing Fields, the pregnant bulk of the Mater Maxima filling the sky above them.

The door of the drop-ship shut with a hollow boom. Bannick was captive in the belly of the windowless craft.

A shocked silence prevailed over the recruits. Loss was heavy in the air. It was a second of limbo, a space between one life and another.

'Right then!' bellowed the sergeant. 'You young gentlemen have four hours, fifty-three minutes before loading of this rotation is complete, and I am afraid to say you will not be relaxing! Prepare yourselves for months of unending pain which I have the sorrowful duty of dishing out to turn you young popinjays into proper soldiers and officers worthy to wear the uniform of the Emperor!' He sounded happy at this prospect. 'You are going to hate me, my young gentlemen, but that is of no account! I will turn each and every one of you miserable dung beetles into warriors, or you will die trying!' He laughed at his own joke. 'Aw, come, come now, no sad faces. You're in the Imperial Guard now!'

INTERSTITIAL

We suffered a grave blow yesterday.

The 42nd advance was turned by orkish cunning. Several (8? Unconfirmed at this date) heavy walkers and a medium-class Titan were deployed by the enemy, resulting in the destruction of fully three companies of the regiment. Many more casualties were suffered by Atraxian and Paragonian mechanised forces. Somehow the Savlar managed to get out in one piece, more or less.

Losses:

Main Battle Tanks (destroyed/ unrecoverable): 19

Main Battle Tanks (damaged – light): 7

Main Battle Tanks (damaged – severe): 4

Main Battle Tanks (operational): 70

Other vehicles lost or rendered inoperable (support, etc): 37

Casualties sustained: 149 (98 dead, 38 wounded, 13 MIA)

Further losses were sustained early this morning when a regimental recovery team came under attack by ork reconnaissance forces. Two apparently salvageable Leman Russ proved to be booby-trapped. The detonation of these by the recovery crew brought down a demi-company of ork fast-attack vehicles. One Atlas lost. Enginseer Rankoun killed, plus four Munitorum tech-adepts.

That I should lose so many of my men at our first engagement is a source of grave shame for me. That they are not my people matters little. Today I attempted to tender my resignation, but General Ban Lo Kism Verkerigen would not countenance it. I am to attempt to rebuild the regiment with the meagre resources to hand.

I fear our attempts at reinforcing the war effort here on Kalidar have come to little. Our journey here overran by twelve months, delaying our deployment by three seasons, and allowing the orks to consolidate their gains. Several of high command are pressing to petition Castellan Evenius of the Black Templars Adeptus Astartes for further aid, but I am not hopeful. The Angels of Death know no master but our lord the Emperor. They are few in number here, and what forces they have are heavily invested in clearing remaining ork nests from the far side of Kalidar in conjunction with the second battlegroup. I fear this conflict goes ill. I shall continue to pray daily for victory.

Extract, Colonel Gueptera Assis Sholana's personal diaries, Commander-in-Chief, 42nd Paragonian Armoured Regiment.

CHAPTER 7

KALIDAR IV, ADEPTUS MINISTORUM MEDICAE FACILITY, HIVE MODULUS
3283397.M41

'So this is him?' Cortein peered through the thick plex window to the room beyond, lurid with ultraviolet light, at the young lieutenant. He lay upon the gurney of an auto-chirurgeon, clan tattoo visible on his right shoulder, a tattoo that matched Cortein's own. Metal limbs were busy about him, pulling pipes depending from tanks of liquid and pushing them into his mouth, forcing his jaw painfully wide. Cortein thought it a kindness the boy was unconscious. He stared for several minutes, watching the chirurgeon. The wards he'd come through to get here were full past capacity of dead and dying men, the medicae personnel overwhelmed. The stench of burnt flesh and suppurating wounds still clung to his nostrils. The shouts and moans had been the worst, men on the edge of extinction, calling for the Emperor's final benediction, finding mercy nowhere.

The viewing room was blessedly quiet, aseptic. Here important men were treated for dustlung by lungwash, a process too complicated and time-consuming to be given to the lower ranks. A commissar stood in one corner, overlooking the lungwash room, his job to oversee the treatment given to the battlegroup's senior officers. The look on his young face made it clear he was indifferent to Bannick's fate, and he did not so much as acknowledge the presence of Brasslock and Cortein.

'He doesn't look like much,' Cortein said finally.

'I would not underestimate him. This is the one,' said Brasslock, 'whose actions aided your escape from the Kostoval Flats debacle.'

Cortein snorted. 'Not my debacle, enginseer. These idiots have no wit at all when it comes to the ork. They read the first passage on the greenskins they find in the *Tactica Imperium*, go no further and are blinded by dogma to what's in front of them. Orks are not stupid. Whoever first committed that to paper was deluding themselves and those that followed. If only they'd read further in the *Tactica*, they'd know.'

'Nevertheless, no matter where fault lies, a debacle it was, and it is thanks to this lieutenant that you lived to see this day at all.' Brasslock's flesh voice caught in his throat, his artificial lungs clicking as they forced air over neglected vocal cords.

'He's just a boy. He's got no place aboard my tank.'

'Your tank? The crewing of prime assets such as *Mars Triumphant* is of great interest to the Adeptus Mechanicus, honoured lieutenant, and we have selected this boy. Our prognostication savants suggest a match higher than the 79th percentile. Magi Rotar and Hammerweld have petitioned Honoured Captain Hannick, and he has acquiesced, accepting the judgement of the Omnissiah. Lieutenant Colaron Artem Lo Bannick is to be your new third gunner.'

'Pressure at your behest,' said Cortein.

'I am but a humble enginseer, Cortein. But I submitted the initial request, yes.'

Cortein shook his head. 'I wish you wouldn't meddle, Brasslock. I need experienced crew, it's bad enough with Marsello aboard, this…' He consulted the file in his hand, 'Bannick, he's been in combat what, once? One does not just walk onto a super-heavy tank crew. It requires training, exceptional dedication and talent. And what will his commanding officer say? The boy's a lieutenant. Becoming third gunner aboard *Mars* will be an effective demotion for him.'

Brasslock coughed his wheezing laugh. 'He will keep his rank.'

'Then he outranks everyone aboard but me; that is no fit position for a third gunner.'

'Then order him to obey your subordinates. You lose your patience with me, Cortein, when I am but the messenger. *Mars Triumphant* itself approves of this choice. A great confrontation is coming, it feels it. This boy will help with that.'

'I don't want to hear any more of that, Brasslock.'

'It informed me itself.'

'Still pushing the line that its time is up?'

'Affirmative. All the signs are there. You know in your heart that it is true. You listen, when you say you cannot hear.'

'You've no idea what's going on in my head, Brasslock. I could do without this.'

The enginseer chuckled, throaty machine grating laced with binaric chitter. 'Take it up with *Mars Triumphant* if you will. If you do not believe me, consider this, skilled tank crew are at a shortage, he is one, and he has no tank. You yourself have often bemoaned the lack of suitable material for your successor. This boy has shown remarkable spirit. He took command of a leaderless rearguard unit. When he chanced upon your duel with the xeno engine he could have turned and run, but he did not. Furthermore, it was only his exemplary judgement and skill that enabled him to save your life, and the life of the holy *Mars Triumphant*, at all. For that we of Adeptus Mechanicus owe him a great debt. You would acknowledge yours if you were not so…' Brasslock searched for the right word, emotional terms employed only unusually by such as he, cold cog and hot gear needing no such designations, 'stubborn.'

'That's why he's getting the lungwash eh? They usually only give that out to higher ranks. You whispered into a few more ears no doubt.'

'My Biologian colleagues attached to the Medicae were only too happy to help.' Brasslock bowed his ever-shrouded head. 'It is such a great shame so many brave soldiers are denied this treatment, but alas, it is complex. That Bannick is receiving it at all should tell you of his exceptional talent. See, he bears the mark of the Machine-God.' A metal tendril rose from beneath Brasslock's robes and indicated Bannick's cog medallion. 'He has all the qualities necessary. Train him.'

Cortein knocked the file against his hand and exhaled hard. Brasslock was right, to an extent. The recent battle had ripped the reinforcing regiments to shreds. Troops that should have helped secure a swift Imperial victory had been fed into a trap. If Hannick hadn't seen that too and ordered the withdrawal, they'd be looking at a full-scale evacuation – as it was they'd saved only a third of the troops committed to the battle. And now here they were, stuck right back where the Imperial army was before the reinforcements had got to Kalidar, the Imperials in Hive Modulus, the orks in Hive Meradon. *I'm not surprised this war is going to the dogs, looking at the way these idiots are running it,* thought Cortein. For a moment he longed to be back rooting out eldar pirates from the Indrani Agri-Cluster. But the Dentares campaign had come to a successful close, so here they were, shipped out, six months back to Paragon, a supposedly ten-month trip out to Kalidar that turned into a two-year ordeal. Three weeks in between with his feet on the ground of a home he'd never thought to see again. How much Paragon had changed, how much dirtier, how much more run down. *The effects of nostalgia?* he thought, *or perhaps the whole universe really is going to hell...* He flipped the file over again. It had so many official stamps on its crumbling card cover that it was nearly black. One of hundreds of thousands like it. He'd had to argue for ten minutes with a pasty-faced Munitorum clerk to get hold of it, then wait another half an hour while it was fetched from the depths of the company records; practically lightspeed for the Munitorum. *Someone other than the tech-priests is pulling strings here. But Brasslock is right,* he told himself as he read through a long list of training commendations, *good personnel are few and far between. This boy's record suggests he has potential.* 'Why does he have to be so damned young?' he added aloud, and shut the casing of the file with a snap.

'They are all young, honoured lieutenant,' countered Brasslock. 'And yet they serve.'

The hives of Kalidar were unlike anything Bannick had seen before. There were no hives on Paragon. Furthermore, the hostile surface of Kalidar would not permit the mountain-sized cities other hive-worlds possessed, with which Bannick was familiar from vidcast and book. On Kalidar, each hive centred on a shaft punched into the crust of the planet, a hole wide enough to swallow a cruiser. The better districts were a third of the way down the shaft, round the sides, their presence marked out by domed parks and palace-promontories extending into the void. The further one went up or down the shaft, the poorer the area, likewise the further away from it into the earth. The domains of the hivelords thus formed a toroid about the middle, a sealed domain of luxury denied the majority of the planet's population. Industry was concentrated round the lip above and below ground, while deep down were the mines, workings following the veins of precious lorelei far out into the desert.

Hive Modulus was on the front line, the nearest of the world's four human-held hives to Hive Meradon, which the orks had snatched from the defenders nearly three years earlier. Swathes of the upper levels of Modulus had been requisitioned by the Departmento Munitorum to billet the Imperial forces, its workshops given over to vehicle repair, yet Modulus worked on under the nose of the enemy, mining and processing Kalidar's rare mineral wealth.

Bannick felt weak after his treatment, his lungs ragged, but had been ordered to report to 42nd regimental command to receive new orders immediately, and so he made his way on the city's spiral uproad, which, with its downroad twin, formed an elegant helix inside the city shaft. Looking down from the road gave Bannick vertigo, so he kept to the inner pedestrian way, away from the harsh light of the sky above.

The road was heavy with traffic. Units of Guardsmen jogged past. Industrial wagons ground upwards laden with tonnes of ore or with the sand that needed to be dredged constantly from the lower levels.

But it was the work gangs of native Kalidarians that fixed Bannick's attention. Every third hour a klaxon sounded and a hundred nondescript doors hissed open, disgorging workers for the shift change.

They went past Bannick in endless streams, their appearance shocking: pallid, slight beings, covered with sores. Most had their rebreathers implanted, their mouths hidden under oxidised metal. Cracked flesh surrounded these metal snouts, tubes that could be attached to nutrient packs dangled from them, the implants preventing the taking of solid food. Thick pipes ran over their shoulders to bulky cylinders upon their backs. They were bald, and nearly all showed the milky eyes of the blind, sight taken from them by Kalidar's abrasive dust. With a jolt of shock Bannick saw that more than half of them bore minor signs of mutation and deformity: withered additional arms, twisted backs, crooked limbs, and worse. Revulsion filled him. They moved in human chains at a shuffling jog, left arm clasping the left shoulder of his fellow to the front, thin metal wires running through eyelets on collars to ensure they would not separate. The collars did not look as if they would come off. The workers were so emaciated he could not tell the women from the men, and their stench was astonishing.

Each work party, hundreds strong, was led by a pureborn overseer, better fed, better clad, the only Kalidarians Bannick saw on the road wearing goggles. Each carried a tall staff in one hand topped with a crackling prod, in the other they rang a bell, marking the steps of the workers with dolorous chimes.

'Stand, wretch! Stand!' the sharp discharge of electricity reached Bannick as he made another slow turn of the spiral road. A party of workers stood, heads bowed, while their overseer set to work on one of their number, collapsed on the rockcrete. 'Stand!'

Bannick watched, the scene momentarily obscured by a road train rumbling up the carriageway. When he could see again, the overseer was stabbing at the worker upon the floor, each jab accompanied by a crack of energy. He turned to go, no concern of his, but a hand grasped his bicep, staying him.

'Does it shock you, lieutenant?' said a voice right in his ear.

Bannick turned to look into the face of a veteran of the Paragonian 23rd, one of three Paragonian regiments brought in from the Dentares warzone and shipped over with the two new raisings from their homeworld. He had a hard face. Bannick was cautious, he wore the markings of a peacekeeper, the

Paragon regiments' military arbitrators, and his eyes brimmed with hostility.

Bannick's brow furrowed. 'Why should it shock me?'

'These workers, they can't speak, can't eat, most are blind,' said the peacekeeper. 'They neuter them, you know that? Does that not raise a little pity in you?'

'Sir,' said Bannick, standing tall, smoothing down his uniform. 'Don't tell me what to think. These workers are genetically impure, beneath human. What of it?'

The older man's face grew harder still. 'That may be so, but tell me, "sir", is it any different for men of purer birth? What about on Paragon?'

Bannick inclined his head. 'At home the workers are cared for as per the teachings of the Adeptus Ministorum. Alms are provided to the poor and those rendered unfit for work.'

'Is that so? Is that so?' the peacekeeper nodded in a way that suggested anything but agreement. 'How many times did you go down onto the shop floor of your own clan workshops? What are you? A Bannick? I recognise the face. Do you think your folks back home treated their workers much better? My family worked hard, until a bad debt cast my father into the prison-foundries of our clan and me into the army. I went to visit my father once. Only once, I couldn't stand it. It killed him soon enough. They aren't much better than this, the debtors' manufactoria, no matter what the clan lords might say about Paragonian virtues. What do you think happens to the likes of them back home? You ever recall seeing a man like that?' He pointed out a man with a tiny head, almost conical, idiot eyes rolling in his face. 'Or like that?' Another, this one with miniature limbs halfway up his ribcage terminating in a pair of backwards feet. 'Think on that. At least here these poor basdacks get to live. At home they don't even drown them before they toss them into the incinerator. This is the way things are son. Live with it, and spare me your hypocrisy. Paragon's no better.'

'I could have you arrested for this,' said Bannick, painfully aware still of the crackles of the prod. Surely, even for a debased creature like the mutant, enough was enough?

'As a peacekeeper I have jurisdiction over you – those are the captain-general's standing orders and as such they supersede anything you might have to say on the matter. Who do you think they'll believe, a boy, an aristocrat's brat, or a proven servant of the Emperor?'

The overseer had stopped thrashing the worker. He knelt down and roughly examined the prone man, then pulled a small pair of clippers from a pouch at his belt, and cut the worker free from his collar. He rearranged his blind slaves, rolled the dead man out over the road way, and pitched him down the central shaft. He returned to his troop, rang his bell three times, and the column set off again.

'Now, do you have anything to say to me?'

Bannick shook his head.

'Good lad, "sir",' said the peacekeeper. 'Now on your way, and think on what you had, and how you got it, next time you dream of home.'

Bannick arrived at the 42nd's regimental HQ five minutes early, but was shown in to see the colonel by his adjutant, a fussy little Guardsman, right away.

Colonel Sholana was short and dark with eyes of a piercing yellow. He came from some world Bannick had never heard of and had an accent he struggled to cope with. Detached from his original unit, Sholana had been put in charge of the Paragonian 42nd Armoured Regiment, there not being enough experienced Paragonian officers left from the Dentares veterans to spare in staffing the new raisings.

'At ease, lieutenant. Come, sit down.' Sholana gestured with a deep-brown hand to the chair before his desk. Bannick sat. 'That's better. I don't stand much on ceremony. I find being cooped up in a tank quite restrictive enough without having everyone leaping to attention all the time, especially when we're talking like now, in an informal little chat.'

Bannick said nothing. He'd heard mixed reports about Sholana's informal little chats.

'Will you be wanting a drink, lieutenant?' asked Sholana.

'No, sir.'

'Well, perhaps it is a little early.' He eyed the decanter of liquor on his desk suspiciously. 'And I will admit, that although I find much admirable in the culture of Paragon, this... glice?'

'Gleece, sir,' said Bannick.

'Gleece. Gleece. Yes. I find it not entirely to my taste. It is a little... thick, I suppose, yes. I rather prefer a good amasec. Still,' he said brightly, 'I suppose I will get used to it eventually, no? I won't keep you, Bannick, so I'll get right to the point. You're to be transferred.'

'Sir?'

'The regiment is not in a good way. We lost half our personnel and a quarter of our fighting vehicles in the Kostoval Flats. Stragglers still trickle in, but...' he raised his hands. 'I trust you understand, this is all in the strictest confidence.' The colonel spun his chair away from the desk, once the property of the refinery manager. The buildings of the facility protruded above the ground, and Sholana's office had a good view out over the refinery's topside grounds, cleared to provide a marshalling yard for the regiment. The green sky was clear and the window shielding was open, showing the red-grey deserts of Kalidar stretching away beyond the mass of buildings of Modulus's surface town. Further out on a large section of desert bulldozed flat was the battlegroup's landing field, cluttered with drop-ships, shuttlecraft and cargo lifters.

'I have been a soldier for many years, Bannick. Morale. That's the thing, low morale can kill a regiment more surely than a well-placed virus bomb, and the 42nd's is at rock bottom. That's one of the reasons I've given leave for this transfer to go ahead.' He turned back to face the lieutenant, reached into a drawer in the metal desk and took out an envelope. He leaned forwards and handed it to Bannick.

'It's a shame to lose you. You showed real initiative out there, although,' he chuckled, 'if I were of another mind I could have you shot for ordering the rearguard to fall back, but I prefer to be… flexible.' His grin broadened. 'Do us proud.'

Bannick opened the envelope. Within was a sheet of onion-skin paper, typed with his new assignment: the 7th Paragonian Super-heavy Tank Company. Bannick's eyes widened. He looked to Sholana, his face questioning.

'You understand, your new position will not be a demotion; although you will be fulfilling the role of third gunner, you will keep your rank of lieutenant. This, though unusual, is the quickest way to the command of one of those behemoths. They do that, you know, bring in new blood, select promising tankers, put them in a junior role, see if they've got what it takes.' He wagged a finger. 'You're going places, lieutenant. Knowing that will give your comrades remaining under my command great cheer. Cortein's a good man, bit of a loner, but I suppose you have to be to command a machine like that.' He paused for a space. 'You've also been put forward for commendation, by me. Congratulations.' He shoved a small box across the table. 'No time for ceremony, I'm afraid. Wear it with pride, eh?'

But Bannick was not listening. He was going to serve aboard a Baneblade.

The rest of what Sholana had to say washed over him. He

found himself outside, clutching orders and medal in a daze. He fished out his aquila and cog from within his shirt and kissed both reverently in turn. Whatever he had done to deserve this chance at redemption, he swore in his heart not to let the Emperor down.

CHAPTER 8

ARONIS CITY, THE SIXTH MOON OF PARAGON VI
2103395.M41

Bannick had only a few days until he was due to attend the Paragonian military academy; a few months later he'd ship out. Now was as good a time as any to tell his fiancée. He drew in a deep breath, and shook. In some ways, telling Kaithalar the wedding was off was far more terrifying than going to war. He rallied himself, and knocked on the door.

'Come in!' Kaithalar Beyn Lo Turannigen's terse voice sounded from the other side of the ornate doors, their wood heavy with gilt plasterwork. Two liveried bondsmen swung them aside, admitting Bannick to the office of the Warden of Clan Turannigen. She stood behind a desk whose impressive size barely filled a corner of the massive room. The curtains were pulled against the eclipse's wan day and the fireplace was filled side to side with burning logs, struggling to keep the chill of the Long Winter at bay. To one side of it stood the Steward of Turannigen, reading silently from a ledger, while next to him an enhanced savant burbled nonsense and accounting figures to no one in particular, piles of printed parchment piling up round his feet, issuing from the records unit embedded in his chest.

Kaithalar didn't look up from her charts as Bannick came into the room. A large fur was thrown over her slender shoulders, her face creased as always in a frown. She stroked at a goblet of gleece as she read and reread the sheets before her. 'Come to apologise, have you?'

A servant moved to take Bannick's furs, but he shooed him away. He hunted around for a chair that was not piled high with sheets of vellum or production flimsies. He gave up, instead shifting the smallest pile he could find onto the floor before moving the chair as near to the fire as was polite and sitting down.

'It's not like that, Kaithalar...' he began, and stumbled to a stop. He rubbed his face, not knowing what to say. The last week had been impossible. Tuparillio's face haunted his dreams. He was drawn and pale, his eyes yellow from too much sleep and wine. He felt weak, but he had no appetite for food.

Kaithalar looked up and stared at him hard. She'd always been a tough one, Bannick had seen that when they'd been at the collegium together, even before her father's death had made her clan productiva and driven the girl from her once and for all. But today, Bannick thought, her eyes were a little softer, there was hurt in them too.

'I've never thought highly of you, Colaron,' she said matter-of-factly. 'You're a rake more interested in bedding bond skirt and drinking your family's wealth than making something of yourself. I pity you for it. I really do. All you male scions are like that, you're expected to be, hanging off the say-so of your fathers until they hand on their office to you and die.' She barked out a sharp, bitter laugh. 'While we girls stay at home and behave like good daughters. Not me, though, not me, no brother.' She cast her gaze around the room at the heaped papers. 'I thought you might be a little different, but you are not. You are a drunken idiot like the rest of them, puffed up with honour. What was it, did Tuparillio look at one of your girlies funny? He was a boy, Colaron, a little boy. You should have slapped him and sent him on his way.'

'It wasn't like that, look, can we not talk about this please? He was intent... he was...' He couldn't tell her. He didn't want to involve her in his guilt. He gave up, exasperated with himself. 'Listen to me. I have come here because I have something to say...'

Her facade suddenly cracked. 'Whatever you say, it's no excuse! No excuse! I cannot have my betrothed becoming involved in common duelling. Barbarism! Have you any idea how embarrassing this is? What shame it is to have my betrothed whispered about as a kinslayer? It's hard enough to run a clan department as a woman as it is, and now I have my future husband rampaging like a sho-beast. I will not stand for it! To think I thought you might be able to cope with this!' she shouted, waving at the mess of documents. 'To help me! How wrong I was.' She punctuated her words by beating upon the table with a delicate fist. Her goblet had fallen, spilling gleece onto the papers. It dripped onto the carpet, unnoticed. 'It is too much to hope for a love match, but in you I at least had hopes for a profitable partnership. Now, because of your behaviour you owe great indemnity, the alliance is in jeopardy and the finances of both clans will suffer. You're lucky I don't terminate the agreement. I need Clan Bannick's backing to secure...'

She is beautiful, thought Bannick, and he felt a tenderness for her that surprised him. *Perhaps it would have been a good match.* 'Kaith,' he interrupted gently. 'You are right. I would be nothing but a liability to you.'

'What do you mean, you "would be"?'

'Kaith, I'm sorry, I… Look, I don't know how to say this. I'm withdrawing from the marriage contract.' Bannick hurried on before she could react, gabbling. 'I have enlisted in the Guard, in the new double founding. I'll be leaving as soon as the Long Winter is done. It's not you, it's this business with… with the duel.' *Say his name*, he thought, *tell her why he called you out…* He couldn't. 'I can't serve the Emperor here, I've proved that, you're right. I will go and fight in His wars and, if He is willing, give service with my body and blood. I'm sorry.'

Kaithalar's mouth dropped wide, then snapped shut. Her features hardened.

'I have to get away… I saw Tuparillio's mother, my aunt, my mother, they know… I…'

'Get out,' she said.

'Kaith…'

'Get out!' she shouted. She scooped up her goblet and hurled it at him. It sailed past his head, cracking the face of a plaster puttee on the wall behind him. The two bondsmen bodyguards re-entered the room and made towards him. Bannick left.

The winter day outside seemed as bleak as his prospects.

CHAPTER 9

KALIDAR IV, HIVE MODULUS
3286397.M41

Bannick was forced to wait for several hours before his liaison showed up; his belongings crammed into his kitbag, he sat outside the barracks of the 42nd Paragonian Armoured Regiment on a poorly made metal chair. He was nervous, whether of meeting the tank or its commander Cortein he wasn't sure. Either one he did not wish to disappoint. As a boy he'd imagined fighting aboard a super-heavy tank, playing a game, imagining himself a hero like his uncle, who'd gone to war while Bannick was a boy. There was a statue in the clan hall, a bust of a man his tutor had told him commanded a super-heavy tank, an honoured man. Bannick had often daydreamed that he was that man.

The man was Honoured Lieutenant Marken Cortein Lo Bannick, his rank in the style of Paragon, for as the Paragonians made machines they especially revered them. To serve aboard a Baneblade was a great honour for Bannick, to serve under a man who'd inspired him even greater, but it was an honour Bannick felt sure he did not deserve, and so he sat there with a mixture of dread and excitement churning in his stomach. He would have laughed at the perversity of fate were he not so on edge. War was supposed to have been an impossibility for him, no matter how much he had played and later duelled, and yet here he was. It was all thanks to Tuparillio. Thoughts ran round his head as he waited, taking his mind off the recent defeat at Kostoval and the disappearance of his foster-brother Kalligen.

The barracks was situated in a food store five turns below the surface, not far from the Medicae facility where Bannick had been treated. The men had complained about how far away they were from their vehicles. It wasn't a problem Bannick had to worry about now, nor did many of his colleagues. There were many empty beds in the enlisted men's dormitory and officers' rooms.

Kalligen's room was empty too. It had been hard to find anyone who knew what had happened to him, so many members of the regiment were dead or injured. He'd searched until he hit upon a crowd of men huddled around a casualty list pinned up on the wall of the mess. He fought his way through, eyes scanning the flimsies to find what he had feared. 'Kalligen, Lazlo Gratimar Lo, 2098231, Lieutenant, MIA' was all it had said. No matter how many times he reread it, it did not tell him anything more.

Eventually he'd tracked down a junior support sergeant attached to Kalligen's platoon. He told Bannick that only two of his friend's four tanks had made it back into the depot, Kalligen's own disappearing into the sandstorm. This last the sergeant had heard from a sponson gunner, sole survivor of Kalligen's three tanks, and currently under the Medicae. Bannick pressed him for more information, but he had little to give.

Missing in action on Kalidar was death postponed. Bannick became morose. Kalligen had been his closest friend for as long as he could remember, an interclan fostering. Clan Kalligen had taken Bannick's older brother, his family had got Kalligen in return. Dark-eyed, cheeky, quick with his words, much to the annoyance of the Bannick tutors and, later, the masters at the collegium. Bannick thought his father would strike him for his impudence, but Kalligen had drawn something warm out in the old man, and he'd become much loved. Bannick remembered how all Kalligen's bravado had gone in the first night when he'd cried for his own folk. Since then they'd been like brothers, and now he was gone.

Bannick silently prayed. *You should have taken me in his stead. He was a better man than I, for all his blasphemy. He didn't deserve to die.* And Bannick thought further that the Emperor was cruel to torment him in this way, no matter his crimes. He waited for grief, but it did not come. He felt oddly numb, more weary than anything else. His callousness depressed him further, his emotions were being abraded by Kalidar.

Death in war is to be expected, he told himself. *I will mourn Kalligen when I have done my duty.*

Exhausted, Bannick drifted into semi-consciousness, aware of his surroundings, the scrape of cheap furniture, the murmur of men on clean-up duty, the scribble of a pen on the casualty listings on the nearby wall as some adjutant or another made an adjustment to the rollcall of the dead, and then he fell asleep.

A boot kicked his, and he jerked awake.

'Hi,' said the man before him, small and wiry with a grin that screamed 'insubordination'. He proffered a dirty hand. Bannick hesitated, shaking sleep from his mind, and took it. He shook it as firmly as he could. It was slick with grease. The man's uniform was equally filthy. 'I'm Radden, first gunner aboard *Mars Triumphant*. Sorry I'm so late, but we've been having no end of basdack troubles with the cannon targeting unit. We got pretty beat up back there at Osnakhem, not as bad as your boys, but still…' He shrugged. 'You want me to take that?' Radden pointed to Bannick's kitbag, and continued talking without drawing breath. 'You're Bannick right? Nice to meet you, damn shame about Vand, he was our third gunner before you, but always nice to meet a new face, it can get a bit anti-social being a tanker, but I guess you know that huh, lieutenant?' Bannick got to his feet and stretched. 'Come with me, come on, come on. I managed to requisition a groundcar, we can drive back in style.' He winked in a way that suggested 'requisition' were a synonym for 'steal'.

He paused as he bent to lift Bannick's bag. 'Sorry, the honoured lieutenant says I'm always gabbling on, can't stop talking ha ha! That's my problem, but I can shoot straight, they all say that about me… What by the Throne have you got in this?' Radden bent down and opened Bannick's bag. He rummaged through it and began tossing objects onto the floor. 'Sorry, but you won't be needing this, or this, or this. Not much storage on board. Say, I better leave this, looks like it has sentimental value. But definitely not this!' Bannick moved to protest, he even considered ordering him to stop, but wasn't sure. In pure rank terms, he outranked Radden, but as first gunner, Radden technically had seniority over him on the tank crew until the honoured lieutenant said otherwise. 'You got a spare rebreather?' He zipped up the bag, leaving a pile of Bannick's possessions to one side. 'No? You're going to need one, we often operate out for long periods. Last thing we need is for you to be jumping every time a bit of dust comes floating in. I'll make sure we get you one. Right then! Ready? Let's go, this way, this way!' The little gunner stopped again, a puzzled frown crossing his brow beneath his red hair. 'You know what, lieutenant, you don't say much.'

* * *

Radden drove the requisitioned groundcar like a maniac, weaving through the traffic with centimetres to spare as he climbed the uproad and took to the ways between the thick-walled buildings of Modulus's surface town. On the flat, he drove even more badly, all the way to the factory where the 7th currently had its home. Long lines of infantry went by in a blur as Radden accelerated, chattering away as he drove. He turned off the overroute without signalling, causing a double-decked ore truck to blare angrily. He powered into a building emptied of ore and foundry vehicles to accommodate the 7th, and skidded to a halt in one of a series of partitioned ore stalls.

'Sorry if I scared you!' said Radden with a smirk, patently anything but apologetic. 'Good job I'm not the driver eh?' He pulled his respirator on. 'You'll need yours on too. The building's not fully sealed. I've been told that on a day like this, it doesn't really matter, but I'm not taking any chances, I don't know about you.'

Bannick followed suit, the memory of the lungwash still raw.

They got out of the car, accompanied by a hiss of escaping atmosphere, and walked past lines of manufactory equipment onto the main floor. The machines that worked there in peacetime had been shunted carelessly to the other side of the half-kilometre wide room, the rockcrete in the middle scarred with scrape marks where they'd been dragged out. In their place was a hollow square about two hundred metres across. One side was walled off by prefabricated barracks buildings, boxes stacked one atop the other, each accessed through a flexible airlock. Store blocks, pallets of spare parts, a small Adeptus Mechanicus shrine, a portable Ministorum chapel on fat wheels and munitions stacks made up two more walls. The fourth side of the square was open, facing the doors to the warehouse.

Bannick breathed a little quicker of the rebreather-fouled air as he caught sight of what stood before them: the remaining three super-heavy tanks of the 7th Paragonian Heavy Tank Company.

'The Baneblade *Artemen Ultrus*, the Hellhammer *Ostrakhan's Rebirth*, our captain's ride – he likes blasting things up close – and of course, the Baneblade *Mars Triumphant*. Ours,' said Radden, indicating each of the tanks in turn. 'As you can see, we took a bit of a beating. Always comes through though, *Mars Triumphant* does, a millennium old and still going strong. Oldest tank in the company.'

Radden glanced at the empty space on the floor, a box of white paint where *Lux Imperator* should have stood. 'They got the Shadowsword though, basdack orks.' The pair of them made the sign of the aquila, Paragon style, sharing for a moment comradeship in the memory of the dead vehicle.

Each tank was more than thirteen metres long, over eight wide, the tallest of them towering three times the height of a tall man. The Leman Russ that Bannick had been trained to command seemed puny in comparison, for every tank here was the equal of a squadron of Leman Russ, or a full-strength platoon of infantry.

And he was going to serve on one. By the Throne, he didn't deserve this.

'Hey, now that's the right response,' said Radden at Bannick's wide-eyed silence. 'Come on, your new posting awaits.' Radden made off to *Mars Triumphant*, Bannick trailing in his wake, unable to take his eyes off the Baneblade.

The two Baneblades were of the Martian pattern and differed from one another only in minor detail – both sported a fore-mounted demolisher cannon, a twin-linked heavy bolter turret beside it. Both had battle cannons as their main weapons in double-hatched turrets, rocket-assisted models with longer, vented barrels that were more powerful and further ranged than those mounted on Leman Russ. Both had a coaxial autocannon beside their main guns, more for ranging than for destruction. Both carried two pairs of twin auxiliary fuel tanks up and behind their track guards, either side of reactor plants that muttered and hummed even as the tanks slept. Both carried a sponson bank of remotely operated weapons on either side, although *Mars Triumphant* had lost one of hers in the fight, more twin-linked heavy bolters with a 90-degree arc of fire to the side and a turreted lascannon atop the sponson with 270 degrees of movement.

It was on the turret the two tanks differed, *Mars Triumphant* carrying a pintle stubber on its left hatch that the other Baneblade, *Artemen Ultrus*, lacked. *Mars Triumphant* had a larger comms array to the turret's rear, more stowage and a periscope mounting carved with two winged battle saints either side of the glass. Indeed, *Artemen Ultrus* was altogether plainer, lacking the decoration and scrollwork that *Mars Triumphant* had, and Bannick guessed it must be because of the Baneblade's great age. This was a revered vehicle, a living relic, a testimony to the persistence and power of the Imperium of Man.

'She is, beautiful, isn't she?' said Radden. 'She's looking a little out of sorts right now, but don't you worry, we'll fix her right up.'

Many panels had been removed from the tanks, revealing the machinery beneath. Lines led from batteries of machines and fuel tanks. Powerloaders stalked noisily between pallets of shells, powercells, spares and rations. Sparks arced from welding torches. Servitors trudged back and forth, or stood in place, precisely performing repetitive tasks. Tech-priests watched over all, interrupting their chants and prayers to deliver sharp rebukes to those less devout, or to communicate with the machine-spirits within the vehicles. Although the full company required forty crewmen to man the vehicles, the number of support staff they required to keep them supplied and functioning was almost quadruple that.

The super-heavies dwarfed all; like chained monsters they rose up from amidst the activity all about them, quiescent, yet clearly the true power in the room. Swarmed over by tech-priests, their cyborg servitors and men of the Munitorum, they were patient, like beasts being cleaned of parasites by lesser creatures. Their aura of strength was almost overwhelming, as if at any time they chose they could rise up and swat away the bustle.

An Atlas recovery tank was drawn up by the damaged flank of *Mars Triumphant*, the shell of a sponson hanging from it. Cables and wires like intestines spilled from a hole in the Baneblade's side. New plates of armour and parts showed where the tank had been hit by the ork Titan's strange weapons and repaired, free of paint, glistening like new scar tissue. The damage had appeared grave to Bannick's eyes in the battle, but ministered to by the tech-priests it seemed a flesh wound, and the tank sat there unperturbed.

Two tech-priests were busy at the side as the sponson came down, one plugged into a panel in the side of the Atlas by mechadendrite. The two screeched binaric in staccato audio bursts at each other as Radden and Bannick passed, their gesticulating speaking volumes as to their disagreement. 'That one there,' said Radden, pointing, 'is Enginseer Adept Brasslock. You'll be seeing a lot of him, and him.' He pointed at a servitor stood to one side, and Bannick recognised it as the one he and Kalligen had seen on the barge. It was equipped for war, a heavy bolter plugged into its shoulder socket. 'That's Urtho, the two are rarely apart. See one, the other will be close by. Take my advice and never, ever lose your temper with Brasslock. Urtho does not take kindly to it. Some say he's got a scrap of personality left in his scraped-out brain, but me, I just think its clever conditioning or something.'

They went round the back of the Baneblade, the tank's reactor powerplant looming above them. Radden showed Bannick the crew ladder, hard by the plant on the left-hand side, and together they clambered aboard. They went up onto the wide shoulder of the main deck roof, upon which sat the turret.

'Here.' Radden banged on a hatch beneath his feet with his heel, 'you can get into the main deck, it's a squeeze, brings you right in over the tech station, only for escape or emergency, annoys Vorkosigen if you use it to get in and out, but don't let that stop you. There.' Radden paused and pointed along the tank to the front, 'fore of the main deck, is another access hatch that leads into the forward compartment up where the driver's station is. It comes down right on the second gunnery chair, so I'd avoid it unless you want to end up in Ganlick's lap, and trust me, you don't. That's where you'll be, sometimes, when Sergeant Ganlick is on other duties or off rotation, but mostly you're in third gunnery, which is all remote-controlled from the command deck. We'll go in through the top, that way you can see where everything is. Ganlick is that ox over there. See?' Radden pointed out a bald head bobbing about near to the hull-mounted demolisher cannon. 'Oi! 'Lick!' Radden produced a small nut from in his overalls and bounced it off Ganlick's head. The body it attached to unfolded to a ridiculous height. Not only was he one of the tallest tankers Bannick had ever seen, but among the biggest of men. That he could squeeze himself into a tank even so big as the Baneblade was a surprise.

'Big as an ork he is,' said Radden to Bannick, 'smells like one too. Ganlick!'

'Frag you, you skinny little basdack,' growled the huge man, and bent back down to his task.

'Hey! I thought I'd introduce you! Be nice! This is Lieutenant Bannick, our new third gunner and brass trainee.'

'Frag him too,' grumbled the sergeant.

'He's got a foul temper that one, only talks when he's after something, but he's as superstitious as they come, so he's not too much trouble inside, because he doesn't want to upset *Mars Triumphant*. See that big medallion on his neck? Bought it for a month's wages the day we got here off some sand-dwelling basdack. Idiot. Supposed to bring protection from ghosts or somesuch. Still, if you want to know something, he can find it out. He might not say much, but Ganlick could get a commissar to spill his guts given enough time, it's a real knack he has. Come on,' he said, and led Bannick up onto the wide turret of the Baneblade. Two large hatches sat side by side, one proud of the other, jutting out of the turret's side to form an observation cupola, the other ringed by a well-maintained vision block, and mounting a heavy stubber on a rail. Two periscope units and targeting arrays were to the front of the turrets, external comms gear to the rear. Radden pressed his forefinger into a slot by the vision-block hatch. A clunk of a lock disengaging came from within. 'We'll get your print patterned inside,' he said. 'All these lock down automatically; just one of the many benefits of serving onboard a genuine Mars-made war machine. Of course, you can still open them by hand from the inside, otherwise we might be in trouble, eh?'

'That's good,' said Bannick. 'These Mars tech too?' he indicated the augur lenses to the front of the hatches.

'Oh, all Mars tech,' nodded Radden. 'Real sophisticated stuff. Vorkosigen, that's our tech-adept, can't make head nor tail of most of it, that's why we have Brasslock, Crampspan and the other enginseers permanently attached to the unit. Well, we had Crampspan…' Radden's normal bluster trailed off at the mention of the Shadowsword's enginseer, no doubt dead with the rest. 'It's the kind of stuff an adept would sell his grandmama to learn about – Brasslock probably had. And you ain't seen nothing yet, lieutenant, oh no.' He hopped through the hatch. Bannick waited for a moment before following on down, having to twist his body to one side to avoid the firestep inside the turret.

Inside there was not enough room to stand. Bannick hunched over, and looked around. It took a moment for his eyes to adjust to the gloom, lit by the red and green of multiple screens and what light came in through the hatch.

'The gunnery deck,' said Radden proudly. 'Where you're standing is where Meggen, my loader, stands when he's up here. This is me, main gunnery.' He grabbed a much-patched, high backed chair set partway into the turret floor and gave it an affectionate shake. 'Right by the main gun. That's my suite. Nice eh? I get the secondary scope directly in – that's the small boxy one next to the big fancy one up there.' He rapped a knuckle against the ceiling, 'though the honoured lieutenant gets the feed off it. Told you the tech was good. The commander sits below, not like in one of your Leman Russ, this, oh no. Too much going on to have him isolated up here in the turret, although of course all the main feeds to his tac displays come direct from the top, gives him a good view.' He pointed up. 'And there is a secondary command chair to the back here.' He pointed to a cramped cubby hole in the observation cupola. 'If he needs a look out top, he can direct us all from up here.'

It was oppressively hot inside the turret, airless, noisy with muted voices and the hammering of engineering works on the outside. 'Meggen's job right there.' He pointed out a shell rack and a boxy shell lift hard to the central turret well. Six shells sat to attention, ready for action. They were half the height of a man, crowding the turret further. Between them, the breech of the gun, access points and the main gunnery station, there was little space to move. 'Ralt sends 'em up from the shell store on the lower deck. Sometimes Meggen gets a bit bored and rattles off a few shots from the stubber. Don't touch it, he thinks it's his,' he added conspiratorially. 'Gets real jealous, so he does.'

'Now, down here.' Radden went over to the turret ladder well, set centrally so access could be had at all times between turret and main decks, the shell elevator hard by it. 'The main command deck.'

They descended into a room, the sides of which formed an irregular octagon, viewing cupolas of armaglass set into each facet. The track units ran under the extreme edges of the deck, the space they occupied creating shelves down either side of the compartment, both full of equipment. Like the turret, it was incredibly cramped and hot. 'This is where Cortein sits.' He gestured to a high-backed seat, multiple tac-displays in front of it. 'And that there,' he said, pointing to another tanker, stripped down to his vest, skin running with sweat, tattoo of the Epperaliant clan clearly visible, 'is Second Lieutenant Epperaliant, commsman and second-in-command.'

'Welcome aboard, lieutenant,' said Epperaliant, and went back to whatever he had been doing. His comms-suite and Cortein's command suite formed a continuous L-shaped run down the right side of the room and across the front, Epperaliant's chair set at right-angles to that of the commander, rails allowing it an easy run up and down the bank of monitors, logic engines and augur readouts. Cortein's station included a chart desk, a highly sophisticated cogitator display capable of three-dimensional map projection, something Bannick had only ever seen in static facilities before. Radden had been right about the level of technology aboard. 'This is you, third gunnery station, all remotes. You'll be primarily responsible for the sponson weaponry and the hull turret heavy bolter, because

Outlanner's always too busy actually driving to fire that. You can actually man all the guns from this station, twitch stick activated mostly.' Radden activated a few screens, dragging his fingers across them, pushed some of the station's bewildering array of controls.

Radden noticed Bannick's expression of concentration. 'Don't worry, it's much more sophisticated than a Leman Russ, but you'll get the hang of it. It'll do half the work for you. Mars tech, y'see? All STC stuff, but not like the templates we have back on Paragon, only the higher tech-adepts can manage this level of systems integration. Make sure you pray to it properly, at least when Brasslock's around. Oh, and don't try and run my gun remotely, okay? What I said about Meggen and his weapon goes doubly for me, just so's we're clear, that's mine and mine alone, and I don't like other people touching it, unless I'm dead, huh? Then help yourself, because I'll be past caring,' he grinned.

'Now, there's space in this second chair for your loader, Marsello. He's just a kid, but he's a pretty good shot, and with both of you working the console you should be able to put out a high rate of fire. Try not to fire off too much in one burst. The bolters don't often go dry, the hoppers have four thousand rounds in them each, but the interior reloading systems don't always work so well. The only reliable way to reload is to clear out and refill the entire system. That's through the sponson access hatch, and they're on the outside. If you do need a reload, that's Marsello's job, just don't send him out in the middle of a firefight. Don't worry about the lascannons too much, they're run directly off the powerplant, so no energy packs there to worry about, though the shunts sometimes burn out. If they do, Marsello or Engineer Vorkosigen can swap them pretty quick. Basically, both of you fight. Anything goes wrong, you carry on firing, Marsello or the tech-adept will sort it. Tech station's to the rear.' He indicated another large station, second only in size to the comms suite, at the back along the longest face of the irregular, octagonal room. The floor stepped up to this, meaning it was not possible to stand at all in that part of the compartment; the tech-adept would have to slide into the depression housing his seat, the back of which nearly bumped the low ceiling.

The whole deck was crammed with tech, the shell elevator and turret well ladder cutting right up the middle so that it was almost unrealistic to expect five men to work in there. The combat stations were so close they'd all be rubbing elbows. There was far less space in the tank than Bannick had expected, a consequence of thick armour, multiple systems and the ten-strong crew needed to operate it all.

'Access to the lower deck is this way.' Radden moved over to a kidney-shaped slot to the front left of the compartment. They clambered down a ladder to a corridor beneath. For the first time, they could stand up almost straight, although Bannick's shoulders brushed either side of the narrow gangway. The air below was even thicker and hotter than in the two decks above. 'The command deck floor sits low, but there are stores under-neath, plus three bunks.' He showed Bannick three openings leading into boxes as small as coffins. 'When we're travelling, we rotate. You get time to grab some shut-eye, do so. We're in demand and can be in the field for weeks.' He rolled his eyes and grinned as he said this. 'Your locker's here too.' He banged on a tiny door. 'Glad I made you leave all that rubbish behind? I thought so. You might want to take that jacket and shirt off later, as I'm sure you've noticed it's very hot in here, but let's meet the honoured lieutenant first while you're look-ing respectable, make a good impression, eh? We've got bunks in the barracks, but we never see them, so if you want some-thing to hand, keep it here.'

He turned round and faced the track unit's inner wall. 'This door in the track unit goes out into the bolter hoppers. From here we can replenish the sponsons during an engagement, there's another in the shell room. Feed magazines in, shell side first, the tank's autoloaders take care of the rest. Or I should say, "should", always jamming, the damn things, so don't rely on it. What did I say?'

Bannick, entranced by the Baneblade, was flustered by Radden's sudden question, but recovered quickly.

'Short bursts,' he managed.

'That's right. But like I say, if we're reloading, that's Marsello's job. This cabling's for the lascannons.' He pointed out thick bundles of power lines heading to the reactor. 'Try not to catch your shoulders on the clasps, they're sharp as razors and they'll make you bleed like a stuck hog. Watch out for the quick release caps, knock one of them the wrong way and you'll have the best part of the batteries' charge running through you. It's supposed to make them easy to swap out, and we do need to, but it's a hazard if you ask me. This way,' he turned and pointed towards the front of the Baneblade, 'is the driver and second gunner's compartment, but we'll leave that, that's Ganlick's and Outlanner's realm. Outlanner's never out of there. Even in base he sleeps in his chair, it's so hard to stop him driving the Honoured Lieutenant's given up, overlooks his gleece habit, because he's the best driver there is in this army, on the sauce or off it. He's there right now, should be if old habits are anything to go by, and we all got those eh?' Another smile. Bannick found himself warming to the talkative gunner. 'Let's go aft, meet the others. Watch out you don't trip on the rails, they're for the shell sled to the demolisher up front.'

They took a few steps up to the rear of the tank, passing a pair of votive recesses, wherein sat small effigies of the Emperor and the servo-skull of the Omnissiah. Next to that, a wall of tarnished brass plaques, the decorative framing of which was obscured by crumbling parchment, Adeptus Mechanicus seals, medals on age-dark ribbons and ancient dogtags. 'What's this?' asked Bannick.

'Wall of honour,' said Radden, as if that explained it, and pressed ahead into the gloom. 'This is the shell locker.' They stuck their heads in through a tiny doorway, the sliding door already open. A low room greeted them, evidently the part of the tank directly beneath the tech station above. Two men with bulging arms, also stripped to their vests, sat playing cards on upturned crates, squeezed into the tiny space between the shell racks, choking out what little oxygen there was with cheroot smoke. Which, even though there was no exposed explosive material, was completely against regulations. Munitions of various sizes stood in racks on the walls, the room so small and the shells so big that their detonation caps were less than half a metre apart.

At the front of the compartment, which Bannick judged to be more or less the exact centre across the width of the tank, stood the base of the shell elevator, a tube with a closeable slot big enough to take two rounds of the tank's metre-long battle cannon shells. 'This is the magazine, the most heavily armoured part of *Mars Triumphant*. Makes sense, eh? We call it the shell store, Ganlick boom box. Doesn't matter does it, as long as we all know what we're talking about, eh? These're Meggen and Ralt, that young 'un there with the clipboard is Marsello. Ralt and Marsello are Clan Meggen too,' said Radden, pointing at their matching clan markings, 'but it gets too damn confusing having three loaders with the same name, so they go by their mother-names.'

'And I was here first,' said the original of the three Meggens, his voice deep and gravelly, a sure-fire sign of long-time lho addiction.

Ralt grunted his hello without taking his eyes off the cards on the crate. Marsello forced his way past the other loaders, however, and shook Bannick warmly by the hand. He was significantly younger than the rest of the tankers, his biological age couldn't have been more than twenty or so.

'See, he's the keen one! He's not been with us long, picked him up to replace the last third loader we had, man by the name of Atrellis.'

'Atrellan,' grunted Ralt.

'Yeah, that was it. You forget, after a while. He's the youngest. New recruit we picked up from Dostan, Paragon colony IV, not far out from the Dentares belt, a few years back. Wouldn't normally take someone this young, but there wasn't much choice at the mining station. We'd had heavy casualties and the top brass didn't want any tank crew entirely made up of greenhorns, so we got lumbered. The battlegroup got about five hundred guys sick of mining, we got him.'

The young tanker ignored Radden's chatter. 'Lieutenant, sir, welcome to *Mars Triumphant*, I'm looking forward to serving with you.'

'If you can show me the ropes, I'd appreciate it,' said Bannick. 'That targeting suite's like nothing I have ever seen before.'

'Of course, sir.' The kid's face lit up.

'Young, isn't he? Told you,' said Radden. 'Right, introductions over, this way, the Honoured Lieutenant's waiting.'

A pace past the shell locker, and the corridor turned ninety degrees and became a shallow alcove. The roof thereafter dipped to form a crawlspace running under *Mars*'s massive powerplant. Jammed into the alcove were two men, oblivious to the furnace heat radiating from the reactor. Bannick was starting to wish he could take his uniform jacket and shirt off, his collar felt two sizes smaller than normal.

'Just make sure they don't burn up again,' one of the men

was saying. 'Those fires are a damn distraction. If one goes down in a storm we'll all choke to death in here, am I clear?' said one. He had no cap or rank badges on; like the rest of the tankers he was only wearing his vest in the hot interior, but Bannick immediately recognised him as Cortein, there was no mistaking it.

'Yes, sir. But I can't rush it. Perhaps if I can get one of the higher adepts to look at it properly and placate the...' said the second, a much smaller man, smaller even than Radden, crouched in the crawlway entrance. He wore the deep-red robes of the Adeptus Mechanicus, stained deeper with sweat and oil, his large eyes blinking often.

'I'll speak to Brasslock, just see what you can do Vorkosigen. Get it fixed and stop talking about the damned spirits. That's not your realm, this is.' He kicked the engineer's toolbox. 'If anyone is going to be praying, it's not going to be you. Last thing I need is the *Mars* going down because you missed tightening a nut and messed up one of the rituals, you understand?' The little man nodded morosely. 'Now, Radden, back with the new boy already?'

'Yes, sir. Sir, Lieutenant Colaron Artem Lo Bannick. This is Honoured Lieutenant Cortein.'

Bannick found himself staring at a shoulder tattoo to match his own. Cortein followed his gaze.

'I'm of Clan Bannick, lad, or I was, I left all that behind a long time ago,' said Cortein.

'Cortein is your matronymic.' Bannick spoke rapidly, nervous. Cortein was a minor hero back home. 'I have met your brother, sir, he worked with my father.'

'Have you now? I suggest you think about dropping "Bannick" too, there's probably a thousand Bannicks within five hundred metres of this post. It's going to drive the brass crazy trying to tell us all apart, half a million Paragonian from five regiments in this warzone, with only a hundred and fifty clan names to go around. Hard enough to know who's who if you're from Paragon. Your loyalty is to the Emperor first and only, and not to either Paragon or your clan, do you understand?'

'Yes, sir.'

'Yes, sir, oh I like that, I like that very much. Keep that up and I might even grow to like you. Now, I'd get yourself familiarised with your station. We're mobilising soon.' He gave Bannick a look.

'Sir?'

'Lieutenant, get out of my way.'

Bannick glanced across at the walls pressing in either side of him. 'Yes, sir. Sorry, sir.' He and Radden backed away. 'Sir…'

'What?'

'I wanted to say thank you for bringing me aboard.'

'Don't thank me, boy, you've got to prove yourself to me yet.'

'Well, whom do I thank? This is a great honour,' said Bannick as civilly as he could. This commander was not behaving in a manner befitting the rank. He fought his irritation; his pride had wrecked his life back on Paragon and he'd tried to quash it, but it was in his blood.

'If you feel the need to give thanks, thank the tank.'

Bannick frowned. 'Sir?'

Cortein laughed. 'I didn't choose you, boy, *Mars Triumphant* did, or so the tech-priests say.'

Cortein pushed his way past. Radden said they ought to go and sign Bannick into his billet. 'Not that you'll ever use it,' the first gunner added. 'This is home now.'

Something made Bannick uneasy as he reached the ladder to the main deck. He turned before he ascended, and caught Tech-Adept Vorkosigen staring hard at him. The little man was almost lost in the darkness, but there was no mistaking the look of hostility on his face. He held an Emperor's Tarot deck in his hand, a small black box with a single button and a screen to display its spread. The box rattled as it ran through a reading and stopped. Without looking at it or taking his eyes of Bannick, Vorkosigen went back into the recess under the engine of *Mars Triumphant*.

CHAPTER 10

KALIDAR IV, VORSANII ARIDITY
3289397.M41

'There they are, green basdacks.' Ganlick spat over the side of the Salamander scout vehicle and offered his magnoculars to Bannick. He was disappointed to be away from the Baneblade so soon, he'd hoped to have got himself a little more acclimatised to the third gunnery station's fire control systems, but he and Ganlick had been sent out a day ahead of the Baneblade to check their target, a medium-sized mining complex overrun by the orks.

Ganlick pulled a stick of hi-energy wafer out of his top pocket. He offered it to Bannick, who waved it away. Ganlick shrugged. 'Suit yourself,' he said, and offered it to the three crew in the back of the scout tank and the Savlar accompanying them. They too declined his offer, intent on their instruments. The four crew of the Salamander had made it obvious they thought the tankers completely surplus to requirements, and were insulted by the implication that Cortein didn't trust them to do their job, though they seemed even less at ease with the Savlar observer. They barely spoke, and had not even offered their names. Bannick was inclined to agree with their stance; the wisdom of sending two of the super-heavy's crew out in front of their taskforce was suspect, but when he'd circumspectly asked Ganlick about this the veteran tanker had just growled at him. Radden had been right about the second gunner – he didn't talk much, leaving Bannick alone with his thoughts on the Salamander. Why had Cortein sent him ahead? To test him? Radden had said something about Cortein wanting his own report on the target, but why two of them? It was dangerous, thought Bannick.

'Well ain't you all a bunch of miserable basdacks,' grumbled Ganlick and stuffed the declined food up underneath his respirator masking. 'I need a piss,' he said. He jumped over the far side of the Salamander's crew compartment. The sound of water striking the sand followed, along with a satisfied gasp.

Bannick had the magnocular's magnification up to maximum, multiple filtration subfunctions within them working hard to clear the scene below of whorls of dust curling in the lazy night wind. The mine head appeared in the grainy green of light amplification, ghost light trailing off the spotlights the orks had set up on its structure as he panned from left to right. The installation was set into a broad pit ten kilometres across. The majority of the mine comprised a tall gantry, some of which had collapsed in on itself. Low buildings lay half-buried in the sand around it.

'This hasn't been used for a long time,' said Bannick as Ganlick rejoined him.

'Well done,' said Ganlick sarcastically. 'Pocket geologian are we now? It's been off the books for about sixty years. That's why the orks got in so close – everyone forgot it was there.'

'Easy to hide in a crater,' said Bannick.

'You could hide four armies anywhere on this rock. No comms, no sats, no pict, no vox, just noise. And it's not a crater, boy,' said the big surly man, putting his magnoculars back up to his face. 'It's subsidence. The crystals form in veins in the sand. The ones lower down, they're older. The sand at that depth is pressed into soft rock, like under the hives. That's where the big crystals are, the most valuable. The newer ones grow in sand that's still loose. Machines work out in spiral from the installation there, scoop them up, chuck the spoil round the rim, move on, sand sinks in the middle. So, looks like a crater, but ain't a crater.'

Bannick did not challenge him on this. The Ganlick Clan were Paragon's foremost mining people, busy deep in the many mountains dragged up by Mater Maxima's gravitic grasp on the moon-world. Even a lowborn clansman like Ganlick would have a deep knowledge of the industry. And, like Radden had said of the surly second gunner, he had a knack for finding things out.

'I'll be glad of this.' Ganlick grasped at his talisman, a lump of ore, hammer purified, decorated with the sail quills of a desert sandpike. 'There's always a resonance round these old workings, I've been told. Kalidar's got it all, dust storms, sandpike, angry sandscum, greenies and ghosts.'

Bannick scoffed. 'That's nonsense. That thing cost you a month's pay, at least according to Radden.'

'Radden's a basdack; doesn't know anything. Some of it is nonsense, granted, but lorelei crystals boy, they're only reason we're here. All about this planet, running through it like silver in the mountains, product of the star-tide from that big blue basdack in the sky. What? You think the orks came here 'cause the sky is green like them? No! Without this stuff, all that hoodoo the Scholastica domeheads pull off wouldn't work half so well.'

Bannick looked at him uncomprehendingly.

'It's witch stuff, city boy,' said Ganlick, as if he were lecturing an idiot. 'They put it in their rods and relays. lorelei has a psychoactive matrix, and some of the best of it comes from here. Why by Holy Terra do you think we're on this sandbox? Why do you think there's so many of his loyal citizens toiling away here? Lorelei, it's the only reason any of us are here at all, and why the brass don't bomb it from orbit and start all over again. I'll bet it's the same for the greenskins. This medallion's made out of some charged ore or other, fragments of the lorelei in it, y'see? Shorts out any residual activity, stops you seeing the ghosts. lorelei's to blame for that too. Sandscum use 'em, stops 'em going mad. Lesson for you there, new meat, always talk to the natives.'

'I see,' said Bannick.

'No you don't,' said Ganlick. 'Emperor! You know, Cortein sent you out here with me because he trusts what I can find out and he wanted to see what you'd do. The report I've got in my head is not shaping up in your favour.'

Bannick bit back his annoyance. Ganlick was enjoying speaking to him, a lieutenant, like this. Cortein had made it very clear to all aboard that, while under his command, Bannick was to be treated as of third gunner ranking, and not lieutenant, until he'd proven himself. For all practical purposes, everyone on *Mars Triumphant* bar the loaders outranked him. It made sense, Bannick had a lot to learn, but with Ganlick it was proving irksome.

'We're done here,' said one of the scouts in surly fashion. 'We have the necessary data. We need to report back.'

The scout handed Ganlick an auspex. The big man flicked through the picts the men had gathered and grunted an affirmative.

'Wait.' The Savlar spoke for the first time all day. Bannick found the Savlar a strange people, their eyes hard, their skin seamed with unidentifiable dirt. They had a chemical odour to them, as if they washed in something other than water, if they washed at all. Radden had told him Savlar was a hole of a world, awash with deadly pollutants.

'They're thieves, dregs,' Radden had said. 'Keep your kit close to you when they're about. Those bulky respirators they never take off? Nitro-chem inhalers in 'em. Stay out of their way in a fight, they can't tell green from man when they're in the gas fugue. They're here because they're survivors. They don't raise them often, too difficult to control, only get 'em in for for places like this. That's how fragged we are.'

The Savlar dialect of Gothic was so thick that Bannick could only catch one in three words. Thankfully, their companion at least switched to a form of standard Low Gothic when speaking to him and Ganlick. 'Let we wait,' he said, his voice sibilant. 'I have no signal from my Savlar command to tell main raider group in place, yes? We go now, we risking very nasty surprises. We go now, I outta range, no confirm.'

Ganlick caught the man eying his medallion speculatively. He narrowed his eyes and shook his head, and shoved the ugly thing down his tunic top. The Savlar held his gaze for a while, and looked away.

'Sir?' said the Paragonian scout.

Bannick looked to Ganlick.

'You're the lieutenant,' said the big man.

'Cortein said…'

'We're not on board *Mars Triumphant* now, are we?'

Bannick hesitated, then nodded. 'He's right, no signal, and we're not going in. We wait.'

They watched then, under the crackling aurorae of the Kalidar night. The wind stilled entirely, dropping off as the temperature plummeted. The change was making the Paragonian scouts nervous. Visibility was improving, and the growing temperature differentials would make them an easy spot on broad spectral imaging equipment. Bannick had to admit he'd been grateful to find the orks did not possess that facility naturally, and that in fact their eyesight was poor all round.

'There's something going on down there,' said Ganlick. The scouts joined the two tankers on the track housing.

The door to the facility, reworked to resemble a fanged maw by the orks, swung open, its groan shattering the desert silence. Light from inside flooded out. A line of fast buggies roared out on broad tyres, their engines puttering in the distance, and swung away towards the south.

Minutes passed. The door remained wide.

A big party of orks, a hundred or more, came out onto the sand. They dragged pierced oil barrels with them and set a broad semicircle of fires within them round the facility entrance. Smaller greenskins the size of children ran to and fro, bringing out barrels of liquor and food. The voices of the orks rumbled out across the sand; they drank and became louder, discharging weapons into the air. The small greenskins roasted something in the fires, ignoring the squeals as others of their number were baited by the orks, one held head down over the flames himself, eliciting great hilarity from the larger xenos as it wriggled and screamed.

'Nice party,' grunted Ganlick. 'Basdack greenskins.'

Then came the men, a line of them, perhaps fifty or so, yokes holding neck and hands, chained together. No respirators or goggles. They stumbled as they walked, urged on by the whips of more orks laughing behind them.

They were driven into a circle of whooping orks. Bannick had to stop himself swearing aloud as one of the green giants ran in and kicked a man so hard in the ribs he flew back three metres and collapsed in the dust. He did not get up again. The other orks were angered by this, and the aggressor was roundly beaten by his fellows as the remaining humans were kicked and shoved into a cage whose bars were lined with jagged barbs.

Bannick soon learned why.

He'd wasted one of their toys.

More orks came up from inside, dragging horrific implements, cruel spikes, tables lined with hook and blade. They selected one of the captives and dragged him out. Human screams, thinned by distance, joined the noise of the orks.

'Throne,' Bannick muttered. 'Throne.' He realised he was saying it over and over again.

'See the green ones, see them play,' said the Savlar in a singsong voice. 'Best not be taken by them, see?' He looked on at the carnage with dead eyes, appearing more curious than anything else. Bannick wondered what kind of world could make a man that unfeeling. 'Glad it's not me, I am. Thank the Golden One it's not me. Greenies are not like in the book, eh, officer man? Not like the book at all.' There was a hiss from within the Savlar's bulky breathing apparatus. He sighed and his eyes took on a glaze.

'*The Infantryman's Uplifting Primer*?'

The Savlar giggled.

'Not fit for burning,' said Ganlick. 'Those basdacks can grow eight feet tall and more. They can pull the head off a man as soon as think about it, and they don't do much thinking. Takes a lot to kill them. The book's full of crap.'

Out into the night, where the sands were painted vividly by the shifting waves of Kalidar's tortured electromagnetic field, a bright star burst quietly.

'Hehehe, signal star,' said the Savlar. 'No vox, no good here. See, greenskins too gwoop to notice, too cruel,' he said, lapsing entirely into his own version of battered Gothic for a space, then. 'Now we go, yes, lieutenant sir?'

Bannick managed to tear his eyes away from the horrors in

the basin below. He had to swallow back bile before he could speak. 'Your men are in place?'

'Oh yes, signal star say so. My Savlar brothers, they no let down, they deep in transit tunnels, like back home Savlar, atomics ready to go they are, as soon as they fight in to ork nest.'

'And all they need is a diversion,' said Bannick. He checked his timepiece, embedded in the back of his leather gauntlet. 'We've got an hour before they move in. We better make sure there's no welcoming party for them. Let's head back to the rendezvous point?'

Ganlick put down his magnoculars. 'Aye to that.'

Mars Triumphant's engine growled and the main deck shook.

'Steady as she goes, Outlanner,' said Cortein. 'Reduce speed to two-thirds.' Cortein flung the levers on the heading wheels, the bell rang. 'Keep us in line with the support. Epperaliant, get on the signals, we're being outpaced again.'

Epperaliant nodded and took his headset off. The night was so clear they'd probably be able to raise the fleet if they wanted to, but Cortein had ordered vox silence until they hit the escarpment. Epperaliant clambered up into the turret, signal lamp in hand.

'The ork encampment will come into view any time now, sir,' said Radden eagerly over the vox. 'Shall I open fire as soon as?'

'Wait for my orders, Radden, they've not got notice of us yet. Let's get everyone in line shall we? I want this little operation to go with minimum bloodshed, no point trying to lift spirits if we lose half our men. Remember, we're here to restore the battlegroup's faith in the 7th. Losing *Lux Imperator* was a great blow to morale, we need to show that the rest of us have what it takes.'

Cortein risked a few coded datasquirts, their carrier waves tuned near as could be to Kalidar's background radiation, ordering the other vehicles into attack formation. Two Leman Russ flanked the tank, both standard-armed with battle cannon and heavy bolters. The three tanks approached the spoil rim around the sunken mine pit, the Leman Russ slowing to one-third to match the super-heavy's speed, trusting that the orks' noise would cover their advance.

'Outlanner, halt. Epperaliant, do we have a ready signal from Lieutenant Strenkelios?'

'Sir,' replied Epperaliant over the internal vox. 'They're in place. But I can see them.'

'Then signal them back. When we come over the depression rim, I want them completely hidden from view, that way the orks will get the full benefit of our surprise.'

The Atraxian heavy infantry were holding a position half a kilometre back from the spoil rim, just one platoon, but heavy infantry well-equipped with carapace armour. Five Chimeras backed them up, and a further Leman Russ – the surprise. In place of its battle cannon, the tank mounted a punisher gatling cannon, a horrendous weapon capable of wreaking great havoc on infantry. Their rarity on Kalidar was much lamented.

The orks in the mine were a fast company, mounted in light buggies and other vehicles that could swoop in, attack and be away again before the Imperials could react. They were a thorn in the side of the Imperial effort, harrying recovery teams trying to claim back wrecked vehicles from the Kostoval flats. With the planet's subterreanean transit network as fiercely contested as the surface, and air transit nigh on impossible in the unpredictable weather, overland routes were the only option for supply convoys, and these were being mercilessly targeted by the orks' light vehicle columns, guided onto them by means command could not fathom.

'I don't need to remind you that destroying this nest has been designated an A-plus priority by command. It's a victory we need after that disaster at the Flats. We've been through worse before, men,' said Cortein, 'and *Mars Triumphant* has seen much, much worse.' He patted the ceiling of the compartment. 'We draw them out, we draw them away, give those Savlar scum time to get in underneath them and blow the green basdacks into the warp and back. Any remnants, we lead onto Strenkelios's men. The orks won't be able to resist us, we're big but we're alone, a worthy foe but an isolated one, a combination of strength and weakness that'll have them scrambling over each other to get at us. That's the trap. Let's not spoil this now. Do me proud.'

'Aye, sir!' echoed the men.

'Come down, Epperaliant, I need you here. Comms silence is broken in the attack group as of now. Sound the order, we advance. Outlanner, take us over the rim, *now*. For Paragon!'

'Aye, sir!' echoed the men.

'For the Emperor!'

'Aye, sir!'

'For the greater glory of *Mars Triumphant*!'

'Aye, sir!'

The light in the main deck shifted to red, signifying combat stations. The engine of *Mars Triumphant* roared out a challenge, daring any greenskin that might be listening to come and try their luck. With a lurch, the behemoth rumbled forwards on Kalidar's hard sands, up the spoil line and into full view of the ork base, Leman Russ flanking either side.

'Gentlemen, we have thirty-two minutes until the Savlar detonate their atomic mines. Fire at will, make as much of a rumpus as you can. Radden, throw one down the throat of that mess and see what it pukes out.'

He stabbed his hand into the holo of the mine-head door, and targeting information sprang up on the gunnery stations' screens.

Bannick and Marsello sat side by side, each one controlling a sponson. Bannick peered at the tank's screens on his station. The weight of the machine's systems pressed in on his consciousness, lending it physical presence as if he sat in a cave with a bear.

The tank rumbled forwards in the dawn light, battle cannon spitting rocket-propelled shells as it went. The Leman Russ joined their own deadly shouts to *Mars Triumphant*'s song of destruction. The heavy bolters were not in range, so Bannick set to picking off lone orks with his lascannon. Through the magnification of his weapon's augur-eyes, he saw the drunken xenos stumbling to their feet, gesticulating and shouting. Several turned to run inside. Bannick wondered how they could survive without respirators. Ganlick was right, they were tough. *That won't help them*, he thought, as he vaporised one of the foul things with a lasblast. He caught sight of the caged and tortured men in the cap and hatred filled his heart. He set to his task with grim satisfaction. Shells exploded amid the xenos. Sand erupted into the air, the orks were in uproar.

Then there were orks everywhere. A stream of buggies, bikes and other constructions came pouring out of the mine's mouth. Radden's shots took their toll as they emerged, but there were scores of them, and they rapidly closed with the heavy Imperial vehicles. Bannick and Marsello opened up with the six heavy bolters at their command. Burning wreckage bounced through the desert, but still the vehicles came on.

'Well done,' said Cortein. 'That poked them. Steady as we go, prepare for all back one-third, let's give it five more minutes then begin to draw them away. Convey my order to our support, Epperaliant.'

Bannick's view tracked over the caged prisoners again. He squinted. There, movement. He zoomed in, picture shuddering. 'Honoured lieutenant!'

'Wait!'

'Bannick, what is it?'

'Quadrant five, movement, non-orkoid.' said Bannick. 'Human prisoners, they're still alive.' He threw up a pict onto the comm desk main screen.

'Emperor's teeth, what have they done?' asked Cortein. At least ten of the men were still alive, trapped in the cage.

'Maybe we can fire, open a hole in the cage?' said Bannick.

'Negative, it's too small a target, we'll kill them,' said Marsello. 'Perhaps we'd better, it'd be a mercy.'

Cortein spoke. 'Dammit! There must be a way.'

Epperaliant yelled. 'We have to stay clear of the mine, the ground's too soft down there to support us. We'll become mired. Let's give them a clean end and commend their souls to our protector.'

'I'm not suggesting risking this machine for the sake of a few men, Epperaliant, but there are other ways,' said Cortein firmly. He chewed his lip. 'That Salamander, boy, how fast is it?'

'Fast,' said Bannick.

'Get it out here.' Cortein magnified a pict of the area, pulling up the cage on his chart desk. He transmitted a datasquirt with rapid finger motions across his command suite. 'Tank two, cover that Salamander when it comes in. I want a wall of fire round it, nothing gets through to harm it!'

'Incoming!' shouted Epperaliant.

The Baneblade shook as if it had been kicked by one of the ork's vile gods, Bannick having to grab at his station to avoid being thrown to the floor. Lights flickered. Epperaliant looked to the ceiling expectantly, but no further blows came.

'Damage report!' shouted Cortein.

'All systems functioning in the green, honoured lieutenant. We've got some energy spiking round demolisher fire control, but it'll hold,' said Vorkosigen, his ever-present tarot reader swinging on a cord by his head.

'Don't risk it, Vorkosigen. Switch to auxiliary,' said Cortein.

Vorkosigen replied. 'Switching to auxiliary. Ganlick, you'll be offline for four, three, two, one – back online.'

'What the…?' said Marsello, eyes wide.

From out of the mouth of the mine came a hulking ork battlefortress, a huge ork armoured vehicle borne on eight fat, metal wheels. Bigger than the Baneblade, it bristled with weapons poking out of gunports lined with the crude glyphs of ork-kind. A massive turret followed the super-heavy's movement, gunsmoke pouring from its barrel. Three smaller cannons manned by smaller greenskins spoke next; triple impacts banged out a tattoo on the hull.

'We'll have to take that out for Strenkelios's sake, we don't want to draw that up towards the infantry,' said Cortein. 'Steady Marsello, don't panic, it's no match for *Mars Triumphant*. Outlanner, forward armour to main target.' Cortein designated the ork battlefortress as such, targeting information relayed to the gunners' stations. 'Take it down.'

All the men spoke now, busy with their tasks, a constant, unhurried chatter that filled the tank, detailing everything they were doing. Cortein heard them all, despite the roar of the engine and the crash of cannon fire, replying, ordering, conducting them like an orchestra, *Mars Triumphant* responding smoothly to the crew's prompting.

'Tanks two and three, concentrate on the smaller vehicles. The battlefortress is ours. Epperaliant, where's that damned Salamander? I want those men out of there.'

'They're on their way sir, the crew are not pleased,' said Epperaliant.

'I'll have them up on charges if they're not here within three minutes. Make that clear to them. Get them down here now!'

'Yes, sir.'

'And request Lieutenant Strenkelios move his Atraxians to the ridge, the ambush is off, repeat, off. He can get his target practice from the ridge edge.'

The main cannons of Mars Triumphant spoke in unison, striking hard at the battlefortress, yet despite its ramshackle construction it was tough and came on, its bestial snout panting fire as it rumbled forwards.

'Damn thing's got armour thick as grox skin!' shouted Radden, stitching magnesium tracer across its front, following it with a shot from the main cannon.

'We're down to two shells up here! Ralt! Ralt! More ammo!' called Meggen.

Behind Bannick the shell elevator rattled as more ammunition was sent up top by the loader down below.

'Bannick, sweep off those gretchin from the cannons,' said Radden.

'Gretchin?'

'The little greenskins! Keep the smaller guns out of commission while we load up again,' explained the main gunner.

Bannick did as he was asked, raking the gunports with heavy bolter fire; it drove the gretchin back, but no matter how many of the skinny greenskins exploded, there always seemed to be more. He switched to lascannon and burnt out a gunport. There was an orange flash from within, and the cannon fell silent.

'Good shot!' shouted Radden, deafening Bannick over the vox with his excitement. 'Now watch this.' The main gun of Mars Triumphant boomed. The side of the battlefortress exploded in flame and two of its wheels flew off, slowing it considerably, although it did not halt.

The duel began in earnest, the titanic vehicles circling each other as buggies and trakks buzzed ineffectually around them. Shot after shot went between the two tanks, to little effect.

'Doesn't this basdack have a weak point?' said Radden.

'I'm on it, Radden! Give me some time!' said Epperaliant.

Bannick listened intently to the chatter, his own eyes firmly on tacfeed and gun cameras. He tracked the left lascannon a full 180 degrees, so that it pointed directly to the rear. Through the weapon's eye he caught sight of a trio of light half-tracks carrying rocket launchers lining up to blast *Mars Triumphant* from behind. He annihilated them one after the other with bolts of searing light.

'Keep it up, Bannick,' said Cortein, in between his endless stream of orders, his fingers dancing over his command suite. 'Keep them off the powerplant.'

A huge ork appeared atop the battlefortress, poking out of a turret hatch, a power claw the size of a man on its left hand. It gesticulated and roared as its tank shot at the Baneblade, a bald challenge.

'There, got it,' said Epperaliant. 'Logic engine suggests this spot. Check your auspex, data coming up now.'

'Doesn't look like much. Ganlick?' said Radden.

'Ready for your mark,' replied the second gunner.

'Load up AP, Radden,' said Cortein.

'Load AP!' said Radden.

'Loading AP!' said Meggen. In the turret, Radden kissed his hand and slapped the shell as Meggen pushed it home.

'Right sponson lascannon offline!' said Marsello.

'Power lines, power lines! Don't fire so often, allow two breaths between, you're overstressing the shunts.' Tech-Adept Vorkosigen began a low chant as he attempted a reroute on the weapon.

'Ready!' said Radden.

'Ready!' repeated Ganlick.

'Fire!' said Cortein.

Radden's shell arced through the air, burying itself deep in the ork vehicle, Ganlick's close in behind. The ork warleader had time enough for one more defiant roar before he and his tank were obliterated in a hemisphere of fire and metal fragments.

'Target destroyed, good work,' said Cortein. 'Time check?'

'Seventeen minutes to detonation,' said Epperaliant.

'Where's that damn Salamander?'

Epperaliant checked over his instruments. 'They've taken a hit.' He pushed his mouthpiece in close and voxed them urgently. A voice, drowning in static, came back faintly. 'Thirty metres behind us. We don't have time, we've done our job, let's pull out.'

'We shall commend our fallen to the Emperor,' said Bannick quietly.

'We'll make time,' said Cortein. 'I want those men out of there.'

Bannick thought for a moment, watching the green silhouettes of ork light vehicles dance round his scope like fireflies. What should he do? He thought back to his youth, to the statue – what would that man do, the hero Cortein, if he could? He spoke up. 'Sir, I'll go. I'll drive it.'

'Will you now?'

'Yes, sir, if the Emperor wills it.'

Cortein appraised him for a long second. 'I have known both pious fools and saints in my time. Which are you?'

'Sir?'

Cortein thought rapidly, came to a decision. 'Go to it. Be quick. You've now fifteen minutes! Outlanner, back us out of here, two-thirds speed, concentrate all fire forwards, Mauser's pattern. Marsello, cover our backs.'

Bannick nodded a thanks to Cortein, and clambered up into the turret and out the top instead, ignoring Radden's questions as he went.

He leapt down from the turret as it swung round, onto the roof of the main deck, then over the side of the track guard. It was a three-and-a-half-metre drop, but Kalidar's gravity was low and he took the impact with a roll. He was up on his feet and running towards the Salamander before he knew it. The roar of the Baneblade's engine was terrifying outside the tank. Guns and turrets swivelled this way and that, spitting fire and death, devastating the orks. A wagon full of orks came caroming through the night, then another, and another. One took a hit from the Baneblade, spinning it to one side. The entire machine toppled over, spilling orks across the sand. They picked themselves up and ran on, towards the spoil rim.

Strenheim and his troops had arrived; a disciplined line of stormtroopers took up station along the depression rim to rain lasgun fire down on the orks, Chimeras at their flanks. The night lit up as a plasma gun sent a small sun burning through the air. It struck and exploded in a miniature nova that immolated an ork biker, droplets of molten steel pattering onto the desert, fused sand glowing hot in the crater left behind. The trucks disgorged their cargo, and the orks ran up the banking. Many died, but several got in close, hurling men this way and that before they were brought down, Strenheim at the front, ordering new fire patterns as he decapitated a greenskin with his sword. More orks came in from the mine, Bannick ran on, the Salamander almost in reach.

The Leman Russ Punisher roared up and over the edge of the depression, its punisher barrel powering up. The tank halted, weapon swinging round.

It was pointed right at Bannick. He hit the deck as it fired. Thousands of white-hot shells scored trails in the night, so bright they left tracks on Bannick's vision. The bullet storm stopped as quickly as it had begun and Bannick glanced behind him to see a wet slick of orkish parts spread in a wide cone behind him. He gave silent thanks and scrambled forwards onto the Salamander.

The commsman lay curled at the foot of his instruments in a pool of his own guts, the commander was missing, the gunner lolled on the floor, trying to staunch the flow of blood coming from a nasty shrapnel wound in his arm. Bannick checked him quickly. 'Hold on!' he shouted into his ear, then pushed his way through the door into the enclosed drive compartment. The driver lay slumped at the controls, dead. Bannick shoved him to one side and took his place.

Emperor, lend me speed, he thought. *If not for me, for those men the orks would have killed.*

He slammed the Salamander into forward gear, gunning its overcharged engines as hard as he dared; it jumped forwards, the hard-packed sand almost as good as a road. Free of heavy armour, the Chimera variant was light enough to keep pace with the ork buggies. Several of these peeled away from harassing the Baneblade and gave chase, wild shots from their heavy stubbers hammering off the vehicle. A thump, and Bannick was face to face with a leering ork face pushing and snapping at the vision slit, before it was snatched away. A buggy attempted to outpace him, its cackling gunner bringing rockets round to fire right at the front of the Salamander, but a lascannon bolt from the right cut it in half, and Bannick's borrowed vehicle bounced as it ran over the wreckage.

Eight minutes.

The sand softened to the centre of the depression, slowing the scout tank. Five hundred metres to go.

The Salamander burst through the fence surrounding the prisoners' cage. Bannick wrenched back on a drive lever, shutting one of the track units off, spinning the vehicle round. He pushed himself out of the seat and leapt over the dead driver.

He tried to ignore the sight of the tortured men pinned to

poles about the enclosure. The scent of burnt human flesh assailed him through his rebreather.

He flew as he ran to the cage door. He pulled his laspistol from its holster and shot a cowering gretchin that stood hissing by the cage door.

The men looked at him in surprise. They stood. They'd had their limbs freed from the yokes, and had the sense to tear some of their uniforms off and wrap them round their faces. Perhaps they'd avoid the dustlung. There were about twelve of them.

Three shots and the lock was broken.

Six minutes.

'Everyone out!'

The men needed little encouragement, those least hurt helping the others.

'Get these men down!' shouted Bannick as the uninjured guardsmen piled the wounded men into the back of the Salamander, dragging the dead body of the commsman out and leaving him on the sand. Two captives, severely wounded, were brought down quickly, screaming as their brutalised flesh tore further. Bannick quickly scanned round the enclosure. Eight more men were dead, three more living, but so enwrapped in spike and chain he had no chance to bring them down in time.

Bannick grimaced as he shot each one in the head. Eyes gouged out, noses cut off, skin flayed. As he gave the Emperor's benediction, his hatred for the orks hardened.

'Let's go!' he shouted, waving the men onto the vehicle. The tank was designed for five to work without hindrance, but there was just enough space for the twelve men to cram in. 'The mine is going up!'

He boarded the Salamander and pushed his way roughly into the drive compartment.

Four minutes.

The Salamander was slower than before, weighed down by

extra men, its tracks turning less surely on the softer ground at the heart of the depression, but it was quick enough. The mutilated corpses of their comrades were soon behind the escaping guard, the spire of the mining installation growing smaller and smaller. As they hit the harder-packed ground towards the edge of the depression, the Salamander's speed increased rapidly. In the back, the guardsmen ransacked storage bins for rebreathers, and clung on for their lives.

One minute.

Bannick swerved the Salamaner round the wrecks of ork buggies. There were only a few left functioning, buzzing round the larger tanks like gnats. The fighting was coming to an end. The orks were finished.

Bannick checked his timepiece and pressed the drive levers for the vehicle's twin engines forwards as far as he could.

Ten... nine... eight... seven...

He drove past one of the Leman Russ, making with all speed to the crater rim; the other was already creeping up and over.

Six... five...

Strenheim's men had fallen back, leaving nought but green corpses to show they had been there.

Four...

He shot past *Mars Triumphant*, its hull going past in a blur. The spoil rim grew nearer and nearer.

Three... two... one...

A low, rumbling boom passed through the tank, a low-frequency shockwave that made the metal of the vehicle buzz.

The ground bucked under the Salamander as the entire floor of the depression heaved up in a bulge, then dropped. The engines screamed as Bannick pushed the scout tank up and out of the sinking depression, sand pouring back past it into the deepened hole. He gained the rim, and pushed the tank up and out of the danger zone. The second Leman Russ followed a second later, toppling towards safety.

Out over on the other side Bannick jammed the brakes on hard, and the vehicle struggled to a halt, engines stinking of burning oil.

Bannick shoved his way out of the scout tank and ran up the pseudo-crater wall. He had to see what had happened to *Mars Triumphant*.

Inside the depression, the facility had disappeared. In its stead lay a sucking hole. Ork carcasses and wrecked vehicles flowed towards it, tumbling down on rivers of sand.

Mars Triumphant hung at the edge of the collapse, metres away from the spoil rim. Its tracks turned implacably, the ground disappearing beneath it, fighting to keep position.

'No!' shouted Bannick.

The tank's engine howled, gears grinding raucously within its track units. Slowly, slowly, the Baneblade made ground, edging forwards, and pulled itself onto the base of the spoil-rim wall. Bannick held his breath as it climbed out, one painful centimetre at a time.

Then the mighty tank slipped, the ground under the right track unit gave way and it yawed alarming towards that side. The sand poured back faster than the tracks could turn, *Mars Triumphant* was pulled down, down into the rushing torrent of dust, buried up to its tracks, then its turret. Black smoke poured from its quad smokestacks as its mechanisms screamed.

The rushing sand swallowed it whole.

Bannick sank to his knees.

The speed of the sand hissing into the altered landscape slowed. Aftershocks rumbled through the ground, the avalanche stilled.

The Baneblade was gone. The cruelty of the God-Emperor hit him like a hammerblow. He'd dishonoured himself, tried to redeem his honour in the eyes of the lord of mankind, for

Bannick believed fervently that He watched all the men that fought for Him. To be picked to serve aboard a super-heavy tank, the very one commanded by the hero of his clan, seemed a vindication of everything he had put himself through – the leaving of home, the disapproval of his father, the loss of his friend, but no, it was not enough, nothing could ever be enough for what he had done. This was all his fault, his doing. The Baneblade had been destroyed to punish him for breaking the codes of his clan, for the death of Tuparillio. He bowed his head in shame and prayed fervently for the souls of the men aboard the tank, and for the chance to expend his life as a useful servant of the Imperium. It was all he had, and all that he could give. He knew it for an inferior offering.

Bannick remained that way for some time before he stood. Reluctantly, he quit the wall and walked down onto the desert floor. The sun was over the horizon now, the wind rising with it. In the distance a smudge of red hinted at another storm on its way.

He was halfway back when mechanical thunder made him turn again.

Mars Triumphant crested the wall of the mine depression, sand streaming from its flanks like water cascading from an ocean leviathan. It reared up high as it took the barrier, engines roaring, a beast bellowing its defiance to the universe, and came down hard. Once off the wall it levelled out, and growled to a stop in front of Bannick.

Sand whispered onto the floor as it stood there, wide lights and augurs regarding him, engine revs breathing. Bannick stared back. He saw *Mars Triumphant* briefly as the tech-priests saw it, not just as a machine with a soul as most men would, a relic and reminder of the power and endurance of the Imperium, but as a living, breathing embodiment of the Emperor's will. It was like looking at a ragged preacher, and catching a glimpse of the holy fire of sainthood beneath the surface. Through the mighty machine's glass augurs and optics, the Emperor could see him stood there, right then, pathetic on the sand. The living god of mankind, clad in armour of plasteel and adamantium, gazed through the machinery before Bannick and judged him.

He was found wanting.

Bannick fell to his knees, overwhelmed.

A clang from above broke the spell, followed by a shout. Bannick stood and stepped back to see Radden's flame-haired head poke from the turret high above.

'Bet you thought we were goners there eh, new boy? Well not us, not while we're riding this! Not while we've got *Mars Triumphant*.' He laughed as he pounded the tank's armour, face bright with the glee of survival. He made the sign of the aquila, raised his medallions to his lips and pressed loud kisses upon them. 'Praise be!' He shouted. 'Praise be to the tech-priests of Mars and all their screw-bothering mumblings! Ha!'

Once news of their success had been conveyed to battlegroup HQ, *Mars Triumphant* and the other units had been ordered to stay put and wait for relief, so they waited and took stock of their casualties and vehicle damage. Shortly after the battle, a group of support staff from the 7th arrived in an Atlas tank, along with it Enginseers Brasslock and Starstan. Two hours or so later, Medicae and Munitorum teams arrived to resupply the group and take the wounded back to Hive Modulus

The last of the casualties were shipped out close to the end of the long Kalidarian day, eighteen hours since the morning when Bannick had watched *Mars Triumphant* haul itself out of the crater, and it was a crater now, the result of a five-megatonne portable atomic seeded in the depths of the disused mine. How many of the Savlar had died fighting in the transit tunnels to place it there Bannick did not know, but having seen the orks at work in the open twice now, he was developing a respect for the so-called dregs, no matter what was said about them.

The crews of the tanks, their support vehicles and the platoon under Lieutenant Strenkelios had formed a camp, lookouts placed in a kilometre-wide cordon. Reinforcements were due to arrive later that day, a recon company with light vehicles who'd scour the surrounding area for outlying groups of greenskins while the attack group made its way back to Hive Modulus.

The weather held, the storm moving away from the horizon. Bannick was assigned to Enginseer Brasslock as he worked over the Baneblade, examining it in minute detail, Urtho his awesome shadow.

'Do you hear it?' the enginseer asked Bannick.

'I hear the ticking of cooling metal, the creak of systems recently deactivated. I am sorry, but I hear nothing more.' Bannick shuddered as he remembered how the tank had appeared after the battle. But now the presence within it had retreated, leaving only metal behind.

Brasslock caught sight of this involuntary twitch, within his cowl ancient eyes creased with a smile and he nodded with approval. 'On Paragon the cult of the Omnissiah is strong, yes?'

'Among the clan aristocracy and others, we depend on the beneficence of the Machine-God, yes.' Bannick pulled out his cog and eagle. 'He is second only to the Emperor in our prayers.'

Brasslock made a rasping noise Bannick supposed was a chuckle. 'You are marked by the Machine-God.' A metal tendril whipped out of the tech-priest's robes and tapped Bannick's chest. 'And you respect Him. You have seen His glory now.'

Bannick nodded hesitantly.

'Then continue to listen, and you will hear.'

Bannick cast his gaze up the side of the war machine, a metal wall that blocked out the merciless Kalidarian sun. 'What will I hear?'

'That *Mars Triumphant* is pleased with its choice. The machine-spirit of the Baneblade is satisfied with your actions, not least in your saving of the little one.' His cowled head gestured towards the Salamander, currently being field-repaired by a team of Munitorum specialists under the direction of an enginseer. 'All machines are sacred. They are brothers. Save one, and all are glad.'

The rest of the crew went over their own systems, Tech-Adept Vorkosigen running general diagnostics on a data-slate independently of the enginseer's efforts. As Bannick followed the ancient enginseer round, he was glad he was in the shadow of *Mars Triumphant*, and not with the Atraxian storm troopers, who laboured in the full glare of the sun moving stinking orkish corpses into a pile for burning; necessary, so he'd been told, to stop their bodies shedding spores. He found it hard to credit, but leave them unburnt and a year later this area would be crawling with yet more greenskins.

Further reinforcements came in three hours before sunset, Honoured Captain Hannick among them, and he and Cortein were locked in close consultation for the remainder of the day. The honoured captain was surprisingly young, thought Bannick, much younger than Cortein.

Later, as the fierce blue sun of Kalidar burned its way into the horizon, they drank. The others welcomed Bannick now, praising his deeds in the battle. Yet he could not share their joy. His dishonour set him aside in his mind, he was sure that the near loss of the Baneblade was a warning to him, a reminder that the Emperor knew of his shame, that *Mars Triumphant* knew, even if his comrades did not. He could not rid himself of the image of the men broken by the orks. Head swimming from the rough gleece the men handed round the sealed crew tent, he made his excuses and went outside, walking without purpose to the edge of the encampment, resenting with every rubber-tainted breath the respirator he was forced to wear.

Bannick stood at the edge of the desert, his breath noisy in his ears. He became lost in thought, watching the day die.

'It is, in its way, a beautiful place,' said a voice close by him.

'Honoured lieutenant,' Bannick said, snapping to attention.

'At ease, lieutenant, the time's not right for that now. The day is done, we won. Now we rest.'

Cortein came to stand by him. Like Bannick, he had his officer's cap and coat on against the cold. They could have been two gentleman soldiers of their clan, taking the air at a Paragonian desert resort, were it not for the reek of spilt fuel and ork corpses burning on the pyre. 'A harsh beauty. This is so hard a planet,' he said. 'So hot, so cold. No soft edges, not like home.'

'No, sir.'

Cortein toed the sand with his boot. 'You can never go back. It is a long time since I signed up; Paragon is not the world I left.'

Bannick nodded. Cortein's brother, whom he had met when he was very young, had died years ago, and he had been truly ancient, even by the aristocracy's standards. 'Your raising took place in my grandfather's time.'

'Time is bent out of shape by the warp,' said Cortein. 'Twenty-four jumps I've made, no more than twelve years total in the immaterium, yet over a century added outside, so thirty years of fighting becomes an age. Go home yourself, you'll see it change. It will not be the same.'

'I did not join to go home, sir.'

Cortein made an affirmative noise. 'Few ever go back. I was lucky in a sense, unlucky in another.'

'I joined to leave, sir, to serve my Emperor as best I may.'

Cortein nodded. 'I was like you once, I too waived my clan exemption.'

'I know, they still talk about it back home.'

'Really now? Well, there's a thing,' said Cortein in a manner that suggested he'd had to sit through plenty of adulatory events on Paragon.

'They have a statue to you in the Great Clan Hall.'

Cortein snorted. 'I saw it. Doesn't mean much. I don't fight for glory, not any more.'

'What do you fight for?'

Cortein frowned, and did not answer immediately. 'I am no longer sure. I have seen worlds where men live and die in squalor, labouring on tasks they do not understand night and day for crumbs of food without succour of any kind. Our kind are beset on every side by all manner of evils – the orks are the least of the horrors this universe has to show, believe me. I spent a decade fighting eldar pirates, decadent scum who thrive on pain, worse than the orks. What they'll do to men, women, children... the more blameless the better... those sights, they never leave you.'

Bannick thought of the tortured men; he doubted he'd ever forget that. It would be some time before he'd be comfortable around the smell of roasting meat. He understood.

'Even they are not the worst. There are things out there that will eat your soul, and then there are those on our own side.' He gave a low, mirthless chuckle. 'Some of them will dispose of you like a rag, tossing you aside when you have served your purpose. So... Brasslock has his Machine-God, the men their own reasons. But me? I fight because that is what I do, and I fight because we must. One of those eldar degenerates, we managed to catch and interrogate one once, he laughed at us all the while, right until he died under the chirurgeon's blades, said we were a crude mirror of what had happened to his own kind, long ago, that mankind was a lower creature doomed to a worse fate. And I will not have that. Perhaps he was right, perhaps the doomsayers are right, that these are the times of ending. You see it sometimes, the way the senior officers will gamble with men's lives, there is a certain…weariness to it all. But I will not. For the High Lords the score of victory is measured in planetary systems, not in the survival of individuals, and it is all too easy to fall into such a mindset oneself. Hannick, for example, he's a good commander, but the machines are his charge, not the men. I took a dressing-down from him today for risking *Mars Triumphant*, not for the first time. He said half of those we rescued will die from dustlung anyway, and he's probably right.'

'If I may?' asked Bannick hesitantly.

'Go ahead, please speak freely.'

'Then why do it, sir?'

'Because half will not die, and they can fight again.' Cortein drew in a deep breath. 'To not fight is to hand victory to our enemies, yet to fight and abandon the spirit that makes us better than these evil creatures is worse than defeat. Men are men because they will risk themselves for one another, that is how we have spread across the stars. We look out for our own. If a single life can be saved, it should be. Every man with a gun in his hand is a bullet in the armoury of the Emperor. Every man counts!' He became fervent. 'We all must make the greatest sacrifice so that the Imperium may endure. Day by day billions die for the very survival of the human race, as I will surely die. To die for the Emperor is glory, for in each kilometre of ground bought by death lies hope for the survival of our kind. Death, boy, holds no fear for me, for the Emperor is at my side. But to throw away the lives of those who can also fight? To waste men and materiel simply because there is always more? That is a grave and odious sin, and I will not stand for it. It is by profligacy that we lose, for one day, if we cast away a tank here, a life there, on and on and on, then there will be *no more*. The mightiest edifice may be tumbled if it is carried away stone by stone. That, Colaron Artem Lo Bannick, is why I fight the way I do, and why sometimes I will take a calculated risk.'

They stood in silence for a space, the aurorae like warring ghosts in the sky above. Cortein turned to face the younger officer. 'Now, I am going for a drink. You will come too. You did well today, you deserve to rest. On board *Mars Triumphant*, we think for ourselves, and we fight for each other. That is why we win. Welcome to the crew, Colaron Artem Lo Bannick.'

Bannick followed his commander. He was glad he had not been asked his own reasons for fighting; he had no wish to describe his need for redemption.

As Bannick came to the tent airlock, he caught the telltale rattle of a tarot deck. He looked towards *Mars Triumphant*, but saw nothing. *Vorkosigen*, he thought. *Only he carries that damn deck around.* Without stopping to wonder why the little man was always watching him, Bannick went inside to sleep.

INTERSTITIAL

Of Paragon, I will say it is most blessed of the Emperor's domains within that subsector, and is holy to the Saint Honoria Dahl, a third-grade sister of Ephesus, cruelly martyred there some four thousand years past at the height of the Age of Apostasy, and whose Late Cheroptidian Revival Basilica will enchant those who enjoy architectural beauty with their worship.
However one may regard it a fine point for the wayfarer to recoup and rest upon pilgrimage, I say to weaker souls be wary, lest resolve in the matter of one's holy journey is sapped, for all things are possible on the sixth moon of the sixth world of that system. Better the drear stone prairies of Uzarn for those intent upon contemplation. Temptation stalks the halls of Paragon.'

Frater Zonecus Tufar's Famous Pilgrimage Guide,
volume XXIII, 'Coreward on the Road
of the Ephesian Saints'

CHAPTER 11

ARONIS CITY, THE SIXTH MOON OF PARAGON VI
2043395.M41

Bannick's father's study was warm and comfortable, yet Bannick felt anything but, the fear in his guts as icy as the Long Winter outside; fear that his uncle would refuse his request.

Vardamon Anselm Lo Bannick's smile became fixed and the conversation stalled. He leaned back a little, firelight catching on the medals upon his chest, glinting off the brass of his artificial eye. For a second, the noise of the ball outside the study intruded between nephew and uncle, shattering the atmosphere of comradeship they had shared until a moment ago. 'Ah, boy,' he said eventually. 'Boy, you have grown so much.' His eye lingered on the scar across Bannick's cheek, and his face was curious with unasked questions.

'You already said that, uncle. Forgive me, but you are avoiding my question.' Colaron Bannick was nervous. He could not spoil his chance, he needed his uncle's influence to lift the exemption. He was tired and twitchy, guilt as heavy on him as his need to escape.

Captain Bannick snorted and sank further into the armchair,

his head disappearing within its wings. If he noticed the younger Bannick's discomfort he gave no indication. Colaron had to lean forwards to keep his uncle's gaze. He looked far older than his father. Vardamon maintained he'd been fighting for over twenty years, although but nine had gone on Paragon, a consequence of shifting through the warp. Transmission back and forth from that otherwoldy ocean into realspace was not readily controlled, and time could flow strangely for those who pierced the veil between. Bannick supposed it was possible that, right now, his uncle was both here and elsewhere in the galaxy, waging war for the Emperor. He tried not to think of it, unsure if such thoughts were heretical or not.

'I ask you again. Please consider my request.'

Vardamon sighed. 'You are set upon this course of action, then? Been dreaming of throwing your life away on some distant armpit of a world for the greater glory of the Emperor since you were a boy, no doubt. Well my advice to you is, don't.' He swirled his glass round in his hand, the vintage gleece within sliding thickly up its sides. He raised it sharply and downed it all, a small fortune's worth of liquor, then immediately leaned forwards for the decanter and poured himself some more. Outside, the shrill, false laughter of some courtly fool eager to please rose above the hubbub.

'Uncle, such talk…'

Vardamon held up a brusque hand in interruption. 'Don't give me all that "you're being heretical" nonsense, boy. I'm in my brother's damned study, in my family home, and I can say what I damn well please!' He fell quiet. When he spoke again he was quieter, and did not look his nephew in the eye. He stared at the flames in the grate of the room, as if addressing them. 'I am not saying that the Emperor does not need soldiers, by the Throne he does, but he does not necessarily need you. The Imperium is beset on all sides by things I won't even begin to describe to you. I'm proud of what I've done, but I would not wish for you to do the same.'

'You have done well from your service.'

'This?' he gestured to his shining dress carapace breast-plate and the medals upon it. 'Or this?' he pointed to the cumbersome augmetic attached to his head. 'Money? Medals? The hope of some land grant on some freshly conquered back-water?' Vardamon glared at him accusingly. 'I could have had all that and more if I'd just stayed at home. I'm the brother of the Auditor of Clan Bannick for Terra's sake, I could have stayed here and lived the high life. Instead I ran off pursu-ing idiot dreams of glory!' He looked at his nephew. There was a cloudiness to his remaining eye. The gleece was making him drunk. 'Little, dear, Col. I'd not have you think me an old fool nostalgic for home, but believe me, the galaxy doesn't get much better than Paragon, and most of it is a lot worse. I wouldn't wish my life on my enemy, let alone my nephew.'

'How can you say that? They sent you home to recruit a new regiment. You're a hero.'

'No,' his uncle said sadly. 'A hero is a dead man. And there are plenty of them in the Paragonian 62nd. Why, practically the whole damned bunch of them are heroes now.' He laughed bitterly. 'Don't make my mistake, don't throw away your clan-bought immunity from the draft just because of some fool romantic ideal. Stay here, work the foundry ledgers for your father, then one day, succeed him and prosper. Serve the Emperor that way, as legitimate a way as battle, huh? Huh?'

He leaned forwards, gleece thick on his breath, the lens of his artificial eye glimmering red. Bannick did not answer. His uncle shook his head. 'Better that than death. Or worse. And believe me, there is worse out there, much worse.' He shook his head, as if to clear it, and drank deeply of his gleece. 'No, no. I will not help you renounce your exemption.'

'But uncle…'

Vardamon closed his eyes and pinched at the bridge of his nose, rubbing round his augmetic. He had become fat and jowly, well-fed, but there was something gaunt about him, as if his skull showed through his skin, grinning in horror at what Captain Bannick had seen, and his face was ruined where the augmetic's metal met the skin. 'What would your father say? What of the alliance with Clan Turannigen? Have you thought of that?'

The two of them sat, the warmth of the fire failing to keep the chill of winter entirely out of the room. Vardamon shuddered, whether from the cold or the memory of battle the younger Bannick could not tell.

'Uncle…' he began hesitantly. He gulped at his own gleece, it put fire in his belly. He needed it, and his voice firmed. 'You are right. I want to serve. And I admire you for what you have done.'

Vardamon rolled his eye in exasperation. 'Have you not been listening to me boy?'

Bannick pressed on. 'But uncle, it's not just that, it's…' his words caught in his throat.

'What?'

'There's been trouble,' he admitted. His uncle would not know of it, not yet. Bannick's father had made sure few had.

His uncle's eyes narrowed, the iris of his brass eye whirring, his gaze once more falling on Bannick's scar. 'What kind of trouble?'

INTERSTITIAL

The conduct of officers, when invited to high table in mixed regimental company, will include the following:

i) The wearing of formal dress, including, but not restricted to, the bearing of dress regulation arms at all times.

ii) The correct use of title, rank and privilege when addressing fellow officers.

iii) Imperial Standard high table manners (see appendix forty-six (46).

iv) Hair length, facial decoration, tattoos, marking, jewellery, fetishes, religious insignia and other affectations will be allowed to only those permitted by individual regimental edict.

v) Standard Low Gothic and/ or High Gothic ONLY to be employed at all times.

vi) Excessive intoxication will not be tolerated, on pain of court martial.

vii) Standards of prior ablutions to accord with, or exceed, washroom discipline six (6).

viii) Elimination of waste to be taken strictly in designated areas.

Excerpt from the Officer's Standard Primer, *Book Four,* 'Manners and Conduct'.

CHAPTER 12

KALIDAR IV, BATTLEGROUP COMMAND LEVIATHAN,
MACAREE'S TABLELANDS
3328397.M41

Being invited to a banquet aboard the Command Leviathan Magnificence was a great honour, but Bannick, who'd been born to such affairs, was impatient for its conclusion. His shining breastplate, the exact same kind as his uncle had worn all those months ago, weighed heavily on his front, his white gloves formed a lump where they were tucked into his sash, and he wished he could undo the top button of his high-necked vermillion dress tunic. The Great Room of Magnificence was cool and ventilated with purified air, not a speck of Kalidarian dust marring its precious wood panelling or the crystal tableware of the long table. Despite being stuffed into his dress attire, the room was the most comfortable one Bannick had been in since his arrival on the planet.

Still, the room was stifling in its own way. Bannick would have preferred to have been in his vest in the stuffy bowels of the Baneblade. Before they'd come, Cortein had remarked that you could never tell which way the cards would fall in the

Guard. 'I've seen men executed for leaving their station they way you did,' he'd said as they'd struggled into their dress uniforms in their tent. 'And I've seen men lauded for far less. In a way, we're lucky.'

Bannick was clever enough not to remark that Cortein had let him go. He was being tested by his clansman; the Honoured Lieutenant's acquiescence to his request had been one such test, he realised that now.

He supposed that he had passed it. The destruction of the orks had given command the morale boost it sought, the return of the men Bannick had rescued even more so. Two weeks more of fighting, and the orks had been pushed back from the outlying mine heads of Hive Modulus, drawing the force on the Kostoval Flats out, finally ending the siege at the Urtis complex. The orks had fragmented somewhat, their heavy walker unit broken up, and since then two more of the large war machines had been brought down, although there had been no further sign of the Gargant.

Cause enough to celebrate, it seemed, and Bannick had been ordered to attend the banquet. His medal had been taken from him, polished, and before the feast commenced, formally re-presented by Captain-General Iskhandrian of Atraxia himself, along with a fine sword.

Bannick's new sword sat uncomfortably at his side, tangling with the legs of his chair every time he was obliged to stand and greet a superior officer, and there were a great many of them. The top brass of every regiment on Kalidar was present in the banqueting hall, the pompous titles of each shouted out by the battlegroup's most senior sergeant as they entered the room: three Atraxian colonels, their marshall, five Paragonian colonels, Paragonian General Ban Lo Kism Verkerigen, the two commissar-colonels of the Savlar regiments, three other high-ranking politicals, Navy liaisons in flounced silk shirtsleeves and bright blue tunics, two tech-priests who sat there not eating a thing, sipping tall canisters of nutrient substitute, Mastraen the Astropath Prime, his aide, the aide's cymunculous, Maldon and Logan, the army's two primaris psykers, a spindly, frog-fingered Navigator in a power-assist harness and an unpronounceable string of names, the High Chaplain Moktarn in his ecclesiastical splendour, on and on, and of course, at the head of the table, Captain-General Iskhandrian of Atraxia, commander of the Imperial Guard on Kalidar. Fifty men, all told. The surroundings were of shameful luxury. Bannick found it hard to credit that they were in the heart of a mobile command fortress, a deadly storm raging outside. Other than that, he thought, it was just like a clan banquet back home, with all present jockeying for position, the room thick with intrigue.

He looked at the faces, all colours, all types, eyes of every shade, bodies of all shapes. Tall, short, squat, slender, augmented, purestrain, modified. Man was infinitely variable, though his nature was not.

He was thankful, at least, that the presentation was over.

Iskhandrian delivered a speech at table, praising late Imperial efforts in driving the orks back, and the Imperial Guard's presence here in what was deep enemy territory.

'Three weeks, gentlemen,' he had said, 'and Hive Meradon will be back in Imperial hands, and the ork nearly gone from Kalidar.'

His words drew a well-measured amount of applause.

Down the table from where Bannick sat, Cortein held himself still. Eyes keen to court intrigue, Bannick could tell that Cortein did not believe a word of what was said. He himself was too cynical to take the speech at face value, but not sufficiently arrogant to think he knew enough about the war to form his own opinion. He resolved to ask Cortein about his opinion later.

Then came the dinner. Bannick had not seen so much food for two years. Courses came and went, accompanied by a variety of wines, liqueurs, liquors and other fluid intoxicants that boggled the mind. Even in the heart of Helwat City on Paragon he'd not seen such variety.

As the exotic beverages flowed, so did the conversation, all of it fascinating. Bannick made sure to restrict his own stimulant intake. He instead dined on the talk of others, dipped in and out of conversations around the table automatically, another aspect of his privileged upbringing he despised, another trait he'd never divested himself of. At least here, unlike on the battlefield, he did not feel so naïve.

'The Savlar require a firm hand.' One of the commissars spoke. He too, Bannick noted, had barely touched a drop of drink. 'That is why all their high-ranking officers are drawn from the Schola Progenium.'

'Such as yourself and Damartes there,' said a Navy man, the medals and pips cluttering his shoulders describing his rank as that of commander. He had an insouciant manner that patently irritated the commissar.

'Indeed,' said the commissar. He struggled to crack the casing on his food, a sand-dwelling crustacean native to Kalidar. He failed and waved it impatiently away. 'Oh, the discipline on the ships of the Navy is well regarded by we of the Commissariat, Commander Spaduski, but the Savlar require something... more exacting, shall we say. Their world is one of sinners, sir, a penal outpost bedevilled by gang-warfare and profanity. What little productivity is wrested from it is done so at the point of a gun. The crime of rape is so prevalent there that it is said that only one in four of every Savlar born on the world knows his father. The world is perpetually shrouded in a toxic miasma, it is a poisonous broil, sir. And it is as only right! For the judgement of the Emperor requires that they who have transgressed be punished. They are thieves, murderers, profaners, heretics, liars and scum, the worst the Imperium has to offer, and Savlar is a fit place for them to suffer their penitence. Yet with the Emperor's guidance we can turn the most unpromising instrument into a potent weapon.'

'I wonder,' said the navy man, taking a long pull at an ornate goblet of rare Zolasian wine. 'How many generations of suffering are required to expunge the guilt of an ancestor? I rather thought it was the threat of returning to Savlar that encouraged them to fight. However, I am pleased to hear they are so motivated by love for our beneficent Emperor.'

'This is an under-resourced war, sir,' countered the commissar. 'The Savlar fight well when correctly motivated. That is all that matters.'

'I find faith like that reassuring,' said another, a broad-shouldered giant. When the man had walked in Bannick had initially taken him to be some kind of priest from a mendicant order, for his appearance was modest and his manner that of an aesthete, and Bannick thought his enormous size another product of man's endless variety. It had not been until the man had been announced by the sergeant as the Brother Arnegis, Lord Steward to Castellan Thieme of the Black Templars that Bannick realised that the priest was actually one of the enhanced Adeptus Astartes, whose presence on the far side of Kalidar was the source of much rumour among the ranks. His cheeks were sharp, his face long and stern and bored, but his eyes were bright as if he found the whole affair on the Leviathan somewhat amusing. These eyes constantly scanned the room, as if searching for threats, and from time to time he would fix one or another of the men around the table with a piercing, assessing stare. All were targets of his judgement, high and lower ranks alike, and none could hold his gaze. The psykers at the table, especially, seemed to draw his attention.

Bannick watched him from the corner of his eye, not wishing to be subject to his scrutiny. Arnegis ate a great deal, methodically munching his way through four portions of food, but said little. Now, however, he had roused himself to interject. 'It is, of course, the larger part of our lives in the Chapter, Emperor be praised, but it fills me with great joy that lesser men than the glorious Adeptus Astartes are still true in appropriate veneration of our blessed lord. One sees so little of it sometimes, and the work of the pure increases enormously as heresy multiplies.'

'Praise be to that!' shouted the ecclesiarch down the table. He held high his goblet. The Lord Steward inclined his head in acknowledgment.

'It is a burden the Black Templars gladly bear.'

'And you, lieutenant?' said an adjutant Bannick did not know. 'I understand Paragon is a jewel of a world, some have it that the people there are soft, yet you men fight well, no need to toughen you up, Kalidar seems to be doing an admirable job there.' He attempted a laugh. No one joined him.

'The conditions here are no suitable topic for levity,' grumbled a sour-looking captain three seats up, and the adjutant coloured. 'I have a score of men dead a day from the dustlung alone.'

'We fight well,' said Bannick. 'But I hold the Savlar in great respect. Throne knows what they faced in order to plant that bomb, but they did, and detonated it to the minute.'

Commander Spaduski nodded as he cracked his sandmite open and swallowed down its meagre flesh. He made a face. Bannick had eaten his with a blank face, it tasted vile, but he had better manners – or perhaps more sense – than the spacefarer. 'A fair point. Our commissar colleague has a point, I will concede. This is an under-resourced war. Other conquests are drawing resources away from every conflict in this segmentum and half the Segmentum Pacificus.'

'There's a force out in the western reaches now,' said Spaduski, 'waging war on places that have never seen the light of the Emperor – a hundred worlds they've conquered, but at what cost? Two-thirds of the Pacificus fleet is with them, hundreds of regiments, five Chapters of the Adeptus Astartes, and every money-grabbing member of the Rogue Trader houses that can scrape together a following trailing in their wake.'

'A mighty army,' said the commissar, 'bringing light to the dark!'

'Aye,' said Spaduski. 'But how many worlds like this do we stand to lose to pay for their illumination?' He gestured down the table with the cartiligenous shell of the sand-mite. 'Look at Iskhandrian there, hollow-eyed from all his work, he's a good commander from all I hear, but this is a hard war, and he is too dogmatic. They are not normal orks, these Blood Axes, they withdraw and plot as surely as any human foe.'

'Sir! He works to the holy words of the *Tactica*.'

'With all due respect, Commissar Van Bast, the *Tactica* is vast, no one can read it all, and then it is merely the beginning of the lessons we warriors of the Emperor must learn. The primary lessons on the greenskin menace within are... elementary. The *Tactica* fails to reveal early enough the full complexity of ork behaviour and clan division,' said Spaduski. 'Lack of true study of our blessed texts is an error I find among my fellow officers all too often.' The embarrassed adjutant nodded enthusiastically and attempted to interject. Spaduski turned away, pointedly ignoring him.

Bannick was careful to appear engaged yet distant. Spaduski's criticism of the captain-general was dangerous, but this near-heretical assertion about the holy *Tactica*, from which most Imperial wisdom was derived, was almost too much. The commissar's expression grew grim. Bannick wasn't sure how the

Commissariat worked within the Navy, but he'd never dare speak so openly in front of a political officer of any kind like that. Spaduski, however, was either too brave, too indifferent, too drunk or too stupid to care. Bannick doubted it was the last. 'We're all at risk down here,' he went on. 'No vox comms up or down. Iskhandria should be aboard my ship, *Terra's Lambent Glory*, safely directing the troops, but the damned magnetosphere forces him down here into this... landship,' he said dismissively. 'Undermanned, and a target. Not that it's much better up there. We lost four cruisers last month alone to ork strikes, a very bad score. They're hiding out in the belts, attacking when we least expect it.'

'Then be more vigilant,' said the commissar.

Spaduski leaned forwards. 'Listen to me, we know this breed of greenskin. I've fought them before, out Valhalla way fifty years and more ago. They can take you by surprise, these Blood Axes, but even I've not seen this. There's something strange going on here. We can't see the ork, but as sure as the Emperor sits upon the Golden Throne, they can see us. That we keep fighting them on the ground as if they'll happily throw themselves at our guns like other orks is extremely unhelpful. The astropaths on board talk of a presence in the warp, something... new.'

'That may be so,' said the commissar. 'But the Emperor will bring us victory.'

'Will He now?' said the Navy man. 'Or is it our own efforts, and our own discernment, good or bad as that may be, that will see us fall or succeed?'

'Be careful of your tone, sir,' said the commissar, his face hardening further. His palm slapped lightly upon the table.

Spaduski held up his hands. 'I merely warn against complacency. Faith is, as ever, the thickest of armours and I wear mine like a second skin. Were it not for the guiding light of our glorious lord, my ship would travel nowhere, and that is the least of all He does for us. Now, if you would excuse me, I am due to report in.'

As Spaduski stood, a primaris psyker who had been talking a few feet away moved down the table and leaned into their conversation, grabbing onto Spaduski's arm and preventing his exit. His eyes were piercing, sparkling with an energy far beyond that which is visible in the face of normal men. His costume was elaborate, implants plugged into his skull and trailing out from his hair. He exuded a palpable aura of might, yet his face was waxy and pale, his remarkable eyes sunk deep into shadowed flesh, an effect multiplied by the high psi-collar he wore. *He is a strong man made sick by the witchlight within him*, thought Bannick, and recalled his name as Maldon, but he smiled brightly as friendly men do. The commissar face's stiffened at the approach of the powerful witch. For all that they were sanctioned, and bore the same gifts as the Emperor himself, albeit to far meaner proportions, psykers did not share His will or His purity. The Space Marine, too, watched him with undisguised suspicion.

The psyker paid neither of them any heed. 'Gentlemen! All this talk of travails! Shall we not change the matter to a lighter subject? Alas, the machines of the Adeptus Mechanicus may struggle with the conditions here on Kalidar, but I assure you that, with the Emperor's aid, we of the Scholastica Psykana can fill the gap. I will gladly announce to you all at this very moment that forty-four of my colleagues, with full staff and a supplementary astropathic demi-choir, are en route to Kalidar as we speak. Is this not so?'

'Indeed it is,' agreed the astropath from his seat down the table, empty eye-sockets dark within the green of his robe.

'There,' said the psyker. 'Where the might of the Martian Omnissiah is stymied, then the will and farsight of the Emperor will prevail. With additional minds to sing the praises of the Emperor, we will be able to cast a full psychic net around Kalidar and bring to an end the communications troubles that have so bedevilled us; to root out this strange aberration allied to the ork. Gentlemen!' he shouted out, as conversation quieted down the length of the table. Bannick caught Cortein's eye, sat twelve seats away. He shrugged, almost imperceptibly. 'To victory!' shouted the psyker.

A mumbled cry of 'hear hear' replied. The hubbub resumed. The psyker did not sit.

'...have so bedevilled us; to root out this strange aberration allied to the ork. Gentlemen!' Maldon repeated, his arm jerking upwards. 'To victory!' Veins stood out on his head, cords on his neck. His face flushed red as if with great effort.

'What are you playing at?' hissed Spaduski. He removed the man's hand from his arm and backed away.

'...to ...vict...' the psyker shook as if palsied, his wine slopping over the sides of his goblet. His hand clenched, the glass shattered, piercing his flesh. Blood and wine spattered the tableware. His eyes rolled in his head, terrified.

'Rrrr... Rrrr... To vic... to viccctorrrrrrrrrrrrrrrrrrrreeeeeeeeeeee.' Maldon shook so hard his features blurred, his voice becoming a hideous burr. Sparks of green crackled from his fingers and breastplate, there was a bang, and the thick collar he wore exploded, showering the diners with broken crystal. The astropath cried out, muscles straining, unable to move; the other sanctioned psyker in the room screamed, blood streaming from his eyes and nose, and he collapsed into his food. Slowly, Maldon rose into the air, a storm of green sparks blazing around him as he was lifted above the table, forced upwards by a cascade of eldritch energy. Chairs scraped as men recoiled, pistols and swords were drawn, bringing leaps of warp-born power to earth through them. Cursing, their owners dropped them.

Maldon hung in the centre of the room's high arched ceiling, drifting in a circle. His face blazed with green energy, blackened jelly running down his cheeks where his eyes had been cooked in their sockets. There was a crack of breaking bone, and the psyker's jaw sagged wide. Mandible jerking in a parody of normal speech, the storm-wracked man spoke.

'Hur, hur, hur,' he said in a voice not his own, a voice guttural and inhuman. 'I see you, I see you all! There is no escape! This world belongs to the green! You are all dead! All of you!' The psyker's hand jerked up, fingers out in a claw, pointing at the occupants of the room. 'And I am coming for you!'

Malton began a hideous gurgle, his broken jaw flapping on his chest, tongue out long and twitching. Green fire shot from his throat as his body convulsed fit to snap his spine.

His head exploded, showering the room with fragments of skull and brain. The green light cut off. Fountaining blood, the corpse of the primaris psyker crashed into the table, scattering the feast everywhere.

Klaxons blared. A blast shook the command vehicle, sending the officers sprawling. A chandelier hit the floor, smoke poured into the room from a vent, then shut off. Green emergency lighting gave the room a ghostly air. The sounds of small explosions came and went. Shouting and feet ringing on metal floors went past the great room's doors.

'Attention, attention,' a vox-borne voice called. 'All hands to battle stations, all hands to battle stations, we are under attack. Repeat, we are under attack!'

Bannick ran after Spaduski through the Leviathan, rebreather case clunking on the back of his breastplate and bruising his hip. All officers in the mess had been ordered back to their posts, scattering to whatever route would take them there quickest. Many of them had made straight for the command deck of the massive vehicle, to direct their troops. Cortein had gone with them. The half-dozen or so other officers junior enough to be leading their troops in the field had scattered to various sally ports and access hatches. No one seemed to know where exactly the orks were on board. It was suggested that if they split up, at least some of them would get out. Spaduski was making for the comms suite, to see if he could get in touch with his ship. Bannick opted to follow him and find his own exit.

With a clatter of feet, Spaduski and Bannick ran smack into a squad of Atraxian Guard Paramount, the high command's elite unit. Weapons were whipped up on both sides, and slowly lowered.

'Sirs,' said the squad sergeant, his face hidden by his carapace mask.

The crack of lasgun fire echoed distantly, roars and the clatter of orkish handguns replying.

'The orks. Do you know where they are?' muttered Spaduski.

'There are a large group of them pouring in through door fourteen…'

Spaduski raised an eyebrow.

'Towards the rear, sir, maybe thirty or more. But reports have individuals roaming the entire ship. They've destroyed our comms array, and done something to the internal surveillance.' The sergeant's melodious Atraxian accent was at odds with his faceless armour.

There was the sound of an explosion. The Leviathan rocked.

'And now they're blasting this place apart from the inside,' growled the Navy man. 'This could go badly. A boarding action is no good thing with these creatures.'

A crackle of vox from the squad, the sergeant spoke into it. 'We're whittling them down, sir. Our comrades in the Guard Paramount are taking care of the main group. We're on our way to the command deck just in case any get through there and try to assassinate high command.' He paused for a moment, listening to vox chatter. 'You,' he said to six of his troops. 'Continue on up to the command deck and reinforce the squad on the doors.' He spoke into his vox rapidly, requesting permission to escort Bannick and Spaduski. 'We're to get these officers to their men,' he said presently. Milite and Tesk, you come with me. Gentlemen, what are your orders?'

'I've been ordered back to my vehicle,' said Bannick.

'I have to try and make contact with the fleet,' said Spaduski. 'Is the main vox array still down?'

'Yes, commander,' replied the Atraxian. 'The orks targeted that first, all our communications capabilities are severely compromised.'

'In that case I have to make it to the astropathic choir. I just hope they can send a message out with their leader in a coma.'

The sergeant said, 'The comms room is this way, on the way to the choir. We'll visit both.' He pointed to Bannick. 'Milite will take you to the nearest sally. After that, you are on your own. The primary duty of the Guard Paramount is to protect command.'

'I understand.'

'Good. Move out,' said the Atraxian. Half his squad made their way cautiously up the corridor, towards the command deck.

'I wish you well,' said Spaduski.

'And I you too,' said Bannick, and he and his escort made off down the way. They jogged cautiously, pausing at every junction while the trooper checked the passages. Bannick stood behind him, sword hilt and laspistol held in palms that had suddenly gone sweaty. The distant sounds of fighting reached their ears every so often, but Bannick was amazed how quiet the giant vehicle was. Its carrier decks were empty, the troops it could carry billeted outside, all the action was going on elsewhere, he supposed, up on the elevated command deck at the top of the fore tower, in the six turrets down the flanks, round the breached accessway where the orks had broken in, anywhere but here.

Milites slowed to a halt, listening to a message.

'Sorry sir,' he said shortly. 'Road out to the second sally port is blocked. Three orks putting up a fight, they'll lock it down, but they don't know how long.' He tapped onto his wrist-mounted augur, brought up plans, looked up. 'We'll go this way. It means backtracking a little,' said Milite. 'But there's an external hatch nearby.'

The trooper led Bannick to one of the wide ways that led down either side of the vehicle, which were repeated on every one of the command centre's main four decks, giving access to the tank bays and troop compartments on the lower two, the various command sections on the upper. The far end of the corridor lit sporadically with the flash of weapons discharge, there was a defiant, alien bellow, shouting, then silence. The trooper held up a hand until the noise dissipated, then led Bannick across the corridor and into a side spur terminating at the inner hull of the command vehicle. A keypad sat alongside a window-sized doorway a metre off the floor bearing a large three.

'Maintenance, I'm afraid, sir, it'll be a squeeze.'

'I'm a tanker, I've got into smaller spaces,' said Bannick. He undid his sword while the trooper keyed in the code.

'I've turned on the maintenance ladder, it should be out of the hull when you get there. It'll deactivate automatically in a minute, and you'll have to drop the last six metres or so in any case. The outer door will open at your biosign, but only once. After that, you are stuck, sir. Inside or out,' he warned. 'Auto defences activate twenty seconds after. You won't have long to get out.'

'Thank you.' Bannick passed his weapon to the trooper and climbed into the service tunnel. The trooper pushed the sword into the tunnel after him and sealed him in, trapping him in the space between inner and outer hulls. Bannick muttered a quick prayer. He crawled off, banging his knuckles on the mesh floor where he gripped his sword. He'd have abandoned the weapon, but he was probably going to need it. The service ducts were silent, the vehicle's innermost parts impervious to the sounds of the battle inside and the storm outside. Bannick crossed another tunnel that cut through his own at right angles, curving off into the darkness. Conduits and subsystems surrounded him, many bearing the seals and parchments left by free-roaming Adeptus Mechanicus repair vermin. He hoped he didn't encounter any. Light was restricted to the twinkling of small system status indicators and widely spaced lumen cubes set into the floor.

He made the outermost skin of the Leviathan in a few minutes. Once there he struggled his rebreather and goggles on and keyed the hatch's single button. A broad sweep scan-laser swept up and down him, tasting his biology. A trill indicated the machine-spirit within was satisfied.

The hatch cracked with a hiss, and the fury of Kalidar came shrieking in, hot wind and razor dust blasting Bannick. The hatch stopped wide with a clunk, opening out onto a scene of eerie blankness.

The dust storm filled the night, the Imperial camp's lights diffracted into fuzzy globes, muffling the outside in a uniform dimness within which darker shapes lurked; the great mesas that gave Macaree's Tablelands its name. There were twenty-four gradings of dust storm on Kalidar – Bannick reckoned this to be somewhere round the fifteen mark. Blown up like this, the fine dust could cause dustlung after a few breaths. When it settled it ran like water, pooling in hollows in the ground, creating new deposits of deadly quickdust. Flows of heavier sand ran above the ground thirty metres below, completely obscuring it, whipped along the surface by the wind, the kind of fanged wind that cut.

From within this maelstrom, he could make out the sounds of fighting.

Holy Lord protect me, thought Bannick. He realised he was afraid, and that relieved him, for if he was numbed to the battle he was dead. He double-checked the seals on his respirator. He dropped his sword over the edge. It bounced once off the sloping fortress wall, and disappeared into the storm.

He swung his legs out into the teeth of the storm, turned round and hung precariously from the hatchway by his hands. He was between two of the Leviathan's side bastions, just below their turrets. These whined from side to side, unable to find a target. For a couple of moments his feet banged ineffectually into the heavily decorated side of the Leviathan, and he began to sweat. If the hatch shut, he'd lose his fingers and then... His fear intensified, empowering him. His foot found one of the hemispherical holes that made up the surface ladder and he breathed a sigh of relief. Quickly he descended, mindful of the time left to him before the hatch and ladder disengaged. He made it to where the ladder gave out, six metres off the ground. Turning, he pushed himself away from the side of the immense vehicle and fell through the air, coat fluttering behind him. He passed into the stream of heavier sand, and landed.

'Thank the Emperor for low-G,' he said. He stood and pulled out his laspistol. He found his sword quickly; already it was covering over with heavy grains of sand. He belted it back on and he pulled it free of the scabbard.

Down here, right in the gullet of Kalidar's latest tantrum, he could hardly see. Sand pattered off his goggles like stubber fire, his ears filled with the stuff. The night, normally frigid, was stifling, the storm's thick air acting as a blanket, trapping the heat of the day.

Vision limited by goggles and sand, hearing muffled, Bannick retreated into a world delineated by the circumscribed glow of the camp lamps. His breathing and heart competed with the roar of the wind. Any minute, he expected an ork to loom out of the night and snap his neck with its brutal hands; more than once he spun round, panic barely below the surface, sure he was about to be attacked.

All he saw were shapes in the night, flashes in the gloom, muffled explosions and the crack of lasfire, amplified by superheated dust exploding in its beams.

Only once did he pass by a firefight close enough to see. A squad of Guard had formed up in the heart of their platoon camp, loosing volleys of lasfire that crackled through the air, felling orks charging them. Others outflanked their small bastion, and melee ensued. Bannick debated joining them, but pressed on, thoughts on his orders, the Baneblade and his comrades.

He came across an ork alone, crouched over something by the tracks of a Leman Russ. He crept up behind it. It was busy for a second, then away into the night without noticing him. He waited a few heartbeats and went to where the ork had been crouched. Explosives, it had been planting explosives. He checked the device quickly, six sticks of pliable explosive matter. As far as he could tell, two blinking green lights and a mechanical clock checking down the seconds on top formed the detonator. Gritting his teeth, he aimed his pistol and put a las-shot through the clock face. The bomb fizzed. He pulled the device free and tossed it as far as he could from the tank. The storm would bury it, they'd have to dig it out and destroy it, but better that than lose a tank.

He recognised where he was then, the edge of the vehicle park, armoured fighting vehicles in precise ranks filling the canyon floor, their blocky shapes hazy in the night. Trails of ork footprints, already filling with sand, curved lazy S-shapes from tank to tank.

Emperor knew how many bombs the orks had planted while the Guard's attention was fixed on the Leviathan.

Bannick pressed the stud at the side of his respirator. Vox static hissed in his ears angrily, Kalidar's snake warning. 'This is Lieutenant Colaron Artem Lo Bannick. Command, come in...' He waited for a reply; nothing came. 'Is anyone there? The attack on the Leviathan is a feint. They're booby-trapping the tanks, repeat, orks are attaching explosives to our tanks.'

No reply. Bannick swore. He searched up and down the bands for a working channel, nothing but the rush of interference and unintelligible chatter. He was about to try again when chatter of a different kind cut across his attention. Heavy bolter fire, coming from the centre of the massed ranks.

The place where the super-heavies rested.

He ran through the whirling dust, towards *Mars Triumphant*. Stooped silhouettes loomed up and then away, orks, guns out, firing. The bolter fire grew louder, the distinctive double report as the guns spat out the round and the accelerant activated, pushing the bolt past the speed of sound.

Bannick threw himself forwards, a line of bolts streaking overhead. He rolled in time to see an ork bearing down on him from the storm. Huge and warty, green skin rendered brown by the dust, it leered evilly and raised a huge pistol. The young lieutenant prepared to die.

The trigger pulled. A click. The ork looked at its gun and threw it aside. Kalidar spared neither side's weapons, it seemed.

It was all the time Bannick needed to aim a sideways swipe at its leg, cutting it deep into its calf beneath the back of the knee, splashing Bannick with dark blood. The ork roared, made to grab him, but Bannick was past it quickly, leaving it limping and shouting behind him in the storm.

He was in the marshalling ground, the broad space at the middle of the camp's vehicle park, a temporary square delineated by the tanks around it. Ahead, in its centre, sat the super-heavies. All three were part-active, heavy bolters blazing as turrets tracked this way and that. Bolter shells spanged off them as they caught each other in the crossfire, the crews trusting to their armour to stop the bolts dead. To the south, the smell of smoke as the tents of the company burned, a broad orange band in the whirling dust hinting at their location.

None of the tanks moved. Their engines required time to energise at best, the exhortations of the company enginseers at worst. Nevertheless, bodies of orks formed a broken cordon of flesh about thirty metres out from them, the barrage of fire from all three super-heavy tanks keeping the xenos at bay. The tanks were sluggish, but far from sleeping.

Bannick shook off a rising fugue brought on by the scent of burning flesh; the bodies of the men he could not rescue, brutalised into unrecognisable form, flashing into his mind. He forced himself to run. Luck was on his side: the orks had evidently been beaten back from the tanks, but he could hear them above the keen of the wind, regrouping, shadows moving in the storm. He had to be quick. He waited for the bolter turrets on *Ostrakan's Rebirth*, closest to him now, to track away, then broke into a run.

He just hoped he wouldn't be mistaken for the enemy.

He sprinted past the bulk of the Hellhammer, veering round its front. He hit the deck once again as a trio of rounds spat from the left sponson of *Mars Triumphant*, waited. No more came. They must have identified him as human – even in the storm the silhouettes of man and ork were easy to tell apart.

He ran to the tank's blunt nose, not wasting time scrambling round to the rear access ladder. Aided by the planet's low gravity, he leapt the two and a half metres onto the sloping front, scrambled up over the demolisher cannon and onto the forward gunnery access hatch. He jammed his finger into the access lock, cursing as it failed to activate, scraping the choking dust from its internal iris. A clunk, and the lock disengaged. He yanked at the hatch, wormed inside, his respirator's snout catching and banging painfully into his face as he dropped within.

The hatch shut with difficulty, the crunch of sand powdering in its seals. The wind was shut away to a distant whisper.

Bannick was stood hard by Ganlick's seat. The low chair, jammed in tight by the forward demolisher turret, was vacant, screens off on the small station. Through the bulkhead's cutaway he saw Outlanner in the driver's chair as always, maskless, unconcerned that he might have got a lungful.

'Lieutenant,' said the driver. 'How're you?' He leaned back. 'You got sand all over Ganlick's chair, he ain't gonna be too happy 'bout that.'

Bannick tore his mask off. 'Can't you get this damned thing moving? There are orks everywhere.'

Outlanner shrugged. 'No reactor power, no drive. Vorkosigen's doing his best, but he ain't got the full-on knowhow. Need a proper coghead for that.'

'Who else is aboard?' snapped Bannick. Outlanner was dreamy, full of gleece. Cortein let him get away with it; Bannick would have wondered why but he'd seen the man drive.

'Me, Vorkosigen, Marsello and Ganlick, he's up on the command deck, firing your guns at the greenies.' The driver sighed. He'd be no help unless they got the engines on line.

'Vorkosigen!' bawled Bannick as he hurried up the gangway. 'Vorkosigen!'

The little engineer's legs and blood-red robe could be seen protruding from out of the engine access. The eyes of the machine-spirit emblem to the side were extinguished, Vorksosigen's prayers croaking out from below the block, in a poor mimicry of his Adeptus Mechanicus superiors. Bannick went up and stood over him.

'Report, Vorkosigen.'

Vorkosigen scooted out, his face oily, spanner in hand. The stare his big eyes gave Bannick was far from friendly. 'Sir,' he said coldly.

'I said report, dammit! Why isn't the plant online? Ganlick is in charge, am I correct? He ordered you to activate, no?'

A pause. 'The plants were powered down to a null state by the enginseers on all the super-heavies, sir,' said Vorkosigen. He deliberately avoided looking Bannick in the eye, staring at the metal of the ceiling behind his shoulder. The tone he used was slow, patronising. 'Usually when we stop *Mars Triumphant* goes into a standing ready state, but there is full maintenance scheduled for tomorrow and the multifuel reactor needs to be entirely cold before…'

'Spare me the explanations, Vorkosigen, can you get it started?'

'No. I can't. I am trying, but I cannot do it without the enginseers. The reactor is rarely let into this state. Only my superiors know the proper rites for full reactivation, this is not a secret aspirants are party to.'

'Why in the name of Terra would they leave us sitting dead?'

'Standard procedure sir, we're due a big engagement. I'm trying to patch in all the back-ups at once. That should buy us more time.' With that, Vorkosigen slid back under the tank's engine block.

'Damn orks picked their moment,' said Bannick. He went forwards again, showering dust from his coat. He hauled himself up the ladder onto the command deck. Marsello and Ganlick looked up sharply, the big gunner in the third gunner's seat. Bannick's seat.

'What's going on?'

'We're running off batteries,' said the second gunner, terse as always. 'Sponsons only, I wouldn't want to draw on the lascannon right now, and we don't want to hit the other super-heavies with those. Heavy bolters are okay, lascannon shots.' He shrugged. 'Anyhow, we'd have four, maybe five shots, then we'd be without anything.'

'Heavy bolters only then?'

'Yes,' said Ganlick.

'Vorkosigen told me that this is standard, seems insane to me. What did he mean?'

Ganlick looked up again from the screen, a swarm of dots at its edge, motion markers blurred with static. The orks were massing. 'The amount of power *Mars Triumphant* and her sisters use is enormous. They'll run off anything…'

'Like the Leman Russ and Chimeras?' interrupted Bannick.

'Yeah, but the plant is much bigger. The reactor has to be serviced every six months or so, but they do it every time they think we'll be in a big engagement or long out in the field. More often, if the fuel or conditions are rough, like here…'

'They're coming back in!' said Marsello.

'Stand ready,' said Bannick. 'Where are the others?'

'Ralt, Meggen and Epperaliant are off in camp at the rec tent. It's their off shift. The honoured lieutenant?'

'The last I saw of him, he was escorting the captain-general back to the command deck of the Leviathan. Captain Hannick too.'

The sound of explosions rumbled through the hull.

'They hit the Leviathan?' asked Marsello, panic in his voice.

'They hit the Leviathan, blew one of the basdack doors off

and got right inside. And they've rigged the vehicle park with explosives, I guess that was them. Seems we're a target as well,' said Bannick. 'Orks have hit the barrack tents, they've penned in our support while another group comes up here to cripple our armour. There's not many of them out there, but they've got the whole camp in uproar, feinting and retreating, burning as they go.'

'A diversion, from orks?' said Marsello.

'We're dead in the sand,' said Ganlick.

The second and third gunners locked eyes.

'You're the ranking officer,' said Ganlick, abruptly. Bannick was relieved and appalled simultaneously – relieved he wouldn't have a turf war with the second gunner, appalled that he was responsible for the safety of *Mars Triumphant*.

'You sure?'

'I point guns and shoot 'em,' said Ganlick. 'I'm second gunner here, but the pips on your shoulder say you're it and Cortein isn't here to say otherwise. Where do you want me? I could go up top and man the stubber, you two keep us clear with the sponsons?'

Bannick thought about it. He looked at the command suite. No use to him with the main guns and engines offline, and it felt wrong to usurp Cortein's place. Better he stay here, where he belonged.

'Okay. Keep your tracking down if you can,' advised Ganlick. 'It's that which'll squeeze the batteries dry. You'll be lucky to hit anything anyway, best we can hope for now is to keep them back.' They squeezed awkwardly past each other. Bannick sat as Ganlick pulled himself up the ladder. Marsello and Bannick slipped on their respirators. The hatch up top opened up and let Kalidar in.

'They're coming! Prepare delta fire pattern.' The vox burst to life, the systems on the super-heavies powerful enough to break through the storm, at least at this short range. Honoured Lieutenant Marteken, the commander of *Artemen Ultrus*, the company's other Baneblade. Bannick felt a rush of relief that he wasn't the only ranking officer with the company and therefore responsible for the whole unit. He reported in rapidly. Marteken didn't have time to respond before the orks were on them.

The orks approached sidewise, using the parking pattern of the tanks against them. They came in fast, firing their clumsy rockets as they ran. Five of these small groups were pinned or scattered, but each one targeted let another further forwards, the super-heavy tanks' arcs of fire compromised by their own bulk.

They're sophisticated for orks all right, thought Bannick, but they're still aiming to get in close. He thought of the explosives attached to the sides of the Leman Russ.

'They're trying to get in with krak!' he yelled into the vox. 'Don't let them into your dead fire zones!'

Green dots swirled all over his tac display, many winked out as bolts found orks and blew them apart. More came in, close to fifty.

A burst of thunder rumbled through *Mars Triumphant*: one, two, three, four explosions in quick succession. Screams filled the vox, the crew of *Ostrakan's Rebirth*.

The vox crackled. 'Hull breach! Hull breach!' Cholo, another man of Clan Radden, Hannick's commsman. There was a babble of panic and crashing, more screams. A wave of strong static washed it out, then a click, Marteken cutting the feed, making the remaining crew of the two operational tanks stay focused.

The guns of *Ostrakan's Rebirth* fell silent. It took a moment for Bannick, intent on playing his own bolters across the advancing orks, to realise that Ganlick's stubber had cut off too. If the orks had got to the tank, the open hatch would give them a way in…

A clumsy thump of boots on metal made him turn. It saved his life.

Crammed into the confines of the tank, like a monster from a fairytale stealing into a nursery, stood an ork. Bannick hadn't had time to register the size and power of the creatures out there in the storm. They were shapes in the murk, the fights he had brief, sight of the creatures lost to the storm. Here, in the dim lights of the tanks, he could see how large orks truly were. It barely fitted in the confines of the command deck. It was perhaps as tall as Bannick, but only because it was so deeply stooped. Had it stood up straight it would have overtopped him by a head or more, and it was far more massive, four or five times his weight, its body a mass of slab-like muscle and ropey sinew. Hands as big as ammo boxes reached down to the floor, talons terminating fingers wide as two of Bannick's own. Its head was huge, a hulking bucket of a skull as large as a man's ribcage, dozerblade lower jaw jutting forwards, lined with swordblade fangs, ropes of drool streaming from between them. Bandoliers laden with shell cases and explosives criss-crossed its barrel chest, uniform camouflaged in the drab red oxides and greys of Kalidar. Its green skin was also disguised, scab, sore and scar all painted over with finger-smears of colour. Round its neck hung a chain of teeth, a crossed-axe pendant dangling from the centre. Its eyes were tiny, picked out a deep red by the lights in the cabin, retinas silvering as it leaned in towards Bannick.

The ork went for him as he dove out of his chair, bringing its knife down hard and shearing the back of his station chair in half. Bannick fell to the floor, knocking the mask from his face. Immediately the stench of the ork assailed him, a strong animal stink, alien sweat and dung, rotting flesh and something like seaweed. Bannick scrambled up, reaching for his holster. He glanced to his sword, no room to pull it free, he prayed his laspistol would be enough. Marsello cried out, distracting the ork. Bannick sent a bolt of crimson light searing into the ork's shoulder. The creature's flesh smouldered, adding the flavour of hot wax and burnt meat to the reek in the room. It roared, more with annoyance than real pain, jaws hinging wide. It kept its eyes on the third loader, but pivoted backwards, bringing its long arm round towards Bannick. The beast's massive shoulder moved slowly, but by the time the motion had reached its hand it was travelling fast as a whip. Bannick dodged his head, narrowly saving him from a broken neck as the ork's backhand connect with his chest like a cannon shot. Bannick was hurled backwards, foot catching on the edge of the down well; he stumbled backwards into the command suite, gun clattering to the floor

Bannick shook the spots from his eyes in time to see the ork's knife wrench free from Marsello's chest, blood fountaining from the hole in his ribs, painting the command deck with his life.

The ork stood, grinning at him. A deep, horrible noise Bannick took for a chuckle came up from its chest. It licked the knife edge with a long pink tongue, Marsello's life-blood trickling onto its sabre-teeth, then gestured to the gun on the floor between them.

The basdacked thing was challenging him.

Bannick grabbed for his pistol as the ork clumsily swiped at him. He seized the dropped weapon, rolled sideways, over the lip of the stairwell as the ork lunged again. He landed hard on the deck, cutting his hand on a bunk door left askew. The ork came to the top of the steps, bulky body filling the aperture. Bannick brought up his gun, loosed off a shot, catching the ork in the arm as it wrestled itself through. It hissed and shook its head, began to descend. Bannick aimed for the head and missed. He scrabbled on his back towards the forward compartment of the tank.

The ork came down, caution gone. It was playing with him. Bannick got up, kept low. The corridor was tight, no place for a fight, but the ork was at an even greater disadvantage, trapped by its huge bulk.

Who was he trying to convince? He was a dead man.

Suddenly, the ork grunted. It turned its head, rubbing at its brutish skull, thick blood trickling from a wound. Behind it, he could make out Vorkosigen, clutching a large spanner. The ork tried to turn to face him. It bellowed in anger as its knife caught on the wall. Too big to fit into a corridor made for beings half its size, it could not twist itself round to get at this new irritant.

Bannick raised his gun for a final shot, trying to pinpoint a weak spot on the beast's chest, some way into the vital organs, finding none. Faced with such a being, the laspistol felt as potent as a child's water gun, a pathetic defence, all the training he'd had as a youth in blade and fist combat useless against it. His heart quailed at the thought of the thousands upon thousands of other greenskins on Kalidar, all wanting to rend him apart.

He stilled his nerves. The ork was trapped, head turned awkwardly back and forth between the two humans, long arms alternately reaching for him, then struggling to get at Vorkosigen. The will to live flared bright in him. In circumstances like this, some men gave up and let death take them.

Colaron Artem Lo Bannick was not among such men.

His eyes lighted on the thick cables running the length of the corridor: The lascannon feeds. He had a chance, there was always a chance.

Darting forwards, he flicked the quick release on part of the cable set, leaving the other end connected to the power supply. The cables swung down, a dull glow shining from their ends. He snatched up the bundle, careful to make sure his hand stayed on the thick insulation.

'Xenos!' he shouted. 'Ork!' The ork did not turn. It was still intent on thrashing its way around to deal with the small engineer who was repeatedly battering it on the skull, his face twisted in terror. Bannick shot it instead, aiming for the face, suddenly thankful for the endless lectures on combat anatomy he'd endured aboard the transport barge. The army might have played down the size and power of the greenskins, but they'd been right about their vulnerable spots.

He had its attention.

The ork clutched at its ear, howling in outrage, and turned to finished Bannick once and for all. Bannick was ready.

'Prepare to receive the light of the Emperor,' he said, steel in his voice, and thrust the live end of the cable into the creature's mouth as far as he dared, snatching his hand back as the jaws snapped shut. Raw energy poured directly from the Baneblade's batteries, energy sufficient to power a lascannon. The ork twitched as arcing sparks ran over it, mouth locked shut by electrically induced muscle spasm. Bannick shot again and again into the ork's face, until it was a las-charred ruin.

The ork leaned forwards in the corridor, too big to collapse, corpse smoking.

Bannick breathed hard and leaned into the wall, laspistol clattering on the metal as he let his arm swing down. His breath was short and shaky, his bowels loose. He felt sick in the aftermath of adrenaline.

The ork seemed bigger in death than it had in life. It certainly smelled a lot worse. Bannick suppressed a smile as he wondered how in the Emperor's name they were going to get the thing out of there. He was struck by the ludicrous nature of his situation. That Vorkosigen was trapped, and would likely have to remain there until they'd chainsawed the stinking cadaver apart, just made it all the more absurd.

Aftershock. Relief. All normal. He'd often wondered why the watchmen and bodyguards back home had had such black humour. As an angry youth, he'd thought such behaviour unbefitting a gentleman like himself. He understood now; it was a coping mechanism, ancient and tested on billions of battlefields. He'd survived again. He would live. It helped one's sanity to find that funny.

From outside came the muffled rumble of tank engines, Imperial. Looked like they'd finally been stirred to action.

Vorkosigen glowered at him over the dead ork, face still blanched with battle-fear. Take some tankers out of a tank, crack them out of their thick armour, and they were as vulnerable as shelled sand-mites.

'Don't think this changes anything!' said the tech-adept, and clutched the cracked screen of the tarot reader to him protectively.

Bannick shook his head. He was getting the measure of Vorkosigen. The tech-adept did not like him, and that was getting to be a problem. He was about to ask him whether he ought to shoot him and solve his problem, when a clang sounded from behind him.

'Lieutenant,' said a voice. Bannick turned to see Ganlick hanging head down through the forward access, eye swollen shut, blood running off his respirator to drip on the floor.

'Ganlick. You're alive.'

'Yeah. Basdack greenie pulled me out of the turret and chucked me over the side like I was a slowtail pup. Didn't come down to finish me off. His mistake. Thank the Emperor I had my knife and pistol on me. I got his buddy. You?'

'Marsello's dead.'

Ganlick shook his head, looked genuinely regretful. That was that, grieving put away to be endured later. The soldier's way.

Bannick inclined his head towards the dead alien. 'Looks like we both lived to tell the tale.'

'Yeah,' said the taciturn gunner. 'Anyways, fighting's moved off aways from us. Cortein's here. Wants to see you.'

Bannick stood up again, reholstered his pistol, nodded his assent. He grimaced as his vox earpiece squealed, static pushed back. The Leviathan's powerful comms suite was back on line. Orders flowed like water, directing a counter-attack.

'And Bannick,' said Ganlick. 'Don't get sand on my seat again.'

INTERSTITIAL

011000011001111010110>01110=37Alpha5[[[
TF01101100<0110001}}IFChecksum14<two=//
thenvocalisation::'hoorah'

Magos Eurakote Steelmaster celebrates the naming of the
Hellhammer Ostrakan's Rebirth.

CHAPTER 13

KALIDAR IV, WESTERN HEMISPHERE ARMY GROUP
CAMP, MACAREE'S TABLELANDS
3329397.M41

The camp was a flurry of activity as Bannick jumped off the skirts of *Mars Triumphant* and onto the sand. He adjusted his rebreather as he walked towards Cortein, who stood next to an angry Hannick.

Tanks ground round and about. Squads of infantry ran past, heading over to the far side of the Leviathan where the last few orks were holding out.

Ostrakan's Rebirth billowed smoke, weapons pointed at useless angles, left track blown off, engine block plating twisted. Already Adeptus Mechanicus enginseer teams were about it, assessing the damage as its blackened, shaken crew were helped off, their dead comrades preceding them in body sacks, stern-faced proctors taking them for their final blessing.

Cortein stood with Hannick, the pair of them staring at the wrecked Hellhammer. 'I don't believe what I am seeing,' said Hannick. 'What did they do to my tank?' his voice was cold and level, mouth twisted into a near-snarl.

'I hear the damage is not as bad as it appears, honoured captain,' said Cortein. He nodded to Bannick as he came up alongside his clansman.

Hannick gave Cortein a hard stare. 'It is not so much the fact of what they did, but that they could do it at all. Where were our sentries? Colonel Gemael, he was in charge of setting camp. Best put the wolves in charge of the flock! Damned fool!'

'The orks used the storm to slip into the camp.' Cortein's face betrayed nothing of what he thought.

'That does not mean that we should not have been prepared. Blast it! Thrice blast it! Dogmatic fools leading us, green recruits, damnable weather! Basdack orks! We should have been laagered!'

'That's unusually strong for you, sir,' said Cortein drily. 'I did suggest we not follow the orders, leave the reactors online, and lay up the crew at hand with the vehicles.'

'You're enjoying this far too much, Cortein,' said Hannick. They'd fought together for years. This was one occasion when Hannick wished he'd listened to his second. 'Bah!' he shouted. 'Look what they did to my tank! How many times have you seen *Ostrakhan's Rebirth* in such a state?' Hannick gestured at the Hellhammer. Fire suppressant was being foamed onto its blast sites, smothering the remaining flames hiding in its cracked armour. 'How many times? Never, never has my engine been so shamed!' He walked forwards a few paces, hands behind his head. 'This was supposed to be clear territory.'

'Sir,' said Cortein. Then to Bannick, 'Do not worry about Hannick. He's a fine battlefield commander but the finer points of logistics have never come easy to him and he can let his temper run. From time to time the dignity of command escapes him.' He paused. 'I am sorry to hear about Marsello.

He would have made a fine tanker, given time. You did what you could, and you are still alive.'

Bannick stood a little straighter, but said nothing.

'It is war,' said Cortein, quietly, 'comrades die all the time, so do friends. Don't worry if you don't feel it. When there's a pause, a quiet time, that's when it'll hit you, the crew'll be there for each other when it does.' He gripped Bannick's shoulder and stood back.

'Sir,' said Bannick.

'Yes?'

'Vorkosigen. He's getting to be a problem.'

Cortein started to speak, but Hannick was making his way back to them. 'Later,' he said.

Hannick turned his back on his wounded tank and ran a hand over his face, stopping at his respirator. He found it loose, and that gave him something to concentrate on. He regained his calm as he tightened the straps and eventually noticed Bannick. 'Lieutenant,' he said. 'You did a good job here, as well as can be expected. As probably the next honoured lieutenant in my command, judging by the rate at which we are losing men, you're to accompany us to an emergency staff meeting. We're all to go, we tankers, so we'll just wait for Marteken and then we'll find out what in the Emperor's name we're going to do to these green whoresons to pay them back for that.' He pointed at his tank. 'I do not take kindly to having my armour so mishandled.'

'Sir! Sir!' Radden and the other tankers came jogging from the direction of the barracks. Ralt had a minor wound to his right shoulder, and clutched at it. Epperaliant carried a las-carbine ready, and looked about him warily, peering into the night. The rest had their pistols out, all had their respirators and goggles on, but, roused directly from the rec tents, most did not have their coats, their bare arms reddened by the stinging sand. 'The orks, the basdack greenskins, they attacked the barracks, thirty or so, like ghosts! In and out of the storm…' Radden panted, out of breath in Kalidar's oxygen-poor air. 'We got them though, we got them all. Thanks be to the Throne that those Atraxian boys fight better than they play cards.'

'*Mars Triumphant*?' said Ralt carefully.

'Fine,' said Cortein. '*Ostrakhan's Rebirth* was damaged, though. We're going to need Brasslock and the Munitorum crews. Where is he?'

'You don't know?' said Radden.

Epperaliant glanced from Radden to Cortein. 'There's something you need to see.'

The Adeptus Mechanicus quarters had been hit along with other key areas of the camp. It appeared the orks had known what to expect from the arcane weaponry of the tech-adepts, for the orkish dead there were larger and more heavily armed and armoured than the bodies Bannick saw elsewhere, and there were a lot of them. Stripes of fused sand marked the ground where the tech-priests had unleashed their ancient power. Warrior-servitors stood blank-faced, weapons ready, uncaring of their broken comrades.

Urtho lay still, his muscular body shrunken in death, child-like in its appearance, curled protectively round the blackened rent in his belly. His heavy bolter had been wrenched from its mount and lay in pieces several feet away from his body. His left shoulder had been reduced to a tangle of wires and bent metal from which a nub of pink-white bone protruded. The interface plug cap had been torn from the end of his truncated humerus, revealing raw marrow to the air. Sheltered from the wind in the lee of an Adeptus Mechanicus shelter, sand had yet to crust over his remains.

A circle of dead orks three-deep lay around the servitor,

many bearing the telltale signs of bolter fire: large craters in their bodies, limbs blown off, heads missing. Those nearer-by had their eyes gouged and skulls crushed. The sand all about was sticky with blood.

'Look like he gave a good account of himself,' said Radden quietly.

Other servitors stomped about, hauling the bodies back, mindlessly repairing the shelter, heedless of the storm.

'Servitor 00897 "Urtho" slew fourteen of the enemy.' Magos Rotar stood with them – Epperaliant, Cortein, Radden and Bannick, the rest having been detailed to see to the tank. 'An above-average score for one of his build model. Unfortunately we believe his bolter malfunctioned. It is a Delta-Ceres pattern, a type known to be unreliable in sandy conditions. Still, his efficacy in close combat was admirable. We will salvage what we can and incorporate his abilities into our next design.' He had no human voice, he spoke as a machine.

'And Brasslock was taken?'

The magos bowed from the waist and augmitted a series of binaric howls, each communications string interrupted as he listened for a reply. Probably carries an internal vox, thought Bannick. The magos's head had been covered, or possibly replaced, it was impossible to tell, by a dark metal dome studded with ocular sensors. One arm bore a large claw, clasping a bloodied, cog-toothed axe, the other was hidden within its crimson sleeve. On his back he wore a heavy servo-harness, the four limbs and the tools at their tips twitching and swaying with a life of their own. This is what they mean when they say the flesh is weak, thought Bannick. There's not much man left in those robes. The magos made him feel uneasy, and he'd been around tech-priests all his life, he bore their symbol about his neck next to his aquila. But this, this was too much.

'His datapipe ceased to display forty three minutes ago;

four minutes, twenty-two seconds after this servitor unit went offline. I answer affirmatively to your query, I believe he was taken.'

'You do not seem concerned,' said Bannick.

'The flesh is weak. Emotional response is born from the flesh. He will live, or he will die. It matters not. His uploads were frequent, his knowledge will live on, that is the primary concern of all the adepts of Mars, the persistence of knowledge for the greater glory of the Omnissiah. Our lives are nothing but filaments in the shining racks of enlightenment. One component breaks, another can be found.'

Bannick fought back an urge to grab the metal man and shake him. He had liked Brasslock. Despite his allegiances he had possessed a deep sense of humanity that this creature did not display. Magos Rotar was less of a man than Urtho had been.

The magos caught his expression, and misinterpreted it. 'Do not concern yourself, lieutenant. There are enough drone units to see to the proper activation of your war machine.' He shrieked again, earsplitting audible databursts. Three servitors ceased work abruptly, turned on their heels as one and walked off into the storm. Dawn was breaking, natural light swamping the electric glow of the camp lights. Still the servitors vanished from view after walking only a few metres.

'Come on,' said Cortein. 'There's not much more we can accomplish here.'

Bannick joined Cortein and Hannick for the army group briefing aboard the *Magnificence*, taking him for the first time into the command tower at the front of the massive vehicle. The tower extended two extra floors above the vehicle's broad back, the majority of the lower one occupied by the Chamber of Strategies, the nerve centre of the Guard force on Kalidar.

The chamber was open to the bridge of the Leviathan, sat fore and above on the second extra floor of the tower, wide windows affording a broad view of the land below, although these currently had their armoured shutters down against the storm, for Kalidar's fury was potent enough to scour even armaglass blind. The bridge was the province of the Leviathan commander, his command crew and staff occupying its twenty-six stations, controlling weaponry, motivation and all other functions appertaining to the governance of the vehicle in motion and in battle. Spaduski had been correct in describing it as a ship of the land. Commander UvTerra stood up there now, issuing orders to his own officers, their activity frantic as they attempted to verify the security situation within and without the vast vehicle, and to begin repairs. The orks had let off two bombs inside, demolished one of the three main entryways, and shattered a track with carefully timed explosions as they retreated.

Rails ran along the circular platform at the back, guarding the four-metre drop down to the floor of the long ellipse of The Chamber of Strategies. The chamber was as crowded with ostentatious decoration as it was with machinery and men. Here the assembled generals and senior staff of the Imperial Army Group directed hundreds of thousands of men in their war against the ork. Bridge and chamber together occupied one complex space, their division from each other effected by their differing heights. Curling stairs ran either side of the room, allowing access between the two, for direct communication between the commander in chief and Leviathan captain were vital. The stairs passed twin galleries of servitor-manned stations around the mid height of the room, where once-free men were plugged directly into the vehicle, their minds wiped, modified brains accommodating many of the complicated systems integration tasks the Leviathan's logicators could not manage alone.

Ranks of other stations, manned by uniformed staff officers, ran either side of the chamber floor, a massive chart desk occupying the middle. A prognosticator-logistician formed of vat-grown man and machine, spider-limbed and gangling, hung from a nest of cables in the roof, from where it could dart down to any point on either raised bridge or lowered chart room. This cyborg was, to all intents, the mind of *Magnificence*.

Electronic comms and tac-suites took up much of the chamber's capacity, where communications operatives waged their own war with Kalidar's ceaseless scream, trying to keep lines of informational traffic open between the hive cities, the Leviathan, the fleet and the various subdivisions of the battle group.

A short corridor at the end of the chamber led to an Astropathic relay, the fortress-vehicle being of sufficient size to host its own psychic communications link. Below the bridge, fire control for the command fortress's macro cannon was situated, the cannon itself taking up most of the four decks at the front of the Leviathan below the tower.

At the request of Sanctioned Psyker Logan, part of the screening surrounding the relay had been removed. Astropath Prime Mastraen himself was within the relay chamber, two other astropaths with him, singing out a screen of psychic interference that wove with the lorelei's natural warp harmonics. They were hoping to drown out the thoughts of the assembled commanders, hiding their plans from whatever was watching. The atmosphere was oppressive with psychic might, the assembled officers experiencing nausea and odd, phantom sensations. They struggled to concentrate on Captain-General Iskhandrian, who stood on a railed pulpit backing onto the Astropathic relay, flanked by two Guards Paramount, their armoured faces a mass of lenses and carapace plating. Clustered around them were five Ministorum priests, quietly muttering prayers, while behind them modified youths waved censers of incense from mechanical limbs. A vat-cherub hovered above, weeping over the scroll of the recent dead.

'This raid was a valuable, if costly, lesson to us,' said the general. He leaned heavily against the dark bronze lectern at the pulpit front, looking more exhausted than before. He was still in his dress uniform, now spattered with ork blood. A team of ork commandoes had disabled the security spirits on a hatch very much like that which Bannick had used, worked their way in as far as the command deck's armoured doors, catching the general and his staff as they made their way up. The Guard Paramount had made short work of the intruders, killing fourteen orks for the loss of only five men, but four of them had been high-ranking officers. Any doubts Iskhandrian had had about orkish cunning had been firmly displaced. Not that he'd admit to ever having had any.

'The orks are far from beaten,' he continued. 'We can ill afford to be complacent. We will not be so taken again.' The gathered men nodded. All had noted the absence of the Atraxian Colonel Gemael, responsible for setting the camp. He had been one of those most vocal in denouncing reports of unusual ork tactics; several troopers had been condemned to death by him for voicing their concerns. Heresy, apparently, because until tonight the official line had been that orks don't understand stealth, because that what it said in the *Tactica*. That it said exactly the opposite elsewhere did not matter much; each volume of the work, and each revision of each volume, had its own adherents. Such inflexibility was dangerous.

'General Basteen and Castellan Sullio have been promoted to second and third in command. Ostilek, Gemael and Tulligen will face disciplinary charges on grounds of treasonous unadaptability. Let us not forget the *Tactica Imperium* teaches us this valuable lesson among the many others it provides us.

Let that be an end to it, and let us bring this war also to an end. Sanctioned Psyker Logan, please.'

Iskhandrian had a good record, had fought the orks before, a different kind of ork, so it turned out, but had a reputation as a hopeless dogmatist. The orks might have struck a blow against the Imperial effort on Kalidar with their raid, but it would be one that rebounded dangerously against them if it shook him out of his dogmatism. Typically, he made no mention of his own mistakes. It would be the lower-ranking generals who would pay; whether they encouraged him or not was irrelevant. The whole thing was wearily familiar, like the machinations of the clan nobility back home. The only difference was that duelling was outlawed in this particular battlegroup. The Atraxians thought it wasteful. Bannick, once a champion of such encounters, agreed.

At Iskhandrian's mention of his name, Logan rose up into the air on a platform at the end of a jointed arm and addressed the officers. 'Many of you were present at the banquet this evening when Sanctioned Psyker Maldon was killed. You may have realised he was slain by a surge of etheric energy, under the direction of an enemy witch.'

Several men in the room made the sign of the aquila.

'The agents of the ruinous powers?' said a horrified aide. 'A rogue witch, working with the orks?'

'Not in this instance,' said Logan. His voice was thick with effort. He shook as he spoke, still unrecovered from the psychic backlash he had experienced earlier. 'The mind we are dealing with is an orkish one, albeit vastly more powerful than the ordinary run of their psykers. Orks are capable of great psychic feats, indeed they are all mildly psychic.' He shuddered, as if he could hear their barbarous thoughts. 'Their state of excitement generates ever greater disturbances in the fabric of the warp. There are those orks who are attuned to this excitation of the warp, those that can channel it and unleash it to great destructive effect. But rarely are they capable of such fine manipulations – they draw in the power of those around them, spew it forth, and then they are spent. Explosive power is their art. Invading the mind of another and bending it to your will is a subtle skill, made all the more difficult if the mind in question is not that of one's own kind. This is something different, something more controlled.

'I have fought orks before, I have felt the minds of their warp-sensitives, I… That it can do this in a situation like this, through the warp eddies and mind-currents produced by the lorelei deposits on Kalidar… The way it knew exactly where our sentries were, the camp's defences, where to hit the *Magnificence*…' The remaining psyker looked from face to face, his own grey, crusts of blood round his nostrils. 'Frankly, gentlemen, this thing we face, it terrifies me.'

There were mutters from the assembled officers. Bannick had heard the rumours of the things psykers had to be strengthened against, the nameless horrors that lived on the other side of the veil of reality, the same hideous creatures the Emperor himself battled against night and day for the sake of mankind's souls. For a sanctioned psyker of Logan's rank to admit such fear was alarming.

Iskhandrian spoke again. 'From consultation with Sanctioned Psyker Lord Logan, and Astropath Prime Mastraen, it has become apparent that the orks are aware of our every move. That is how they knew just where to spring the ambush at the Kostoval Flats. How they knew where we would be tonight, even amid this storm. They have known of our exact disposition time and again, and they are intelligent enough to deploy that knowledge in battle. It is imperative that we destroy this capability.'

'We pray to our most beneficent Emperor that the precautions we have taken to shield this briefing from the prying mind that watches us will be sufficient,' said Logan. 'All of you here who are not to take part in the captain-general's plan will have to remain in the Chamber of Strategies until the culmination of that plan.'

'We will detail this plan to those it truly concerns at the end of this briefing,' said Captain-General Iskhandrian. 'Firstly, new intelligence has come to light regarding the orks' reasons for invading Kalidar. I absolutely encourage you to think about this outside this room as often as possible. If some ork witch is peering into our minds, it will serve us well if they know we know what their ultimate objectives are here, and even more so if they become aware that we have means of blocking their information-gathering. Procurator Actual Eskolios will proceed with this brief.'

One of Iskhandrian's aides came forwards and took the place of the captain-general and his guards. He was an effete man in the immaculate uniform robes of a Munitorum official, a backroom quill-pusher who'd not set foot outside the command vehicle, thought Bannick, and judging by the muttering that greeted his appearance, he was not alone in his assessment. But when the Procurator Actual looked at the audience, he met the eyes of many of them, and those that stared back saw a keen mind. He cleared his throat delicately, poured a goblet of water from the lectern's carafe, drank it, and began.

'Gentlemen,' he said, without preamble, his quiet voice carrying across the hubbub of the command deck. 'I will first provide you with some background information regarding the habits of the ork. Please be aware that all information is classified. By all means think long and hard on what you are about to hear. But speak of it, and I will hear of it. And when I do, things will go ill for the man that talks out of turn.

'The ork has been the enemy of mankind since time

immemorial, whatever encounter sparked our struggle against their kind now lost to time. It is doubtful any peaceful resolution could have been achieved. The orks are born warriors.' The chart table burst into light, a life-size depiction of a mature greenskin leaping into the air, where it rotated. Pict-captures of orks in battle, sub-types of orks and their machinery slowly turned round its feet. 'Bigger, stronger, and tougher than any man, save the Angels of Death, they are far deadlier than we prefer to acknowledge. Tell your average man the truth, and we would quickly run out of soldiers.'

Bannick thought of the *Imperial Infantryman's Uplifting Primer*, issued in its billions to soldiers across the Imperium, his own copy thrown on the floor and abandoned by Radden when he came to collect him to serve on *Mars Triumphant*. Propaganda, pure and simple.

'However, you have faced them in battle, and killed them. You know that they are not undefeatable. Perhaps you will forgive our white lies.' Eskelios smiled, his lips weirdly pink on his papery face.

'It is speculated by the Magos Biologis of the Adeptus Mechanicus that the orks are a survivor species, an artificially created race designed by a long-dead civilisation. The whys and wherefores of this are not relevant here; what is relevant is how this affects their distribution, and actions. Part of their survival mechanism is the way that they spread themselves; it is common knowledge that orks are to be found across the known galaxy. Everywhere man goes, there is found ork, and if there is no ork, it can be guaranteed that there will be soon.

'The orks migrate in waves, and if they retreat for a while the next tide mark will always be higher than the last.' The chart table's display changed, showing a small world, icons and text designating it as an ork planet. 'Orks will arrive on a world like this. They will increase in number, they will fight the original inhabitants and, when victorious, amongst themselves. War will intensify, until one ork establishes himself leader of all. The orks will then leave. They direct themselves only insomuch as they invade planets conducive to furthering their crusade – resource-rich manufacturing worlds are preferred targets. A crusade, having gained momentum, will assault systems with ever greater strategic value, some psychic mechanism attracting more orks to the flag of the conqueror. It had been assumed that this was the case here, with Gratzdakka's attack on the Kalidar system. The standard approach to such an infestation of this class of world is abandonment, virus bombing, then reoccupation.' The chart table cycled through a number of scenarios that could trigger an ork war-migration.

'But that does not take into account the lorelei. The deposits found here are vital to the production of psychically attuned weaponry, making this world valuable to the Imperium. Richer worlds have been condemned to the rightful purge of Exterminatus when thus overrun, but ongoing crusades have need of the resources this world produces. Every day, the Imperium pushes further and further into the unknown, and in the dark we meet strange adversaries with great powers of mind, taxing our own psychic capabilities. This world is therefore strategically vital.'

Bannick had suspected as much; it wasn't hard to fill in the picture of why they were there, as Ganlick had said. Kalidar had little to offer, the system's abundance of minerals common throughout the Imperium. Except the lorelei.

'The lorelei. That is the reason we fight here. Until now we assumed that the orks had come here by chance, an inconvenience.

'We now think differently. This invasion is something away from the orkish norm. We believe that they too have come for the crystals.'

The chart table flickered, and suddenly the room was filled with a four-metre representation of the ork Titan that Bannick had faced on the Kostoval Flats, eyes glaring, as terrifying as it was in real life. Pict-capture of the Titan taken from a command vehicle somewhere on the front cycled over and over, ending after thirty seconds with massive weapons discharge in a flash of white.

'We suspect that the ork engine utilises large numbers of the crystals in its emitter arrays,' continued Eskelios. 'Until the attack on Maldon and the raid, we suspected that this was just the passing fancy of one of their maverick engineers, a machine to tap into the warp, perhaps. We have seen it before.' A diagram of a bulky weapon, front-mounted with a propeller-like arrangement, each terminating in an iron-bound ball. 'Or to magnify the abilities of a group of their shaman-psykers. But the attack, coupled with the constant foreknowledge of the orkish forces, led us to suspect one mind. Astropath Prime Mastraen confirmed this today. Behind the psychic noise put out by Kalidar's lorelei deposits, and the roar of the orkish war-call, we have detected a single, powerful mind looking at us from the immaterium. This is why we are not able to break the deadlock here on Kalidar. The same psychic signature has been detected from this ork Titan,' he indicated the engine, huge and scowling at the centre of the room. 'This situation has to change.'

Eskelios stepped down.

'For some time,' Logan spoke again, 'our Schola Psykana prognosticators have been unable to see a clear course. We had thought their foresight to be somewhat affected by Kalidar's, ah, unique circumstances. Now we believe it to be partly the influence of this mind, partly because they had not all the variables to hand. Having taken these factors into account, we are now able to plot a path through the uncertainties of this war to victory. There is great interference in the warp. It takes more than natural interference to accomplish this on the local scale, as we see here. This witch is employing a device, we are sure.' Grainy picts of the ruined surface town and central well of the conquered hive flickered onto the chart desk's display. 'The centre of the hive has been gutted. The orks are moving large amounts of material into the cavity. These picts were taken four days ago by a specially adapted Lightning fighter on a reconnaissance run. Our commsat network about the world has been severely compromised by the ork fleet – aircraft, as you know, gentlemen, are limited in the time they can spend in Kalidar's atmosphere. Our good fortune, in this case, because the ork air defence is rudimentary – they do not think we can put up significant airpower.'

They'd be right about that, thought Bannick. Dust, crazy EM fields, solar flaring and contrary, multi-level laminar windflows had put paid to any attempt to dominate the skies of Kalidar.

'But this Lightning came back, engine fans glassed, with these pictures. It shows some kind of device that we now believe to be a psychic amplifier. This device, part contructed as it is, is to blame for our growing difficulty in utilising psychic communications, but we fear it might also have… darker purposes. This must be our primary target. However, it is protected by a grade omicron psychic umbrella.' Graphics whirled up, depicting a cross-section of the hive, a visualisation of the device at its base. 'This effect is more potent a defence that a fourteen-layer deep void shield array. The ork witch is undoubtedly the source of it, until he is dead….' He shook a little, and mopped at his brow. 'Strike at his engine, kill him, and we disable the field.' He dipped his head. 'And that is all I can tell you at this time.'

Another of Iskhandrian's aides took to the podium. He read out a long list of names. 'Those men whose names are upon the list I have delivered must leave the briefing. We repeat that none of this be discussed outside this room.' He repeated the list. The greater part of the group filed out.

Bannick's name, and Cortein's, were not on that list.

Iskhandrian took to the podium again. 'Gentlemen, I shall now detail to you the plan...'

INTERSTITIAL

ii) In the event of a challenge being issued, so long as the challenger and instigator of the challenge holds valid license, legally ratified by two members of recognised enforcement agencies, to engage in personal combat with a man of equal social standing and rank, should any harm come to either party, neither the challenger nor the challenged shall come under the scrutiny of the law for their actions; both shall be held as righteous in thought, intent, and deed, no matter the outcome.

Paragonian constitution,
'Codicils Regarding Rightful Duelling'

CHAPTER 14

ARONIS CITY, PARAGON VI
2005395.M41

Bannick staggered out of the cathedral. The day was dusk-dim. On the horizon, Mater Maxima sank from sight, a thin corona of hard light on its bloated curve a promise of the Glory Seasons to come, but promises kept no one warm.

Glory, when the sun was unobstructed, was weeks away. Frozen Paragon would continue to inch its way around the gas giant, a process that took the best part of two Terran years, the moon-world's own axial tilt seasonally plunging the temperatures deeper. On the light side of the gas giant, during the Glory Seasons, the Paragonians termed these seasonal variations individually: Growth, Little Summer, Second Growth, Little Fall, Little Winter, twice the planet went through these before Mater Maxima smothered it with the darkness of eclipse and the Long Winter began its twenty-three months. The years of the Long Winter also contained a series of five seasons, but the Paragonians had no names for them. Winter was winter, and it was long and cold at that.

Bannick's lungs burnt with the chill. He clamped the body of a slowtail, a small animal native to Paragon, between his teeth, breathing through it to warm the air. He regretted losing his gloves in the Gardens of the Vermillion Moon. His body shivered, but he paid it no attention, his dishonour worse than the chill.

He walked along frozen canals. Paragon was turning its back on what little light Mater Maxima let by, and true night was falling. A few skaters sported on the ice, a skiff ground by, hull raised up on winter blades, but people were hurrying home, bundles of fur barely recognisable as human. Bannick wandered slowly, feet leading him where they would, one thing on his mind and one thing only.

Tuparillio, lying dead on the grass, blue stained crimson.

The insides of Bannick's nostrils were raw with the cold, the clouds of his breath transformed to ice crystals. The chase hadn't given him chance to put his furs on properly. His teeth were beginning to chatter. If he didn't get inside soon he'd be found frozen hard as stone by the Dawn Watch.

He thought about finding somewhere quiet and letting the Long Winter do its work. He was empty inside, shame chilling him far more than the cold. He doubted. He did not deserve to live.

But Bannick did not stop. He wandered through icy arcades. The night grew blacker. Powdery snow began to fall, so cold on the skin it pricked like needles. The canals broadened out, became the floating harbour, the buildings rippling upwards, pregnant with the promise of warmth and comfort, and Bannick knew where he was.

The House of Mostinick rose up before him. Had it only been a day since he was here? It seemed a lifetime ago.

It called to him, its drink and girls and machine-breathed warmth. Comforts of a life he'd lost yesterday.

He looked at his fingertips. He'd left his gloves behind. They were blue, as numb as his heart. *Get inside!* part of him urged, *Live and serve!* and he obeyed, dragging his feet up to the carven gates. Unbidden, his hand rose up and pulled upon the bellcord.

A vision panel slid back. The eyes it revealed widened and the door opened.

'Master Artem Lo Bannick! What has occurred to you? Quickly, in! In!' The door master peered out into the street, checking to see if Bannick had been seen; it would do his master's business little good if the gossip casts picked up on his dishevelled appearance, for it would lead to pressure from the boy's clan.

The door master ushered the shivering aristocrat in, and the door rumbled closed on toothed wheels. Sealed, the door master activated the inner-entry of the heat lock, and warmth, lho-smoke, music, and laughter came washing out.

'Have you been mugged sir? Shall I call out the Night Watch? Were you hurt?' the door master, used to shepherding young nobles drunken into the night, had adopted something of an avuncular air towards his master's clients. He grasped at Bannick's shoulders. Bannick pushed his hand away when it strayed too close to the stick bandage on his cheek.

'I'm fine, I'm fine. Thank you, Colleteno.' He adopted a light manner, trying to approximate the way he'd been every other time he'd been when patronising Mostinick's.

'Oh, sir! Thank the Lords of Terra you are unhurt!' As he fussed at Bannick's fastenings Colleteno tipped a nod at a flunky within the inner-entry. Moments later a string of servants came back, bearing hot gleece and active thermal clothing. Bannick let them remove and stow his furs.

'Drink sir, drink!'

Bannick clumsily took the gleece goblet. He drank as the servants placed the vest on him, clipping its battery to his waist. Pain erupted along his fingertips as the vest and gleece cup warmed his body, his cut cheek burning.

'Thank you, Colleteno.'

'That's better, sir. The colour is returning to your face.' He took Bannick's goblet, and frowned at the bandage. 'Are you sure you are well, sir?'

Bannick moved his face out of the light. 'It's nothing. I cut myself on my calf skating on Zero Night.' He tried for a smile, but it cracked his face like ice breaking on water. 'I had taken a lot of gleece.'

'Very well, sir. Your friend Master Kalligen is here. Shall I inform him you have arrived, Master Bannick?'

Bannick nodded. A servant departed, bearing the message.

Bannick followed a girl into the dim red lighting of the House. The inner-entry clunked shut, leaving Colleteno to his vigil on the gate.

In a small welcome suite he was led to a large padded chair. He sat, and more servants, all female this time, attended to him, bathing and rerobing him in soft indoor clothes. He batted them away when they became amorous. He began to feel better.

He waved off their offers of further services, promises to fetch his regular girls. 'Not tonight,' he said. 'I would like to join my friend. Take me to him.'

One of the girls took him back out into the House. Stairs twined languorously round the bulging, fluidly formed walls, leading to the other entertainment levels, each one more debauched than the last

Down on the ground floor, people sat and drank, ate, smoked and gambled. Aside from a bathhouse out the back, the floor was dominated by a single room, divided into booths by curtains and screens. Large carven buttress roots from the tropical jungles held up the ceiling. A band played tranquil music in one corner.

Lazlo Kalligen sat at the back of the room, screened off by

swags of gauze and fretted wood. He smiled when he saw his friend, but his eyes were troubled, and he was paler than usual.

'What the blazes have you done to yourself?' he demanded.

'It's nothing,' said Bannick, and his wound throbbed.

Lazlo stared at the bandage on his cheek. 'Duelling?'

Bannick nodded. It was enough.

'You won again, I take it?' Kalligen took a drink. 'I knew you'd get yourself hurt eventually, good as you are.' Ordinarily cheerful, Kalligen was subdued, no outburst of heretical irony for his friend today. 'I would have come out to meet you but, you know, I've got a drink.' Glazed eyes and a slight slur to his words said it was the latest of many. 'Gleece for my friend,' he said to the server. 'Warmed, quickly now! He looks, well…' he peered at Bannick in the gloom. 'You look like shit.'

'Where did you get to last night?' said Bannick, and slid himself onto a velvet-upholstered bench opposite his friend.

'Ah, sorry. I met a young lady who proved most… interesting.' Kalligen gave a tired chuckle. 'I'm not in a good way myself, really, really not. I better enjoy this drink, because it's the last I'll be getting for a long time. They don't like the cadets drinking. I'm attempting to fill up on all the drinks I'm going to miss out on. I reckon I've about five thousand to go. Fancy helping me out?'

A tray bearing a salver of heated gleece and a goblet arrived at the table. Bannick poured himself a drink and gulped it down, surprising himself with his thirst for it. Let them bring more.

Kalligen sat up, his face bordering on petulant. 'Aren't you going to ask me what this is all about? "Ooh, why the melodrama Lazlo? What ails you?" And so forth? The usual friendly business?'

'No, I'm not. Your behaviour is nothing out of the ordinary.' He looked around the bar, searching for accusing looks but finding none.

'Hey! Pay attention! I'm suffering here.' Kalligen leaned forwards, picked up his own jug and eyed it speculatively. He tipped a few drips into his cup, put the salver aside and grabbed Bannick's off his tray, filling up the goblet carelessly, slopping the daily pay of a foundryman's worth onto the table.

'Fine. What's wrong?' he asked. 'The training lasts three months, you'll be back in here in no time, with a nice haircut and shiny boots to impress the ladies with; not even you can drink five thousand servings of gleece in three months.'

'Ah, now my foster-brother, that is where you are wrong.' Kalligen's eyes glistened in the dark. 'I won't be drinking for some time, and certainly not here.'

'Lazlo, I'm not some doxy who'll give you a sympathy fumble. The planetary defence militia never leaves its homeworld. That's why it's called a planetary defence militia. It's for defending the planet.'

Kalligen blew out a shaky breath. It was his turn to peer into the dimly lit room. Certain they were not being overheard, he looked his friend in the eye. 'Col, I'm not going into the militia. They're calling a general draft, I was told this morning. Apparently my father's known for days, but he didn't want to spoil "my last Zero Night".' He rumbled out his impression of his father, serious and gravelly. 'There'll be a general newscast announcement tomorrow. Your uncle's coming back. The 322nd Armoured, 62nd and 84th Mechanised Regiments and the 7th Super-heavy Company are coming home, along with a bunch of offworlders.' He took a gulp of gleece. 'They've already broken warp and are inbound from the Paragon Reaches. The Dentares war is over, but they need fresh meat for some place called Kalidar. Seems home is on the way. All militia applications have been transferred to the Departmento Munitorum for processing with immediate effect. My clan exemption's invalid, because apparently I already agreed to be a soldier.' He gave a pained smile. 'So I'm not going into the militia. I'm off into the Throne-blasted Guard, Emperor save me. I'll never be coming home again.'

A sudden thought seized Bannick. Perhaps the confessor had been correct, opportunity did present itself at the behest of the Emperor. Maybe this was it, his chance to atone, to serve.

'Who are they taking?'

'Does it matter?' Kalligen shrugged. 'Anyone, everyone. It's to be a double raising, a tank regiment and mechanised infantry, plus fill-ins for the holes in the ranks of existing units. I've a cousin in tithing, he's been up every night all week banging psych-messages out through the astropath relay to the sector Munitorum central officium. Reading between the lines, and he always does, our boys took a real hammering out there. You know they prefer to keep troops from certain worlds together, they need reinforcing before they're redeployed, a surprise visit home after a victorious war will do a world of good on the propaganda fronts, we're on the way to Kalidar... I'm sure the Lord is happy about that too, after all that business with his brother. It all makes perfect, perfect sense. For them, at any rate. For me, well, I'm shafted.' He looked up quickly. 'You tell anyone this, they will execute you, and me, so please don't, there's a good fellow, I'd hate to die at home when I can be gunned down out there in the stars. For the Emperor!' he added loudly, raising his goblet. There were murmured acknowledgements from the rest of the room. 'See, I'm going to be a bloody hero!' He slammed back his drink and threw the cup onto the table with a clatter.

Bannick's mind raced. He was sure his killing of Tuparillio would be adjudged dishonourable. Ever since the fight, he'd been wondering what he could do to get away from his actions, and atone for them. This was a sign, this is what the Emperor wanted for him. 'Lazlo, I am going to come with you.'

'What?' shouted Kalligen. Eyes and faces turned towards them, a break in the noise of the bar. He dropped his voice to a hard whisper. 'Are you insane? Next year you're to marry the warden of Clan Turannigen! You'll be Clan Auditor of Bannick *and* Head of Turranigen before you're sixty, and then it'll be half a century of dancing girls and fancy banquets before you can even think about dying. By all means, give all that up so some stinking alien can turn your head into a drinking cup!' he slapped the table hard and pushed himself back, exasperated. 'You're tired, you look like death. It's pre-wedding nerves, that's all.' Kalligen spoke quickly, reassuring himself more than Bannick. 'Some way to serve the Emperor outside of a ledger. Boyhood nonsense. Don't do it. Let me out there to die alone, I'll be happier knowing that you are still having a good time. It'll be a comfort in my foxhole. Anyway, your father will never approve.'

Bannick knew all too well what his father was going to say, on a great many matters. 'The duel, Lazlo.'

'And? What's that got to do with anything? You duel all the time!'

'Not any more,' he said, and he told him how Tuparillio had died.

Kalligen drew in a deep breath. 'Looks like the two-headed eagle shat on both of us, my foster-brother. And for that, I need a basdack drink. Pass me the jug.'

INTERSTITIAL

By the flicker of the tarot, the common body of men scries
the will of the Master of Mankind, and takes direction
from its readings of his divine purpose for all, each and
every one. All can be enlightened. All can know the truth!
Reader prices start at 27 Estrillian Newmarks.
Customisation options numerous.

Extract from an Atraxian catalogue of devotional items.

CHAPTER 15

KALIDAR IV, PENUMBRIC BADLANDS
3335397.M41

Bannick awoke, disoriented, to a thick fug of stale air and fumes. It was totally dark, he was trapped in a slender space that jounced and bumped. Was he dead? He'd been dreaming of Paragon, the sun on the sea in the Glory, a party on the shore with Kalligen, warm girls, hot sand, the cold of winter a distant memory. He hadn't prayed so much then, it hadn't seemed so important, and for a few seconds it wasn't important again. It seemed like the last three years had not happened at all, and he was the boy he had been, and that war was a distant story that filled him with the need for glory and pushed him on to drill and drill with his swordmaster; that the duel he fought had not been fought, and fighting was still a game.

The bunk – he was in one of *Mars*'s three narrow bunks, mattress slick with the oils of engines and other human beings. The smell brought him crashing into the present.

His mind cleared to the squeal of drivewheels on track as *Mars Triumphant* rode up onto rocks and crushed them to powder. His head took longer to attain clarity than it should, the after-effects of the drugs they'd all been forced to take lingering long.

They were two weeks into their journey, and still he wasn't over the drugs. A sleeping mind would tell the ork witch little, the confusion of human dreams too obtuse a puzzle to solve. All aboard but Outlanner had been tranquillised for three days. Bannick wondered if orks dreamt. Only the drivers and Captain Exertraxes, the man in command of the expedition, had remained awake. Cortein, designated second in command, had been put under, growling darkly while the medics hyposprayed him. He and Bannick had been dosed right there and then in the Chamber of Strategies, the crew shortly after.

Exertraxes had their path as a series of the waypoints, the coordinates to the next stage of their journey contained in a sealed envelope to be opened when a waypoint had been reached. The drivers had been told nothing of their destination, only that Exertraxes was in command and that they were to follow his orders to the letter. Once they'd arrived on the forbidden zone around the basin, a place so thick with lorelei they thought not even the ork witch could see there, it didn't matter who knew what. Three days later everyone else came round, stiff and sore from being unconscious at station, bladders painfully full or accidentally voided in sleep despite the anti-diuretics and hibernation shots. The dreams the lorelei brought had them screaming in their sleep as often as not, or more perniciously activated long-dormant memories of happier times, making the men surly and withdrawn when they awoke to the reality of their situation.

It was an unhappy start to an unhappy journey.

The storm that had begun the night of the ork attack howled with obscene vigour round the task force – *Mars Triumphant*, a company of Leman Russ, a platoon of fifty mechanised

Atraxian heavy infantry and support vehicles, a lonely file of metal winding its way slowly across the immense desolate spaces of Kalidar, its cargo of men trapped inside, helpless as canned meat.

Once they were within the psychically turbulent penumbra of the Ozymandian Basin, those of them that hadn't been at the briefing had been told where they were going: Hive Meradon. Orktown. Right to the heart of the enemy's lair. It was the kind of suicide mission you'd like to be asked to volunteer for, but they hadn't been, and that didn't help the mood aboard the tank. Bannick was thankful he wasn't crammed into the back of one of the convoy's Chimeras. The squads in them had not been able to disembark since they set off; too risky. The wind out there would flay you alive.

He felt the need to pray now; he wondered how he had ignored it for so long as a boy and hoped it would not go against him. He did so, beseeching the Emperor for His aid in the coming battle and thanking Him for His continued protection.

Religious duty discharged, Bannick yawned and rubbed his eyes. He checked his timepiece; he'd had his five hours, his turn to go on watch in the turret, to relieve Radden. He reached up over his head, grasped the handles and twisted, opening the bunk hatch. He pulled himself out, a difficult manoeuvre for the corridor was barely sixty centimetres wide. He looked at the place where the ork had been dismembered, metal shiny where it had been scrubbed clean. Who'd done it, he didn't know, because he'd woken up in his chair and they were on the move. He was glad it hadn't been him. He banged on the lids of the other two bunks. From within Ganlick mumbled and Ralt swore. Bannick pulled himself up the steps into the command deck without waiting for them. Meggen, Cortein and Epparaliant were on the command deck, eyes straining against the shifting patterns on the tank's screens. Meggen sat in Bannick's chair, its back hastily repaired with wire and tape. Bannick looked at the station where Marsello had died. It too, was spotless, scrubbed out by an anonymous maintenance crew.

Nobody spoke, no one had shown the desire to for a week. The intense closeness raised tensions in the crew. Radden's incessant chatter had gone from mildly annoying to deadly irritating. The click of Vorkosigen's tarot deck drove them all to distraction. Ganlick had given up speaking at all, Ralt muttered obscenities round his lho-cigars, Meggen refused to come out of the shell locker, where he sat staring at the five lorelei shells they been issued with as if they'd suck his soul out. Not talking was the men's way of coping. Too much conversation would provide a gap for their tension to get out, and once it did, there'd be no putting it back; they were Paragonians to a man and they would fight. Even Radden had finally, mercifully, shut up.

It was oven-hot in the tank. The comfort of the crew, though low on the list of Adeptus Mechanicus priorities, had been taken into account by the Baneblade's aeons-dead creators, the air coolant and filtration systems being extensions of the machinery that allowed the tank to operate in myriad inhospitable environments. But *Mars Triumphant* was a thousand years old. Despite its venerable age, it had been imperfectly built to corrupted schematics, and Kalidar taxed its systems to the limit. The dust, finer than cosmetic powders, clogged the filtration units' intakes. Before the mission, they had been changed every other day. But time and the storm were against them. They could not get out and make camp. The air they were breathing was the same air they'd been breathing for a week, carbon dioxide processed over and again by the tank's ancient scrubbers. The air should have been dry and acerbic, but it was thick with unfiltered scent, the smell of men trapped in close quarters with each other, of rations and excretion, of stale breath and staler sweat. Lho-smoking was regarded as unhealthy back home on Paragon, but Bannick was glad of Ralt's habit, for it masked the stink of the tank. All the men were stripped down to vest and trousers. Sweaty, grimy, oily, no signifiers of rank to mark them apart, they all looked the same, gunner and lieutenant, commsman and loader: tired-eyed, dirty, jumpy.

Only Cortein spoke, only then to give orders or request data. He looked up from his scopes when Bannick came in, the others didn't.

'That time already?' said Cortein. 'The others?'

'Coming,' said Bannick.

'Fine.' Cortein peered at his chart desk for a while, a scratchy wire frame holograph of the landscape rolled over it. He pulled up a larger-scale representation of the terrain. The boulder-strewn plateaus and crazed canyons of the badlands round the edge of the Ozymandian Basin were beginning to peter out. 'We're coming up to level ground. It'll take several hours to cross before we reach the next shock ridge. I've decided to postpone full crew action until the next sleep cycle. We have to be prepared, all of us, before we go into the Ozymandian Basin proper. I'm moving up your rest period, Meggen.'

Meggen sagged with visible relief. 'Thank you, sir.'

'Bannick, before you relieve Radden, get down and tell Outlanner I want him asleep inside of half an hour. Ganlick can drive for a while.'

'Yes, honoured lieutenant.'

Bannick went down the stairs, backing up to let Ralt past, tapping Ganlick's shoulder before he went up.

'You're wanted up front,' he said. Together they went forwards, matching their footfalls to the judder and sway of the tank as it left the badlands.

Outlanner never came back from his driving position willingly, sleeping only when Cortein ordered him to, his mind wholly on the task of guiding *Mars Triumphant* blind through the storm. His eyes were intent on his main auspex scope. Smaller screens relayed real-time images from the tank's augur lenses, several of them dead from battle damage or dust scouring. Outlanner sat back in his driver's chair, a man at ease with his surroundings, fastidiously making small adjustments to the tank's heading, jinking it past outcrops and boulders with millimetres to spare. Bannick watched, fascinated, as he did whenever he came up front while Outlanner was driving. He'd not have thought it possible to move such a large machine with such precision.

'You two just going to stand there breathing? You're distracting me,' said the driver.

'You're coming off. Ganlick's taking over. The honoured lieutenant wants you asleep in half an hour.'

'Or what? 'Lick can't handle this kind of terrain.'

'Or he'll come down and read you a bedtime story, then he'll court-martial your sorry hide,' growled Ganlick. 'Move over.'

'This shock ridge is nearly done. We've a clear run before we hit the next, the last before we head down into the basin proper,' said Bannick.

'Move over,' said Ganlick.

Outlanner grunted. 'If you can handle it. Give me a moment.'

A few more nudges of the tank's drive levers, minute adjustments. He waited for a short run of clear terrain then locked the levers in position and stood. 'You're on.'

'You been drinking, Outlanner?' said Ganlick as he pushed past.

'Don't need no gleece.' He tapped at his temple. 'Driving keeps this occupied. I only drift when I'm bored. Nothing boring about this.'

Ganlick gave him a sour look, got into the driving seat and disengaged the drive locks. The motion of the Baneblade changed, becoming less smooth. Small bangs and squeaks sounded as Ganlick clipped rocks.

'Told you,' said Outlanner to Bannick. 'Too rough for 'Lick.'

Bannick put out his lip thoughtfully. Outlanner had a point. 'You sure you'll be okay?' he said.

'Those pips might give you the right to tell me what to do, but I've been on this tank for thirteen years. I can drive plenty good enough, don't listen to Outlanner. Besides, these canyons will give out soon enough, like you say. The Basin's an old impact crater, see? No, before you say it, not like where we fought the orks at the mine. This is the real deal, big old rock hit this place millions of years gone, hit it so hard it vaporised the planetary crust. These ridges are frozen rock ripples, like on water, you get me? It'll flatten out soon enough when we go into a trough, they're all full of sand. Damned dust is good for that, at least.'

'Fine, Ganlick.' Bannick and Outlanner made to go.

'Hey! Bannick!'

Bannick turned back. 'What?'

'You watch out. You see anything weird, you tell me, okay? This place is full of lorelei, pressure-formed by the impact, denser than the usual crystals, unholy work between the sun and the smash. It'll start to mess with our heads when we get close in, it's a psychic tar pit. You think the dreams we were having were bad? This place has much worse to throw at us, so I been told. They've tried to mine it plenty of times, always fails. Terra, they even tried building a hive out here, but the fields are too intense, messes up your mind, makes everyone a psyker, so they say! Armour will help, so will these.' He nodded at lorelei crystals hung round the cabin. 'Some kind of fracture pattern in the crystal generates the mind-fragging stuff. Having some of it about you interferes with its wave-front, at least some.'

Bannick smiled, Ganlick never ceased to surprise him. 'How do you find this stuff out, Ganlick?'

'Like I said, I ask around. You want to get yourself one of these.' Ganlick picked his sandscum amulet up off his chest and waved it. 'From what I hear, you'll start listening to me once we been through the basin.' He looked back at Bannick. 'Like looking into the warp, so they say, and there ain't nobody wants to do that.'

Outlanner and Bannick left Ganlick to it. Bannick helped the driver into his bunk. He grimaced as he closed it up. Hot-bunking wasn't pleasant, but at least they had bunks on the Baneblade. Leman Russ crew on forced advances were expected to sleep at their stations, if they slept at all.

He was about to go back up to the command deck when the clatter of Vorkosigen's tarot reader caught his attention. He suppressed his irritation. Cortein had told him to leave the little tech-adept alone, so he had, and he would.

'You're going to get us all killed,' came a voice from the gloom aft.

'Vorkosigen, leave it be,' said Bannick. He steadied himself on the tank walls as Ganlick clipped a rock. A deep boom sounded in the tank, like a bell tolling. The charms and fet-ishes of the aeons dangling from the ceiling and walls jingled nervously.

'You are going to kill us. These cards, the cards come up. They come up every time.' Another rattle. 'It's you, I'm sure of it.'

Vorkosigen stepped out from the munitions store, a cutting laser in one hand, tarot deck on the other, face lit from below by the light of the screen. 'Look!' he thrust the reader at Bannick. It was a cheap thing, fashioned from plastic, non-Paragonian, an unfamiliar design. The reader screen was cracked, scuffed to near opacity. Bannick watched as the the card icons rattled by with a noise like bone dice in a cup. Vorkosigen had it arranged in a standard nine-card 'H'-spread. The first card stuck. Guilliman's Wrath. A double-meaning card, for the wrath could be directed either way. The Blind Seer, the Extinguished Star, the Nova, the Lords of Terra, the Young Warrior, the Fortress of Faith, the Dishonoured Scion…

'I'm sorry,' said Bannick, holding up his hands, eyes fixed on the cutter the engineer held. 'I don't follow the tarot…'

Vorkosigen jabbed the tool threateningly towards Bannick. It was off, but he could activate it easily enough, and then it'd cut through plasteel. 'Look at the screen!'

'I said I don't follow the tarot,' repeated Bannick slowly. It was simple truth.

The cards had all locked into place. A grating, malfunctioning machine voice began to recite the card names, a precursor to a reading.

'Never mind! Watch again!'

Vorkosigen shook the deck. Again the cards rattled past.

The first card stuck. Guilliman's Wrath, top of the left stick of the 'H'.

'What do you see?'

Bannick shook his head.

'Look closely!'

Bannick watched the cards rattle into place again. 'It's the same reading,' he said.

'It is. Again.'

Once more the cards rattled. The first to come up was Guilliman's Wrath. The others followed suit.

'And again.' Vorkosigen rattled the card reader in Bannick's face, stepping closer in towards him. Bannick glanced at the cutter.

'A malfunction,' Bannick said calmly, although a chill ran down his spine. 'The reader looks in need of repair.'

'Its functions are unimpaired.' Vorkosigen dropped it, pulled a smaller reader from his belt, higher-tech, better made. 'Look at this. Look!' He pressed the button. The screen swirled and cleared, displaying the same reading. He pushed it into his belt, pulled out another. 'And this.' A third reader, truly ancient, its cards tiny illustrations on multi-faceted shapes, no backlight. Vorkosigen pumped its trigger lever. The shapes bounced around the box, coming to rest in the shape of an H reading. The same reading.

Cold sweat trickled down Bannick's back.

'Need to see more?' he hissed. 'I've got four more, all ages, all types, all the same reading. That's not chance. The Emperor is telling me something.'

'Why would the Emperor want to tell you anything?'

Vorkosigen's face reddened and he barged into Bannick, pushing him up against the wall. He was surprisingly strong. His bulging eyes looked up into Bannick's face. 'You basdack aristocrats are all the same,' he snarled. '"Why would he talk to you?" What makes you so special, you arrogant pig? A-a-a! Make a noise and I'll cut your warp-cursed throat. Do you know how many wars this machine has fought in? How many lives it has saved? Do you?'

Vorkosigen's big eyes darted about, resting on stencilled warnings, piping, charms hung five centuries before his birth. 'The Emperor is telling us to be careful. You basdacks, think you're above us all, we who make the machines and do the work...' he spluttered, spraying Bannick with froth. 'It's we clansmen that hold the Imperium together, not you and your rituals and fancy uniforms! While you were up in your feather bed with your cheap sluts, my family was deep in the bowels of your forges, hammering ceramite. What do you know of hard work, of suffering? I bet all this, this stink, the noise, the heat, the shifts, I'll bet it's all a nasty shock to you. Me? I was born into it. And you come in here, all stiff sleeves and peaked cap, looking like you own the place... It's *you*, you misbegotten fool, the tarot is telling me to be wary of *you*. The cards, they're all of destruction, of death, the Fortress of Faith toppled – *Mars Triumphant* toppled, and at the heart of it the Young Warrior, the Dishonoured Scion, *you*. The naïve, the highborn, the feted, the man that smashes it down in the name of glory. Sound familiar?'

Bannick held Vorkosigen's eyes. What if he were right? The tarot was one of the few levellers in the Imperium. Highborn, lowborn, spacer, planetsider, scum... It did not matter who you were, or where you were, as long as you had a reader, anyone could scry for the Emperor's will, and sometimes he did communicate with his servants, even the lowliest, or so it was said. Bannick regarded the tarot with deep suspicion. He was too worldly to take it at face value. But he was a man of faith, the saints' tales were full of proofs of its efficacy, and he had sinned terribly. He was unfit to serve on so potent an instrument of divine will.

'You're going to get us all killed and I am not going to let that happen. The Emperor does not want it to happen, and by his name I will not let *Mars Triumphant* die.' Vorkosigen slid the switch on his cutter. A thin beam of light leapt across the gap between its two prongs. The heat of it curled the hair at Bannick's throat.

'How?' Bannick gasped. 'How do you know? What am I going to do? How can you be sure your interpretation is correct? I would never do anything to harm this tank or its crew, or to endanger our mission.'

'The tarot doesn't tell me that,' hissed Vorkosigen, 'only deals in generalities, doesn't it? The Emperor has a lot on his mind, as big and as powerful as that is, it's a bit too much to expect him to come here himself and give me a personal prophecy, isn't it? That's why we have the tarot, and thanks to that I know enough. You, this tank, a poor match.'

Bannick moved quickly, jamming his left hand up under the cutter, turning his head to one side, bringing his right elbow over to knock the tool away from his face. There was a sizzle of flesh and a blossom of hot pain along his ear as the light beam sliced a sliver of it away. Vorkosigen stumbled. Bannick pivoted, shoving hard. The little tech-adept bounced off the wall, kicking the first tarot reader away, setting it off.

'What do you know about the Emperor? What do you know? What do you know of what life is like for the rest of us? Nothing! You know nothing at all!'

Bannick punched him with the heel of his hand. Vorkosigen fell with a cry, the contents of his belt scattering. Bannick was on him in an instant, pinning his arms with his legs, punching the defenceless head of the tech-adept repeatedly. All the rage, all the pain, the fear, poured out of him. Tuparillio, Kalligen, the war, the suffering he had seen, but most of all that he had been born as he was, son of a clan master, imprisoned by duty and responsibility as surely as if he were bound by chains.

The tech-adept stopped moving. Bannick's fist stilled and his shoulders slumped. Vorkosigen was stained and bloody, like his cousin had been.

'No, it is you who knows nothing at all,' whispered Bannick.

'What in the name of the thrice-blasted apostate is going on here?' Cortein, shouting from the top of the stairs.

Bannick looked up, Vorkosigen at his feet, blood on his fists.

On the floor, amidst spilled tools, three tarot readers clattered to a stop, their inevitable readings clicking into place one after another.

INTERSTITIAL

'Boys play gladly as men at war. In war, terror reduces
men to boys once more.'

Sayings of Solon

CHAPTER 16

ARONIS CITY, PARAGON VI
2003395.M41

The door shut behind Bannick with a soft click, yet it reverberated off into the cavernous interior of the church, accentuating the silence by its intrusion.

The double-headed aquila dominated the wall opposite the doors. Ranks of dark-wood pews, the faces of saints on them worn to nubs, lined a broad aisle leading to the altar. The columns of the nave loomed over him, trees in a forest of stone fruited with carvings, their tops vanishing in the gloom. Hanging from the unseen ceiling was a statue of the Emperor Resplendent, winged and armed with sword and shield, gilt age-darkened, so that the statue glittered only just so, a tiny glimmer in the boundless dark of the rafters, where winged things swooped on the edge of sight, chittering litanies and disturbing the sepulchral air of the place.

Bannick's breath rasped in his ears, the rush of the air in and out of his lungs an imposition upon the stillness, and without thinking he held his breath until his body forced him to exhale. His cheek throbbed, his head felt light from the shot the medicae had given him.

A flurry of cloth and the sound of a book closing, and a priest rose up from a pew far forward of Bannick. His insignificant size by the eagle revealed the true scale of the place.

'I shouldn't have come,' he muttered to himself.

'Loyal servant of the Emperor, may I help you?' the priest made his way from where he'd been sitting to the central aisle. An object rose off the pew and followed him with the thrum of antigravitic motors.

Bannick made to go.

'No wait! Stay a while,' called the priest. 'All are welcome in the house of the Emperor.'

'… peror … peror … peror,' echoed the stone.

Determined to leave, Bannick found that he could not, simply could not lift his legs or turn away. He looked upwards. The Emperor glared down at him.

The priest reached him. 'Good day to you, if there is such thing as one in the Long Winter.' The priest smiled, his voice was warm, not stern as those of some Bannick had met. His face was round, broader at the bottom than at the top, with a rack of fleshy chins. Dark smudges sat under his eyes, and what little hair he had was cropped close to his skin. He wore the long white surplice, thick with the embroidery of a third-rank confessor. A servo-skull bobbed by his head, motors whirring as its metal eyes zeroed in on Bannick's face. 'I do not think I know you, my son. Forgive me, Aronis is a large city, it is hard for me to keep the faces of all our congregation in mind.' His face became concerned as he took in Bannick's swollen face, the stick bandage over his cheek.

Bannick tried to speak, but his mouth was dry, he swallowed, licked his lips and tried again. 'I have not been to the church for many years,' he said.

The priest placed his hands into his broad sleeves. 'In that case, introductions are in order. I am Confessor Pyke, late of the Zoroman Orbital Habitats in the Vertheni system. And this is my predecessor, Confessor Zumanzi, whose remains have had the singular blessing of being crafted into the device you see accompanying me.'

'I…' stuttered Bannick. 'I am Colaron Artem Lo Bannick.'

'Of the opticals clan? Hmmm, I suppose had I been here longer I would have been able to tell. There is a certain look, I am told, to each of the clans, but I as yet do not see it. All the children of Man are equal to me.'

'You are not here long?' said Bannick, seeking refuge in this mundane exchange, anything to push the image of Tuparillio's face from his mind.

Confessor Pyke shook his head. 'No, not long here, not long anywhere, in truth. The Ecclesiarchy do like to move us so, keeps us from putting down roots. But one mustn't complain, one's duty is to the church and to the Master of Mankind.' The confessor glanced back to the eagle, then smiled at Bannick. 'And one is happy in one's work. Tell me, why have you not been to church for so long, my son? Our praises warm the Emperor, trapped in the cold machinery of His Golden Throne, our strength is His strength, and His strength is the pillar that holds up the Imperium. Would you deny succour to our lord?'

Bannick had no answer.

'I suppose you have not unburdened yourself of sin, either?'

Bannick shook his head. 'I have had nothing to confess,' he lied.

'Oh, my son.' The priest smiled and inclined his head, placed a plump hand on Bannick's shoulder. 'I am sure you have. What you mean is "I have nothing to reveal bar minor transgressions that I would prefer the law does not know of."' He looked meaningfully at Bannick's wounded face. 'And that is perfectly understandable, all young men are the same. But looking at you now, this has changed, has it not?'

Bannick nodded. His knees felt weak.

The priest came forwards and took his elbow. 'Take heart, my son. There is little that the Emperor will not excuse if a man offers true service, body and heart, soul and mind. There is nothing higher in this world than to serve the Emperor, and in so doing, serve man.' Both of them raised their eyes to the effigy of the man-god suspended above.

'Yes,' Bannick managed.

'Good. Be warmed, young man, in this coldest of seasons, be warmed in the knowledge that through service lies glory. But first, yes, first we must pray so that we may know what service will aid in the repentance of our transgressions. There is nothing quite like sharing a burden to ease one's heart and the mind, no? Come with me, to the altar, let us there offer up ourselves to the Emperor.'

Bannick offered no resistance.

'I'm afraid shriving requires a donation, no problem for a man from such a wealthy background as yourself, but all these candles do not pay for themselves, alas.'

Together they walked into the long aisles running down either side of the nave where Confessor Pyke took him to the altar. They knelt together in prayer before Pyke bade Bannick tell of his sins to the God-Emperor.

There, in the dark and cold of the house of the Lord of Man, Bannick told of how he had become a murderer.

INTERSTITIAL

Hive Meradon is the administrative capital of the Kalidarian southern hemisphere. A hole in the sand that produces 36 megatonnes of processed lorelei pellets per annum for the Scholastica Psykana and Adeptus Astartes Librarium, there is nothing else remarkable about it at all. If I do recommend the locally caught, magnesium-seared sand-mite, it is only because it is practically the only palatable thing to eat there. At all costs, avoid the 'salad'.

Heironymous Squeam,
Minor Industrial Worlds of the Segmentum Pacificus,
a Precise Guide.

CHAPTER 17

KALIDAR IV, HIVE MERADON
3335397.M41

Brasslock shifted from consciousness to unconsciousness so often he was not sure which was which. At the moment, he thought he was awake. His mental processes were coherent. There had been no sudden relocation or arbitrary change in causal events. Processional phenomena went one to the other without non-logical shifts. The existence of the room he occupied was objectively apparent by the level of detail available to his senses; the grains of dirt under his flesh hand, the hum of distant machinery, the trickle of dust on his face, the smell of unwashed bodies and suppurating wounds, the moans of prisoners, the clank of chains as they shifted listlessly, attempting to find a little comfort for their tortured bodies; these were not the soft-edges of a dream, where sensation came and went on a whim. The floor he lay face down on was the same floor he lay on a minute ago, the dark the same dark. He was not dreaming. He wished he were.

He pressed his flesh forefinger into the metal. Grit moved

in the ridges of his fingerprint and he took a slow, painful breath. Real, all too real.

The Adeptus Mechanicus lived by two contradictory creeds; faith, and reason. Faith in the Machine-God and His knowledge, reason the key to unlocking the deep truths underlying His gifts. Prayer was the appropriate adjunct to both.

When the orks came, he had thought he was about to die. He should have been dead. But he was not. Reason told him that, while his faith told him that it could not be any other way. He was a servant of the Omnissiah, and he lived because He willed it.

He ran a diagnostic with his cranial implants. His augmetics were sluggish to respond, the external sockets and cabling damaged by the blows rained down upon him by the orks when they took him. He was relieved when the contents of his intelligence core memory dumps showed continued viability. To have lost the contents of his ingrams would have been too much.

He remembered the orks' foul breath and rough hands, their hulking mass, his panic as they grabbed him. Poor, faithful Urtho smashed down and torn to pieces as the servitor tried to defend him.

Pity and fear. Weaknesses of the flesh. His augmetics attempted an emotion suppression, unsuccessfully. He'd never been able to let go entirely of his human frailties, and in truth he had never wanted to. Under the plasteel and the wiring, he was a man, all the servants of the Omnissiah were. He was not an adherent of the subsects who regarded all trappings of the biological frame to be shameful failings. Was not the body, after all, a marvellous machine itself? Was not the flesh-form that worn by the most holy Emperor Himself? The Magos Biologis argued thus, even as they tinkered with its genetic underpinnings, tireless in their endeavours to improve upon it. How were the tech-priests to serve man's Imperium if they left humanity entirely behind? He had read the secret histories, the chronicles of the Blind King and his uprising against the High Lords of Terra, how he had sought to use the powers of the Machine-God to rid the universe of all organic human life. This unholy course of action had been disastrous for the Imperium and the Adeptus Mechanicus both, yet still some of his colleagues failed to see the lessons of the past.

There were those of the Adeptus Mechanicus who tried to sever themselves from their biological origins completely, adepts like Rotar. But not Brasslock. For him, the perfection of the will of the Omnissiah was the operation of machinery and humanity in balance, not in discord, neither side attempting to usurp the other, but both locked in a perfect reciprocal circle, benefits flowing between them without end. Knowledge as the tool of man. Best trust in metal, in cog and gear, best be a machine, but always with a human heart.

Brasslock was a man, forever would be a man. As an adept of Mars Brasslock had complete faith in the process of cause and effect, felt it inevitable, and was calm in the face of his circumstances. They were as the Omnissiah and Emperor intended. As a man, Brasslock felt fear.

The orks had hacked away most of his augmetics. They had stopped trying to pull out his mechadendrite assembly when they discovered that to do so would kill him. Likewise, his internal heart, lung and nutrient mechanisms remained intact, although not one part of him remained untouched. Curious ork specialists, one dressed as some hideous parody of a medicae doctor, the other wielding a variety of surprisingly delicate machine tools, had gone over his body for hours. Strapped to a table, unanaesthetised, his augmetics had fought hard to keep the pain at bay, but had failed. The agony of that examination remained with him, reduced to a dull throb now, but there. When he moved, bone and metal ground and pain flared high, especially around the crude sutures of the wounds they'd inflicted. This was as nothing to the sensations he'd suffered as they'd pulled him apart.

He felt feverish. The beginning of infection, he thought. That would probably kill him if the orks did not do the job themselves.

His mechadendrites themselves had been scissored off, the stubs of them twitching infuriatingly as they malfunctioned, a deep itch he could not scratch. Much of his right arm assembly had gone. They hadn't been able to undo the locking mechanism for the multitool prosthesis he had been wearing. In the end they had become impatient and wrenched it out, damaging his nerve circuitry interfaces. After that they'd proceeded to dismantle his entire limb, piece by excruciating piece, only stopping when they'd severed the pressure lines that went deep within him. These acted as a secondary circulatory system and, when cut, his machine components had almost bled out, but the ork mechanic had been quick. He sealed the rupture and refilled the lubrication tubes with some filthy orkish oil. He felt polluted, the vile distillates of the greenskins within the holy Omnissiah's gifts!

They'd become agitated when it looked like he might die, a flurry of activity had erupted around him, the smaller gretchin xenoforms, humans too, working fast. They'd been more cautious after that, for a time.

The pressure in his machine circulatory system was too low, the oil of entirely the wrong kind. His intelligence core's mental interface was alive with warning sigils. His breathing laboured and machine heart beat erratically. His legs were practically non-functional, he could move them, but there was not sufficient pressure in the hydraulics to bear his weight. One of his eyes had been smashed in with the butt of a powerdrill by the mechanic, wires pulled and teased by poking ork fingers. It was as if the beast had been trying to understand how it worked, to see what made Brasslock function, but this could not have been so, orks were animals.

He drew some comfort from the knowledge that they, xenos and masters of nothing but the crassest mechanisms, would never understand, and that even if they did, they lacked the blessing of the Omnissiah's faith to make His blessings function correctly and with joy. They did not know the correct prayers, the rightful rituals to ensure proper operation. One only had to look at the ork machines to see that, the way they rattled and banged and puffed black smoke, forever on the brink of catastrophic malfunction. This provided some comfort.

Brasslock was restricted in his movements. One weak flesh arm was left to him, the two smallest fingers of that hand broken. He could move his torso slightly, but the weight of his broken augmetics dragged at his ancient flesh. He was effectively a cripple, and unlike the others in the room about him, he wore no chains or binding. The orks judged him to be no threat. Face down on the floor, he awaited his death.

The orks would not leave their prisoners alone. Time and again they returned. Many men went out and were not brought back, others died in the cell from the horrific injuries they returned with.

Brasslock was unrobed – naked, humiliated, broken and bereft, his only succour the small array of blinking icons telling him of his pains, the last gift of the Omnissiah remaining to him.

Next time, they would take that away too. He prayed as hard as he could to the Omnissiah and the Emperor both that he would die before that happened.

For the first time in two centuries, Brasslock knew what it

was to be truly human. Without the power of the Machine-God's gifts, he was helpless and feeble, an old man. Had his tearducts not been removed decades before, he would have wept.

'Brother,' came a voice. 'Brother?' A hand fell on his flesh shoulder. Brasslock started. The prisoners did not talk to one another for fear of reprisals from the orks. When they did, they did not address Brasslock, superstitions surrounding the tech-priests keeping them distant.

'Who is this who calls me brother?' he managed. He could not see the man's face.

'It doesn't matter much,' whispered the man, sitting near the crippled tech-priest. 'We're all brothers here.'

The tech-priest turned his head a little. The room was too dark for a man to see, but the light amplification enhancements of his remaining ocular augmetic provided him with a green, blurry version of sight.

The man who called him brother sat, knees drawn up, hands clasped round them. Light reflected from his retinas and teeth, giving him a ghostly air, intensified when he moved, the lighter parts of him leaving streamers of greenish-white across Brasslock's vision field. His uniform was stained dark, his hair wild, face smeared with something; all came out as darker greens to the tech-priest's eye, but he appeared remarkably unharmed.

'You, you are not fettered,' croaked the priest with his flesh voice. His augmitters, including his vox grille, had been stripped from him.

The man looked himself up and down as if surprised. 'No, I suppose I am not, but then iron cannot bind any man who has faith in the Emperor, is that not the case?'

Brasslock turned his head away. 'I find your faith uplifting,' he said, not sure if he believed that any more.

'And so you should, Enginseer Brasslock. I once had none,

but in circumstances such as mine, it becomes something of a necessity.'

'Indeed,' said Brasslock.

A cruel shout in guttural Gothic came from outside the room, telling them to shut up. A metal object banging on the door. Other prisoners hissed, urging the tech-priest to silence.

The stranger ignored them. 'Brasslock, do not let them break you, no matter what. Do not give up your secrets!'

Brasslock did not respond, weary to the bone. He was drifting into sleep when it occurred to him that he had not told the man his name.

When Brasslock lifted his head to ask him if they'd met before, the man had gone.

INTERSTITIAL

The amount of lorelei present in the Ozymandian Flatlands estimated by the previous Geologian Surveyor team has proven to be, if anything, a grievous understatement. The combination of tidal effort, stellar radiologic bombardment and the trauma to the crust of the impact event has created lorelei deposits of unparalleled purity and quantity. Our recent calculations indicate that an amount of raw crystals equal to half the entire crystalline resource of Kalidar is present in fracture lines throughout the basin. Although deep compared to some of the other deposits – sand harvesters would be entirely ineffectual – the concentration of the veins make viable the establishment of deep mining, at a cost in lives and materials easily borne, no greater, we perceive, than five billion Imperials annually, lower caste and mutant slave deaths at >20,500.

It is the recommendation of this committee that the founding of a new hive be undertaken in the heart of the basin as soon as possible, better to exploit this most precious of resources.

Ozymandian Basin geological report, M40.

CHAPTER 18
KALIDAR IV, OZYMANDIAN BASIN
3338397.M41

'Steady! Steady! Outlanner, hold the line down the middle!' Cortein shouted into the internal vox.

'I see it sir, I see it!' the driver's voice crackled back over the speakers. 'Got to bear left a little, there's a fissure there in the rock to the right, it might give.'

Mars Triumphant's engines grumbled loudly as the tank struggled down the slope into the basin, its great weight working against it on fractured rock and sand covering the sides of the basin.

Cortein nodded to Epparaliant, who waited expectantly at his comms station. He turned to his unit, hands playing over the controls for the tank's laser pulse data systems, warning those coming behind them to follow Outlanner's lead.

Behind *Mars Triumphant*, the other vehicles of the taskforce came on: a thin line of Leman Russ, one after another, five of the nine accompanying the larger tank. Behind them, two Chimeras, then the first of four Trojan supply vehicles. Tethered behind it was a large flatbed carrying vast fuel drums, also tracked, another Trojan attached to the end to stabilise its progress. Then Exertraxes's command Chimera, bristling with antennae rendered useless by the storm, another Chimera, and Captain Verselleo's command tank. Following them came another paired unit of Trojans guiding a second flatbed trailer, this stacked high with ammunition. The rear was brought up by the second of Exertraxes's platoon lieutenants in his Chimera, two of his squads alongside him. Then came an Atlas recovery vehicle, currently home to the taskforce's enginseer and astropath. Finally, two standard armed Leman Russ battle tanks, turrets reversed, acting as a rearguard.

'This is not easy,' came Outlanner's voice. The storm blew on. The wind could be heard even inside. The internal vox crackled like gunfire, external vox swamped by static. *Mars Triumphant* shifted abruptly to the right, metal groaning, equipment jangling. All the crew were on duty. Even Vorkosigen, bruised and subdued, sat at his station, Meggen hanging from the central well ladder, keeping a watchful eye on him. Every one of them, bar the loader, scanned their station pict screens, gauging how much space they had on the treacherous mountain path.

'Steady, Outlanner, steady. Four degrees left, forward three metres, back five degrees,' said Cortein, adjusting the heading dials.

'Sir.' The tank juddered as it shifted, creeping forwards a centimetre at a time.

When they'd reached the barrier range, it had taken a day to find a gap through the worn mountains around the crater. Exertraxes's first lieutenant, Polikon, found this path and had driven its length once before returning with the information for the rest of the convoy. He and his command crew had then descended a second time in their Chimera, and now waited at the bottom.

Bannick was deeply thankful they only had to do it once.

Whatever had inflicted this wound on the surface of Kalidar had been enormous; the ring range about the Basin towered high still after a million years of erosion. Polikon had found a cleft, a canyon blasted by unnumbered sandstorms through a weakness in the stone. Its sides were rippled and it hooted and whooped in the storm. At the end of the canyon-pass came the descent, a fifty-degree path of rock and sand. The men were unnerved by the voice of the canyon, its eerie song adding to the dread anticipation of what awaited them within the basin itself.

The lorelei visions, the ghosts of Kalidar.

Bannick's eyes struggled to make sense of what he saw through his pict-feed. The air was a shifting mosaic of sand streamers, the landscape beyond it tilted and jumbled rocks worn smooth as eggs. The chart desk at Cortein's station showed the situation as best it could, but without direct sat-feeds and orbital locators it was impossible to trust it. The maps it ran from may or may not have been accurate, and they could not be sure of their position. Right now it was about a kilometre off, said Cortein, but they could all see the steep escarpment around the basin, an endless sea of sand. Eppa-raliant, meanwhile, followed a rough chart made by Polikon.

'Sir.' Epparaliant looked concerned. 'According to Polikon's charts the path narrows to less than twenty metres ahead. There's a tilt of fifteen degrees to the right on it. It's going to be dangerous.'

'Yeah, yeah, I know. Hang on, this is going to be real tight.' Outlanner's voice was strained.

'Steady as she goes,' said Cortein.

Bannick held his breath as they approached the narrowing, a featureless sheet of tilted rock. *Mars Triumphant* shifted up jerkily as it breasted the lip of it, treads scrabbling on the stone. Outlanner eased the tank forwards. Hitting then passing a point of equilibrium, *Mars Triumphant* fell slowly forwards, skidding sideways as it did so.

The crew were thrown to the side. The tank slipped on, its path lubricated by the rivers of sand poured over it from the desert above. *Mars Triumphant* juddered sideways, tracks squealing, closer and closer to the edge of the path. Outlanner swore fluently as he wrestled with the Baneblade. The vehicle did a slow turn and came to a rest.

Bannick took a look out of one of the right sponson bolter cameras and experienced a rush of vertigo. The right side of *Mars Triumphant* hung over nothingness.

'Throne,' whispered Meggen, catching sight of the display.

The engine turned over quietly. Metal ticked and creaked at the unusual distribution of the super-heavy's weight. The wind howled louder.

Cortein punched his vox. 'Stop the convoy. Exertraxes, call a halt! I repeat immediate halt!'

Epperaliant frantically worked the signal pulse, passing the information behind. Too late. There was a clang and *Mars* shifted further, lurching dangerously on the precipice.

'Hard contact,' said Epperaliant calmly.

'What are they doing?' growled Cortein. He punched the vox again. 'Back up, back up now, tank five!'

A rumble of static. Words. 'Ne... ...ive. We... r... gro... ed.'

'Dammit! Listen to me,' said Cortein. 'Outlanner, hold position. Vorkosigen.'

'Sir?'

Bannick could feel the tech-adept purposefully not looking at him. Once the story came out of his assault on Bannick, Cortein had put him on immediate report. He'd be fortunate to escape with his life when they returned.

If they returned.

'We need more traction,' said Cortein. 'Give it to me.'

'I can up the reactor output, adjust the drive mechanism to increase the torque on the engine, sir. It'll be an increase of…' he went over some calculations, referring to multiple instruments as he did so. 'Five per cent or so, sir.'

'Better than nothing. Do it.'

There was a burst of vox, a rush of horrendous interference. Epperaliant winced and began trying to isolate a signal. 'It's Exertraxes, sir, he suggests he send the Atlas forwards to help pull us out backwards to try another path.'

'That an order?'

'No, sir, it's a suggestion.'

Cortein thought briefly. 'No. Tell him there's not enough room for them to start dancing tanks round each other,' said Cortein. 'Outlanner?'

'We'll never get the Trojans and supply trailers back up, and there's no telling if any path would be better than this one. We're nearly there. I can do this, I am sure of it.'

Epperalient scanned forwards on the map. 'He's right, honoured lieutenant. We've only a hundred metres of path left to go. Once we get over this, we'll be running on easier ground, I say it's worth the risk.'

'Relay a negative then, commsman. Bannick, keep an eye on our right.'

'Sir.' Bannick could not tear himself away from the terrifying pict view.

'Ready?'

'Ready,' said Outlanner.

'On my order,' said Cortein. 'Three, two, one… Now.'

Outlanner gunned the engine and engaged the drive units. There was a squeal of metal on rock. The tank, with more traction to its right, spun towards the edge again. Bannick grabbed onto his station in anticipation of the fall.

'Got you!' said Outlanner's crackling voice. The tank lined

up obliquely with the path, both tracks on hard stone. *Mars Triumphant* suddenly lurched forwards, Ganlick cursing as he banged his head on the demolisher cannon breech, Outlanner expertly shifting power back and forth between the left and right drive wheels until the Baneblade was back in the centre of the path.

Tank five was not so fortunate.

As the Baneblade crawled forwards millimetre by millimetre, the crew watched tank five on *Mars*'s aft screen. Smoke poured from the stacks on its engine, flat ribbons of black carried horizontally off by the gale.

'You're overgunning your engine! Power down, man, power down!' shouted Cortein. Epperaliant hammered out a semaphore on the signal laser.

'Ca… n… ion' came a panicked voice.

Tracks spinning, tank five skidded backwards and sideways. Panicked shouts came over the vox, broken by Kalidar's own scream. Slowly it slid, treads spinning ineffectually, first one track, then the other, the driver desperately trying to mimic Outlanner's success and failing. The Leman Russ hit the edge, the front of the right track going out over the precipice. The shouts and orders emanating from tank five became ever more desperate. The roar of its struggling engine fought high of the storm. A bang sounded as the whole of the right track unit went over the edge, crashing the hull into the rock.

'Dammit!' yelled Cortein into his vox horn. 'Turn off your engine! Deactivate now! Shut it down!'

The driver of the tank either never heard or was too panicked to pay attention. Both tracks spun wildly, right-hand unit treading air. Tank five shifted further and further off the road. On the vox they heard the vehicle's commander bellowing to the driver to stand down. Too late, the tracks disengaged. Tank five hung for a moment, before pitching sideways and falling from the path, the shouts of its crew turning into screams.

The loud, metallic bangs of its progress down the mountainside fought with the wind, grew distant and indistinct, then stopped.

Silence fell.

The wind blew on.

Silence reined on the command deck. To lose men that way seemed worse than in battle, somehow.

'Poor basdacks,' said Raggen. Meggen made the sign of the aquila. Bannick muttered a quick prayer, commending their souls to the Emperor. Epperaliant spoke urgently into the vox. 'Tank five! Tank five! Come in! Come in!'

'Anything?' asked Cortein.

Epperaliant turned away from his station and shook his head slowly.

'That's a loss we can ill afford,' muttered Cortein. 'Outlanner, get us off this mountain. Vox ahead to Polikon if you can, commsman. Get him to drive round and see if there are any survivors. And tell the rest of them to take it slowly! I don't want to see any more men die today.'

INTERSTITIAL

'Thou shalt not sully the shell of the divine engine.
Thou shalt not sully its mechanism.
Thou shalt not countenance the use of sullied components.
Thou shalt not be complicit in the sullying.
Thou shalt destroy the sullied.'

Adeptus Mechanicus cant

CHAPTER 19

KALIDAR IV, HIVE MERADON
3339397.M41

Brasslock's struggling cranial implants allowed him to keep track of the time, a chronometer ticking on remorselessly within the lower left field of his remaining ocular implant. Without it, he would have had little idea how many days had passed. Food was delivered sporadically, if at all, and when it came it was rancid, doled out by cackling gretchin who spat in it and dropped it upon the floor, or by terrified human slaves. The light in the room never changed, nor did the air.

They came for him at the start of the Kalidarian night, two brutish orks, bigger than any he'd seen yet, clad in thick plates of armour decorated with garish camo patterns and glyphs of crossed axes and stylised, howling maws. He shrank away as best he could, but they hauled him off the floor as if he were a child and dragged him out of the prison cell. He resolved to die nobly, for any further tampering with his machine gifts by the ork specialists would surely kill him, and he was determined not to give them the satisfaction of seeing him break.

Nevertheless his heart quailed when they approached the examination room.

They passed it without slowing.

He was too surprised and relieved to be afraid, and thanked the Omnissiah and Emperor in equal, fervent, measure.

Brasslock was dragged along corridors and up stairways he had not seen before, the service ways of a large complex.

Up one stairwell, through a door, then into what had been a richly appointed corridor. Toppled offworld furnishings and objets d'art from across the galaxy lay about, smashed into pieces, the soiled carpet was scattered with bones and filth, the walls daubed with crudely realised ork ideograms, candelabra hung with grisly trophies.

Brasslock recognised a palace when he saw one. There were few men in the Imperium who could afford such luxury.

He was dragged onwards, past broken transport ways and ballrooms turned into barracks for ork troops, from where smells of roasting meat and screams came intermingled. Past shattered windows looking upon gardens made wasteland by war, along a processional route studded with lines of spikes upon which were impaled the rotted bodies of militia soldiers. Always they were in the shadows, intermittent fires or buzzing vacuum bulbs dotted here and there, the power out in much of the building.

Then to a great cavern, whose armaglass wall lay in pieces on the ground amidst burnt-out vehicles and charred corpses. His implant whirred its iris tight shut against the sudden return of light, although the storm made a drab day.

Up steps, patterned carpets soaked brown with old blood, through massive doors rent by explosion into a hall, once the throne room of a hive governor, now the lair of the ork conquerors of Meradon.

The room was crowded with enormous orks, bigger than any

two of their common troopers put together. All were dressed in filthy uniforms draped with braid, high-peaked caps upon their tiny craniums, parodies of Imperial uniforms, like apes on parade.

Scurrying lesser greenskins and human slaves ran to and fro, bringing food and drink to ork nobles lounging on broken human furniture too small for their bodies. With horror, Brasslock saw free men here too, not slaves, armed, walking warily in between the orks. Pirates, mercenary scum. A smattering of other xenos there were also, some in chains, living trophies bruised and torn, others clearly in the pay of the greenskins.

They stood talking at one another, men, aliens and orks, in the harsh, guttural tongue of the greenskins. Occasionally, two orks might shove and gesticulate angrily, hands straying towards blades, but it stopped there. All, no matter how large they were, or how decorated their uniforms, were cowed by the being sat at the end of the room.

Upon a throne fashioned from skulls and helmets, before a great, curved window that allowed views from the very top to the very bottom of the conquered Hive Meradon, sat the Arch-Skarlord Gratzdakka Wur Mekdakka, the king of Orktown.

The Arch-Skarlord was as big as an alpha ambull, muscles like anvils rippling under its well-tailored uniform: long coat, high cap, boots polished to a mirror shine. A rack of medals to shame a warrior-saint sparkled on its chest, gold rings covered every finger. The ork warboss's face was long, with a massive jaw full of yellowing fangs. Its skull, like those of all orks, was low and small, brows heavy, cheeks high and pronounced. Its forehead sloped back sharply, and yet in the caverns of its eye sockets red glimmers hinted at a brand of feral intelligence. A feather sat incongruously in the band of its peaked cap, its sabre-teeth were capped with precious metals, and a necklace of similarly decorated fangs was slung about its neck, a heavy, vulgar pendant bearing the crossed axes of its clan hanging in the middle of the chain.

Mounted behind were two enormous power axes, identical, crossed above his throne, a variety of helmets, including those of the Adeptus Astartes, strung between. Banners of every kind were arrayed either side of it – Imperial from a dozen different military organisations and a score of worlds, orkish types of every kind, alien flags of obscure origin. Gretchin servants, similarly uniformed to their master, were ranged about him, fanning him, feeding him, shining his boots. The ork king idly cuffed one away, and stuffed food into his mouth, his cunning eyes never leaving Brasslock as he was brought towards him. Either side of the throne stood two massive bodyguards, caps with shiny peaks pulled hard down over their eyes, standing motionless, their power axes tall as they were, crusted with old blood.

It was before this creature that Brasslock was thrown, his damaged legs shoved under him so he was knelt upon the floor.

A gretchin standing on the skull of an unidentifiable creature leaned in close to its master, long fingers cupped round its mouth, whispering. The warboss gave a curt nod.

Gretchin hauled at a long chain, pulling a nearly naked, hairless fat man to his feet from behind the throne. He wore a collar about his neck. The lesser greenskins prodded him forwards. The warboss gestured with a claw, nodded. The man shuffled forwards, flesh wobbling.

'WaaskruzdreknakaaGratzdakkaWurMekDakkagrubgrub-nardeffskragnaffgulgul,' said the warboss, its voice so deep it made Brasslock's bones vibrate.

The fat man looked upwards and drew breath. 'My lord and master, the great Arch-Skarlord General Gratzdakka Wur Mekdakka, king of Hive Meradon, Conqueror of Kalidar, the mighty, the powerful, the foe-bane, the git-kicker, would speak with you.' The man's voice stridulated, the voice of a eunuch. A large gretchin hissed at him, yanked at his chain and gestured for him to go on. 'I am Dog. I will speak for the general. I will translate.'

Another stream of rumbling, barbarous syllables poured from the ork.

'My master commands that these gifts shall be yours.'

Gretchin servants came forwards with a torn tapestry wrapped in a bundle, and tipped its contents onto the floor. All gaudy objects, some priceless, some junk, the orks having little idea of human concepts of value. Three terrified women in tattered finery were dragged in chains from the back of the room by an ork in a leather smock. The greenskins understood certain human traits, at least.

More orkish, Dog translating, bored eyes cast up to the ceiling. 'And he will see to it that you are restored to your former functionality, only much improved.' A gaggle of ork mechanics in the crowd guffawed, one tipped a salute at the enginseer. 'You will be the envy of your mekboy friends.'

Further harsh ork words.

'You must tell him the workings of this mighty tank, and all this will be yours,' translated Dog.

'But not my freedom?' croaked Brasslock.

'No, never that,' replied Dog, and his face betrayed a hint of sadness.

The warlord spoke, so then did Dog.

'As you can see, we are not as other orks. We understand. We plan, we fight good, we fight better than other orks because we think. We work and fight with others, for more victory, more teeth, and more fighting. Our machines are the best. Our boys are the best. We take your tanks and make them more powerful. We respect you as favoured foes. I, Gratzdakka, offer you the chance to join my mekboys. War and gold will be your forever reward,' said Dog, speaking over the warlord's rumbling offer. The warlord raised a hand and beckoned to the two ork minders. They hauled Brasslock to his feet, his legs jamming and clicking in protest as they dragged him to the window displaying the shaft of Hive Meradon. Gratzdakka spoke again.

'But first, you must fix this, and fix it good,' said Dog.

A massive mechanic came close to Brasslock, its stink choking the enginseer's artificial olfactory bulbs. With a look of pride, it pointed down to the plaza below the window.

'Mekgramekamek,' it said proudly, unfolding a long arm to indicate the plaza below, its hot, malodorous breath washing over the enginseer.

There, surrounded by industrious greenskins of all sizes, cloaked in scaffolding, sparks spraying as thick plates and other orkish improvements were welded and hammered into place, was imprisoned the Shadowsword, *Lux Imperator*.

Brasslock looked back to Dog, to Gratzdakka. Lines tracked across his vision as his remaining eye malfunctioned. 'I... I cannot. I cannot do it. I will not. I refuse.'

Dog sighed. 'You should have agreed.' He began to address Gratzdakka, but the huge greenskin stood up from his throne, towering over everything else in the room. It strode over to the enginseer, shoving Dog to the floor as he came. The translator slave scuttled back to lurk amongst the warlord's gretchin.

The two ork minders stepped back warily, releasing Brasslock who sagged halfway to the floor on his damaged legs. Gratzdakka came to stand over Brasslock. It regarded the human, fists on its ape-like hips, for a few moments. Standing there, legs too short for its body, dressed in imitation Imperial gear, the ork would have been ridiculous, funny even, if it weren't a monster from wildest nightmare.

Gratzdakka coughed, looked round the room, then grabbed

at the enginseer, his hand fitting round the tech-priest's chest. Thus grasping him, the giant xeno hauled him into line with his eyes.

'Now that,' said the general in thick, broken Gothic, syllables mangled by its alien throat, words whistling between its fangs, but understandable, nevertheless, 'is a real, real shame. I tried to be nice little human, I tried. You fix that.' He pointed. 'You get this.' And again, filthy claws jabbing at the proffered treaures. 'That's how you trade in the Imperium.' He pronounced this 'Imperroom'.

'Eh, eh?' he shook the enginseer, his grip round Brasslock's ribs like a vice. 'Yeah. So that's how I do it. Shame, shame. Now I am gonna have to ask old Greeneye to take a look in your head, and you are not going to like that one bit, squishy. I'm having me killy wagon, it doesn't matter if you like it or not. Nah.' The general dropped Brasslock to the floor.

'Take him away, and get Greeneye!' he roared. 'Tell him it's weirding time!'

INTERSTITIAL

'They're here, Emperor forgive me, they won't stop looking at me, they won't stop looking at me! My eyes! My
eyes! Make them stop!'

*Last recorded transmission of Hive Kimeradon
Constructor team, M37*

CHAPTER 20
KALIDAR IV, OZYMANDIAN BASIN
3339397.M41

The convoy made it down the mountain as night fell with no further losses. In the lee of a slab of rock where the storm was somewhat blunted, the strikeforce set up an encampment, men in protective gear working outside, risking the storm to put up airlocked tents. When Polikon had reached tank five, he had discovered that one of the men had, incredibly, survived. It was a small stroke of luck, but it raised their spirits as they went about the business of assessing their vehicles for storm damage. The hundred and fifty men looked forward to their first proper sleep in some time. Few enjoyed it.

The nightmares they suffered that night were but a foretaste of things to come. In the morning, they left hurriedly, talking little, many of the men casting nervous glances over their shoulders as they broke the tents down with haste.

As the convoy trekked further into the Ozymandian Basin, the sense of someone watching him never left Bannick. He'd look up from his monitors, or start from his maintenance duties, sure someone had hissed in his ear, or called his name from far away. One time he swore he saw someone standing in the shadows as he bent to retrieve rations from the storage lockers, sure it was Vorkosigen – he meant to send him off, but when he'd turned round there'd been no one there.

The men, who'd been avoiding looking one another in the eye for the last week, suddenly began talking again. They went reluctantly to the bunks when their rest rotation came round, and spent time they should have been sleeping playing cards, talking, whatever they could do to drive the phantoms away from the edge of their perception. All except Ralt, who'd come white-faced from his time in the bunks and refused to leave the turret.

Bannick was deferring the nightmares by playing cards with Meggen in the munitions locker when the alarm klaxon sounded. 'All hands to stations.' Epperaliant's voice crackled over the vox system.

'What in the name of Terra is that all about?' muttered Meggen round his cigar, although there was no disguising his relief at the thought of something to focus on.

'We'll find out soon enough,' said Bannick. He put his middling hand down on the ammo box they used as a table and went above. Meggen moved over to the shell lift and began unclamping shells, ready for action.

Cortein was on the vox, rapidly delivering orders to the convoy, when Bannick came onto the command deck.

'What's going on?' he asked as he slid into the third gunner's station.

'Exertraxes has veered off course and some of the Leman Russ company have followed him. He's gabbling some nonsense about the spires of Elidia,' said Epperaliant, not looking up from his station. His hands moved quickly over the tac displays, relaying orders via datapipe to the other vehicles in the convoy. The esoteric piece of Scholastica Psykana equipment added to his station displayed graphs spiked with worrying indications of psychic interference.

'The lorelei?'

Epperaliant nodded. 'Evidently.'

'By the Throne! Listen to me!' shouted Cortein, addressing the rest of the convoy. 'Do not listen to the captain, he is under the influence of the crystals. Do not follow him!' Cortein turned back from his station. 'I've stopped most of them, but three of the Leman Russ went after him. There's swiftdust all over this place.' The Baneblade was out at the front, a suite of Martian sensors probing the ground ahead.

'Seismic readings say he's heading right for a swiftdust patch, honoured lieutenant. It's fifty metres deep and then some, readings give out. If he goes in there, we'll never get them out.'

'Exertraxes, come in, come in!' said Cortein. A burst of static, perhaps a hint of shouting lost in the electric noise, then nothing. 'Can you boost the signal?'

'That's it,' said Epperaliant. 'It's this damn storm. It's overwhelming everything that I've got. Only the tightest databeams get through coherently, and I have to send those by pulsed laser individually to each vehicle.' A pause. 'He's in, honoured lieutenant, he's hit the swiftdust.'

'Emperor's Teeth. Outlanner, swing us in as close as is safe. Epperaliant, call up the Atlas. Bannick, I want you and Ganlick outside on this.' Cortein looked to the outside views given by the pict-captors on the exterior of the tank – front view, weapons, sides and rear – all of them showing sheets of red and grey sand blowing past. 'I can't see a damn thing in here. You'll be my eyes. Full protective wear, be careful.'

'Yes, sir.'

'Good, now get on it.'

In the turret, Ganlick and Bannick donned additional gear. Heavy trousers to go under their coats, gauntlets to the elbow that locked down their uniform sleeves, plus fours over their boots, covering the space between sock and footwear, hoods with holes for mouth, nose and eyes and long necks that tucked under the coats. Over this they put on their rebreathers. They fastened belts with carabiners about their waists, tested their voxes, gave Radden the thumbs-up and made for the main hatch.

Radden closed off the central well, and he and Ralt put on their own respirators and goggles. Then Bannick and Ganlick flung back the hatch.

Immediately, the turret was filled with swirling sand, the narrow opening the wind forced itself through turning the storm's tendril into a bucking dust-devil. Papers and flimsies tore around the room. The wind dropped a little as Ganlick forced his large frame out of the top, then again as Bannick followed.

As his head emerged from the hatch, it felt as if the wind would tear it off. Everything was a hideous grey, a lighter smear where the sun stood shrouded being the only point of reference. Ganlick hauled Bannick up out of the turret and slammed it shut. He grasped Bannick's shoulder and guided him off the turret, into the lee of the metal where the wind was slightly less ferocious. He patted and turned Bannick, unspooled a loop of line from his shoulder and clipped it to Bannick's belt, then to his own.

'To the tank?' shouted Bannick, gesturing at a handhold on the vehicle.

Ganlick shook his head. 'Not enough line,' he shouted back, his voice nearly drowned by Kalidar's angry roar. They were stood only a metre apart, but Bannick could barely hear him.

'Stay close!' shouted Bannick. He looked around. 'That way, the Atlas!' he jabbed his finger three times to make sure Ganlick understood, and away they went.

The storm had been raging for weeks, shrouding the entire planet in a pall of sand. With the sun obscured, the temperature had gradually dropped far lower than the usual stifling Kalidarian norm; nevertheless, Bannick and Ganlick sweated hard as they pushed on through the sand, hunkered down against the wind snatching at them with sharp fingers. The wind did not blow constantly, but buffeted them with cruel fists, first from one side, then the other. One moment Bannick would be leant hard into the wind, the next he'd feel himself stagger alarmingly forwards as the storm's blasts switched direction. Merely walking was not an option; to stand straight in the teeth of such a gale would have quickly resulted in both men being thrown on their backs, so they crouched and scuttled at an unnatural stoop, legs spread wide, an exhausting mode of locomotion.

The sandy cargo of the tempest scrabbled at their clothes, a million tiny claws seeking to scratch them, and Bannick's skin crawled in rebellion at the sensation. From time to time a shower of heavier grit, blasted high up into the air over some distant plain, would rain down. To the men it seemed directed with malice, an attempt on the part of the angry world to lay them low. The plastics of Bannick's visor were scored and pitted within moments of leaving the security of the Baneblade. He had a sudden recollection of his first battle here on Kalidar, when he would not risk his periscope glass. Time and the war were wearing away his defences, shelling him layer by layer, until now here he was, lost in the teeth of another storm, his protection gone from armaplas and ceramite to heavy clothing. He entertained the terrifying thought that this might be stripped away also, leaving him naked in the sands.

The shapes of the tanks came and went as they marched, grit rattling from their hulls, faint red blinks coming from their vision arrays, laser-pulsed data flickering from tank to tank.

It was sophisticated technology, not often fitted to the humble Leman Russ, these tanks being specially equipped for the strikeforce.

A flat-topped tank loomed out of the storm, the tracery of a crane arm hard against the buff sky, its metal drawing a chorus of eerie shrieks from the wind.

Ganlick staggered as Bannick stopped and the line connecting them went taut; the second gunner had not noticed the Atlas, head down against the wind. Bannick went to his aid. Bannick indicated the Atlas, and they both halted.

'Sir, sir,' said Bannick, shouting to hear his own voice above the storm. 'We've reached the Atlas, orders please?' Bannick could not stop a small plea entering his voice. A burst of static replied. He leaned into his comrade, resting his rebreather directly against Ganlick's, trusting that direct contact would carry his voice through rubber and plastic. 'Nothing from Cortein.'

Ganlick replied, muffled. 'Let's go aboard, see if we can communicate via pulse.'

Bannick nodded.

Together they made their way round the recovery tank's rear traction spade, to one of the side access hatches. Bannick drew his pistol and slammed the butt hard on the door four times.

Half a minute passed. The door ground open and the mask of a rebreather appeared. They were beckoned inside. They wasted minutes struggling through the narrow door. Eventually inside, the door clanged shut and the tank roared as the engine gunned, sucking the dust-laden air into its purification filters. The tank's commander gave a thumbs-up, and they removed their masks.

'What's the situation?' asked the tank commander. Behind him sat a gaunt-looking driver. On a pile of equipment sat Valle, the taskforce astropath. Valle was the only sure means for the group to communicate with command, although until they left the basin his powerful mind was useless. He sat with poise, his calm, eyeless face framed by green robes, at odds with the vehicle's operator, who lay bound and gagged on the floor to his right, terrified eyes rolling white. The commander followed his gaze.

'Hmmm, yeah. Tokkan there started up pretty soon after we got into the basin,' he said.

'I sense your concern,' said the astropath serenely. 'He will be fine once we leave the basin. Such a concentration of crystalline lorelei has unfortunate effects upon the weak-willed, but the visions can do no direct harm. His affliction will pass.'

'We're all affected,' said Bannick. 'Exertraxes has gone into the swiftdust, raving. We've got to get him out. You had a data-pulse on the situation?'

'Not yet, but we've got a burst of it on the vox, here and there amid the static.' The commander nodded to his driver, who turned to a comms panel and tapped out a message. Moments later a thin line of flawed paper spat from the console. 'Cortein says this is the case, sir. He's assumed command. They say that Exertraxes has minutes at best before he goes under.'

The commander sucked in his lower lip, pulling at the stubble on his chin with the upper. 'We can't go in there, we'll sink in seconds.'

'How do you ordinarily pull a tank out of the dust?' said Bannick.

'Someone takes a line in – men sink less quickly than tanks. Usually him.' The commander moved his head in the direction of his operator. 'And he's not going anywhere. I could go, but…' he shrugged.

'We'll do it, we're suited up already,' said Ganlick.

'Sure?' said the Atlas commander, but he wasn't seeking a reply. 'We'll need to reposition…' He looked to his driver.

'Location's up on the tac display sir.'

'Fine. We'll disengage the hook and begin to unspool the wire. When we drop the spade and dig in, that's the signal to go. Move slow and wide, don't rush or you'll be sucked under.'

'Vox is useless in this,' said Bannick. 'Send a message to Epperaliant to tell the others not to use their voxes at all. Then we can send a signal like this.' He activated the vox in the mask hanging from his neck. Three bursts of static came out. 'A quick double like this means there's trouble.' He demonstrated. 'Pull us out if so.'

'Very good,' said the Atlas commander. 'Set out straight from the back of the tank. Use the cable as a guide. We'll line up as best we can. There's a couple of sets of sandshoes stowed there.' He indicated a rack to the rear, where strapped contrivances like broad-woven baskets hung. 'Good luck. May the Emperor watch over you.'

'Come on Bannick, let's go,' said Ganlick, making for the internal door that led through the track unit. 'Basdack coward, should have gone himself, it's his damn job,' he muttered to Bannick as they secured their masks, uncaring whether the commander heard or not. Then, 'Anything happens to me, and it looks like we're not going to make it out, cut the line, save yourself. Got it, sir? I'll be doing the same.'

Bannick nodded.

Outside, they stood back as the Atlas ponderously swivelled round, back pointing at the swiftdust. There was a dull clunk and the hook's lock disengaged, leaving it to swing loose in the wind, and the engine died. The winch wound round, depositing several loops of cable on the ground. Bannick and Ganlick took up the hook, dragging the woven metal rope behind them.

'This is heavy,' Ganlick said, complaint heavy with interference.

There was a whine of hydraulics, and the spade at the rear of the vehicle descended, pushing into the sand until the rear of the tank rose slightly.

'That's the signal,' said Bannick and pointed emphatically, unsure if Ganlick would have heard.

They walked out from the Atlas, Ganlick carrying the hook, Bannick taking up station ten metres behind him. That way, should they wander off course the cable would kink and alert them. More cable unspooled as they walked.

Up ahead, Ganlick slowed. He'd hit the swiftdust. The dark bulks of armoured vehicles resolved themselves. Two Leman Russ were reversing slowly from the swiftdust zone. Another was mired further out, but figures swathed as he and Ganlick were knee-deep in the dust, attaching tow cables that ran back to a fourth tank almost invisible in the dust storm.

Ganlick had stopped and was donning the sandshoes. Bannick took the opportunity to do the same, laying the cable down while he struggled them on. He'd worn similar broad footwear to walk on snow back home on Paragon; the idea being that they increased the surface area of the feet and so stopped them sinking so easily, but the fastenings were unfamiliar to him, and it took him three tries to get them on. He stood, and Ganlick gestured for him to follow. One of the men to the rear of the swamped Russ looked up and waved, an offer of help, Bannick shook his head and waved them back.

Bannick was in the swiftdust moments later.

There was little to warn him. A shift in the stability of the sand, perhaps, a feeling of looseness, but it was hard to tell with the surface being so motile if that was an actual effect or a sensation born of fear. There was no colour variation between the normal sand and the swiftdust, although the latter was usually smoother; this subtle visual clue to the danger was obscured by the storm, both by the lack of visibility and the tendrils of windblown sand that curled at ground level like snakes.

Soon though, he felt the effects. The sand began to drag at his feet, and he noted that they sank further than before, even with the sandshoes on. He twisted and pulled, the exhausting rhythm he'd learnt as a boy on Paragon coming back easily to him – it was hard work, but he had the cable to lean on, and that helped with the buffeting of the storm winds. He could not see the stranded Chimera, so instead followed the indistinct shape of the large gunner.

Swiftdust was the bane of life on Kalidar and could suck a tank under in minutes. The constant storms on the planet generated immense amounts of static electricity. Much of this energy was dissipated in ferocious dry lightning storms. But sometimes it lingered, suspending the talc-like dusts in a mixture not unlike quicksand. Within one patch its consistency could vary from near solid to thick liquid, and rapidly fluctuate between. Although here and there across Kalidar there were stable seas of it, the stormy nature of the world meant that any hollow in the landscape could harbour a pocket of the stuff. The Adeptus Mechanicus had devised a complicated means, employing a forest of copper rods and capacitors, to draw away the electricity and collapse the dustfields, but it was a time-consuming and imprecise affair, only used where a swiftdust field had formed in front of a large group or blocked a key line of advance.

Bannick was concentrating so hard on his feet, sure that any lapse would result in his immediate death, that he ran into the back of Ganlick.

Ganlick pointed. The rear of the Chimera, canted at a forty-five-degree angle, protruded from the sand. Frantic banging came from within. The rear door ramp was part open. A hand waved in the air, ungloved and raw. Bannick grasped it.

'Get back inside! Shut the door or you'll all suffocate! We're going to tow you out,' shouted Bannick over the vox. A crackling greeted him, but the hand withdrew, and the door shuddered shut by a few centimetres, sand blocking its full closure.

He and Ganlick were up to their knees now, the eddies caused by the slowly sinking APC dragging them under with it.

Bannick flailed his way over to his fellow tanker, grabbing his shoulder, leant his face against Ganlick's. 'We don't have much time, Ganlick, they'll not get that door shut.' Bannick glanced at the rivers of dust pouring inside.

'Where do we attach this?' shouted Ganlick. 'The tow points are too deep under, I can't fight it through.'

Bannick ran his eyes quickly over the sinking vehicle. The top of the turret's antennae array were slipping out of sight into the unrippled dust surface. Soon the whole thing would follow.

His eyes locked with Ganlick's. 'Run it through the grab handles,' he shouted.

'They'll never hold.'

'They'll have to. Give it to me.'

Ganlick reluctantly handed the hook over.

'Boost me up onto the roof, I can't get up myself.'

Up to their waists in the sucking dust now, Ganlick struggled to shove Bannick onto the Chimera. Bannick kicked off the sandshoes, and that seemed to help.

After an exhausting minute, Bannick was atop the tank. Bending the cable into a loop as best he could, he pushed it through one of the four grab handles still visible on the vehicle's angled sides, wiggling it frantically, working against both its own thickness and the friction provided by the sand. He tugged it through, pulling the hook against the handle, then thought better of it and wrapped a free loop of line round the hook. He then tugged as much slack in as he could through the handle, and passed the loop over the top hatch, and into another handle, then back over, digging dust out of the way to get to the third handle as it vanished into the red-and-grey desert floor.

By the time he reached the last handle and passed the cable through one more time, only the top hatch and the very rear of the tank were still above the level of the dust. He looked behind the tank. Ganlick was up to his neck in it, one shoulder free, hand gripping the lip of the cracked back ramp.

As quickly as he was able, Bannick grabbed at the hook and its loop of slack, and ran it under and over the cable criss-crossing the top hatch. Finally, he hooked the hook into the middle and closed its catch. He looked to Ganlick, who nodded.

Bannick stepped back as far as he was able, sand and dust pouring over his boots. Three bursts on the vox. A moment of silence, then the cable leading back to the shore sprang free from the dust with a thrum. It quivered in the air, a shriek rising from the storm as it cut itself across the line. Distantly, Bannick could make out the roar of a powerful engine labouring.

The Chimera stopped sinking, then, as the Atlas growled in the depths of the storm, it began to re-emerge.

Bannick felt a surge of relief as the command tank's aerials came back out of the dustpatch.

He looked to Ganlick, and his heart turned cold.

The motion of the tank was forcing the big man under the sand. Bannick dove backwards, landing hard on the Chimera roof.

"Lick! 'Lick! Take my hand!' he pushed his arm out. The meaty fist of the second gunner sought his once, twice, failed. His head was disappearing.

Bannick swore, thrust his outstretched arm into the liquid dust, found a gloved hand. Tugging with all his might, he guided it to the cable, helped the big man hook his fingers round it. But they were both weak, and Bannick did not know how long Ganlick could hold on, nor what forces were exerted on him by the sand as the Chimera was dragged free.

An indistinct babble on the vox, a hiss. 'Cut the rope,' said Ganlick, distant, as if already dead, his soul carried away into the warp.

'No,' replied Bannick.

Bannick inched forwards, grabbing with one hand at the web of cables he'd made, gripping Ganlick's wrist as tight as he could, hoping he could hold on long enough, that the respirator could provide the second gunner with sufficient air to keep him conscious until they were free, but it was no good, Ganlick was being dragged under the Chimera as it was pulled back.

With agonising slowness, the Chimera was tugged towards solid ground, still Ganlick clung on.

'Colaron.' The call of his name, the clarity of the voice cutting through the roar and fury of Kalidar, made Bannick start so hard he nearly let go of Ganlick.

His head whipped round. There, standing in the air, unaffected by the storm, stood Tuparillio, unchanged from the day Bannick had seen him last, the day he had killed him.

The phantom vanished as a screech of tortured metal rent the air. One of the grab handles suddenly gave. The Chimera lurched as cable spanged taut. A chunk of metal hurtled through the air, narrowly missing Bannick's face as he was thrown free. He landed in the dust, and was immediately sucked into the sand. His legs felt as if they were locked in rockcrete.

Ganlick's hand slipped from the cable.

He was going to have to cut the rope linking them.

He reached for his knife, strapped about his waist, but by now the swiftdust was pulling hard, rushing to fill the void left by the departing APC, and he was in up to his chest. He could not get to his blade. Vainly he reached for the Chimera, but it slid by his outstretched fingertips.

He sank deeper.

His arms became pinned, the dust covered his chin.

Grains of sand jostled with one another over his goggles, fighting to slay him. Bannick finally succumbed to panic, struggling against the sand as the roar of Kalidar's angry magnetosphere howled in his ears through his vox headset.

The swiftdust pulled him into the dark.

Epperaliant thumped down onto the command deck from the central ladder, dust showering from his outer gear. He unwrapped the scarf from about his face, removed his goggles and rebreather and breathed in the tank's thick fug as if it were as sweet as mountain air.

'Exertraxes is secure, sir,' he reported. 'Valle has helped him, he's chanting the liturgy like a priest in peril right now.'

'The Leman Russ?'

'They hauled themselves out, sir, it was close, but there have been no further losses.'

'Except Ganlick and Bannick,' said Cortein.

'I'm afraid there's no sign of them, sir,' said Epperaliant.

Cortein sat straight in his chair. Three men down on *Mars Triumphant*, with Vorkosigen riding a knife-edge of madness. Not good. Not good at all.

He pressed the button on his vox horn. 'Attention!' he shouted, hoping to batter the voice of Kalidar aside with his own. 'Cortein speaking. I'm taking command,' he said. 'I want regular sound-offs from each vehicle every ten minutes until we're out of this mess. Keep an eye on your crewmates and squad members. If anyone starts to act strangely, restrain them immediately, no matter what their rank. Drivers to rotate every third hour. These measures are to continue until I say otherwise. Prepare to move out.' His finger left the horn button. 'Epperaliant, relay that by signal laser and signal lamp. I want the whole convoy clear on this.'

'Sir.'

Cortein looked to his instruments as Epperaliant sent out the orders, lost deep in thought, Ganlick and Bannick gone. He exhaled hard, sat up straight. Their mourning would have to wait. He had a job to do. 'Outlanner,' he said, 'take us out of here.'

INTERSTITIAL

'The Emperor does not forgive easily. Mercy is not His
purview. Those that fall from His grace face a long and
hard climb back into favour...

'There is one sin that offends the Emperor more than
any, and that is the rejection of duty. To reject the duty
the Emperor grants to us all is the most egregious of all
acts. To do so not only invites eternal damnation for the
individual, but for each and every human soul that turns
their back upon their allotted task, the burden falls harder
upon those faithful who heed their calling. And thus the
risk for all increases. To the individual, this may seem
a small increment, a tiny drop, but hearken! Is not an
ocean filled drop by drop?

'Let it be known that for those who serve, the Emperor
has nothing but love, that to give oneself wholly to
the Emperor's way, to trust in His judgement in His
assignation of tasks for you, is the greatest act a man can
perform. No sin is so grave, no crime so unforgiveable,
that the stain cannot be wiped away by toil in the name
of the greater glory of the Master of all Mankind. To you,
delivered from the dark by the good offices of our Lord
Solar, you who have dwelled so long without the light of
our lord and saviour, there can be only one choice:
Serve, serve, serve!'

*Ecclesiarch Ponpus Theriodes, prior to the
Goodholme Burning, M41.*

INTERSTITIAL

The lorelei has a melting point of 1137 degrees. It is
smelted, purified first by manual scraping and then by
rotation in a centrifuge. This process is repeated until
a purity level of greater than 99 parts per 100 lorelei to
other material has been achieved. The molten liquid is
quickly cooled and processed into pellet form. The rapid
cooling of the material prevents the reformation of the
crystalline matrix that gives the lorelei its psychoactive
properties, and so it is rendered safe for transport to other
centres of manufacturing. Once delivered, the pellets are
remelted, psychically cleansed, and cast into the desired
shape. It is allowed to cool very slowly – it can take over
a year to grow the finest psy-matrices used by the holy
orders of the Emperor's Inquisition, the Scholastica
Psykana, and the Librarium of the Adeptus Astartes. Only
then is it checked, rechecked, blessed and sanctified,
before being employed in a manner befitting the purpose
to which it is intended.

An Introduction to the Arts of Psychoactive Crystalline
Form, *page 93*, *'Kalidarian lorelei'*, *by Magos Eko.*

CHAPTER 21

KALIDAR IV, HIVE MERADON
3343397.M41

Blazing green eyes, a scarred head with wild plumes of crackling hair, rough hands. Something violent and questing pushing deep into his mind, tearing, ripping and pulling.

Brasslock's memory was disjointed, shattered by psychic aftershock. He did not know where he was. He would lose consciousness and awaken in the cell, seemingly lying there for weeks and weeks, floating on a sea of pain, sometimes becoming delirious, his mind full of visions of marching orks dressed in parodies of Imperial garb, profaning the name of the Emperor, scarring the souls of machines with their crude additions. The faces of his colleagues and friends, his enemies and rivals, the ork warboss and countless other foes poured through his mind.

Once, he started awake. He was at a desk in the scriptorum adjoining the tech vaults of the scholam on Marcellus. The room smelled comfortingly of metal, rust, old paper and age-brittle flimsies, of film-fungus and degraded data crystal. He was a young novitiate and had yet to receive his first external enhancement, the scars above his new ingram still itchy. For several minutes he took in the sights of the room, and began to think that his career, two centuries of study and war, had yet to happen.

Pain shattered the vision. Clumsy fingers of green fire scrabbling through his consciousness.

Somehow he clung on to his personality, to his very soul, because through it all, close to hand, was the stranger from the cell. In the light, Brasslock saw that he was an officer, one from the Paragonian regiments, the stains upon his uniform a mixture of blood and oil. Brasslock stopped asking himself why the orks could not see him. He realised his mind was malfunctioning, already the bonds between flesh and machine in his skull were coming undone. It would not be long before the synapses of his brain began to unravel. The stranger's presence was doubtless the first sign of that.

Still, he took strength from the stranger, who silently urged him to resist.

In the examination room, they tortured him in between bouts of psychic examination, burning and cutting what little remained of his flesh, running high currents through his components. Before, the pain they had inflicted on him had been a by-product of their childlike curiosity. Now they were trying their best to hurt him.

His legs were wrenched free, the pain circuits of his gifts laid bare and attached to horrible machines. The agonies the mechanic and torturer inflicted upon him were as nothing compared to the pain and sense of violation from the acts of the ork they called Greeneye.

When he came in, that first time, Brasslock thought he might die of fright. Greeneye was tall and gangly. His head seemed far too large for his scrawny body, a wild, straggly beard of crimson dangled from his jutting chin, similar hair, fine and artificial-looking, sticking up from all angles on his head. He carried a thick copper stave, chained to his wrist and leg, topped with the double-headed axe common to these orks. His uniform was a crazed motley of clashing camouflage schemes, a hat that looked like it had been take from the head of a cardinal crammed onto his crazy mop. Bells, also copper, jangled where he walked, and random cracks and sparks of energy shot from him, earthing themselves in anything that happened to be near.

When he entered the room, the gretchin assistants of the two ork specialists slunk back, ears flattening against their heads underneath their fatigue caps. The orks themselves seemed cowed, behaving in a subdued way, as if they were seeking to placate the ork sorcerer.

Greeneye himself was manic, cackling insanely, twisting his copper staff between his hands. Two stone-faced ork minders kept two steps behind him at all times, heavy clubs in hand, ready to strike should his powers run out of control.

The ork witch drew near to where the remains of Brasslock were pinned, arms spread, to a tilted torture bench.

Hello human, a voice sounded in his head. *We are going to get to know each other very well, you and I.* Mind to mind, without the interference of vocal chord and language, the ork expressed itself clearly, yet Brasslock could sense seething energies of great potency and violence behind its words. *I'm the one in charge here. Shhh!* The ork drew a finger across his lips and smiled wickedly. *Don't tell! It was me who wanted to come here, to Kalidar, for the crystals. The crystals give me power. Power to build a Waaagh! that no creature, man or ork has ever seen before. I will magnify the Mork-call, I will sing loud the shout of Gork through the green wyrd. This is what your Emperor does, with his light, with his fire. So shall I! A great green fire no ork will be able to resist, no ork will stay behind, a green tide, half the galaxy wide!* The ork spread his arms and clacked his teeth. *You have seen my Gargant? Seen its power? It is only the beginning.*

A flash. Brasslock found himself deep within the bowels of Hive Meradon, right at the bottom of the shaft. High above, a coin of light shone. Work teams of humans – highborn shackled next to mutant slave caste – orks and gretchin laboured hard on a monstrous machine. Despite its crude build, Brasslock recognised the machine as a psychic resonator, similar to those used to amplify the signals of astropaths in relay stations. Smelting machinery, taken from one of the hive's factories, glowed red-hot two hundred or so metres away, clanking conveyor belts pouring unprocessed lorelei crystals into seven deep crucibles. Blistered men and women, many maskless, worked long poles like rakes, scraping impurities from the top. Goggled orkish overseers whipped and cajoled, as did other men.

Always, there were those who were willing to betray their own.

Ork mechanics oversaw the process, barking orders, pointing, working massive spanners to bolt the frame of the machine together, welding and riveting. Others, bigger, dress ornate and decorated with glyphs of axes and spanners, looked over the smelters, making sure no bored ork threw in a prisoner for their amusement and contaminated the crystal. Near the crucibles stood a large, ribbed vessel that could only be a mould, to shape the lorelei into its final form.

But to do that, I need Gratzdakka, said Greeneye, and the vision melted away. *And he wants your tank, your* Lux Imperator, *for himself.* The ork pointed at the young officer. *He cannot help you. But he can watch.*

'Now,' said the ork aloud in shattered, throaty Gothic. 'Hold still, 'cause this is really going to hurt.' With that he reached forward a gnarled, scabby hand, placed it over Brasslock's face and took a deep breath.

Brasslock screamed as he felt the sinews of his mind forced apart.

Time ceased to have any meaning shortly after. The chronometer in his eyepiece was dead, although the eye still functioned. The ork mechanic had been careful to leave Brasslock's machine senses and organs more or less intact, as had the medical specialist with his organics. No point torturing him if he could not experience it, or if he died before they had the information. The ork witch never spoke to him like that again, only probed and probed and probed until Brasslock felt his skull would burst.

Finally it stopped.

He was back in the cell. Every nerve ending, every circuit, burned with pain. He was on his back, hand held crooked over his chest. His lungs wheezed and clicked. Supposedly good for a million breaths more, Brasslock sensed that they would not last long.

His friend, the stranger, stood over him. 'You did well,' he said. 'But I am afraid they have the information they need to repair the power transmission systems of *Lux Imperator*'s volcano cannon.'

'I am sorry.' Brasslock felt for his ingrams. They were shocked and truculent, ghostly overlays of corrupt data clogging them. His intelligence core flickered and buzzed, doubling his thoughts, his mind and back-up operating out of sync, the after-effects of a brutal data rip.

'You delayed them. The mechanic could not find the ingrams, the witch could not read them when he did. It took them several days to acquire the data, several days that will help our cause.'

'Now, they will let me die?' said Brasslock.

The stranger looked sorrowful. 'Be strong, Enginseer Brasslock, be strong.'

An ork came and took him soon after. The ork took his hand and dragged him away without effort. He did not weigh much now. He had been reduced to a blackened, scarred torso, one arm attached, metallic spine all that remained of his lower body.

The ork pulled him through endless corridors and stairs, until finally they brought him into the half-light of the storm raging above the hive's central shaft. He was in the marshalling yard before *Lux Imperator*, its hull defaced with blue and black zigzags, iron maw framing its cannon, jerry-rigged turrets jutting out from its track units.

Brasslock could feel the torment of the machine-spirit trapped within.

Other orks joined the one dragging him. They lifted him high. It was then that Brasslock saw the spikes, two long, thin slivers of steel on the front, to the side of the cannon's barrel.

The defiled engine of *Lux Imperator* growled, and the orks cheered.

The wagon would soon be ready for war.

INTERSTITIAL

The amplification of low-grade psychic ability is a side effect of lorelei presence. Naturally occurring crystalline matrices can amplify inborn abilities to noticeable levels. All slave workers are to be checked thrice weekly for incipient witch activity. Those according to standard human phenotype are to be incarcerated and maintained in lorelei-shielded holding cells for the next Black Ship rotation. Those deviating by more than 14 points on the Godolkind Purebreed Guide *<NOTE this is an increase from previous norms of 11 points deviation>* from standard forms are to be immediately liquidated. Standard human populations in the upper hives are to be checked twice weekly, this order *<59>* is now applicable to all grades and ranks. *<Cross ref. Adeptus Arbites case 9,000,873aSigma>* …caution must, however be exercised. In areas of naturally occurring psycho-sensitive crystalline matrices, non-psychic designated personnel may be subject to visions, poltergeist activity or outbursts of hysteria. *<See cross ref. 'The Ghosts of Kalidar'.>*

Extract from amendments to general orders relating to the tithing of emergent psykers on Kalidar, by order of the planetary lord, Imperial Governor Cann. M41

CHAPTER 22

KALIDAR IV, REMAINS OF HIVE KIMERADON
CONSTRUCTION SITE
3344397.M41

Down and down went Bannick, sucked deeper into the choking dust. His rebreather's cycling circuits kicked in when no further air was being drawn from outside. A beep sounded in his ear; the unit's small carbon dioxide scrubbing facility would keep him alive for twenty minutes, no more, and then he would begin to suffocate.

A more pressing problem – he almost laughed at the irony – was the weight of the sand. The deeper he went, the tighter the squeeze of the swiftdust. He found it hard to breathe. He had to force himself not to pant, as hyperventilating would use up his air supply all the quicker.

Down he went. Another beep sounded, ten minutes left. The pressure grew on his limbs, squeezing at his head. Black spots swam in front of his eyes, and he felt consciousness slipping away from him.

Something below him gave. The pressure on his chest abruptly eased and he sucked in a great gulp of tinny, recycled air. He felt himself pick up speed, the sand rasping as it rushed past him.

He burst into an open space, carried by a torrent of sand. Flashes of murky light came and went, and he felt himself fall. He had enough time to make himself go limp before he hit a pile of sand. Over and over he rolled, down a slope, equipment banging painfully into him as he windmilled without control to a stop.

The rope attaching him to Ganlick was taut. It had acted like an anchor, preventing him from falling any further into the pit, which continued down another one hundred metres to form a shallow cone.

He stood with care. He was bruised, but unharmed. He pulled at the rope, using it to haul himself up the slope to where it disappeared into the sand. He pulled at it, but it might as well have gone into rockcrete. Frantically, he threw himself down and dug at the sand like a dog, using his hands as paddles. Sand poured into the hole he had made, endless streams of it; he dug faster, eventually hitting cloth, shoulder – Ganlick.

Diverting the flow of sand away from his comrade with his body, Bannick struggled to free him. Eventually, he had the top half of Ganlick's body free.

Bannick cradled Ganlick's head. He was dead. At some point his mask and hood had come free, and his nose and mouth were full of sand. His cropped hair and new beard were thick with the stuff, eyes caked with it. As best he could, Bannick brushed the second gunner's head and face clean and closed his eyes. He bowed his head in silent prayer then laid his comrade gently down.

Not taking his eyes from the dead man's face, he stood, unsheathed his knife and cut through the line binding them together. He thanked the Emperor. Ganlick had saved Bannick's life through his death, anchoring him and preventing his further fall down the sand slope into the quickdust at the bottom of the shaft.

Only then did he step back from the sandfall and take account of his surroundings. He was in a deep shaft, like that found in one of the hives. It was dim, but the storm-muted sky at the top cast enough illumination for him to see. He realised then that he must somehow have come across the unfinished city Ganlick had told him of a few days before.

The builders had excavated side tunnels and the shaft before they had pulled out. How deep they had delved, Bannick did not know, for they were but black holes in the rock. The wind moaned across the shaft aperture, rising and falling, and a shower of fine dust rained down constantly, torrents of thicker sand shushing down in short bursts, but down sheltered from the wind the air was still.

Platforms and girders protruded from the walls, mountings for construction and excavation equipment or moorings for structures never built. At the top of the slope where Bannick stood, the rock of the shaft wall was visible, the double helix of the up and down roads also visible within. The roads were rough tubes bored through the soft rock. No plating or cladding had ever been installed, and each one was awash with sand and choked by rockfalls, their lower portions hidden by the sand in the pit. The sky above was darkening, going from featureless buff to grey. Night would come soon. He did not want to be left blundering about in the dark.

He made his way up the side of the pit to the edge of the road, testing the ground ahead of him with one foot every few paces. Finally he gained his objective, climbed over the road's rough-hewn lip, and dropped down. He caught his breath, checked his equipment, and thought upon his next actions.

Not knowing what else to do, he partook of the meagre rations in his belt pouches, and fell asleep, exhausted.

* * *

Bannick awoke to bone-numbing cold. His teeth chattering, he curled as tight as he could and tried to keep warm. The persistent feeling of being watched that he'd had ever since they had come into the basin plagued him, and try as he might, he could not dismiss it from his mind. Time and again he lifted his head and looked around the dark. It was so dark he could not see. He had a small supply of flares in his belt. He needed to conserve all his supplies, he told himself, but in the end the feeling of eyes upon him became too much, and he scrabbled up to his knees, fumbled with shaking hands in a belt pouch, and pulled out the flare.

He struck it against the rock. It flared bright, his body shivering gratefully at its sudden warmth. He held it high and stood, peering into the dark beyond the circle of light cast by the flare. It hissed as it burned, dripping molten compounds onto the floor.

He turned round. Something moved beyond the light.

The flare guttered and died. His eyes flared with after-images.

He struck another flare. Light burst out again.

Standing in front of him, his face almost touching his own, stood Tuparillio, eyes dead, skin the blanched the white of the exsanguinated. He stared deep into Bannick's face, his eyes boring into his soul.

'Proud you were, and callous,' he hissed. 'Murderer.'

Bannick's nerve broke. He shouted and fled, his flare casting wild, flickering shadows on the inner wall of the road as he ran upwards, round its gentle curve. He dodged past rockfalls and sandpiles, flying in the low gravity. The flare burnt out and he cast it aside, running blind, stumbling. His dishonour had followed him.

Something caught his foot, turning it and casting him to the floor.

Bannick's insides turned to ice. Behind him, bobbing up and down, came a light.

'Tuparillio! Tuparillio!' he shouted. 'Forgive me, please forgive me!'

His voice echoed round the pit. Still the light advanced, a will o' the wisp, coming implacably for him, the ghost of the kin he murdered.

He pulled out his laspistol, the small charge light on the side providing an infernal cast to the dark. He held it level, then looked at it in horror. What good was a gun against a phantom, would he try and murder his cousin a second time? He cast it aside to clatter from the roadside wall, screwed his eye shut. 'Oh Emperor, forgive me, I ask only to serve, forgive me. I was proud and I was arrogant. Tuparillio…' Tears tracked their way down the dust on his face, wetting his mask under the respirator.

A hand fell on his shoulder.

'No forgiveness, hush, hush, no need. Wake, wake, open eyes! Open eyes!'

Bannick did as he was bade. A man stood over him; a man of a kind. His kindly eyes were too widely spaced, lopsided mouth studded with twisted teeth. One arm was hulking and massive, a lantern on a staff clasped in malformed fingers, the other terminating in a hand with only four fingers, currently resting upon Bannick's shoulder. A mutant. Any disgust Bannick felt was swamped by relief.

'Hush hush,' said the mutant, his voice adendoidal from the air filter plugged into his nostrils, a long rifle, a hunter or sniper's weapon, slung over his shoulder. 'It is the ghosts, yes? You have seen them, the ghosts of Kalidar?' Bannick nodded mutely.

'No worry, I here now.' The mutant shook his sand-crusted coat. Shards of crystal stitched onto it in a complicated pattern jangled on his chest. 'Ghosts go away.'

INTERSTITIAL

'Fear the mutant, loathe the mutant,
destroy the mutant.'

*Edict of Ecclesiarch Thanatos, Prelate-General
of the Red Redemption*

CHAPTER 23

KALIDAR IV, REMAINS OF HIVE KIMERADON
CONSTRUCTION SITE
3344397.M41

Bannick could not pronounce the mutant man's name, so settled on calling him Olli. The creature did not seem to mind. 'You big brave soldier of the Sky Emperor, you want call me Olli, you call me Olli! Is no problem! Scum-speak hard for you? Olli take you to Bruta, yes. He'll know! But first, you take this.'

In one scabbed hand, the mutant held out a talisman.

'You, you took that from Ganlick,' Bannick said, the revulsion he had at the sandscum returning.

'Yes,' the creature's face was innocent. 'I have offended you? Is good talisman.' It waved it at Bannick. 'He no need it now. It keep ghosts away. Is good.' It adjusted the long rifle slung over its malformed shoulder and peered at him earnestly.

Bannick looked Olli up and down: beneath his filthy robes, he caught a glimpse of Ganlick's boots, his belt, canteen and knife…

A surge of the old Bannick rose up in him. How dare this

impure creature defile the resting dead? The brave and pure that fought to keep this planet free of ork conquest? His muscles tensed.

Olli looked dismayed, and took a step backwards.

Bannick stopped himself. What was he thinking? The sandscum was only trying to survive, and although it was impure, a mutant, Olli was his best chance of living too. What else was he going to do? Walk out of the top of the hive into the quickdust fields? Ganlick would not begrudge him the talisman.

He reached out his hand. He opened his mouth, and struggled out, 'Thank you.'

'That good talisman.' Olli tapped it with a too-long finger. 'No bother you, not now.'

'It drives them away?'

Olli laughed. 'Oh no. It stop you seeing them, is all. They still there!'

Bannick shivered and looked around the dark outside Olli's faint circle of lantern light.

'Come now, we go. Is long way!'

Beckoning, the mutant set off up the road, lantern swaying, light catching the edges of rockpiles on the broad way.

Olli chattered on in its pidgin Gothic, pointing out this or that, things half hidden in the dark, covered over with sand. Much of it Bannick could not understand, but Olli did not seem to mind that either.

Half an hour later, Olli beckoned Bannick into a side tunnel, an unfinished transit tube run out from the shaft to serve the planned hive's broader spread.

'Come come, come come!' said the mutant.

Bannick hesitated. The mutant peered back at him with a puzzled expression. It did not seem to mean him any harm. Lacking other options, Bannick followed.

They walked for some time. Bannick noticed the occasional sign of habitation. Scuff marks in the sand, footprints, flat rocks with black circles on them, rags, broken bits of metal and at one intersection they came to, piles of bones.

'Orks come here, kill many sandscum, but we kill more!' Olli laughed wetly then stopped. 'Hmph, so sad, many hearths with no head now, who will feed the children?' he shook his head.

'You leave your dead?'

'Yes, yes!' said Olli. 'Of course. Leave dead, sand-mites come, we catch sand-mites, for food, for oil!' He shook his lantern. 'We use many things from sand-mites, when bones clean, then bury in house of dead. Not before.' The mutant searched the skeletons, turning the bones over carefully. 'No mites here now, shame. I have dry.' He patted his pouches. 'We eat later. Too dangerous here.'

'How long until we get to this Bruta?' asked Bannick.

'One day, maybe little more.' Olli stuck out his lip and waggled his head from side to side. 'We rest tonight, then we go on. We live far away now, where orks cannot find us. Is hard for us to go up.' He pointed to the rocky ceiling, 'to hunt sandpikes, and we hungry, but we have just enough, and they will not follow so deep.'

'Why were you so close to the central shaft?'

'Sky hole? Because things fall in there! Especially in the storm. Fleetlizards, sandpike, easy food. Sometimes things more interesting, like you my friend!' he laughed. 'Come, we go. Is not safe here. From now, you step in my steps, understand?'

'To leave one trail?'

'Yes, yes!' Olli nodded approvingly.

On they went, further and further from the shaft. The tunnels carved in the abandoned attempt to construct the hive gave out, and Olli led him to a dead end.

'Now, you wait here.' The mutant pulled out a small lamp, a

little cup with fat and a wick in it, and lit it from his lantern. Then he scuttled off back the way they had come, stepping only where they had stepped before. Moments later he returned, pulling a weighted blanket across the sand they had walked through, obscuring their footsteps. To Bannick's eye it looked even more obvious than their track had.

'Olli leave meat,' the mutant explained. 'Further up tunnel, one, two, three places.' It held up three crooked fingers. 'Only small pieces, but many sand-mites come, from there, there, maybe there.' He pointed to loose piles of debris, and small holes in the rock. 'They leave many, many tracks. Hide us good, and their piss stink too! Orks no smell us.'

He checked over his work. Satisfied, he led Bannick behind a pile of rocks that obscured a tiny slit, a tighter squeeze than any tank hatch.

'Through here,' Olli said. 'I go first.'

The mutant handed his lantern and pole over, and wriggled into the gap.

A hand reappeared a moment later and beckoned. 'Come, come!'

Bannick looked at it doubtfully, then struggled through into another tunnel. The scrape marks of primitive tools were evident on the soft rock walls, the workmanship rough, but the tunnel ran true.

'Now we in real sandscum land!' said Olli proudly. 'No one know this here, not from outside.'

'Not even the hivers?' asked Bannick.

Olli spat. 'No! They hunt and kill us as often as they trade, but they no come here, they 'fraid of ghosts.'

'So why help me?' said Bannick.

Olli turned back and smiled. 'You have soft face, not hurt by sand. You are tall, not short. You are not of Kalidar. You wear uniform of Sky Emperor! You kill orks?'

'Some,' said Bannick.

'Then you help sandscum, so Olli help you.'

The tunnel led into a series of round tunnels that looked like they'd been melted from the rock. The work of a Kalidarian life-form, Bannick guessed. These tunnels formed a messy labyrinth that cut over and through itself, but Olli followed it unerringly ever downwards. The deeper they went, the lighter it got, bioluminescent fungus growing in ever-greater blue splotches, until in places the entire tunnel was a tube of light. Traces of other animal-life and plants became apparent. On the surface, Kalidar was a blasted wasteland, but wherever life could find a foothold, it invariably did. The tubes gave out onto a great cavern, the rock here harder than the compressed sand that covered most of Kalidar's surface. It was hotter down here, and Bannick was not altogether surprised to find a forest of woody plant-animals that retracted into themselves as he and Olli passed, their sudden movements stirring the pools of steaming water they clustered about. Small animals scurried from them. Olli fell quiet and peered between the plant-animal stems cautiously, but whatever he feared made no appearance.

High up on the other side of the cavern, Olli led him to a shelf of rock with an overhanging lip. The mutant dragged a boulder over to the foot of this cliff, just large enough to allow them to climb up to the shelf if they stood on it. Olli uncoiled a length of rope from his pack and carefully rested the rock on top of a loop of it, then pulled the loop of rope over the back of the rock. He gestured for Bannick to clamber up, then followed himself after passing Bannick the rope.

Once up, Olli pulled hard on the rope, causing the boulder to flip over and roll away.

'There, now we safe,' he said. 'Nothing can get up.' He dusted his hands off. 'We eat.' From his pack he produced a small stove made of salvaged metal, pumped it to prime it and lit it.

Bannick understood the blackened marks he'd seen on flat stones in the upper caverns. There were plenty on the rock platform. Olli poured in water from Ganlick's canteen, and added some dessicated lumps of sand-mite meat and some kind of plant material. Then he went to the back of the shelf, and produced more food, bedrolls and extra lamps from a niche in the rock, hidden by a flat stone.

'This is a safe haven for your people?' said Bannick.

'Oh yes, yes!' said Olli. 'The cavern quetlings, they not get us here.'

Bannick nodded, raised his own canteen and took a much-needed draught. He recapped the bottle, then noticed Olli looking at it longingly. He realised then that the mutant had used all his own water in preparing the meal for the pair of them.

He eyed the mutant dubiously. Olli was unclean in body and therefore in spirit, his body covered in sores. There was no telling what diseases he carried.

That had not stopped him from helping him.

Slowly, Bannick extended the canteen towards Olli.

The man's eyes lit up with gratitude. Licking scabbed and dry lips, he took the bottle, and drank his fill.

Bannick woke twice in the night. The first time was to an unearthly howl, followed by a terrible animal squealing. Exhausted, he drifted to sleep again, only to be stirred awake a second time by the sound of weeping.

He propped himself up on one elbow. 'Olli, are you all right?' he asked.

The mutant started, his long rifle jumping on his knees. 'Oh! Oh, is you, sky-soldier.' He wiped his face. 'Is nothing. I think of my wife. She dead now, long time since. I long for her still.' The mutant cleared his throat. 'You go sleep. We have long journey tomorrow.'

Bruta was short and slight, as many Kalidarians of the lower castes were, a result of poor nutrition and low gravity. He was otherwise untouched by mutation, and carried with him an air of authority. The other inhabitants of the ramshackle cave town Bannick found himself in paid all deference to him.

His office was made of rough-hewn stone, but its walls were lined with books and other data storage media. A half-metre statue of the Emperor stood on a table towards the door.

'Lieutenant,' he said. 'The best I can do for you now is to offer you quarters and lodging. I cannot spare men to guide you back to your unit. I cannot risk leading the orks into this refuge.'

His accent was that of the lower orders of Kalidar, yet he spoke clearly and intelligently. A self-educated man.

'And if I choose to leave myself?'

'Then you will be restrained.' Bruta's face bore an ugly triangular scar, where his implanted rebreather had been removed, Bannick guessed. It twisted as he smiled apologetically. He fixed his one good eye on Bannick, the other milky and blind.

'The war is at a crucial stage,' said Bannick. 'I was on a clandestine mission when I was separated from my men...'

'Your drive across the basin? You intend to attack Orktown, I assume? To take back the hive? A fool's errand. You are surprised,' said the man, 'yet we sandscum have spies. The servants, the servants of servants, the maintenance crews, the work gangs... Our agents are everywhere, for all have reason to hate the ruling classes here. Your departure was noted and passed on. Our influence goes deeper than you think. I've had men on sandpike trailing you the entire way.'

'I see,' said Bannick.

'Do not worry, your secret is safe,' said Bruta. 'We want the orks here no more than you. But I cannot allow you to leave. This refuge remains secret, thus far. Your departure will risk our safety.'

'You will not help us, help the Emperor then?'

'Why should we? You have seen the conditions we are forced to work under, we of the lower castes?'

'Yes, I have,' admitted Bannick.

'And?'

'I realise you do not have easy lives.'

Bruta looked him up and down. 'Look at you, born into some wealthy caste somewhere.' He waved his hand angrily in his direction. 'I can see that from your bearing, not unlike the way our hivelords strut. I recognise a lord or whatever you call yourselves when I see one, there's no hiding it. We are no different to the other men who make up the population of this world, no less in the eyes of the Emperor. But look, see my face? A scar from the device implanted upon me as soon as I stopped growing. I would have been bred twice, then forced to work the mines until I dropped. The mutants have it worse. By all rights, they should hate us all, we pure-born, and yet they do not. When I escaped my work detail a band of them took me in, brought me here to the only place where I have ever been shown kindness. Tell me, lieutenant, why should I risk the lives of my people helping those who have done nothing but oppress my kind?'

'Because the Emperor wills it to be so,' said Bannick.

'If that is the case, He can come here and ask me Himself,' said Bruta. He shook his head, and genuflected towards the statue, muttering an apology. He leaned on his desk and dropped his head. 'You make me forget myself. Please, stay here, be our guest, not our prisoner. We have a hard life, but it is more of a life than many on this world enjoy, and freer. We could use a man like you.'

Bannick shook his head. 'No. I have to go, it is my duty, I am under orders. Think, mayor Bruta. What will you do if the expedition fails? If the orks continue to guess our every move? There is a mind...'

'The ork witch?' Bruta asked. 'I have heard of him. He is a monster, by all accounts. Only the concentration of lorelei in the basin above keeps him ignorant of our location.'

'There you are.' He held out his hand. 'But do you not think that he will find you eventually? If the Imperium loses this world, and it falls under ork dominion for all time, what will become of your people then?'

'They will not let us fall. I have it on good authority that Kalidar is of some importance to another Imperial crusade.'

Another surprise. 'It is, but of minor importance. There are to be no new reinforcements, did you know that?' Bannick was risking his life sharing such information.

Bruta frowned. 'No, no I did not.'

'The Imperium is stretched thin in the Segmentum Pacificus, Bruta; there's more to the galaxy than your cave, and though it might seem a long way away, it affects you, even here. Many regiments and battlefleets have left for the galactic west. If this world cannot be secured by what is available, there will be no more raisings, do you understand? Kalidar will be virus bombed, and even you, here underground, will not survive that. Then new workers will be brought in, and the cycle will continue, only you and yours will have been wiped from history.'

Bruta ground his knuckles into the desk, then spoke. 'I am sorry. I will not aid those who would kill us by throwing our lives away. If you will not agree to remain of your own volition, you will be held until such time as I can be sure that you pose no threat to this settlement.'

'Listen! We have tanks, we are...'

'I have made my decision. Lieutenant, I am sorry.'

He rang for his guards, and they took Bannick away.

Bannick sat on the dry sand floor of his cell. It was as light in there as it was outside, both the inner walls of the prison and the cavern itself being covered in the luminescent algae and plant-animals. Outside, he could hear the quiet noises of a village, the sounds of draught beasts, small machines, the occasional snatch of laughter or speech. The scent of dung, growing things, and the peculiar meaty smell of fires fuelled by the plant-animals wafted in through the barred window; Bruta had made a haven of peace in the heart of a war.

Bannick had been well treated, far better than his hosts would have been by the Kalidarian elite, or his own army for that matter. Some sandscum were employed as native scouts and light cavalry, but they were held in derision by the normal men of the army group. And why not? When had he ever treated a mutant any better himself?

He thought back to his youth, light years behind him.

Perhaps incarceration here was a fitting fate for him. Obscurity and inevitable old age, or disease and a pointless death. For had he not been prideful? Had he not, in his hearts of hearts, hoped for glory to wash away his sin of dishonour? He should have focused on serving the Emperor, and not himself. He'd been given every chance, after all. Pride was not a sin, not when it could be used to serve, but it was when it took one away from the Emperor's purpose. He'd hoped to keep some of the fruit of his labours for himself. His stupid boyhood lust for glory, he'd never be rid of it.

He groaned and knocked the back of his head against the wall.

I'm sorry, my lord, he thought to himself. I'm sorry.

Time passed. He took to pacing back and forth. Lost in

thought, he continued to do so for some time.

The door opened; Bruta, flanked by nervous-looking men.

'If you promise not to run away, I could use your help,' said the mayor.

'Why?' said Bannick. 'Have you seen the sense of my argument?'

'Orks,' said Bruta. 'You are the only professional soldier I have here. Care to lend me your skills?'

Bannick shrugged. 'It's better than sitting out the war in this cell.'

'Good.' Bruta nodded behind him. Bannick's weapons and equipment were tossed onto the sand. 'We're leaving in two minutes.'

Ork speech boomed up and down the transit tunnel. There were fourteen of them, clustered about the body of a six-legged creature Bannick had learned was a sandpike, the carnivorous pseudo-lizard that the sandscum hunted for mounts and for meat. They'd made camp in between two piles of sand, off the old track beds. Here and there pieces of rotting monotrack could still be seen, half-buried in the sand, six hundred years since any train had used them.

Two of the orks were arguing about how best to joint the beast. Others looked at them, then got on with their tasks, two of them cutting up plant-animal stalks and bleeding them ready for burning. Another ork, larger than the rest, was playing with its knife, idly throwing it into an unfortunate example of Kalidar's wildlife pinned to the floor before it. It growled something in the deep clatter the orks had for speech. One of those arguing stepped forwards, rearing up a little, hunched shoulders unbending, but its comrade threw a long arm across its chest and shook its head. The big ork, the leader, grumbled something at them and laughed, then went back to its desultory tortures.

'Damn them,' whispered Bruta. He, Bannick, Olli and two other inhabitants of Scumtown hunkered down to the rear of the ork camp, twenty or so more sandscum waiting up the tunnel on the other side of the xenos. Olli had insisted on accompanying Bannick, his long rifle out and ready. 'If they're here,' continued Bruta. 'They're too close to town. Chances are, they've found it already.'

Half a kilometre behind, back the way they'd come, the transit tunnel had been ruptured by an earthquake in the distant past. Through a series of crevices and worm-tubes, the city of the sandscum could easily be reached.

'Where does this line go?' asked Bannick.

'It's a spur, not been used since the abandonment of the hive construction project,' said Bruta. 'The end of it we blew a long time ago, it should be choked by rubble.'

'But they're in, so I ask again, where does it go?'

'Eventually?' said Bruta grudgingly. 'Right into the heart of Orktown. Right into Hive Meradon, a hundred and fifty kilometres away.'

'These types,' Bannick said. 'They're commandoes of some kind, scouts. The same kind attacked our camp a few weeks ago, staging a raid that crippled the command Leviathan. If they get an inkling you are down here, they'll go back for more of their kind. We have to kill them now.'

'If they haven't found the entrance to the town…'

'They soon will, or others like them will, look.' Bannick pointed to a pair of strange, brightly coloured snuffling creatures tethered to a rock. 'Scent beasts. I reckon they already know you are here.'

Bruta snorted, lips twisted in thought. 'You are right,' he said eventually. 'We'll do this quickly and quietly, the sandscum way.' He turned to the men with them. 'Olli, Branka, Suumsta, you stay here with the lieutenant. Listen to what he says, it might save you. Bannick, once we've begun firing, outflank them, take them by surprise, and we'll cut them down in a crossfire. Don't let any of them escape or we're all dead.' He patted Bannick on the shoulder and withdrew.

One of the scent beasts became agitated and started to strain in the direction of Bannick's hiding place, the other taking up its calls of alarm. Bannick's breath caught as the big ork looked right at him. For a moment he thought he'd been seen, but the ork returned its attention to the creature on the floor. It toed it with a steel-capped boot. Dead. It got up and kicked the yapping scent beast, which slunk low and whimpered.

From his vantage point, Bannick saw an ork sentry go down, two men burying long knives in its neck, sawing and pulling back until its head came off. Sandscum filtered out past its twitching corpse, taking up firing positions, ready to engage the orks, opening up the rear to Bannick's men.

Bruta appeared, raised his hand, looked to his men. He dropped it, and they opened fire.

Primitive autoguns spat bullets streaking towards the orks. Their guns were feeble things compared to the las-weaponry of the guard, but their aim was good, and two of the orks were sent sprawling, holes drilled in their skulls, before they could react. The big ork bellowed orders, and the orks formed a circle, throwing themselves down against the walls of the sandy depression containing their camp and opening up with their large-calibre guns. A pair of them set up a large stubber-like weapon on a tripod. The gun efficiently deployed, the ork loader knocked its comrade on the helmet, and it let rip. The sand in front of Bruta's group exploded in a series of dust explosions as the orks played their heavy gun back and forth across the transit way. Several sandscum fell, the tunnel raucous with gunfire and screams.

'That makes things difficult,' said Bannick. He waved the

sandscum forwards. 'Olli, how far can you kill with that rifle?'

Olli grasped his long-barrelled weapon to his chest and pointed at himself eagerly. 'Long, long way. Olli best shot in town.'

'Then get up on that rock there.' Bannick pointed out a large boulder stone slumped in from the side of the transit tunnel. 'Keep them guessing where you are. Pick them off, go for the ones engaged with Bruta. Take out the leader first, then the heavy gunner. Headshots only, nothing else seems to drop them. Open fire at my signal.'

Olli nodded eagerly and hurried off, casting excited glances in the direction of the orks.

'You two, follow me,' he said to the others, and they set off at a loping run, bodies low, making a wide circuit round the edge of the clearing in the tunnel, heading for a pile of rocks where their weapons would be in range. They threw themselves behind the rockpile. Bannick risked a quick look over the edge. Two more of Bruta's men were down, another ork lay twitching. That left eleven greenskins to twenty sandscum. The situation was a stalemate, both humans and orks pinned in place by each other's fire. For now the humans still outnumbered the xenos, but the orks were levelling the odds.

Bannick looked up to Olli's position. The wiry mutant was pressed against the rock, rifle out and ready, almost invisible in the gloom.

'You two, as soon as Olli kills that gunner, the orks will notice we're here. When I say, give them everything you've got. We've got to take their numbers down and stop them from engaging us at close quarters. Understood?'

The two sandscum nodded.

'Right.' Bannick looked back to Olli, and waved a hand.

Immediately, the mutant hunkered down over his rifle sight, taking his time. Sure of his target, he fired a single shot.

The report of Olli's gun was lost in the chatter of the ork's stubber. Bannick watched as the big ork stopped in mid-shout and slumped forwards against the sandbank it sheltered behind. Quickly, before the others noticed, Olli fired again, and another ork's brains scattered across the sand.

The noise of the stubber abruptly shut off, the orks realising that they'd been outflanked. One stupidly raised its head. Fire from four sandscum autoguns riddled it, making it dance to their clatter.

Eight orks left.

The sandscum on Bruta's side tried to move forwards, but were driven back by bullets.

Two of the beasts were gesturing at Olli. He'd been spotted. They rolled over the berm and scooted along the transit tunnel floor.

'Open fire!' bellowed Bannick. Bright red beams of light stabbed from his laspistol, the crack of its discharge joined by the report of the sandscum's single-shot rifles. Bannick's laspistol only seemed to annoy the orks, and they turned to face this new threat, bellowing as they charged, axes raised. The combined fire of the three men brought them down, the last dying as it hit the rockpile, sending its head-sized pistol clattering over to land at Bannick's feet.

Olli, meanwhile, had been busy. Two more orks had fallen to his long rifle. The orks knew he was there now, and fired at him, but he was out of the effective range of their guns. Bannick saw two bolting together some kind of rocket launcher they'd pulled from a pack, working together intensely, ignoring the battle around them.

'If they fire that in here, it will bring the roof in,' hissed Suumsta.

'We go in now, then. Ready? One, two, three, go, go, go!'

Bannick and the sandscum vaulted over the rockpile,

screaming warcries from cultures born light years apart, yet all the same in the eyes of the Emperor. Bannick fired his laspistol as calmly as he could, aim, squeeze, aim, squeeze. He went for the orks' knees or elbows, hoping to knock them down for a few moments, the weapon lacking the power to penetrate their thick skulls at such a range. Suumsta went down, torso ripped open by ork bullets; his comrade Branka, enraged by his friend's death, ran full pelt into the camp roaring madly. His crooked legs seemed no hindrance as he cast his rifle aside, drew his long sandscum knife and leapt straight onto an ork's back, howling as he stabbed and stabbed into the thing's thick shoulders. The ork grunted in pain and tried to pluck the man from its back, but the sandscum would not let go, sinking his blade into the ork over and over, until it stumbled, and fell.

Bannick was into the thick of the fight shortly afterwards. He played his lasbeam over the orks' faces now, seeking out eyes and open mouths. He missed his sword, left on *Mars Triumphant*; the knife he carried in his left hand felt puny.

If I am to die here, he thought, then so be it.

He dodged between grasping orkish hands, but found himself caught and yanked back. He fell to the floor, an ork looming over him. It held him down with one hand and pulled its own blade with the other. Bannick rammed his knife into its chest, the point skidding over broad ribs before it found its way into the softer fibres of the intercostal spaces. The ork did not slow. Bannick brought up his gun, but the ork let go of Bannick's uniform and slapped the pistol from his hand. It drew back its knife, and Bannick prepared to die.

The ork grinned a millisecond before Olli's shot entered its left eye and smashed the back of its skull outwards, showering Bannick in globules of brain and blood. The ork swayed for a moment before collapsing with murderous weight onto the lieutenant, trapping him under a warm mountain of stinking, alien flesh.

When the ork was levered off him, it was all over. Two men grabbed at Bannick's hands and hauled him to his feet. Bannick coughed as he drew breath into his lungs. Pain flared along his side. He pressed his chest. No ribs broken, but he was badly bruised.

Sandscum and ork bodies lay everywhere. Olli sat calmly on the sand berm carving notches into his rifle while his folk walked from ork to ork, plunging their long, sawtoothed knives into eye sockets or shooting through skulls at short range, making sure the tough creatures were truly dead.

Bruta stood in the midst of it all. 'Twelve men dead.' He shook his head. 'And we had them outnumbered and surrounded. If they ever find Scumtown with any numbers, we're finished.' He looked to Bannick, who stood there pained and dishevelled, clutching his side. The mayor looked up the tunnel, at the corpses, his face set. 'You were right, lieutenant, we don't have any choice. We'll take you back to your tank.'

CHAPTER 24

ARONIS CITY, PARAGON VI
2003395.M41

Silence fell across the Gardens of the Vermillion Moon, as if the plants and animals within were holding their breath. Tuparillio's seconds looked on, slackjawed. The corpse of the boy lay upon the blue grass, red staining it black. Bannick stood over the boy, sword arm extended, poised as if to tackle another blow. He clutched at his cheek, blood and tears leaking between his fingers, the pain making him faint. The wound was a lash of agony.

Tuparillio was on his back, one arm thrown out, sword lying on the grass, the other hand clutching at the hole in his chest. His mouth was wide as if he were about to ask a question, his eyes clouding. Blood covered him, there was so much of it. It soaked his clothes to his knees, made his face half-crimson, the other half snow-white, like a carnival mask. His hair was matted with blood.

'You killed him.' Tolsten broke the silence, Bannick did not know nor would he ever know the boy's clan name or patronymic, some friend of Tuparillio's, some nobody. 'You killed him after he won.'

The other boy in the garden, a Sankello, sank to his knees and stared at the corpse. Bannick looked from Tolsten to the other second, Tolsten glancing between Bannick's weapon and his face, the other boy shaking.

Bannick continued to stare as the medic came to him, injecting his arm with a painkiller, wiping blood away from his face. The medic pressed a stick bandage over the wound, and the pain receded.

'I... I...' Bannick looked at both boys, then back to the corpse. He was still holding his sword, a present from his father. He cast it aside, he couldn't bear to hold it. His limbs began to shake.

'You'll rot for this, Colaron,' said Tolsten.

A hammering came at the heatlock outer door. The noise shook the Sankello boy out of his shock. 'The watch,' he said.

The door panel began to fizz as the watch burned their way in. Acrid smoke polluted the air of the garden. The inner doors of the heatlock cracked open, a pry inserted in the gap, forcing them wider, pushing them into their wall slots. Freezing air blasted into the greenhouse park.

Bannick panicked, he ran to his furs, but woolly-headed from the anaesthetic he misjudged the distance and scattered half of them on the grass. He snatched up what he could and fled.

The doors slid open. The wrath of winter spilled in. Five watchmen, armed and armoured for the winter patrols came with it. 'Stop! Halt in the name of the Watch!' shouted one.

Bannick ran.

Tolsten's voice followed him. 'He went that way! That way! Stop him! He killed Tuparillio!'

He sprinted through the garden, plants whipping him in the face. His gloves tumbled from the bundle in his arms. As he started back for them, a stun baton sped through the air past his face, changing his mind.

'Stop! Stop!' the watchman called.

Bannick reached the back of the courtyard. There was another doorway there, a service entrance. He reached it and stabbed at its lock. The door ground open, showering rust as it slid into the wall. He ducked through. More baton rounds bounced off the wall. He flinched. He hammered the buttons on the panel inside. The watchmen drew near. One of them reached the door as it began to close, attempting to force it, but the mechanism was too strong and he snatched his hands back before his fingers were crushed.

Bannick locked the door with his clan override code. It would hold the watch for a few minutes.

He pelted along the corridor, ducking to avoid runs of rusty geothermal pipes bringing warmth up from the heart of the tidally stressed moon to heat the park.

He reached the exit to the heating plant and tugged his overtrousers on. He'd dropped his vest. From back the way he had come he heard the sound of pursuit. They'd got through quickly. The information did not faze him, his mind was numb with the anaesthetic, blunted along with the pain. Part of himself urged him to stop but he could not.

He dragged his outer boots up quickly and went for the door, a single, not a heatlock. The handle lever was unheated, and as he grabbed it the cold of the Long Winter shot up his arm. He threw back the lever and the door swung open onto the gloom of the day.

Lungs burning, Bannick threw himself into a shelter, a small beehive-shaped building with a slender entrance. He disturbed a pair of lovers, their outer garments partly unwrapped. They left hastily, fleeing the bloodied young man.

Bannick slumped onto the curved bench inside. An array of geothermal pipes formed a fan behind the bench. Bannick sat there on the knife-edge boundary between the cold of the Long Winter and the warmth of Paragon's heart. His body shuddered, and he stirred himself to rearrange his furs. He peered out of the door of the booth. There was no sign of the watch.

He sat back on the bench, shivering, feeling the cold now the danger had passed. What had he done?

He was on the deserted central plaza, tall buildings all around it, its summer garden buried under snow, fountains frozen. Few people came here to relax during the Long Winter, activity shifting to the frost fairs on the city's complex of canals.

A bell rang across the square, marking out the hour to Imperial Time.

Bannick had not thought about the church for a long time. Terra was a long way away, the Emperor incomprehensibly distant. Although Bannick had always been aware that his survival rested upon His broken shoulders, the idea that the Emperor was directly aware of him was nonsensical. The needs and demands of the Paragonian aristocracy, of honour, were far more immediate.

And now he had dishonoured himself.

Bannick sought the cathedral among the buildings opposite, there, facade thick with snow. Built early in the post-Crusade period it was the most ancient structure on Paragon, now somewhat overshadowed by the needle spires of the corporate clans. Still it was tall, three stately towers reaching upwards towards Terra and the Emperor's Golden Throne.

A door opened in its front, one of two small entrances flanking the cyclopean gates in the centre. A cone of orange light spilled onto the dirty snow, framing a man in priest's robes who hurried off.

Bannick stood. The light called to him; even after the door had closed it seemed to him that he could still see it. He left the booth and walked across the square, his footsteps ever quicker as he drew near the church door.

CHAPTER 25

KALIDAR IV, HIVE MERADON
ADMINSTRATIVE PERIPHERY
3349397.M41

Cortein stared hard at his readouts, a welter of metero-logical information streaming down from augur-sats above, information relayed by the fleet. Comms chatter, some of it long-range, hissed through the command deck's speakers, the howl of Kalidar's static reduced to a sibilant protest.

'They're sure the storm has passed? Are you certain?'

Epparaliant nodded. Screens on the comms station showed clear skies, a wall of dust retreating on the horizon. 'Yes, sir, the storm is over. Electomagnetic activity is back down to Kalidar standard. The sunspike is over, fleet metereologians confirm it. Vox communication is possible. We'll be able to speak to command once the attack commences. If the fleet come in overhead, we'll probably be able to get them too.'

Cortein sighed and sat back, then let the convoy know the good news. Over the vox ragged cheers went up from the other tanks, joining with that from *Mars Triumphant*'s crew.

'How far are we from target alpha?'

'Forty kilometres, sir.'

'Any sign we've been noticed?'

Epparaliant checked screens, trying to make sense of degraded datafeeds coming in from orbit. 'No, sir,' he said eventually. 'There's no sign of ork activity in the immediate vicinity.'

Cortein checked his counter. Twenty hours until he was due to launch his attack. 'Tell the men, in person, that we're to make camp. Nothing elaborate, we'll be leaving in eight hours. Hold vox silence, all vehicles. Essential comms only.'

'Yes, sir.' Epparaliant checked his watch. 'All crew synchronise time.' He looked up to the tank's chronometer, displaying the countdown to the rendezvous. '011.36 in three, two, one.' The men on the deck adjusted their timepieces. Epparaliant sent out a quick databurst via laser. 'I've let them know I'm coming.'

'Good. Suit up, standard defence pattern, rotation of twelve sentries.'

'Yes, sir.'

'When that's done Epparaliant, you're first in the bunk.'

Epparaliant, pale with tiredness as all the men were, nodded his thanks.

The sandpike raced through the sand, half-submerged, six legs performing a twisting paddle. Its back, arrow-thin, undulated from side to side as it moved, diamond-shaped head rising and falling as it nosed through the desert floor. Only the quilled vane on its back and the saddle before it carrying Bannick and Olli were completely clear of the ground. Bannick's legs were crooked back, but the sand whispered by millimetres from his toes. Olli wielded a long prod, gently poking the visible part of the pseudo-lizard's head to guide it.

'They go where they want without stick. They go down, they dive in the sand. Forget about us!' the sandscum had explained. The vane on their back picked up on the planet's chaotic magnetic field, or so Bruta had told him, helping them navigate. Their eyes were little more than eight patches of photo-sensitive cells, sealed with tough flaps as they swam. He'd thought they were fast while they were scuttling through the endless passages of the sandscum's hidden realm, but it was nothing to the speed they managed through Kalidar's quickdust. There they were fastest, avoiding the harder packed ground if they could. Bannick understood now why the scum were not often seen, the sandpikes and their riders travelling the areas the men of the Guard avoided.

Wind whipped the scarf over Bannick's respirator and pulled at the turban and sand-coloured robes he'd been given. They'd emerged from a rent in the transit tube into green day, the storm gone. Bannick had almost forgotten what the sky looked like, the sun bright over the Ozymandian barrier range far away.

There were thirty or more other sandpikes, all bearing a pair of warriors, including Bruta. Scouts had joined them, reporting the location of the Imperial convoy soon after they'd left the wrecked transit tunnel. Bannick had no idea how they communicated. None of them had voxes.

Presently, the dust began to thicken into sand. Islands of sun-shattered rock appeared with increasing regularity. Eventually, the dust gave out, and the lizards were forced to run.

Bruta called a halt in the lee of a hill. Soundlessly, the sand-scum dismounted, cast their cloaks about themselves and seemed to become one with the desert floor. The sandpikes made for the nearest dustpan, and sank into it without a trace.

'They never see us,' said Bruta. 'Ever.' He beckoned Olli and Bannick and together they made their way to the brow of the hill.

'There's your tank, Bannick.'

Bannick looked down the escarpment at the tanks below. They were in a wide circle at the top of a bowl-shaped rise in the land, sand dunes masking their presence to the west and east, the hill hiding them from the south. *Mars Triumphant* sat at the most vulnerable point, lascannon turrets and bolter mounts tracking back and forth. It was a good position, with broad fields of fire. Bannick counted the vehicles. They'd not lost any more, and he was thankful.

'It'll be difficult to get down there without being blown to bits. There should be a sentry up here. In fact, I'd put one right there.' He pointed out a large rock across from them.

'Ah,' said Bruta, and pulled Bannick back below the ridgeline, then round the hill. A sandscum dressed in Imperial garb leapt atop the rock. Beneath it, half-dressed, hands on head, covered by two grinning mutants, sat an Atraxian trooper.

Bannick pulled his sandscum robes off, revealing his battered lieutenant's uniform underneath.

'I'm going to need the password, private,' he said.

'How do I know you're not a spy?' said the Atraxian, his lilting accent defiant.

Bannick risked pulling the respirator from his face.

'You, you're from the Baneblade?' said the Atraxian, eyes widening. 'Another ghost? We were supposed to be clear of that.'

Bannick held out his hand. The private looked to the sandscum who nodded their approval. He reached out and grasped Bannick's hand in his own.

'You're alive!'

'Apparently so, private, apparently so,' said Bannick.

The briefing was getting heated, Mayor Bruta annoyed with Exertraxes, who paid little attention to the man's knowledge.

'No, no.' Bruta shook his head. 'All this area now is quickdust, you go through there and you'll be dead within metres, all of you. Here, this is the way you have to go.' He traced his finger through the chart desk display. Wind lifted the sides of the tent slightly. They hadn't bothered to seal it, yet all within had their masks off. Bruta insisted it was safe.

'You say this route is poor? The path you indicate takes us right through the Utrazi Pans.' Captain Exertraxes, wan after his ordeal in the Ozymandian Basin, otherwise recovered. He stood in the full carapace plate of his regiment, cropped grey hair fuzzing a skull scored with the scars of twenty years of service. 'A thermal sink exists below the desert there, pressurised gas jets out unpredictably, enough heat in each one to cook a crew in its tank. No. The pre-planned route was pronounced clear of quickdust before we left.

'Captain,' said Bruta. 'This area is well known to us. We use it often as it offers easy passage for our mounts. It fills seasonally – after the storm it will be full again. This way is better.'

'It's impassable.'

'If you are not sandscum; we know the way.'

Exertraxes rubbed at his face, irritated and tired. He scratched where his rebreather had worn a red mark on his face and sighed tiredly. 'Cortein, what do you think?'

'Sir.' He pointed to broad band of red sigils and flashing dots around the periphery of Hive Meradon. 'The orks have mined this area, augur-sat pict-capture before the storm showed some degree of fortification, albeit ramshackle, heavier fortifications here, here and here. The same with the area around which mayor Bruta says is now dust. But here.' He tapped at the matrix projector of the chart desk, causing the image to shimmer. 'Outside the Utrazi Pans, there's nothing. The orks are lazy. They do not expect anything to come through there at all. I'd trust this man's expertise in this field. Local knowledge has saved me on more than one occasion.'

'We will get you through,' said Bruta. 'I swear.'

Exertraxes looked from man to man, weighing what each had said. 'Very well,' he said. 'We take the pans.'

'I have these.' Bruta beckoned his lieutenant, who was standing guard at the tent flap. The man walked over, and unrolled a cloth on the table. 'Sandscum amulets, made from lorelei crystals. They stop us from seeing the ghosts, very effective. They will offer some protection from the ork witch.' He looked to Exertraxes. The Atraxian thought for a moment then nodded.

'Very well, give them to all the men who will have them. I leave it to their individual consciences whether or not to be involved with such... practices.'

'Go then,' said Bruta.

Bruta's lieutenant nodded, scooped up the cloth and left the tent.

'Perhaps now...?' suggested Cortein.

'Yes, yes, the full orders,' said Exertraxes irritably, and took out a sealed envelope, crisscrossed with warding patterns inscribed there by Sanctioned Psyker Logan. 'No doubt you have some inkling of them already, that we are to draw the orks into attacking us, sow confusion, attempt to isolate and destroy the ork witch engine while the main group assails the forward quarters of Hive Meradon.' He said, distractedly, as he broke open the seals, 'Supposition is ever the sport of idle men...' His voice trailed off as he read. From outside Bannick caught Ralt protesting loudly about the amulets.

'...n't do Ganlick much good did they? No thank you,' he heard. Then Exertraxes spoke again, bringing Bannick's attention back into the tent.

'Ahem,' said the Atraxian. 'Very well. As you know, we are to assault the hive surface town.'

'Our full orders?' asked Cortein.

'See for yourself.'

Bannick took and read the paper aloud. '"Seek and destroy ork super-heavy walker [Titan//Class 3] designated Gargant." Nothing new there,' he said. '"Eliminate targets of opportunity.

Take and hold workshop Alpha 143. Await relief." That's it? Aren't we going to link up with the rest of the battlegroup? For how long are we supposed to hold out?' asked Bannick, passing the sheet on to the other officers in the tent.

'Until we are relieved,' said Exertraxes firmly.

'They mean until we are dead, do they not?' asked Bannick. He and Cortein stood on the hill overlooking the camp, taking the opportunity to stretch their legs. They watched the bustle of men below them preparing for battle, replenishing fuel and munitions from the flatbeds. The tractors and supplies were to wait here, under sandscum guard, until further orders came through. The relief on the faces of their crews was obvious, no matter how they tried to hide it.

'Probably,' said Cortein. 'I'm not going to lie to you. We are to be a valuable diversion and keep their ork witch occupied while the hammerblow falls on the main front. If we are unlucky, then we will all die. That's war.' He shrugged, then gave Bannick a tight smile. 'You appear concerned. I've been in tighter spots than this before. You yourself have cheated death already this week, it can become a habit.'

'Perhaps Vorkosigen's reading of the tarot is right,' said Bannick, following the progress of the tech-adept as he checked the weapons of the Baneblade below. He experienced a sudden shiver of unease at the memory of the screens with their identical spreads. 'Perhaps I am the doom of *Mars Triumphant*.'

'*Mars Triumphant* is old, far older than is easy to understand,' said Cortein, looking out over the desert. They were dead men walking the pair of them, unable to hold each other's gaze for long. 'All things must come to an end, and its time will come eventually. The important thing for us is to concentrate on delivering a couple of shaped lorelei charges into the guts of that ork witch Titan, fry it and the mind controlling it; with that down the brass can concentrate on the rest of the ork army and that device. We can worry about surviving afterwards. Anything should happen, keep your head down, keep your wits about you, you'll be all right.'

Bannick liked to think he'd become accustomed to Cortein, his morals, his overwhelming sense of duty, his air of command tempered by his concern for and comradeship with his men, his sharpness, but there was something different about him today. 'Cortein, you don't think you'll live this out, do you?'

Cortein turned to look at him, his look black, and Bannick worried he'd spoken out of turn, then turned back to the desert, where the night was setting in in earnest. 'Brasslock told me that the machines know. They know when their time has come. Before he was taken, he told me that *Mars Triumphant* was preparing to die. He was very angry on the barge when the orders came through for immediate deployment. He wanted to give its spirit some time to prepare, he wanted to pray with it.'

'Do you think it's true? Does she know?' asked Bannick.

Cortein shrugged. '*Mars Triumphant* has guarded me now for these last thirty years. Everything she does is not so easy to explain by the push of buttons.'

Bannick became aware of the cog nestled next to his aquila. He nodded. 'Once, I was a less faithful man,' he said. I did not believe that the Emperor really watched over us all.'

'You do now?'

'Not entirely, though more than I did, for certain. But I find it hard to believe that a machine is capable of such spiritual feats, no matter how old, or powerful its spirit. Such superstition is for bondsmen and tech-priests. The Emperor is our lord, not the Omnissiah, but if I can change my mind about one thing...' He shuddered as a chill passed over his back, and the image of *Mars Triumphant*, huge and growling as if it studied him, came into his mind. 'I can change my mind about that too.'

The vox in Cortein's respirator crackled, message slurred by the remaining static in the air. 'Cortein! Cortein, come in!' panic overwhelmed the interference; Bausillak, the Atlas commander.

'What is it?'

'Valle sir, it's Valle! Green fire! His head, it's burnt up, sir, it's… Oh Throne! he's dead sir, he…' Shouting and the sound of fire-suppressant cylinders being let off crowded his voice.

Cortein clicked the vox off. 'You get that, Bannick?'

'Yes.'

'Damn ork witch.' He spoke back into his vox again. 'Bausillak, keep it quiet. You let anyone else know, I'll shoot you myself.' He made an adjustment to his vox settings. 'Epperaliant? Epperaliant come in.'

'Sir?' came the commsman's voice.

'Did you ask Astropath Valle to send out a message?' he demanded.

'No, sir, why?'

'To your knowledge, has he attempted to contact HQ?'

'No, sir, not so far as I knew. Orders said no contact until just prior to the assault,' said Epperaliant. 'He knew that.'

The bustle in the hollow below sounded suddenly inadequate, insectile, the quiet sounds pathetic in the vastness of the desert.

'They know we're coming.' Cortein swore. 'Perhaps you are right about Vorkosigen's tarot, Bannick. Maybe after tomorrow, we'll get the opportunity to ask the Emperor ourselves.'

CHAPTER 26

KALIDAR IV, HIVE MERADON SURFACE TOWN
3355397.M41

'Incoming, incoming! For the Emperor's sake, pin down that squad of tank hunters before we lose another Chimera!' Epperaliant shouted over the vox.

The Baneblade ground through the surface town of Hive Meradon, buildings semi-ruinous from the ork conquest, streets deep in sand. Ork defenders assailed them from all sides, but the Baneblade thrust like a spearpoint deep into the deserted settlement, trailing Atraxian Heavy Infantry in its wake.

A torrent of fire poured all over the Baneblade, streaking tracer bullets and corkscrewing rockets ricocheting madly from all over its hull. The giant tank trundled forwards, Bannick dealing out death to countless orks with its heavy bolters, hands twitching over the sticks. Ralt sat in Ganlick's old position, collapsing buildings with the demolisher cannon like houses made of cards, Radden up top whooping as he let the main armament fly again and again. A loud detonation sounded, and through one of his gun augurs, Bannick caught sight of a tower toppling to the ground.

'Exertraxes! Quadrant 4B, our left flank, ork AT squad moving in close.' Epperaliant shouted.

Bannick swung the left pair of bolters out, raked the building as he went past, sending their mass reactive munitions through windows, forcing the ork rocket teams back, and then they were past; he hoped it would be enough to allow the heavy infantry to finish them off. His gun arrays were cluttered with targets, and he struggled to manage both sponsons effectively on his own.

'Keep your fire accurate and brief, Bannick! You're burning through your ammunition,' shouted Cortein. All of them shouted, the noise in the tank the worst Bannick had ever experienced; without the internal vox phones on his ears, he'd not be able to hear anything.

The super-heavy pushed on. They'd overwhelmed the light defences at the edge of the surface town with little difficulty. Bruta had been correct, the segment of the town facing into the dust sea had barely been fortified. Hive Meradon sat on a scarp, the trailing edge sinking into quickdust land and the Pans, the front rising into cliffs a hundred metres high, the main hive shaft bored right through the centre of it. The main ork defence line was along the cliffs. Although the cliffs provided a natural wall, they fronted hard desert, the only direction from which heavy armour could safely approach. The Baneblade and its small strikeforce, having braved the quickdust to the rear of the scarp, had evaded their main redoubts and trenchlines.

Now they crunched their way through the town. As at Modulus, the surface above Meradon's subterranean bulk was covered with a sprawl of mostly low-rise buildings, thick, windowless walls sloped against the planet's ferocious weather. They rose higher in the quadrant they were aiming for, a manufacturing and servicing area for the large foundry vehicles the Kalidarians used to sift the surface sands for lorelei. The factory the orks had co-opted to manufacture their potbellied Titan and heavy walkers was at the heart of it.

The Baneblade flattened small buildings as it went, going right through the larger ones. Sheets of hardened plastics, girders and rockcrete bounced from its hull, shaking the vehicle. In its wake, treading the trail of destruction, men of the Atraxian Heavy Infantry walked, supported by their Chimera APCs, eyes out for ork ambush teams either side of the way. More and more orks were flocking towards the Baneblade, and the forty infantry remaining seemed pitifully few. Far to the rear, the company of Leman Russ battle tanks sat behind a lake of quickdust, operating as substitute artillery, shelling the surface town mercilessly, blasting orks and buildings alike while the sandscum operated like phantoms around them, goading ork buggies, infantry and bikes, luring them away from the town into dust traps and ambushes.

Cortein had control of the forward heavy bolter turret, letting off light bursts as targets presented themselves.

'Epperaliant, prepare the notification. We are approaching our target.' Cortein pressed the vox. 'Cortein to HQ, Cortein to HQ, We are in the surface town, repeat, we are in the surface town. Approaching secondary target.'

Epperaliant sent of a series of encrypted data packets, confirming that the attack was on time and they were in position.

That done, they were on their own.

Below, Meggen laboured alone, supplying both heavy cannon as best he could. Even with two men down, Bannick marvelled at the efficiency with which the crew made the tank work: Radden mercilessly picking high value targets, blasting clanking ork walkers and light tanks into scrap, Ralt tossing the demolisher cannon's shells into the bases of occupied buildings, Outlanner guiding the vehicle round obstacles that Bannick would never have seen, Epperaliant doing half a dozen things at once, gathering information, sending out datasquirts, fielding and prioritising incoming communiqués and acting as a de facto tac officer for the whole taskforce. Vorkosigen hunted out problems and locked them down as quickly as they arose. They were elite tankers, the best of the best, man and machine operating in concert, and Bannick was proud to be one of them.

They'd come through the dustpans unscathed, the sandscum's lizards picking out a safe route for each vehicle, their odd senses attuned to the area's unpredictable eruptions of gas. Bannick had watched geysers carry sparkling cargos of dust and steam high into the air, their range increased by the low-G environment so it seemed the plumes would reach orbit, and he remarked to himself again that despite its deadly nature, Kalidar had its fair share of beauty.

He doubted he'd miss it if he survived long enough to leave.

He reduced a squad of ork anti-armour infantry coming in from the left to puffs of red mist and gristle. No matter how many they killed, the orks came on, firing wildly and roaring, no hope of penetrating the tank's ceramite and plasteel armour, yet attacking all the same. Bursts of light from explosions and weapons fire flashed through the slit windows situated round the cabin, strobing the dimly lit command deck with dazzling regularity.

'Steady now! Three degrees left, Outlanner, we're losing our bead on the factory,' warned Cortein.

The Baneblade gained a broad square littered with the detritus of orkdom – stinking pits of ordure, crude shacks, slave pens – *Mars Triumphant* ground over it all, heading to the factory and yard. Behind a high wall, ork heavy walkers congregated like fat lords at a bar.

'We don't stand much of a chance against that many,' muttered Epperaliant.

'We only have to kill one!' shouted Radden over the vox, and laughed.

'Keep calm, Epperaliant,' said Cortein. 'Status report!'

'There are two operational here, three under repair or construction, I'm getting energy spikes indicating two more elsewhere.'

'Is our main target there, is the Titan among them?'

Epperaliant scanned his bank of instruments, checked the pyskanum equipment bolted to his desk. 'No, sir. The auspex can't pin the Titan down.'

'Dammit! Where is it? We should be able to see it!'

A heavy walker tottered and wobbled as it pedalled round to face the Baneblade, head bobbing comically. Another blew black smoke from its engine units as orks and gretchin swarmed aboard.

The active walker levelled its guns at the tank.

'Prepare for impact!' shouted Cortein.

A tattoo of hammerblows rocked the Baneblade as the ork heavy walker gatling cannon opened up. Klaxons blared, sparks flew from instruments. Bannick's right flank lascannon became unresponsive.

A rocket launched itself from the heavy walker's left shoulder, lumbering into the sky on a pillar of dirty flame, but *Mars Triumphant* was too close, and it overshot them, impacting deep in the surface town somewhere behind, its shockwave flattening buildings in a broad circle. Debris rained down on the tank.

The heavy walker lumbered forwards, crushing the wall round the factory yard, and the second followed, both spitting wildfire at the super-heavy tank.

'We can't take this!' shouted Vorkosigen, and shot a black look at Bannick. 'The tarot was right!'

Radden howled with glee as he decapitated the trailing heavy walker with his cannon. It waddled round in circles, crushing everything about it.

'There are at least two remaining, Radden, and we have no idea where that basdack ork Titan is! Contain your jubilance,' growled Cortein.

'We're not going to survive this,' said Ralt.

Light flared. A bolt of indigo energy punctured the sky with a roar as air ionised into plasma. It struck the lead heavy walker square on its flat shoulders, cutting it in half diagonally. Flame welled up from within its guts, and it exploded with titanic violence that made Bannick's teeth rattle.

Epperaliant looked up, excited. 'The Navy! Sir, the Navy are on the comm…'

'How did they sweep the orks out of orbit?' asked Bannick.

'Praise be to the Emperor that they're there at all,' said Cortein. 'Put them over the vox, Epperaliant.'

'Commander Spaduski of the heavy cruiser *Emperor's Lambent Glory*, glad to speak with you, Honoured Lieutenant Cortein,' crackled a voice. 'Our main battlegroup is engaging the majority of the ork fleets out in the belt junction. With them out of the way, we are free to strike. Imperator Exultis! Our lance batteries are at your disposal. We might not be able to engage the primary target yet, but that's no reason for us to sit up here on our hands.'

Cortein spoke. 'Please, commander, carry on as you were. Target those heavy walkers, we'll send you precise bombardment coordinates.'

'On its way,' said Epperaliant.

'With the Navy at our backs,' continued Cortein, 'we're in with a fighting chance.'

'Will proceed. Emperor protect you all, Spaduski out.'

Epperaliant sent data helping the ship target its weapons more accurately, bringing beams of high energy stabbing down onto the factory, obliterating the dormant heavy walkers. Orks came running from the burning remnants of their war machines and the factory. Bannick and Cortein cut them apart with their heavy bolters.

'Sir, datasquirts coming in, the rest of the battlegroup have engaged to the south of the city.'

A lull in the battle followed as orks were drawn away to face this larger threat.

'Exertraxes, are you there?'

'Cortein.'

'Our secondary objective is accomplished, thanks to the Navy, but we have yet to find the witch engine. With that still operational and the witch alive, the main attack does not stand much chance of disabling the ork device.'

The vox crackled. Exertraxes's voice faded out for a moment. '...under heavy assault, we'll attempt to support you if we can.'

'Negative, captain, get yourselves holed up somewhere,' Cortein said. 'We can do it on our own, their infantry is disorganised now, they're beginning to panic.'

'"No armoured vehicle should proceed without infantry support",' replied Exertraxes, quoting directly from the *Tactica Imperium*.

'*Mars Triumphant* is more than an armoured vehicle, Exertraxes, it is the wrath of the Emperor incarnate. There's no need for you to throw your lives away.' The vox buzzed loudly as another lance beam cut downwards into the surface town, its discharge playing havoc with the already tenuous vox signals.

'We will proceed with you. Hannick warned me about you, Cortein. We will gladly serve the Emperor with our flesh and blood if need be. We'll be with you in a few moments.'

Cortein grunted. 'Very well. Epperaliant, find me that Titan.'

'I've finally got a bead on it, damn thing was hiding in one of the ore towers. It's heading away from us. We are going to have to take it before it gets to the main battle line.'

'Lance strike?' said Bannick.

'I can't get an accurate enough fix on it at this distance sir, and the lances aren't that precise without ground-level targeting data,' replied Epperaliant. 'We're going to have to get closer.'

'Outlanner, follow Epperaliant's lead,' said Cortein.

'Aye, sir!'

'Sir?' said Epperaliant, his eyes widening. 'I'm getting an Imperial recognition signal. It's... it's *Lux Imperator* sir!'

'Where? Where! Quickly, we have to get out of this square,' Vorkosigen spoke up. 'The orks, they take things, make them their own, defile the holy works of the Omnissiah. They will turn our own against us!'

'They took Brasslock...' began Cortein.

'If they've prised the secret of how to make its volcano cannon work out of his tin head,' said Radden, 'we'll be sitting ducks.'

Cortein leaned forwards into the internal vox horn urgently, 'Outlanner, countermand my last. Get us out of this square by the shortest route possible and into cover.'

'Aye, sir.' The tank ground round slowly, heading towards a roadway next to the burning heavy walker factory.

'It's coming in from the west, sir.'

'Exertraxes, stay out of the square, they've a looted superheavy bearing down on us right now.'

Exertraxes voice came back sharply. 'I know my business, Cortein, stay put. If what you say is true we'll take it on together.'

'Continue on your course, Outlanner.'

'You sure, honoured lieutenant?' the driver asked.

'If we're in this square when *Lux Imperator* arrives, we'll be atomised. Our only hope is to get into the buildings where it will not be able to bring its volcano cannon to bear on us directly, and where we will be able to get within effective range.'

'A deadly game of Missionary's Search,' said Bannick.

'Exactly, you're catching on quickly, lieutenant. Vorkosigen get all power rerouted to the engines.'

'*Lux Imperator* is three blocks distant, sir,' said Epperaliant.

'Push it, Outlanner, as hard as she'll go!'

The engine's ever-present grumble became a growl, then a roar. The twitch stick interfaces for Bannick's weapon systems went limp, their energy stolen away to feed the engine. There was a crack and a shower of sparks, Bannick smelled burning, another klaxon blared, adding its clamour to the host of chiming alarms. A handful of screens on the tac and comms stations flickered and went out; red lights flickered urgently on the tech console.

'Report, Vorkosigen!'

'Left augur bank's burnt out again sir,' said Vorkosigen.

'Do we have fire?'

'Not this time.'

'Leave it then! Get everything you have into those engines.'

'Exertraxes is entering the square, sir,' said Epperaliant. On the gun augurs of his left side heavy bolters, Bannick saw the Atraxians marching into the square in good order, las-beams flashing out to topple orks hiding in buildings, Chimera turrets tracking rapid bursts of las-light in broad covering fire patterns as they drove alongside the dismounted troops. They made towards the Baneblade.

'He's hailing us sir.'

'Put him on,' said Cortein.

'Halt, Cortein! Halt!' yelled the captain. 'You are disobeying a direct order. Damn you! Hannick warned me about this, I'll have your whole crew court-martialled.'

'Not very grateful is he?' said Radden from the turret. 'We saved his behind, if I recall.'

'Sir, I repeat, get out of the square, *Lux Imperator* is bearing down on our position. Spread your men, and get into cover,' urged Cortein.

'Don't order me, Cortein,' came the captain's reply.

'Look!' shouted Radden. From the flickering corner of his damaged lascannon display Bannick saw a tall building collapsing in a tumble of great masonry blocks, the picture maddeningly incomplete. A long barrel emerged, followed by the bulk of *Lux Imperator*, and it went out of his view.

'*Lux Imperator* is here,' said Epperaliant.

'By the Throne,' said Vorkosigen, making upon his brow the sign of the holy cog. 'What have they done to her?'

Rubble bounced down from the building as the Shadowsword pulled into the square. An iron maw had been welded round the base of its main weapon and additional turrets sprouted along both sides like mushrooms. Bold checks and firespurts had been daubed on over a garish camouflage scheme. Crossed axes had been nailed to it in several places and the glyphs of the orkish language ran in broad stripes down its flanks.

Cortein drew in a sharp hiss of breath. 'Epperaliant, get me magnification of the frontal armour.'

Cortein's screen fizzed as the main turret periscope focused on the fore of the giant tank, fixed, magnified, blurred, and cleared. There was a man, a man reduced to a shattered torso, pinned to the vehicle's hull below its squat, immovable command turret.

'Is that Brasslock?' asked Epperaliant.

'Emperor save us all,' said Radden.

Some of the orkish extras had been torn away by the vehicle's entrance, the remains of their occupants smeared across the tank's crude new colour scheme. The majority had not, and the multiple new guns it possessed opened up on Exertraxes's Atraxians.

'Idiot!' muttered Cortein, eyes to the periscope mask. Images of dying Atraxians filled his command screens, while on the chart desk the icons signifying squads and tanks winked out. 'They should have sent Strenkelios.'

They did not, because he was not as expendable, thought Bannick.

'Twelve dead to that initial volley sir, one Chimera down,' said Epperaliant.

'Forces remaining?' asked Cortein.

'Thirty-one, five Chimera APCs operational.'

'Have they seen us?' asked Cortein.

'Negative, we're hidden by the debris in the square. Exertraxes has their full attention.' Epperaliant looked up. 'I'm getting an energy spike, *Lux Imperator* is charging its capacitors.'

The Baneblade's turret had swung round as they'd travelled, keeping the main scope and pict augurs on the defiled super-heavy.

The Baneblade carried on its course, Outlanner keeping chunks of heavy walker, ork huts and piles of rubble between them and the Shadowsword. The captured super-heavy was to their right and rear, Exertraxes directly across the square from it. The Baneblade drew closer to the relative safety of the burning factory complex.

'Sir, the Atraxians are getting cut to pieces,' warned Epperaliant.

'Outlanner, keep us on course, that large structure, nearside of quadrant three, turn us round as soon as we're out of *Lux*'s direct line of sight.'

'Will do, sir.'

'And get the fleet back on the vox! Feed them *Lux Imperator*'s coordinates, see if they can help. Radden, get ready to distract *Lux Imperator* as soon as we're within three lengths of the factory.'

'Sir!' said Radden, and servo-motors whined as he kept the turret fixed on the captured tank.

Cortein bellowed down the vox, sharp and commanding, ordering the remaining Atraxians to hit cover round the square, while Epperaliant conducted frantic chatter over the uplink with the Navy. The sound of munitions and lance blasts howling in from high orbit could be heard over the din, but they were growing fainter, the Navy's attention moving towards the second battlefront opened by the main battlegroup.

'Capacitors charged!' shouted Epperaliant.

Bannick, his weapons useless, turned to watch the battle on the comms and tac screens. The additional ork guns on the Shadowsword continued to fire. Lines of smoke and explosions erupted along its side as Chimera multi-lasers raked it mercilessly, but they were powerless to penetrate the super-heavy's plasteel armour.

The volcano cannon discharged. Inside its body, four-tera-watt capacitors simultaneously released energy rapid-charged by the vehicle's engine. A linear sun burned through the Kalidarian air. There was a rush of noise, a sonic clap as superheated air burst outwards from the volcano beam. Dust and debris blew out in a brief hurricane. The sensors of the Baneblade were overloaded, screens blinking out, slit windows round the deck turning into slots of painful white, and Bannick threw his hands up to his eyes. A titanic explosion followed as rocks and metal were instantly vaporised.

A Shadowsword's main armament was designed to punch through void shields; it had enough energy to the cut the limbs from a Titan, one of the great, planet-shaking engines of the Adeptus Mechanicus. Exertraxes's men had no chance. A shockwave blasted out, toppling weakened structures round the square, followed by a giant ball of flame bellying from the impact site as the oxygen in the air ignited, setting everything in the square on fire. The Baneblade shuddered as the firestorm passed over it, more alarms ringing out from the damage-control systems.

The fury of the blast died back. Fires burned everywhere. The Baneblade crunched through the destruction, debris on its hull ablaze.

'Damage!' barked Cortein.

'Minimal,' replied Vorkosigen. 'We've lost half our augurs. Dynamo three is burnt out, but I should be able to keep energy levels up to normal.'

'Main cannon functional, I think we lost the stubber.' Radden.

'We've lost both antennae sir, comms are offline, we're onto short-range vox and signal laser only,' said Epperaliant.

Ralt spoke. 'Demolisher okay.'

'Drive operating within optimal parameters,' reported Outlanner.

Bannick spoke in his turn. 'I've lost a lascannon, right sponson bank, the rest of the tertiary weapons are functioning. Ammunition at sixty-four per cent.'

Meggen's voice buzzed over the internal vox. 'No damage to the magazine, honoured lieutenant.'

'Good. Did we get the fleet before we lost comms?' asked Cortein.

'I informed them of the super-heavy threat, sir, but they're concentrating on the other front, and I can no longer send accurate telemetry to them, even if we had it,' replied Epperaliant.

'We're on our own then. How long until the next blast?'

'At least two minutes, sir, if their capacitors are operating at full capacity,' said Vorkosigen. 'Possibly more, we've no way of knowing what the orks have done to *Lux Imperator*'s main systems.

'Very well. Gunner Ralt, time to let them know we are here.'

'Yes, sir!' motors purred. The main turret view adjusted itself as Radden drew a bead on the opposing tank. It was still facing away towards where Exertraxes's men had been, oblivious to the Baneblade. Magnesium autocannon rounds drew lines in the air, ranging the shot for Radden.

'You… you used Exertraxes as bait?' said Bannick.

Cortein nodded. 'He came into the square against all sense. When he did that, it was either us first, then him, or we could use them to buy us time.' Cortein looked hard at him. 'I cannot save everyone, Bannick, no one can.'

The main cannon barked once, the characteristic boom and roar of the rocket-assisted shells shuddering through the tank. The shell hit the ground by the Shadowsword's right track, blasting a plume of rubble into the sky.

'Damn it!' shouted Radden over the vox. 'I can't get at it, it's hull-down in the mess back there.'

Bannick squinted through his own rangefinders. The Shadowsword was lower to the ground than a Baneblade, its turret and command deck combined and set directly into the main hull. He could barely see its flat top over the debris choking the plaza.

'As long as they know we're here,' said Cortein, and Bannick realised he was attempting to goad the orks to follow them into the maze of streets and wreckage around the square, where its volcano armament would be of far less use than the Baneblade's battle and demolisher cannons.

'Take us in and through the factory, Outlanner.'

'Aye, sir.'

The Baneblade burst through a sloping, storm-proof wall whose few apertures gouted flame, and into the inferno.

Rockcrete boulders and girders clanged down on the tank. Everything inside the building was on fire, the walls, ceiling and machinery. Opposite their entry point, the far wall of the factory had collapsed. The top half of a heavy walker had fallen through it, its steel glowing in the heat. The temperature rose higher in the machine, and Bannick feared they would cook, but Outlanner slammed the right track off, executing a sharp ninety-degree right turn. *Mars Triumphant* burst through another wall, went up and over a pile of rubble choking the street beyond.

On the main turret screen, Bannick caught sight of the Shadowsword as it ground round on its wide treads. Radden loosed an opportunistic shot off at it. The shell went wide, bringing a wall down on the far side of the square.

'That's right Radden, keep them interested,' said Cortein. 'Any sign of the Titan?'

'Negative,' said Epperaliant. 'Not much activity round here now, most of the orks have been drawn off by the main assault.'

'We've done part of our job, at least,' muttered Cortein. 'Outlanner, take us on and round, broad sweep, drawing outwards, I want that tank in the mess with us, then get me behind it.'

'Sir.'

The demolisher boomed and punched a hole in a sloping wall, the Baneblade battering its way through the gap and into the building on the other side of the street from the burning factory. Within, it was dark and quiet, scattered debris between ranks of autoservicers the only sign a war raged outside.

'Redirect energy to tertiary weapons again, engineer,' ordered Cortein.

Bannick's twitch sticks came back to life.

'Keep going, Outlanner.' Cortein peered at the scope screens. 'No sign of it. Have you got the location, Epperaliant?'

'No, sir, wait! There!'

A wall caved in as the Shadowsword burst through into the building sixty metres behind the Baneblade. Ork cannon fire hammered into their rear, exploding one of *Mars Triumphant*'s auxiliary fuel drums, a burning slick of promethium spread behind them.

'Damn them!' shouted Cortein.

The view shifted as the turret tracked round to point directly backwards, cannon barrel automatically staying level as the tank went up and over a machine, turning it to scrap. Radden shot off a shell. It impacted square on the hull of the modified Shadowsword as it swivelled round to bring its volcano cannon to bear. Pieces of armour and orkish equipment smashed into the building's machinery. Fire was beginning to take hold in this building too.

'Get us out of here!' shouted Cortein.

'I'm out of ammo!' shouted Radden.

The shell lift rumbled up the central well by way of reply.

Bannick swung his remaining lascannon round to point rearwards. He had the chance to loose of one bolt of energy before Outlanner turned the tank to the right, obscuring his line of fire with the bulk of Mars Triumphant's hull. He swung out the heavy bolters on the right flank, raking the Shadowsword with explosive bolts, concentrating on the weaker ork turrets ranged on top of the track units.

The Baneblade slammed through another wall, taking this one at a bad angle, jarring the tank and the crew. When Bannick recovered, they were outside on a broad expressway, on the upper of two levels, one curling round as it went to join the up road coming out of the hive's central shaft.

'Which way, honoured lieutenant?' asked Outlanner. The road into the hive formed a four-lane chasm in front of them, running under the square, the higher road they were on once having taken traffic off it and into the factory complexes, although it was filled now with vehicle wrecks. 'Down or back into the square?'

The square was nearer, but wide open, the expressway off-ramp worse – for a couple of hundred metres they'd be exposed.

'Get us back into the square, Outlanner. We're wide open up

here. Stick to the rubble.' Cortein pulled up a desk holo of the far side of the square and highlighted a tightly packed group of buildings. 'Radden, we have got to paralyse that tank! If it can't move, it's helpless.'

'Sir!'

Outlanner swung the tank round, the nose of it squealing against the off-ramp guard wall, pushing rubble and wrecked ground vehicles into the drop below as it turned right again and headed back towards the square. The tank crushed car after car, grinding their frames and their dead occupants flat. A large truck blocked their way. Ralt blasted it with the demolisher, and *Mars Triumphant* shunted its burning carcass sideways into the concrete canyon beside them.

'Incoming!' yelled Epperaliant. The sky filled with smoking trails tipped with fire as Imperial artillery began a long-range bombardment. A building's parapet on the other side of the sunken expressway exploded. It was soon followed by others. Through this rain of deadly shot, *Mars Triumphant* rumbled on.

There was a shuttering roar behind them, and the wall they'd exited from collapsed entirely, the Shadowsword trundling through it. Radden fired a shot at it as it tried in vain to turn to face the other tank.

'It's stuck, sir,' said Epperaliant, then: 'Watch out! Orks!'

Greenskinned warriors were coming in some numbers from the damaged building on the far side of the expressway. Bannick flung his bolters out to maximum rotation, holding them at ninety degrees to the side of the tank. The orks held themselves tight to the retaining wall on the opposite off-ramp, and began to send rockets hurtling toward the super-heavy tank.

'I can't get at them sir!' Bannick said. 'Cover's too tight!'

'Suppressive fire! Stop them taking too many shots.'

The Shadowsword retreated into the building, seeking another way out. The clang and boom of ork rockets on the hull died off as the Baneblade made the square. The orks pulled back from the wall, and made to follow.

Mars Triumphant crushed rubble to powder as its engines hauled its enormous bulk back into the ruined square. Shells rained down all around, the air was thick with smoke and shards of shrapnel. They were re-entering the square a third of a kilometre from where'd they'd left it, diagonally opposite where Exertraxes's men had been vaporised. A large crater cooled in the space where the Atraxians had been, although according to datafeeds, some of the men and vehicles had survived and retreated into the buildings fringing the plaza.

'*Lux Imperator* incoming!' said Epperaliant. 'It's moving parallel to our course.'

'Get us over the square,' said Cortein. 'I want us out of its way again.'

'No, no, they've stopped. I'm getting an energy spike. They're charging the capacitors!'

'Where is it?' said Cortein.

'Two-fifty metres, a hundred and twenty degrees rear right.'

Orks came out of the buildings to the tank's left. Bannick drove them back with heavy bolter fire. The orks withdrew, and a trio of clanking ork dreadnoughts shouldered their way out of the ruins. Bannick fried one with a lascannon shot. Return fire from their strange armaments shattered his bolter bank.

'Honoured Lieutenant Cortein,' he shouted. 'We've got a problem. Ork walkers, coming in. I've lost left bolters.'

'Capacitors at eighty-seven per cent!' said Epperaliant.

'They can't hit us if they can't see us,' growled Cortein.

Radden spoke up. 'At least the bombardment's stopped.' The tank rocked as he shot off another shell. It hit the orks' left flank, killing half a dozen and driving the rest back into cover. The shockwave toppled one of the remaining walkers, where it lay kicking its legs ineffectually, unable to right itself.

'No it hasn't,' said Epperaliant.

'Emperor,' said Cortein.

Across the square, ruins fell inwards with a rush, a grinning ork head fashioned from metal hoved into view atop a broad-bellied body, crackling orbs on insulated poles jutting from its back. A dome of energy flared into visibility every time a shell hit it. The scale of the ork witch's power had grown, for the shield encompassed much of the square. The ork infantry became agitated and excited at its appearance, rushing forwards in the cover of their walkers.

'Greeneye,' whispered Cortein.

'*Lux Imperator*'s capacitors are charged sir! They're moving again, what are your orders?'

Cortein had no time to reply. The cabin air took on strange taste, aluminium on the back teeth. There was a wash of green light, and Bannick gripped at his skull. A voice called his name, his head split and chaos reigned in his mind.

CHAPTER 27
ARONIS CITY, PARAGON VI
2003395.M41

'Colaron! Colaron, damn you! At least look like you are here with us.'

Bannick blinked, confused. He stood on the blue lawn of the Gardens of the Vermillion Moon, flowers nodding in a steady, machine-generated breeze, the warm air thick with their scent. One of Tuparillio's friends stood by the door, keeping watch, a medic by him.

Surely this had all passed? Bannick felt confused for a space, and his eyes – two human eyes – fell on the flowers. Amid the orangey-red of healthy blooms, a dead flower stood out, petals crumpled, as red as unoxygenated blood.

'Colaron!' said Tuparillio.

Bannick shook his head, the sense of déjà vu evaporated.

'Is your arrogance so great,' said Tuparillio, 'that you bring no second?'

Bannick swallowed, his tongue dry with the after-effects of Zero Night. He remembered now, the duel. 'Tuparillio, why are we doing this? We can stop. Record a no show on my part.

Don't make me fight you. You've not got a chance.'

Tuparillio pulled off his winter jerkin, exposing a lean torso shadowed by lines of muscle. Another youth Bannick knew to be called Torsten handed Tuparillio a black jerkin of hardened leather. He shucked it on. 'Proud enough not to register a win in my favour I see. Do I matter that little to you cousin? Do I matter to you as little as Kaithalar?'

He took his sword from the hand of Torsten, and began stretching his muscles out. 'Stop wasting time. Get your sword and glove on.'

Bannick reluctantly pulled the thick moulded glove onto his right hand and took up his rapier. 'What is this all about, Tuparillio! I'm betrothed to her.'

'And yet you mock her. You don't deserve a woman like that, you and that orphan basdack Kalligen, always laughing at her and poking fun, you have no respect for the woman who will be your wife.'

'Come on, Tuparillio, you know what Lazlo's like, he doesn't mean any harm, he's got a sharp tongue on him. He just finds her serious, is all.'

'Sharp as a snake, and his bite is as deadly. Many times have I suffered his sting, mocking me all my life, the pair of you, and now you make a woman of honour your own private laughing stock because you are too juvenile to commit to her and the great service she will do you and our clan.'

His cousin's face was angry, so hard with rage the muscles in it shook. There was more to this than a young man's sense of outraged honour. There was something else. Then it hit Bannick. Tuparillio had been acting peculiarly around him for months ever since the betrothal. The poetry he was rightly famed for had become a furtive, unspoken affair. No recitals. He understood the object of his works, he should have seen this coming and he cursed. 'You're not in love with her, Tuparillio, are you?'

he asked hesitantly, trying to be gentle, his sword tip drooping to the floor.

The boy flushed red, and Bannick recalled the number of times he'd seen the look of anger on the boy's face recently, the amount of time he'd been sitting on his own, brooding. He and Kalligen had had much sport of him. He'd been younger than him, after all. That's what boys do. But they weren't so young any more. 'Oh come on Tuparillio!' he began to laugh, but the stare the boy gave him cut his laughter short.

'That's of no consequence!' Tuparillio spluttered, and Bannick knew he'd found the truth. 'I've called you out because I'm sick of your venality, you are a shame on our clan and on our way of life.' He began to adjust the setting buttons at the hilt of his blade. The length of it rippled as the molecules of the metal rearranged themselves, giving the weapon a razor edge.

'Tuparillio, what are you doing? You don't have license for sharps!' No wonder he had called Bannick here; the master of the duelling fields would have stopped the fight. 'Dammit, listen to me! You're my cousin, for the Emperor's sake! Let's stop! If we must duel, let us do it blunt-bladed, with masks. Satisfy your honour safely.'

Tuparillio advanced.

'You, his seconds, are you going to stop him?'

The boy Torsten folded his arms and gave a slight shake of his head, Tuparillio's other friend, a Sankello, looked away. The medic stood by looking bored.

'Scared now too?' the younger man sneered, and he came at the older Bannick with sudden viciousness.

Colaron Bannick reacted with time to spare, but barely, moving his arm up so that his blade was perpendicular, point to the ground, the arc of the first position. It blocked Tuparillio's weapon, a subtle correction to its course that sent it whisking past Bannick's side. Bannick was in a fencer's crouch by then, and responded swiftly, extending his arm and simultaneously moving his blade in a circle to the fourth position, moving quickly forwards, trying to tangle his cousin's blade and wrench it from his grasp, but the younger Bannick moved back almost as quick, twitching his sword twice in quick succession to block a deception and a thrust from Bannick, returning in kind with two of his own.

Two more quick attacks, and the two cousins found themselves body to body, swords crossed between them. 'You've been practising,' said Bannick.

'Solely so I can teach you a much-needed lesson,' hissed Tuparillio. 'Why do you not sharpen your sword?'

'Because I don't want to kill you, you damn fool!' said Bannick, and a push from both sides forced them apart. They regained a good distance from one another and began to circle, each looking for an opening. Bannick to disarm his clansman, Tuparillio, Bannick realised, to kill him.

'I don't understand!' shouted Bannick, parrying three wild attacks easily, the blades clanging loud in the still garden air.

'No, you never did. For you it was play, wasn't it, all the jibes and the jokes and the mockery!' He executed a near perfect lunge that came within a whisker of skewering Bannick's kidney. A jink to the side and a seventh-position parry saved him. Three quick compound attacks nearly got through Bannick's defence, and he was forced to weave a web of steel about himself. They were sweating in the humid air of the Vermillion Gardens, but both were fit, and now they were warmed up, their sword play increased in accuracy and tempo.

'Sharpen your blade!'

'No,' said Bannick. 'You will have to kill a defenceless man.'

'You are hardly that!' said Tuparillio, and intensified his attack.

Their blades kissed and rang, rattled back and forth, time and again Bannick attempting to remove his cousin's blade. Time and again Tuparillio foiled his attacks and executed an aggressive response.

Talking ceased as Tuparillio pushed home his advantage. Bannick tried every trick he could think of to disarm him, still not willing to sharpen his blade edge enough to cut, still holding back, hoping that the watch would get here and break up the fight before either of them got hurt.

They forced each other back a series of paces, the blue grass trampled dark by their circling. The sap from it was making the lawn slick and treacherous.

'If you are not willing to fight me properly, cousin,' said Tuparillio, 'I will kill you.'

Bannick opened his mouth, but no words came. He would have to hurt Tuparillio to bring this madness to a close.

'Sharpen your blade!'

Bannick looked to the hilt buttons. 'No,' he said.

'Then you will die,' said Tuparillio. He undid the top of his tunic, and pulled out a main-gauche, prongs running either side of the blade, designed to catch and trap an opponent's sword. Tuparillio attacked again, feinting with one blade, then another, trying to step inside the reach of Bannick's sword, where the shorter weapon could be employed. Bannick saw what he was doing, and kept his distance, backing away across the lawn.

'Tuparillio, stop!' he parried an overhead swipe, dodged sideways as the dagger swished through the air.

'You can only win by killing me, so do it! Do it! I have nothing to live for, you've taken and scorned the only thing I care for!'

Blades rang from one another. 'I will not be the agent of your suicide, cousin.'

Tuparillio tried and tried again to force a way past Bannick's guard, but could not. Bannick was the superior swordsman, but he was holding back. There was a chance here that he might get killed if he didn't think of something soon.

Tuparillio's anger gave him an edge that Bannick doubted he'd have found at other times. His attacks became wilder and unpredictable. If Bannick had been fighting to win, he could have killed him a dozen times.

Then the younger Bannick leapt, both blades drawn back, the dagger whisked past Colaron's face, the sword following in a swift circle. He parried one, and not the other. The sword swept across his left cheek, bringing with it a rush of heat and a stinging pain.

'Tuparillio, stop!' he heard Torsten say. 'You have bloodied him, you have won. Honour is satisfied.'

Tuparillio did not listen. With a cry of anguish he leapt high into the air, both blades drawn back, one then another coming towards the older Bannick.

Bannick parried one, then another. Without thinking he lunged, years of training under the duelling masters and the experience of dozens of fights taking over.

The point of his blade, dull as it was, was still sharp enough to kill, and it found its way past Tuparillio's quick counter-parry, and through the younger man's jerkin. Thick blood gouted from the hole in his chest as he slid down the blade, spraying red across the lawn as he slipped from the sword onto the grass.

Tuparillio was dying as he hit the ground. He lifted his head weakly from where he lay, blood staining his teeth. 'You kill your kin in an illegal duel. You dishonour yourself,' he said. 'Now Kaithalar will never marry you.' He smiled triumphantly, and died.

Bannick did not move, sword out still, staring at the body of his cousin.

CHAPTER 28

'Bannick! Bannick!' Hands shook him, Epperaliant. 'Are you all right?'

'Yes,' Bannick said. 'Yes, I think so.' He patted at himself, then withdrew his hand sharply from the sandscum amulet about his neck.

'They're hot,' said Epperaliant. 'Bruta was right, thank the Emperor. The witch shorted out the reactor and knocked us all for six, but we're alive.'

The interior of the tank was dark, all systems down. A few pale warning lights shone in the dark, shafts of light coming in through the viewing slots shone bright shapes on the walls. Cortein stood upon his seat, looking through the glass.

'The orks want *Mars Triumphant* as a prize to join *Lux Imperator*,' said Cortein. 'I'm sure of it. That witch tried to knock us out and leave the tank unharmed. Their infantry's coming up now.' He jumped down and sat back at his station. 'I say we give them a surprise. Vorkosigen, prepare to restart the engine on my order.'

'The others?' asked Bannick, seating himself by his dead fire-station.

'Me and Meggen, we're unhurt,' croaked Outlanner.

'My damn head is splitting,' coughed Radden in the turret.

'Ralt?'

Epperaliant shook his head. 'He would not take the amulet.'

Cortein spoke. 'We have to be quick. Bannick, keep an eye on those orks.' Bannick nodded and clambered up to peer through the viewing slits.

'Meggen,' Cortein shouted down the stairs to the lower deck. 'Get the lorelei shells up here.'

'Lift's out sir!' shouted Meggen. With the internal vox down, they were having to rely on their own voices. Meggen's reply was muffled by the armour plate of the tank.

'Very well. Bring one – it will have to do. Radden?'

'Sir?'

'Get down here and help him, you're going to have to carry it. We can't activate the power systems until we're ready to go. Load it.'

Radden clanged down from above, and made for the stairs down.

'Quietly!' said Cortein. Rumbles sounded from outside, muted battle. It seemed too quiet. 'Bannick, what are those orks up to?'

'They're advancing from three sides. Cautiously, sir, three loose groups covering each other. The nearest is about a hundred metres away and they're not charging in. The last walker is stationary. Malfunction?' The vehicles of the orks were ramshackle.

Cortein shook his head. 'They're holding it back, in case we prove troublesome,' said Cortein.

Bannick went round the cabin, clambering over equipment where he had to, peering out through the command deck's slit windows. He quickly checked the buildings round the square. 'There's no sign of *Lux Imperator*,' he said, moving to the very front of the cabin.

'They must really want *Mars Triumphant* whole,' said Epperaliant, touching the amulet hanging around his neck. 'I pray that the witch cannot see us in here.'

'I doubt it,' said Cortein. Meggen, chomping on one of his never-ending supply of cigars, and Radden appeared, wrestling the lorelei shell in its special casing up the steps into the command deck. Cortein moved over to help them, grasping one of four inset handles round the top. 'If they knew they'd try hitting us again. We have to assume the witch cannot see us.'

The three men manhandled the shell up the ladder into the turret as Bannick kept watch.

Cortein came back down the ladder of the central well and paused. He looked to his jacket hanging on the back of his chair, his cap on the desk. He picked them up and deliberately put them on, pulling his hat tight, buttoning his jacket to the top.

'Bannick, see to those orks as soon as we power up. Outlanner, take us directly towards that Titan. Radden, prepare to fire the main cannon, scramble that witch's brain and get those shields down. Meggen, take Ralt's place up front. Bannick, as soon as you've dealt with those orks, I want you playing the lascannon on the left arm, got it? Meggen, get the demolisher on the right, strip it of its secondary armament. We've got one chance to hit this beast, one. And we'll have the fight of our lives trying to do it. Are we ready men?'

'Sir!' said the surviving crew of *Mars Triumphant*.

'For the Emperor, For Paragon, For *Mars Triumphant*,' said Cortein. 'Now get into your positions. Vorkosigen.'

The little tech-adept blinked his bulging eyes nervously, his skinny arms bare and slick with sweat. 'Sir?'

'You can activate the reactor?'

'Sir. It is dormant, not offline. I can awaken it. I am ready.'

'Very well,' Cortein watched as they moved back to their stations. 'On my mark, tech-adept…'

Muttering the prayers of the tech-priests under his breath, Vorkosigen flicked the switches and toggles that would arm the reactor for reactivation.

'Sound off!' said Cortein.

'Turret ready!' shouted Radden.

'Secondary weapon ready!' said Meggen.

'Tertiary weapons systems ready!' said Bannick.

'Tech ready,' said Vorkosigen.

'Comms and tac ready,' said Epperaliant.

'Driver ready,' said Outlanner.

Bannick looked round the cabin, at Marsello's empty seat, at the scorch damage from shorted systems. He saw Cortein doing the same. Their eyes locked, and Cortein gave him a brief nod.

'Command ready,' said Cortein, concluding the roll-call. 'On my mark, three, two, one. Activate main reactor!'

Vorkosigen bent right over his desk as he depressed the twin activation sigils, prostrating himself at his station before the Omnissiah.

A click, a thrum of engines. A bang.

Mars Triumphant roared into life, screaming defiance at the fat ork giant stood before it.

'Open fire!' bellowed Cortein. 'All weapons!'

On the railed platform atop his Gargant, Greeneye surveyed the battle. He liked much of what the Imperium had. He liked this world, so he grabbed it, and like Gratzdakka, he liked their wagons, so he took them.

Before him the big battlewagon sat, the humans inside fried

dead by the power of his own Morkishness. He could not feel their silly minds, but he had his boys move in slowly just in case. He was not a fool, not like the warboss. He'd seen the humans try to outflank the orks' position, try to attack from two sides at once. He laughed at their pathetic attempts to stop him from seeing them. They were weak, and would be destroyed.

Outside of his protective psychic umbrella, artillery shells hammered down on the surface town, killing orks and men alike as they fought. Pink beams burst through the clouds and scorched whole buildings to vapour, fusing the sand into glass. But he was safe, his power, augmented by the nearly finished Mork shout, focused by the mek know-wots within his Gargant, protected him as well as a squiggoth-hide shield would deflect a stone spearhead. If only Gratzdakka knew how powerful he had become, he would have him killed, but it was much too late for that, and much too late for Gratzdakka.

Greeneye watched the orks approach the tank, the Killa Kan behind them wiggling about like a squig with a broken back was hilarious, and he roared with laughter. Green energies arced from his hair, his eyes bulged, and he howled with joy. War! War! War! All was chaos and destruction about him. The humans had no hope, this world would be his, and then another, and another, and another, his armies swollen by orks drawn in by the power of the Mork shout! He laughed and laughed and laughed, gretchin oilers and crewmen scurrying fearfully away from him.

'WAAAAAAAAAAAAAAAAGGGGGGHHHHHHH!' he howled, and laughed some more.

There was a lurch in his Gargant. Through the open hatch Greeneye heard the captain shouting orders in the head below and the heavy smack of ork hand on ork skull. Weapons fire followed. Greeneye opened his eyes, drawn back from his dreams of conquest.

How could this be? The human wagon was grinding forwards over the rubble, dragging its battered shell towards him! As he watched, the big shootas on the front and side opened fire and killed many of the boys coming forwards. A blasta atop the wagon lanced out, burning a hole right through the last killer kan, stopping it dead in its tracks.

'What's happening!' he shouted into the speaking tube attached to the rail. 'Stop them! I want that wagon!'

Greeneye's Gargant opened up with its cannons and rockets, blasting holes in the ground all around the human wagon, hammering into its hull, shells dragging sparks from its hide, pulling chunks of it away. The little turret with its funny heavy shootas on the front crashed away, the armour on one side buckled, but it still came on.

He ceased to think as an unquenchable fury took him, the unreasoning violence that existed in every ork, a need to smash and burn and win and conquer, to kill and kill until there was no one left, no one left at all but orks, and then they'd fight some more.

His powerful mind swelled with it, drawing energy directly from the immaterial realm of the Great Green where Gork and Mork laughed and clapped at his anger. Lightning arced about him, fizzing from his head, skittering up to the great copper spheres high above the Gargant's back, amplifying his power. He felt the mind of every ork on the planet, each alight with war and violence. He drew upon them, every one, and those beyond Kalidar, and beyond this system, the great green sea of eldritch energy that surrounded the orkish race, protected it, generated by their exuberance and lust for conquest. Time slowed and Greeneye ceased to see the material world, looking instead through his mind's-eye, seeing the world reflected in the green of the weird.

Through a crackling haze of sparks, Greeneye looked down; the power was building in him, surging to be set loose. He could not hold it for much longer. Unable to speak, he slammed his palm down. It fell slowly, although Greeneye knew it was moving fast, until it connected with a big button, activating the wailing siren that informed the captain of the Gargant's warp cannon that it was time to deploy.

Greeneye laughed and laughed as he felt the deck vibrate beneath his feet. Below him, the Gargant's tongue would be jutting out, ready to unleash the fury of Gork and Mork on the stupid humans below him, fury that flowed through *him*.

The big cannon on the tank turret ground upwards. Greeneye laughed, at it. So pathetic! It belched fire, and Greeneye stopped laughing.

Something was wrong. There was an absence in the scene before him, in the world painted in shades of violent green, a black streak, a shell from the gun, a shell his weird-eyes could not see.

When it reached the Gargant's warp-born energy field, the shell did not stop. Greeneye felt the strange shell pierce his psychic defences, green energy rippling as it broke through.

Greeneye did not know it, but his anger was born from fear, the fear of a race which died millions of years ago, a fear that drove them to grasp at any means of survival, in no matter how debased a form. That fear flared in him now as the shell continued on into the Gargant's armour, smashed through it and exploded inside.

Pain erupted in Greeneye's alien mind and he lost control of the energies he wrestled with. He tried to force them through his weirding staff, to earth everything at once and save his head. Energy poured from him and through the Gargant. One of the copper globes exploded and Greeneye fell screaming to his knees.

* * *

Fires burned unchecked in the cabin, Vorkosigen frantically trying to activate the suppression systems. Bannick was down to one bolter bank and one lascannon, on opposing sides of the tank, and his twitch sticks were becoming more difficult to operate. His displays popped and fizzed, most of his augurs were out, yet still he fired.

'Lorelei shell is away!' shouted Radden, and *Mars Triumphant* shifted as its main cannon fired.

Bannick watched on his lascannon screen as the shell impacted on the ork Titan's armoured belly, punching a hole in the armour and exploding within. Fire rushed out of the hole, and the Titan shook. It ground to a halt, but its head and arms continued to operate, hammering the tank with weapons fire.

'Reactor's hit!' shouted Vorkosigen. 'We're losing power!'

'Look!' shouted Epperaliant.

The impact of the shell was a small thing to so large a machine as the ork Titan, but the lorelei in the shell, shattered and spread throughout the machine by the explosion, had done its work. The lightning playing around the head of the machine went wild, felling one of the focusing arms. Green fire played up and down the ork engine. A gun exploded, a turret fell, a lifeless ork with no head coming with it. The ground began to shake as shells from the Imperial bombardment once again found their way to the surface.

'Meggen, Bannick, now!' Cortein shouted.

Bannick aimed at a large rocket launcher on the Titan's left shoulder, his lasbolt flew true, and the whole array went up as one. A second later, a demolisher shell slammed home, tearing the right arm from the machine.

'Keep it up! Keep it up!' yelled Cortein.

'What readings I can get say the main psychic shield over the hive shaft is still up, sir!'

'We have to keep at it until the witch is dead!' yelled Cortein.

Psychic energies, less potent and unfocused by the machine now, began to assail them.

'Sir, *Lux Imperator* coming in to our rear!'

'Can it get a line on us?'

'Too much intervening debris sir,' replied Epperaliant.

'Outlanner, keep it that way!' ordered Cortein.

Demolisher and main cannon shells impacted in a quick tattoo on the Titan. Fire billowed out from the cracks within its armour plates, and it slowly began to slump forwards.

'It's nearly finished!' whooped Radden.

'*Lux Imperator* is drawing near,' shouted Epperaliant.

'I see it,' Outlanner shouted, and the Baneblade shifted leftwards.

'Transmission efficiency down to fifty-four per cent and falling!' said Vorkosigen.

The Baneblade shuddered, Bannick's sticks went limp. 'I've lost fire control.'

A bow wave of green energy washed out from the immobilised Titan. A flickering echo of it passed through the tank, arcing between components and shorting out electronics, the chart table ruptured and exploded, showering glass round the deck. Alarm after alarm blared for attention, Vorkosigen wept as he tried to aid his charge. From the turret above, Radden's shouts became agonised screams.

'Radden!' shouted Cortein.

Something massive impacted the frontal armour, the tank shook hard. *Mars Triumphant* ground round counterclockwise as the left track unit locked.

'Outlanner's down, sir!' shouted Ralt. 'The demolisher's gone.'

'Meggen, Ralt, get up here now.' Cortein looked to everyone. 'Listen to me, you are all to get out.' He stood from his chair. 'I'm staying here to finish the job. That witch must die. The shield over the entrance to Hive Meradon must come down.'

Epperaliant stood, 'Sir, I must protest…'

'I am ordering you to abandon this vehicle with immediate effect. Will you refuse a direct order, Second Lieutenant Commsman Epperaliant?'

'No, no, sir, but… I can't leave you… I can't…'

Cortein placed his hand on the shoulder of his number two. 'Leave now, Epperaliant. Go with Bannick. He'll need looking after when all this is done. Serve him like you have served me.'

Epperaliant wavered for a moment, then clicked his heels together and saluted. 'Sir.'

'Now get rebreathers and gear for the crew. Bannick, get Radden and get away from here as quick as you can. Once I've killed the witch, things are going to get hot here, they'll blast the hive from orbit, keep down and stay low.'

Ralt and Meggen came up, Ralt's face blackened, one eye swollen shut. 'Honoured lieutenant?' he asked.

'Get your survival gear, you're leaving.'

Ralt hesitated, then nodded. Meggen spat out his cigar, and said nothing. He grasped the Honoured Lieutenant's hand as he passed. Taking respirators, coats and weapons belts from Epperaliant, they flicked open the hatch above the tech station and clambered out.

Bannick dragged Radden down from the turret. He was unconscious, his eyes shut, face badly burned. He was in a bad way, but alive. As gently as they could, Bannick and Epperaliant pulled a rebreather over his mouth.

Cortein moved over to the stairs, grabbing for support as the tank juddered. He picked a belt of frag grenades from the shelving round the command deck's periphery and slung them over his shoulder. 'Vorkosigen.'

'I'm won't go. I can't.'

'Tech-Adept…'

'Sir, I can help you. You need me! *Mars Triumphant* needs me…'

Cortein nodded. 'As you wish. Keep us going for as long as you can.'

Vorkosigen immediately turned back to his console, trying to keep the reactor online.

'Honoured Lieutenant Cortein!' called Bannick.

Cortein looked at him.

'It's been an honour.'

Cortein dipped his head. 'Get out of here, Lieutenant Bannick.'

Bannick nodded. Epperaliant passed up out of the hatch, leaned back in and took Radden under the armpits. He and Bannick manoeuvred him out of the hatch, and they were out into the battle.

The others were running ahead of Bannick and Epperaliant, who moved as fast as they could with Radden's arms slung over their shoulders. Bannick risked a look at the tank. It had stopped turning on the spot, Cortein evidently in the driver's seat. Green flares stabbed down at it. A rocket spanged off its thick armour. Then it stopped, the engine dying, and that was the last Bannick saw for a few moments, for he stumbled and was forced to look to the path before him. They ran on, the battle receding behind them, shells exploding left and right. A trio of atmospheric fighters roared overhead, a rare sight in Kalidar's turbulent skies, bombs dropping, hitting some target hidden to him. Sounds of a large battle were becoming apparent, as the Imperial battlegroup forced its way towards the strikeforce's position. But in the square, only the three vehicles fought. Ork and human dead lay in pieces all around. Bannick and Epperaliant, lungs labouring under the stinking rebreathers, dodged around a burning Chimera. They were skirting the edge of the volcano cannon's crater where the Atraxians had died.

Then they were closing on the building line. He could see a number of Atraxians peeking out from shell holes. Arms waved at them frantically. A burst of automatic fire came in from the left. Ralt went down, dead. Lasfire sprayed out from the Atraxians in the building, covering them, and then Bannick was inside. He and Epperaliant collapsed against a ruined buttress by an Atraxian, as friendly hands took Radden away.

'How many are you?' gasped Bannick.

'Twelve,' said the Atraxian. 'Suicide mission. What do you expect? But we nearly did it.'

'Don't count the honoured lieutenant out yet,' said Bannick, and he rolled over to look at the scene.

'You can count us out,' said the Atraxian. 'We've got three dozen orks out there closing in on us. They've been a little timid of our heavy bolter.' he nodded to a shell hole where a two-man weapon team hunkered down. 'It won't last. When they rush us, it's all over.'

Bannick looked out. Things appeared hopeless. The ork Titan burned merrily, but gunfire and psychic attacks still issued from it. *Mars Triumphant* sat, dead. *Lux Imperator* was lining up for a shot, rocking as it twisted a little left, a little right, to gain a good firing solution. From the edge of the square, Bannick could see through the burning ruins to where shells and ship lance beams battered ineffectually at the psychic shield protecting the heart of Hive Meradon.

'Have you got a spare rifle?' he asked.

Delirious with pain, Brasslock moaned. But his physical agony was the least of his hurts, for one of his charges was about to destroy the other. He was cursed enough to be aware of that.

'Hush now, brother,' said the stranger. He hung in the air before the tank, insubstantial as smoke.

'You...' hissed Brasslock. His iron lungs were almost dead.

He did not have long to live. 'You have returned to me.' It was some comfort.

'You can help,' said the ghost. 'Even now, your friend Cortein struggles with *Mars Triumphant*. He intends to sacrifice himself to kill the witch.'

'But, he will surely be destroyed by *Lux Imperator*,' sighed the tech-priest. He was tired, the world was greying around the edges. He was dying. The tank's hull vibrated underneath him with the clangs and shouts of excited ork crew rushing to and fro as they prepared to fire the cannon.

'You can stop that.'

'How?'

'Reach out, speak to the machine's spirit,' said the ghost. 'Calm it, make it disobey its new masters.'

'I cannot,' said Brasslock. 'I have not the augmitters now, and I cannot pray.'

'Have faith, tech-priest. Faith will be enough.'

And Brasslock reached out. His mind was foggy, but its boundaries seemed less hard than they had been, as if his consciousness no longer stopped at the limits of his skull or intelligence core. Away from himself, he felt a huge and powerful spirit, caged and enraged – the machine spirit of *Lux Imperator*. It roared helplessly as rough ork hands twisted at the levers of its metal shell, Brasslock felt its pain and sorrow at the changes wrought upon it. Softly, Brasslock reached out, chanting the litanies of calming in his mind, soothing the beast within the machine. He encircled it with his prayers; it calmed.

He felt the capacitors as a reservoir of light. He touched them, felt a greater presence still guiding him as he bade them vent their energy through the hull of the tank. Like waters through a ruptured dam, four terawatts of caged electricity leapt joyously through the skin of *Lux Imperator*.

Orks howled as they cooked, and Brasslock felt the spirit of the tank sigh with release. All activity within ceased. He himself was untouched.

'There,' said the stranger. 'I must go to my rest now, Enginseer Adept Brasslock, but I am sad to say you must remain. The Emperor has uses for you yet.' The ghostly young officer began to fade away. 'For me, tell my friend Bannick he is right to pray. He always was.'

Brasslock gasped, and sank out of this world. *Lux Imperator* was still.

'Vorkosigen!' there was no reply. Cortein kicked at the tank's controls. 'Move damn you. Move!' he roared. 'I will not die without purpose!'

The tank's engines remained silent.

A blast jolted him, and he looked around the machine he had lived and fought in for thirty years. It was close to the end now, a millennium of combat drawing to an end. *Mars Triumphant* was battered, plates buckled, cables and piping hanging loose, the raw air of Kalidar blowing in from where the heavy bolter turret had once sat.

Cortein took a deep breath, shut his eyes, then opened them and spoke. 'I am no tech-priest, *Mars Triumphant*,' he said, 'but I ask you to listen to me now. You and I have fought together for three decades. I have served you well, and you have served me in kind. Let us go now together in fire and vengeance, and bring destruction to the enemies of the Emperor.'

He mouthed a prayer to the Emperor and Omnissiah, reached for the throttle and twisted it.

Mars Triumphant juddered, the engines engaged. Tracks grinding against buckled skirts, it shuddered towards the crippled Titan.

Cortein smiled. 'Thank you.' He locked the drive levers on full ahead and went aft, ducking stoved-in armour. He had to feel his way by touch, the lights were down, and the air clogged with smoke. Only a few alarms sounded, muted and dim, for the tank, like him, had accepted its fate.

In the shell locker, Cortein wrapped his belt of frag grenades around a high explosive shell. He sat there in the gloom, shaken from side to side as the tank grumbled across the shattered plaza.

He thought of his life. Of home. Of the men who had served with him, and who had died, all in the service of the Emperor.

Now it was over. He had done his best. He prayed to the Emperor that it had been enough.

There was a lurch as the tank's front clanged against the Titan. Cortein depressed the firing button on one of the grenades.

'Emperor save us all,' he said.

Orks ran at them. Bannick fired his borrowed lasgun and the Atraxian heavy bolter chattered. *Mars Triumphant* began to move.

'The honoured lieutenant!' said Epperaliant, snapping off a shot. 'He's still there.'

They watched as the injured tank drove itself into the ork Titan. There was a pause, then a bang. Secondary explosions followed, and *Mars Triumphant* tore itself to pieces, its munitions store going up violently. The tank half lifted off the ground before it was lost to view in a boiling fireball that engulfed the Titan, the pair of giant vehicles detonating with an ear-splitting roar.

Orks and men threw themselves flat as detritus rained down all over the square.

When Bannick looked up again, the psychic shield was gone, shells falling unimpeded from the Imperial artillery right into the shaft of Hive Meradon.

Almost immediately the air above the hive crackled violently as the atmosphere was superheated to roiling plasma by five simultaneous lance strikes right down the throat of the hive. A series of explosions rumbled from deep in the shaft. Sudden flames rushed into the sky and the ground under Bannick's building bucked and shook, large chunks of rockcrete pelting down from the semi-ruined structure, crushing men within. As suddenly as it had begun, the lances snapped off, the air rushing in with a thunderous boom. The orks assaulting the building stopped and turned to see, the men within too surprised to shoot them until Bannick shouted orders and lesser bolts of light snapped out to reap their own harvest of death.

The lances snapped on and off again, sometimes two or three of them at a time striking simultaneously, vaporising strongpoints. The remaining ork heavy walkers, the Titan's lesser kin, trundled round to face a threat they could not assail, and were torn in two by the stabbing light.

In between the beams, the air filled with shapes, teardrops of metal screaming down from the sky, retro-thrusters burning fiercely to slow their descent only a hundred metres above the ground. The pods hit hard, petal-doors blowing open with explosive force. Men, as tall as any ork, made inhumanly bulky by the black armour they wore, stepped out in groups from their drop-pods, laying intricate killing fields of fire with their boltguns. The orks assaulting Bannick's position turned to face this new threat, or fled.

'The Adeptus Astartes! The Black Templars!' one of the Atraxians in the building said. His voice rising to a shout, 'The Emperor be praised! The Emperor be praised! The Angels of Death are here!'

The other men took up the shout. The noise of battle cannons from over the hive's central pit became louder and louder as the main body of the Imperial Guard drove deep into Orktown. Their secret weapon gone, distracted by Cortein's attack, assaulted from above, the orks crumbled.

The war for Kalidar was over.

CHAPTER 29

KALIDAR IV, HIVE MERADON SURFACE TOWN
3359397.M41

Bannick and Hannick stood by a shattered wall on the fifth floor of the tallest surviving building in Meradon's surface town, where a temporary command and medical centre had been established.

He took in silently the information presented to him by Hannick.

'I'm sorry, but you couldn't be allowed to know,' said the honoured captain. 'Valle himself volunteered, he was the bait. Any mind of that magnitude was bound to attract the attention of the witch, and we had to make it look like we were trying to hide him. We needed the orks looking the wrong way and *Mars Triumphant* was a credible threat. We had to have them concentrating on you, so the Black Templars could redeploy and the fleet could position itself in order to destroy the ork device. With the witch bending all his efforts to finding where you were, he effectively made himself blind to our true intentions.'

Bannick nodded.

'We are all asked to make sacrifices, but they can be hard to take,' said Hannick sympathetically.

'It isn't,' said Bannick. 'I serve.'

Hannick carried on regardless, carried away by his own emotions: guilt, maybe, or grief. 'We are engaged in a war of survival. The Imperium is beset on all sides. This is a small battle, and it needed to be finished quickly lest it rapidly escalate into something with far wider consequences. You did well. You played your part. You did your duty, as did your fellows. Mourn them, honour them with your service.

Bannick looked across the ruined surface town. The central shaft of Hive Meradon was marked by a wide column of grey smoke. The shells of heavy walkers burned amid the wrecks of the hive's low surface buildings. Recovery crews worked on abandoned armoured vehicles, a pair of ornate Ecclesiarchy charnel trains made their solemn way back and forth, bulldozing wreckage, recovering corpses, burning ork carcasses and delivering the Emperor's final judgement to those xenos they found alive.

'So the war for Kalidar is over?' said Bannick.

'Almost so. With the warboss dead, the orks will fall to fighting themselves. It is their way. If we manage it correctly, and do not provoke them into reuniting by allowing a new warlord to rise, we will be able to pick them off band by band. The Black Templars are now fighting their way into the hive to clear it. It is too valuable a source of lorelei to destroy, and it is there that the warlord's lieutenants are concentrated, many of the bigger orks, the candidates to take over. It is dangerous, but the Black Templars more dangerous still. The orks lack leadership, and as Meradon is their main stronghold, that should very much be that.' He peered over the drop to the street below, where victorious Guardsmen rested. They smoked and joked in the swaggering way of all men who have fought a hard battle and lived to tell the tale. 'Nevertheless, there's a century or more's work here for clearance teams, burning up spore infestations so the greenskins do not re-emerge as a secondary feral wave, but at least in that regard Kalidar is on our side.'

Hannick sighed, arched his back and clasped his hands behind it. He looked over at Bannick.

'The Munitorum believe that the mines here will be operational again within the month. Can you believe that?'

Bannick said nothing. The wheel of war and oppression grinds on, he thought bitterly.

'As for us, we are finished here,' said Hannick. 'The battlegroup is to be split in half, and we are to be redeployed. Rebellion on the plains of Geratomro or somesuch.'

'Where?' said Bannick.

Hannick smiled. 'The Imperium is vast, Lieutenant Bannick. For us, the men who are privileged enough to serve with such machines as *Mars Triumphant*, the war will never end. We go where we are sent, no matter if we have heard of it or not, and we fight until we fall.'

'But, *Mars Triumphant* is destroyed. Surely I will be returned to the Paragonian 42nd?' said Bannick. 'My secondment is pointless now, there is nothing for me to serve upon and no one to serve with.'

'Nonsense,' said Hannick. 'You are a member of the Paragonian 7th Super-heavy Tank Company, now and forever.' He paused. 'Until your own heroic end at least. A hard service, but what service! We are to meet with an Adeptus Mechanicus manufactory fleet on route to our new assignment. We are to be resupplied. A new Baneblade is probably being assembled up there as we speak. My command is to be returned to full strength.' The young captain seemed happy with that. 'Brasslock lives, as do Meggen and Epperaliant. There's nearly half a crew there, including you. Continuity is the key.'

He didn't mention the others, thought Bannick. Poor young Marsello, or brave Ganlick, Vorkosigen, Radden, dying in agony in the ruins an hour before medicae teams got to us... So many good men dead. And he thought of the billions more that died day in, day out, all over the Imperium, fighting for the continued existence of the human race. What else could he do but serve?

He kept these thoughts to himself, and instead said, 'It is an honour to fight for the Emperor, a double one to serve upon such machines.'

'I'm glad you agree.'

The two men watched the destruction on the plain below for a space. A wide trail of dust churning in the air marked where three full companies of Atraxian Heavy Infantry in Chimeras made their way to the hive entrance to bolster the Marines within, unarmoured trucks bearing units of Savlar Chem-Dogs trailing in their wake. The wind carried the occasional sound of explosions or crackle of gunfire, the noise of tank engines reduced to insect whines. After the fury of the orbital strike, it was almost peaceful, and Kalidar for once was quiescent, sated by the violence wracking its surface.

'I had a cousin once,' said Bannick suddenly. 'A man I loved as a little brother, a boy I read to, and played with, and protected.'

'Indeed?' said Hannick, unsure as to where this was going. 'And what happened to him?'

Bannick looked his commanding officer in the eye. 'I killed him. In a duel. He'd fallen in love with the woman I was required to marry, and did not take too kindly to my and my foster-brother's lack of respect for her. He challenged me, perhaps hoping he would win and could marry her himself, perhaps because he knew he would lose and could die honourably. I don't know why, but it was my hand that ended his life, no matter what his reasons. I slew him. I became a great shame to the clan, a kinslayer. For so long I thought I could never forgive myself the dishonour, but I realise now that I fixated upon that to save myself the truth. I killed a boy I should have saved, and shamed a woman I could have loved.'

'You joined the Guard then, as atonement?'

'Yes, sir. Yes I did.'

'There are billions under arms in the Emperor's armies, Lieutenant Bannick. All have stories, reasons why. Some will be far worse than yours.'

'Do you think, sir, that the Emperor will forgive me, if I serve well?' Sadness overwhelmed him, not for himself, not any more. Cortein had told him there would be a time to mourn, to think of Radden, and Marsello, and Lazlo, and Tuparillio, all of those who had died or who would die. He realised now that he had traded guilt for sorrow of an altogether greater kind. Tears moistened his face, tracking through the dust on his face. 'I do not seek honour. Honour killed my cousin, a good young man. How many more of us will die for honour, or pride? Do you think all this is worthwhile? If we are to survive as a species, is all this worth it?'

Hannick looked embarrassed and toed the floor with his boot, hands behind his back. 'Those are questions for a priest, not for an officer, but I for one am glad you fight with me.'

They fell silent.

'I must away,' said Hannick eventually. 'I am to meet with our remaining tech-priests to discuss the salvage and redeployment of *Lux Imperator*.'

'It is repairable?'

'They believe so,' said Hannick. '*Mars Triumphant* will be recovered also, eventually, but I believe it will be given the final rites of the Machine-God and dismantled. It is past saving. I am sorry for that too.' He sighed. 'Well. *Ostrakhan's Rebirth* needs telemetry testing, I am told, to see how its repairs held out. I expect they will. She may be needed yet. She has never let me down yet, not once. Reports to write, records to file. If only war were just fighting, eh?'

'Sir,' agreed Bannick. 'Sir?'

'Yes?' said Hannick.

'May I ask who I am to serve under? Am I to join the crew of *Ostrakhan's Rebirth*?'

Hannick shook his head. 'You don't understand, Honoured Lieutenant Bannick, you really don't understand it at all.'

'Sir?'

'Congratulations, Bannick.'

With that, the honoured captain went to tend to his men and machines, a wheel within a wheel within an innumerable number of further wheels, whirring mindlessly on, each one serving the Emperor's war machine.

Bannick stayed, his first war done. High above the town, he watched Meradon burn, grief thick in his weary heart.

Greeneye sat and watched the sands blow curling fingers over the shattered remnants of the human battlewagon and his own felled Titan, *Mars Triumphant*'s smashed hull intertwined inextricably with it, the surface of Hive Meradon smashed to pieces about them.

He smiled at the destruction. The orks had lost, but it had been a good fight, and there would be many more.

The sand, he thought, each grain was like an ork, each streamer of it like a warband. Each storm like a Waaagh! – and the desert was huge.

There were billions of orks in the galaxy. Greeneye could feel them out there, a wall of fury and violence pressing on his mind, their mass shunting aside the other gods, blotting out the psychic howl of the devourer, dimming the light of the human Emperor's beacon, the psychic presences of other species candles to the great bonfire of orkish might.

Orks were meant to rule the galaxy, to burn it up and burn it up again, an eternity of warfare that made better and better orks that would one day bring the universe to its knees!

Yes, there would be better fights.

Greeneye was not like other orks. When he looked into the sand curling over the blackened metal, this is what he saw. He did not trouble himself over the next meal, or the next fight, or the impulsive need for cruel amusements at the cost of the weak.

Greeneye had vision.

He could hear the sound of men and their machines close by. They had retaken their city, killed and scattered Greeneye's tribe and were returning it to the dull grey order of humanity. Soon they would come here and cut up the machines, take their parts away, but not yet.

Greeneye stood. In his powerful mind he could already hear the stirrings of sporelings out in the sands, a new generation of orks to fight for him, and him alone, free now from Gratzdakka, hacked down by the black-armoured warriors.

Hidden from human sight by flickering warp fields generated by his insane mind, Greeneye strode off into the desert, copper staff gleaming in the sunlight. If they knew he lived, the humans would hunt him, they would stop at nothing to kill him, but he was Greeneye, the most powerful weirdboy ever! They would have to find him first, and when they did, he would kill them.

He was free, and he would make the galaxy shake at the sound of his name.

EPILOGUE

ADEPTUS MECHANICUS FORGE SHIP
'PATTERNMASTER',
SEGMENTUM PACIFICUS BATTLEGROUP 9876
REDEPLOYMENT FLEET
3480397.M41

The manufactory ship pulsed and shook as a thousand thousand triphammers rang out the birth of war's child, the bringer of ruin, the mightiest battle tank in the galaxy: Baneblade, fifteen metres long, as tall as three men, a moving fortress, hammer of the God-Emperor, bearer of firepower to equal a squadron of lesser tanks.

A choir of tech-adepts and servitors sang the praise of the machine as the final blessings and unguents were applied to the components of the vehicle. Honoured Lieutenant Colaron Artem Lo Bannick watched as Enginseer Brasslock, body now more machine than man, worked with his red-robed fellows to conclude the naming ceremony of the mighty tank.

Behind it hung rack upon rack of part-assembled war machines, awaiting final construction on the long shop floor of the forge ship, a space-borne manufactory cathedral, dedicated to the works of the Omnissiah.

Bannick watched with mixed emotions as the Magos Activator ran through the final checks. There would be no field tests for this vehicle. The proving of its systems would come in battle, and it would fail or protect him according to the whim of the Omnissiah and Emperor.

Bannick muttered his own prayers under his breath.

The ceremony went on for hours, the choir singing loudly, the magi making their arcane pronouncements in ancient Gothic and binaric, their meaning lost to the Paragonian.

Eventually, it reached a climax, and Bannick was beckoned over by a tech-priest who stalked on a hissing, five-legged carriage.

'You are ready?' the man-machine barked through his vox-grille.

'Yes,' said Bannick.

'It is a great honour we do you.'

'I thank you for it,' said Bannick as he was led into the machine by a servo-skull.

In form, the new vehicle was different to *Mars Triumphant*, its internal layout varied too, somehow more cramped, the equipment less sophisticated. A lesser pattern, Brasslock had muttered to him, but mighty enough.

Already the walls and ceilings were crowded with parchments, blessings and devotional texts as Bannick made his way down the stairs to the lower deck corridor. He was directed rear by the servo-skull, to where a young tech-adept stood, tools in hand, by the blank wall of honour. With a bow of his shorn head, the tech-adept set to work.

Bannick watched as a brass plaque bearing his name was placed at the top of the board, the very first commander of Baneblade 3411/214/A/Episilon/Phraxes.

Above the panel where his name was being attached was inscribed the given name of the new tank, flanked by skeletal figures and angels, promising doom to all those who would deny man's right to rule the stars now and forever more.

The Baneblade *Cortein's Honour*.

ABOUT THE AUTHOR

Guy Haley began his career on SFX Magazine
in 1997 before leaving to edit Games Workshop's
White Dwarf, followed by SF magazine *Death
Ray*. Since 2009 he has been a wandering writer,
working in both magazines and novels. He lives in
Somerset with his wife and son, a malamute and
an enormous, evil-tempered Norwegian Forest Cat
called, ironically, Buddy.

WILLIAM KING
WARHAMMER
40,000
THE MACHARIAN CRUSADE
FIST OF DEMETRIUS

An extract from The Macharian Crusade: Fist of Demetrius
by William King

On sale May 2013

A scribe approached and spoke to Macharius with the mixture of precision, formality and reverence that the Lord Solar inspired in those around him. He was doing his best to ignore the shuddering of the ship – and the possibility of instant death – as he brought news of another victory. It seemed that the worlds of the Proteus system had surrendered, bringing another three planets, ten hive cities and nineteen billion people back into the Imperial fold. Macharius nodded an acknowledgement, turned and said something to another clerk, recommending the general in charge of the campaign for some honour or other, and walked on.

Two more uniformed clerks approached and saluted. Before they could even open their mouths to speak, Macharius rattled off orders to commanders who were five star systems away, instructing them as to which cities to besiege, which worlds to offer alliances to and which governors to bribe. He seemed to have no difficulty dredging up any of this knowledge. It was all there in his head, all of the details of an infinitely vast campaign, the like of which had probably not been fought since the Emperor walked among men. He ordered that more reinforcements be sent to aid them and kept on walking towards the furthest tables.

Sometimes he looked up and gazed upon the surface of the burning planet with a look of longing in his eyes. I felt a certain sympathy for him then – Macharius was a warrior, born to fight. He commanded this great force, but I suspect that he missed the thrill of physical conflict, the feeling of danger, of taking his own life in his hands. His thoughts were drifting to those final battles taking place on the world beneath us. His thoughts were drifting to the ancient artefact he had coveted for so long.

I could tell that he wanted to be there. I could also tell that he had something else on his mind, something to do with his current obsession with prophecies and divinations and ancient relics that he shared with Drake. It seemed like a bond that drew the two of them together, although the inquisitor has never struck me as a superstitious man. Quite the opposite, in fact.

Here on the galaxy's farthest rim, superstitions were common. These worlds had been far from the Emperor's light for a hundred generations and all manner of strange, deviant and heretical faiths had sprung up. All manner of weird beliefs had infected the populations, and some had even taken root among our own soldiers, although you would have thought them immune to such corruption. Clusters of prophecies had begun to gather around Macharius himself. That was easy enough to understand. The Lord High Commander seemed invincible, gifted with near-supernatural powers of foresight.

There were some who claimed he was blessed by the Emperor. There were others who thought he was a supernatural being. Reports had started to arrive of shrines being set up to Macharius on dozens of worlds, and not just by those unbelievers whose temples to false prophets had been overthrown.

The ship shook. We looked at each other for a moment before we went back to pretending that nothing had happened. An officer in Naval uniform walked over.

'A glancing strike to the void shields, Lord High Commander,' he volunteered. 'Nothing to worry about.'

'I am not worried,' Macharius replied.

'I doubt they could possibly know this was the Imperial command vessel,' said the officer. He was clearly more disturbed than Macharius as this possibility occurred to him.

Macharius nodded and the officer pulled himself together, clicked his heels and saluted. As the Lord Solar strode by, his mere presence seemed to reassure people. Worried frowns disappeared from the faces of scribes and star-sailors. Commanders must always look confident and that was something that Macharius managed supremely well.

We made our way towards one of the great command tables with utter casualness. Indeed, so relaxed was our approach that I knew that we were approaching the spot in which Macharius had the greatest interest. I had learned to read the subtle signals of his moods by then. Or perhaps I delude myself. Few men ever truly knew what the great general was thinking.

Ahead of us was the command sphere for the current conquest. On its flowing surface was a representation of the continent we could see through the dome above us. Instead of being lit by the fires of burning forests, the sphere showed representations of armies as glowing patterns – ours were green and the enemy forces were red. Various runes indicated the composition of the units. Ours glowed steadily to show that we were certain of their composition. The enemy forces pulsed with varying speed to indicate the degree of certainty as to their position and strength.

Around the table stood a variety of ranking commanders, and Drake. He was, in theory, an observer but stood with the air of a man who was actually in charge, at least until Macharius arrived. The high inquisitor was tall and slim, with a pale cold face and dark hair which now had a tinge of grey in it. Obviously the juvenat treatments had not taken so well with him, or perhaps he was simply much older than he had appeared when we first met and the drugs' effects had started to weaken.

I did not know much of the inquisitor's personal history and he never volunteered anything to anyone in my hearing, even

Macharius. He was a man much more used to asking questions than answering them. Uneasiness seemed to radiate to those around him in the same way that confidence emanated like solar rays from Macharius.

The high inquisitor looked up in recognition as Macharius approached. I suspect that Macharius was as close to a friend as Drake ever had, if 'friend' is a word you can ever use in the context of an inquisitor. I had seen too much of his business over the past ten years to believe that he looked at the world with much humanity.

Macharius nodded a greeting and went over to stand beside the inquisitor. The two men were of similar height, but otherwise were as different as two people could be. Macharius was physically powerful. Drake was slender, ascetic and deceptively frail looking. Macharius wore the elaborately braided uniform of the highest ranking Imperial Guard officer. Drake wore a plain black tunic and a scarlet cloak with a cowl. Around him, a group of storm trooper bodyguards lounged like attack dogs. They eyed us as warily as we eyed them.

Drake nodded to me, which was not something calculated to make me feel any easier in my skin. He had taken an interest in me since Karsk, as he took an interest in all those close to Macharius. I had often been summoned into his presence to answer questions about the general's moods and health. I had reported these conversations to Macharius, of course, and he had told me to answer truthfully. He clearly believed that I had no secrets about him to reveal to the inquisition that they did not already know, and I suspect he was right.

Macharius turned to the adept who stood by the command altar. 'Give me a view of sector Alpha Twelve,' he said. 'Close magnification.'

'In the Emperor's name, Lord Macharius,' the adept responded. He intoned a litany and moved his hands in some ritual gestures over the altar. We looked now at a three-dimensional map of a strange city. All around it was a clear, flat zone, where the cold forest had been burned early to provide a fire-break. The buildings were ziggurats, sheathed in metal, glittering in the light of twin suns. They looked as much like fortresses as temples. They bristled with turrets, blister-bunkers and other fortifications.

War raged. Men in the uniform of the Imperial Guard fought with fanatics in the green and purple robes of the local temple wardens. Blood flowed in the streets. The natives fought stubbornly, with the courage of zealots prepared to die for their misguided faith.

They were going to. That much was obvious. Inexorably, Imperial Chimera, Basilisks and Leman Russ tanks pushed through the streets surrounding the step-pyramids, moving in the direction of the gigantic central temple. Macharius looked at the colonel who had been liaising with the ground forces.

'My orders have been conveyed,' he said. There was a question in his voice, which was not like him. Normally Macharius gave a command in the full expectation of it being obeyed and then moved on. He did not check on subordinates unless something had gone wrong, in which case he moved swiftly and ruthlessly to correct the errors.

'The ground commanders have been specifically instructed not to bombard the central temple. The soldiers know there is to be no plundering – on pain of death – and that demolition charges and heavy weapons are not to be used within the precincts of the Great Temple, Lord High Commander. I made your orders very clear on those points.'

'Good,' Macharius said, and the man seemed to swell with his praise. Like everyone else on the command barge, he knew Macharius would not forget his efficiency, or forgive his failures. He had gained credit in the eyes of the most important man in the Crusade Force and rewards would eventually and be disbursed.

The ship shook again, more violently this time. It seemed like there had been another glancing strike from a planetary defence battery. It made me uneasy. I did not like to feel that any moment I might be vaporised and that there was nothing I could do about it. This was a battle fought with weapons so gigantic that ships with the populations of small cities could be destroyed in an instant and an individual warrior could have no influence on his fate. Give me a ground battle, or even trench warfare, any time. At least there you could take cover, and take a few enemies with you when you met your end.

The glow-globes flickered. A smell of ozone filled the air. Somewhere in the distance someone screamed. Another voice barked an order. I suspect the screamer was being clapped in irons or assigned to a punishment detail.

'It seems like the enemy might be finding their range,' said Macharius. He chuckled and everybody else around him did the same. It was not that what he said was particularly funny, but when a general makes a joke, no matter how feeble, his subordinates laugh. It did dispel the tension.

Drake had ignored the near miss. He had been staring at the battle-map with total concentration, as if he could achieve a spiritual revelation if only he looked hard enough.

'We must have the Fist,' he said in a voice so low that only Macharius and those of us standing close to him could have heard it.

'Do not worry, my friend,' said Macharius. 'We shall get it.'

'We *must*,' said Drake. 'It may be one of the Imperium's most sacred artefacts – a relic from the time when the Emperor walked among us, a thing perhaps borne by one of his most trusted primarchs. A worthy gift for potent allies.'

Macharius smiled. He seemed to be considering something for a moment, which was unusual. Normally, for him to think was to act, and to act with a decision and correctness that most ordinary men could not achieve with hours or days of contemplation.

'In that case, I believe I shall go and collect it myself.'

Drake shook his head like a man hearing something he had feared, but which he had hoped not to have to deal with.

'Is that wise?' he said. It was phrased like a question but it was really a statement. Drake was one of the few men who would have dared to question Macharius. It was a thing that was happening more and more in those days, as if a rift were slowly opening between him and the Lord High Commander, as if he, so seemingly secure in his faith, was starting to have doubts in Macharius.

In this case, I was with him, for I could tell from the rare and slightly unsettling grin spreading across the general's face that Macharius was serious. He really had decided to go planetside and lead the assault on the temple.

I suppose Drake knew as well as I did that once Macharius had made up his mind there was no possibility of deflecting him from his purpose, but the high inquisitor was not a man to easily admit defeat.

'You should not put yourself at risk, Lord High Commander,' said Drake. I suppose he was thinking that he would be in trouble with his superiors if anything happened to Macharius. After all, he seemed to have taken on some responsibility for the general's safety after the events on Karsk.

'I have no intention of doing so,' said Macharius. He was already striding towards the exit of the command centre, and all we could do was follow in his wake, like tiny satellites of a gas giant or a cometary halo whirling around a sun.

Anton shot me a look that I knew well. A grin that was considerably more crazed than Macharius's flickered across his face and was gone before anyone but me could have seen it.

Drake shrugged and began to stride along beside Macharius. His storm troopers moved in his wake, some of them even surging ahead as if they suspected that danger might lurk in every corridor of the command vessel.

'I shall accompany you then,' said the high inquisitor. 'You may need my services down there.'

'As ever, I welcome your company,' said Macharius. 'But admit it, you are just as keen as I to get your hands on the work of the ancients.'

A cold smile appeared on Drake's face, one of the few I had ever seen. He was a forbidding man in a position of fearful power, and I doubt anyone ever mocked him the way that Macharius did. Perhaps he enjoyed the basic human contact. It must have been rare in his life. 'I am certainly keen to know whether it is the thing we seek.'

The battle-barge rocked again under the impact of another

planet-based weapon. I was suddenly glad that we were on the move, heading towards the shuttle bay. It would be good to feel ground beneath my feet again and air in my lungs that had not been recycled through a ship's fallible systems a thousand thousand times.

It struck me then that, for all his courage, perhaps Macharius felt the same way. Even for a man as brave as he undoubtedly was, waiting on a ship under attack, when any moment its walls might explode and you might be cast into the chill vacuum of space, must have been a nerve-wracking experience. I asked myself if it was possible that he was as anxious as I and just hid it better.

I dismissed the idea as ludicrous.

Order the novel or download the eBook
from *blacklibrary.com*
Also available from

GAMES
WORKSHOP®

and all good bookstores